MAN WITH
THE MUSCLE

BY
JULIE MILLER

DID YOU PURCHASE THIS BOOK WITHOUT A COVER?

If you did, you should be aware it is **stolen property** as it was reported *unsold and destroyed* by a retailer. Neither the author nor the publisher has received any payment for this book.

All the characters in this book have no existence outside the imagination of the author, and have no relation whatsoever to anyone bearing the same name or names. They are not even distantly inspired by any individual known or unknown to the author, and all the incidents are pure invention.

All Rights Reserved including the right of reproduction in whole or in part in any form. This edition is published by arrangement with Harlequin Enterprises II B.V./S.à.r.l. The text of this publication or any part thereof may not be reproduced or transmitted in any form or by any means, electronic or mechanical, including photocopying, recording, storage in an information retrieval system, or otherwise, without the written permission of the publisher.

This book is sold subject to the condition that it shall not, by way of trade or otherwise, be lent, resold, hired out or otherwise circulated without the prior consent of the publisher in any form of binding or cover other than that in which it is published and without a similar condition including this condition being imposed on the subsequent purchaser.

® and ™ are trademarks owned and used by the trademark owner and/or its licensee. Trademarks marked with ® are registered with the United Kingdom Patent Office and/or the Office for Harmonisation in the Internal Market and in other countries.

First published in Great Britain 2011
by Mills & Boon, an imprint of Harlequin (UK) Limited,
Eton House, 18-24 Paradise Road, Richmond, Surrey TW9 1SR

© Julie Miller 2010

ISBN: 978 0 263 88567 5

46-1211

Harlequin (UK) policy is to use papers that are natural, renewable and recyclable products and made from wood grown in sustainable forests. The logging and manufacturing processes conform to the legal environmental regulations of the country of origin.

Printed and bound in Spain
by Blackprint CPI, Barcelona

Julie Miller attributes her passion for writing romance to all those fairy tales she read growing up, and to shyness. Encouragement from her family to write down all those feelings she couldn't express became a love for the written word. She gets continued support from her fellow members of the Prairieland Romance Writers, where she serves as the resident "grammar goddess." This award-winning author and teacher has published several paranormal romances. Inspired by the likes of Agatha Christie and Encyclopedia Brown, Ms Miller believes the only thing better than a good mystery is a good romance.

Born and raised in Missouri, she now lives in Nebraska with her husband, son and smiling guard dog, Maxie. Write to Julie at PO Box 5162, Grand Island, NE 68802-5162, USA.

Prologue

The acrid stench of fear and burnt flesh tainted her expensive perfume and quickened his pulse as he put out his cigarette on her sculpted cheekbone.

Her silent scream spasmed through her and she gurgled beneath his hand on her throat, sputtering words with no sound. Her eyes pleaded, wept, their vain tilt not so pronounced as they'd been out on the terrace yesterday evening, laughing at him in the moonlight.

His gloved hand was dark against her alabaster skin. He carefully tucked the cigarette butt into his pocket. It was a lousy, disgusting habit, but tonight had called for something special. He brought both hands to her neck, squeezing a little harder, then easing his grip before closing off her airway again—teasing her, tormenting her with the false promise of freedom.

Just as she had tormented him with her promises.

No more. *He* was the one with the power over her now. *He* was the one in control of their destinies. He couldn't be hurt. He couldn't be used. He wouldn't be denied. Strength surged through him. Dominance. Superiority. His hands jerked around her throat as the anger consumed and cleansed him.

His breath came deeper, stronger as hers constricted.

He straddled her chest and sat, feeling her writhe helplessly, weakly, futilely beneath him.

"You're not so high and mighty now, are you, Gretchen?" He pulled up his stocking mask, wanting her to see his eyes, to know *he* was the one who'd put her in her place. "You want to rethink saying no to me?"

She nodded.

Tears and desperation and the blood on her cheek made her look vulnerable, more human than the icy beauty who'd led him on for so many months—smiling at him, sharing conversations, accepting his gifts—yet ultimately dismissing him as if he was of no more importance than a piece of furniture. For a moment, he paused to tenderly brush aside the damp golden hair that stuck to her forehead. She looked beautiful, stretched out beneath him, begging to do his bidding. This was how it could have been between them—how it should have been. He wanted to kiss her. He nearly did. But no, he wouldn't leave even that little trace of DNA. He was too smart for that.

Too smart for all of them.

Stupid bitches.

"Too late." With a snap, he crushed her windpipe. In a matter of seconds, she was dead.

When the spark faded from her eyes, it took his rage and need with him and he breathed a sigh of relief. He reached for his bag.

Precisely three minutes later, he set about the tasks of cleaning her wounds, untying her wrists and ankles and rewinding the electrical cords before returning them to their storage compartment inside the bag. He wrapped her in her pink silk robe and carried her into the adjoining room where he laid her on the bed and arranged her just so, crossing her hands over her heart in sweet repose, draping her hair over her damaged cheek, carefully removing one of her diamond earrings and closing her eyes.

"Goodbye, sweetheart."

He returned to the opulent, oversize bathroom where he'd surprised her and quickly rolled up the drop cloth he'd used and cleaned any other signs of his presence there. Finally, he stripped off the tan coveralls he wore, packing them and his gloves inside his bag. When he was certain the upstairs hallway was clear, he hurried down the back steps and locked the bag in his vehicle outside. The music from the violins, viola and cello filtered through the crisp night air and masked his footsteps as he flicked the cigarette butt into the storm drain at the curb.

Then he straightened his jacket and jogged around to join the others at the mansion's front drive, ready to be shocked and outraged when some poor unlucky soul discovered Gretchen's body.

And the message he'd tucked beneath the covers beside her.

Chapter One

"You're the saddest bunch of heroes I've ever seen." The chiding female voice cut through the buzz of lively conversations, three different television broadcasts and the chattering clacks of pool balls breaking across a table behind Alex Taylor. "You got the guy. The D.A. will put him away."

"Let's hope." Alex slid onto the green vinyl seat in front of the Shamrock's polished walnut bar and pulled some cash from the front pocket of his jeans. Not even the bright blue eyes and sympathetic smile of Josie Nichols standing on the other side could shake him from the mood he was in. "I need to order some beers."

"Hello?" The bartender slapped her washrag on top of the bar with a purpose, demanding his full attention before glancing over at the flat-screen TV hanging in the corner behind her. "You hope? KCPD's standoff with that gangbanger Demetrius Smith is all over the news. Getting him and his lieutenants off the streets just made Kansas City a hell of a lot safer. If I can walk out to my car at night and not have to worry about getting mugged or raped or caught in the cross fire between his gang and someone else, then I'd say you got the job done. You should be celebrating. Not bringing down the mood of the bar."

"Smith's gotten out with nothing more than a slap on the wrist more than once. Evidence disappears. A witness decides not to testify." Alex closed his eyes and shook his head, seeing the gangly body of a ten-year-old boy cradled in Sergeant Delgado's arms as he crouched down behind an alley fence, waiting for their commanding officer's all-clear order. He'd have thought the kid was sleeping if it hadn't been for all the blood on Delgado's uniform. Two bullets in such a tiny body—and there'd been nothing they could do. Alex opened his eyes, sharing a bit of the grim truth that was forever etched in his memory. "Smith was laughing when we brought him out of that house. An innocent boy died today, and he was laughing. Like he wasn't even accountable for what happened. He's got connections we can only guess at. If the D.A. doesn't make the charges stick—"

"That won't happen this time," Josie insisted. "I can feel it in my bones. Smith's going to prison. That makes you heroes."

Try telling that to the mother of the boy they hadn't been able to save. If they'd cleared the house where Smith and his buddies had been holed up ten minutes sooner, Alex and his team of SWAT—Special Weapons and Tactics—officers might have been able to get him to a hospital before he bled out. Calvin Chambers didn't even have any gang tats on him. And he sure as hell hadn't fired any gun. He'd been an innocent kid cutting through the wrong backyard at the wrong time.

Alex knew more about gang life than young Calvin probably had. He'd had the remnants of the Westside

Warrior tattoo he once thought meant he belonged to something important lasered off his back a decade ago, after he'd been adopted into a real family as a teen. Once he'd been Alexis Pitsaeli, street punk and foster home nightmare with no father to speak of and a mother who prized her drug addiction more than her child. Up until Gideon and Meghan Taylor had set him straight and loved him enough to make him a Taylor, too, Alex had been headed straight to prison or an untimely death.

If Alex hadn't been adopted into the Taylor clan, it wouldn't have surprised anyone to find him shot dead in a gangbanger's backyard. But Calvin Chambers?

He swallowed the bile of irony and rage and guilt, and laid a twenty on top of the bar. "First round's on the new guy."

He nodded back to the corner table where Captain Cutler and the rest of his five-man SWAT team had taken up residence to lose the stress of the day to booze, camaraderie or the company of one of the pretty ladies who seemed to get a thrill out of flirting with the cops who frequented the Kansas City bar. Raucous laughter from the corner table bounced off the walls. Great. He'd missed the joke. It had probably been on him, anyway. Though he'd been on the force for five years now, he'd only been a member of SWAT for eight months. It was like surviving his rookie year all over again.

"Five drafts and some pretzels," he ordered.

Josie shook her dark brown ponytail down her back and pushed the twenty dollars beneath his fingers. "You need to learn the rules of the house, Taylor. On a night like this, the first round's on me." Apparently, she was more intuitive than a cheerleader. "I'm sorry about that boy. I know it's hard to lose anyone on a call like that. But you didn't shoot him."

"I didn't get him home safe to his mom, either."

A bit of temper flared in the bartender's cheeks. "Smith and his thugs are the only ones you should be blaming. You and Rafe, Trip, Holden and the captain ought to all be commended for stopping those losers. That drug house was just outside a school zone. Kids walk by there every day. Bringing guns and drugs and violence into a family neighborhood just…galls me. As far as I'm concerned, we're lucky no one else died. And we owe that to you and your team."

Josie shivered from the top of her head to the hem of her jeans as the emotions worked through her system, and Alex felt his lips curve with half a smile. "So how do you really feel about it?"

She reached across the bar and flicked his shoulder with the towel. "Don't you get smart with me, Taylor." Rocking back on her heels, she pointed a big-sisterly finger at him. "And stop battin' those baby browns at me. I can't help it when I get my Irish up."

"Yes, ma'am." Somehow, she'd successfully broken through the gloom and doom that had settled around his shoulders. Yes, a boy had died tragically today. But many more would be safe because of his SWAT team's actions. For the sake of Josie's smile, he'd look on the bright side.

"There'll be no *ma'am*ing around here, hotshot. Heck, I bet I'm younger than you. What are you, twenty-six?"

"Twenty-seven."

"Ha." She tapped her thumb against her chest.

"Twenty-four. So no *ma'am*s. And put your money away—it's no good here."

When she turned around to pull out five frosted glasses and start drawing beers, Alex stuffed the twenty into her tip jar. He didn't know Josie all that well, beyond the fact she was a slain cop's daughter and could play a mean game of pool. But he'd seen the thick backpack and textbooks that meant she was in school, and suspected that tending bar at the Shamrock was how she supported herself. He wasn't going to let her big heart and true blue loyalty to KCPD keep her from putting food on the table.

While he waited for her to set up the tray of drinks and pour a bowlful of pretzels, Alex let his gaze wander back to the news broadcast on the television. Michael Cutler, the leader of SWAT Team One and the man who'd recruited Alex from a list of prospective beat cop candidates to join KCPD's most highly trained and specialized response team, was finishing up a recorded interview with the reporter. Cutler's tall build and salt-and-pepper hair cut a commanding figure as he answered the blonde woman's questions. Cutler was a good ace—he reminded Alex a lot of his own adoptive father, Gideon Taylor, the fire department's chief arson investigator. He was no-nonsense, tough, but fair.

Cutler handled the interview with the same confident air of calm with which he ran the unit, explaining their mission to assist the drug task force in storming the house while protecting the security of the officers on the scene. When the reporter asked whether he thought the cops or someone in Smith's gang had shot that boy, a pointed glare from Cutler indicated the interview was over.

With the reporter on live back in the studio, Alex

watched the tape continuing in the corner of the screen, showing Trip and Sergeant Delgado escorting a hand-cuffed Demetrius Smith into the back of a police car while Captain Cutler and Holden Kincaid stood guard over Smith's two compatriots being loaded into another black-and-white. Alex was nowhere to be seen in the camera shot. He'd had the inglorious duty of stowing gear and coordinating cleanup with the task force.

A gofer with a gun and body armor. Despite eight months of training and working together, he was still definitely the new guy. Any friendship, respect or trust Delgado, Kincaid and Trip showed him was on a strictly trial basis. He had yet to earn anything more permanent.

As the reporter turned to do a live interview in the studio with Kansas City's D.A., Dwight Powers, Alex's thoughts wandered. He half suspected that the main reason he'd gotten the SWAT position over several other older, more tenured candidates was because he was a Taylor. In addition to his dad's work in conjunction with the police department, his uncle Mitch was chief of the Fourth Precinct. His uncle Mac ran the day shift at the crime lab. He had two other uncles who were cops, and one who was an FBI agent assigned to the Kansas City Bureau. His uncle Brett, the only one who wasn't involved in law enforcement, was married to a cop.

His adopted brother, Edison Pike Taylor, worked in the K-9 unit. His two youngest brothers, Matthew and Mark, while still in college, were both already on their way to similar careers.

With a powerful, venerated family history like that, it made good press within the department to assign one of the next generation of Taylor cops to KCPD's premiere

SWAT unit. But it didn't mean a thing to the members of his team.

Especially when a cop had to die for the position to open up in the first place.

Not only was Alex the new guy, he had the unenviable task of replacing a well-loved friend who'd been shot down in the line of duty. He had a lot to prove no matter how he looked at it.

Better content himself with fetching the beer.

The wry thought faded when another photo popped up on the TV screen beside Smith's booking picture. The woman looked delicate, pretty in an icy-hot way. Striking light red hair. Creamy skin. Wide, slightly full, could-be-sexy-if-they-weren't-pressed-so-tight lips. She was a stunning contrast to Smith's mahogany skin and shaved head. She was all class, all uptown, compared to Smith's decidedly downtown street style.

Beauty aside, noting her knowing arch of one auburn brow, Alex could tell there was some fire under that buttoned-up suit and cool facade, as well. He'd bet those lips softened like honey when she smiled. He wondered what it would take to get her to smile, what a man might do to ignite the fire beneath the surface of her skin.

Alex's pulse shook off the last of its doldrums and beat at a healthy tempo. Nothing like a little sensual delight to take a man's mind off his troubles. He tuned into the story—something about the attorney taking on Smith's prosecution—trying to catch the name of the flame-haired fantasy.

Audrey Kline. Audrey. He grinned at how well the old-fashioned name fit her tailored suit and pearls. Was she another reporter covering the story? She must be new to this station since he hadn't seen…

Wait a minute. *Assistant District Attorney* Audrey Kline?

Alex's pulse tripped over a warning as recognition kicked in. He leaned in slightly, tuning out the noise of the bar around him and reading the words scrolling across the bottom of the screen.

Audrey Kline—daughter of Rupert Kline of Kline, Galloway & Tucker, Attorneys at Law. *That* name he recognized. Rupert Kline was one of the—if not *the*—most revered lawyers in Kansas City. His firm often represented the wealthiest of clients and, more than once, had poked holes in the tightest of KCPD's cases and gotten various slime bags freed or released from jail time with little more than a slap on the wrists.

The enemy was arguing Smith's case?

"No way." Alex's Latin blood hummed through his veins as irritation mixed with the initial attraction he'd felt.

What the hell was the D.A. thinking, putting a pampered society princess in charge of prosecuting Demetrius Smith? Did he really think some rookie wannabe was equipped to handle one of Kansas City's most important cases? Nailing Smith for any number of charges, from drug trafficking and assault to witness intimidation and murder, would put a substantial dent in the city's gang activities and violent crime stats.

He hadn't risked his life to bring Smith in—Calvin Chambers hadn't died—so that Red there could play at her daddy's game and get her picture on TV. Audrey Kline was too young, too pretty, too…fluffy…to be taken seriously and win the case.

What was she doing working for the city when she could be handling contracts or civil suits at Daddy's law firm, anyway? Was there some kind of political agenda going on here? If that murdering SOB Smith got off because Dwight Powers wanted to do a favor for her father...

"You okay, Taylor?" Josie was demanding his attention again.

Alex checked his temper as well as his hormones as the bartender scooted a bowl of pretzels across the bar. "Yeah. Just caught up in the news of the day, I guess."

"I can change the channel," she offered.

He shook his head and stood, tamping down the frissons of unexpected frustration and desire still sparking through his system. "I'm good. I'd better get back to the party."

"If you take this to the table, I'll bring the drinks over in just a sec." She pointed to the waitress standing at the end of the bar. "I need to get her order filled first."

"Sure."

Audrey Kline's picture disappeared and Alex cursed himself for breathing easier. *Stupid move, Taylor.* Twisting his shorts into a knot over some woman he'd never even met and a case that was out of his hands.

He tucked his money clip back into the pocket beneath his badge. Must be the guilt of the day combined with the pressure of the past year that left him feeling the need to connect to the right woman and get some of this pent-up frustration out of his system. He wasn't getting anything but a friendly one-of-the-guys vibe from Josie, and he was cool with that.

But Audrey Kline? One head shot on the news and he'd been thinking of ways he could peel those pinstripes off her. So maybe he'd been a little obsessed with work lately, and hadn't really dated since he'd accepted the SWAT gig. Needs that had been put on hold for too long, simmering too close to the surface, were the only reasons that made sense when it came to explaining his instant awareness of the red-haired attorney and his knee-jerk reaction to her assignment to the Smith case.

Logic said there could never be anything but distance between a rich daddy's girl like her and a streetwise cop like him. She probably owned shoes that cost more than his monthly salary. Unless she went slumming for some secret kind of sex life, he could guarantee that a former gang member turned weapons and recon specialist for KCPD wasn't the kind of guy she'd even deign to notice—much less want to connect with.

And an attorney who lacked the *cojones* to go after Smith and win wasn't the kind of woman *he* wanted to be with anyway, right?

Carrying the oversize pretzel bowl in one hand, Alex made his way between a row of booths and two pool tables, sparing a moment to trade winks with a cool blonde. *That* was who he should be gettin' the hots for. She was interested, willing—and not responsible for bringing Demetrius Smith to justice. But he moved on with a thanks-but-no-thanks smile when giggles and chatter erupted around her table. Too perky. Too easy. While Alex wasn't averse to spending time with a beautiful woman, he just wasn't in the mood for light and playful and meaningless tonight.

Besides, he had a feeling that if he didn't deliver these snacks soon, he'd drop even further down that invisible hierarchy of prove-you-deserve-to-be-here attitude he got from the members of his team.

"Pretzels are up," Alex announced, setting the bowl

on the table and sliding it to the middle. "Josie's bringing the drinks."

"Thanks, shrimp." Joseph Jones, Jr., nicknamed Triple J and often shortened to Trip, stuck a finger into the thick paperback book he was reading and helped himself to a handful of the salty twists.

So Alex was only five-ten. He hated the nickname Trip had stuck him with. Of course, as tall and power-fully built as the tank-size Trip was, anyone under six feet probably seemed small. "At least my mama knew more than one letter of the alphabet when she was coming up with names."

Trip looked up from his book as the others, including Holden Kincaid on his cell phone beside him, laughed. "Good one, peewee."

Yeah. Like that was better than *shrimp*.

"Thank Josie." Alex pulled out a chair and took a seat between Sergeant Delgado and Captain Cutler. "She saw us on the news. She wouldn't take my money."

"What? Hell." Rafe Delgado glanced over his shoul-der at the bar where Josie and her uncle, the Shamrock's owner, Robbie Nichols, were busy serving drinks. "She can't afford that."

"I left a twenty in the tip jar for her," Alex assured him.

"Can't even get one lousy order straight," he grum-bled. The lanky, dark-haired sergeant spun his chair around and shoved it under the table. "I'm going to see if I can at least save her the trip over here."

"She's the one who offered to—"

But Rafe was already striding away. Alex turned at the strong hand that squeezed his shoulder. Captain Cutler's typically stoic expression was eased by a fatherly smile. "Let him go, son. It's not personal."

The reprimand sure felt as if he'd insulted Josie in some way. And he hadn't meant to. "I paid her for the drinks, I swear."

"I know you did. And somewhere under the strain of having that boy die in his arms this afternoon, he knows it, too." Cutler swatted Alex's shoulder and pulled away, including the other two men at the table with them in his explanation for the sergeant's abrupt departure. "Josie's a hell of a lot prettier to look at than any of you. With what we've been through today, I don't blame Rafe for choosing her company over your ugly mugs."

"Sarge likes her?" Alex asked.

"I think it's more of an overprotective big brother thing," Cutler explained. "His first partner when he joined KCPD out of the academy was her dad. He's watched her grow up."

"So no hitting on Josie or Delgado will cut you off at the knees, shrimp." In one smooth motion, Trip pointed a warning finger at Alex and scooped up half the pretzels remaining in the bowl. He glanced over the top of his book. "And you can't afford to be any shorter."

Alex flicked a pretzel across the table, hitting Trip in the middle of his forehead. The book went down on the table. Alex caught the pretzel that came flying back at him and crushed it in his fist, crumbling the dregs down into the bowl.

"Oh, you da man, Taylor."

"That's right, big guy. I'm the man."

"Children…" Captain Cutler warned with a smirk of his own.

Alex's and Trip's respective pretzels were dutifully

stuffed into their own mouths. The silliness of the interchange lightened Alex's mood, and while Trip went back to reading with a grin, Alex turned to spot Sergeant Delgado plucking the tray of beers from Josie's hands and trying to squeeze a word in through the argument his actions triggered.

They were finally shaking off the grim events of the day. SWAT Team One was going to be okay. Alex was fitting in. No one was on his case for being too new, too young, too short—too lucky to have this job because he was a Taylor—too anything. He shifted his shoulders inside the black cotton sweater and leather jacket he wore and relaxed against his chair.

"Liza said to tell everyone hi." Sharpshooter Holden ended the call to his wife and set his cell phone on the table. "I'm leaving after the first drink. I have orders to come home with cookie dough ice cream or not to show up at all." He tapped his cell phone and grinned in a boyishly excited way that belied his ability to go stone-cold still to make a kill shot or bring down a suspect. "With the way her appetite's kicking into high gear, I think we could be having the baby any day now."

Captain Cutler chewed around a pretzel as he spoke. "I thought Liza wasn't due until Christmas."

"It's practically Thanksgiving already."

"In two weeks. You're hopeless, Kincaid."

"Oh, and when you and Jillian decide to start making babies, you're going to be all cool, calm and collected about it?" Holden challenged with a grin.

The captain smoothed his palm across the top of his short, salt-and-pepper hair. "I have a teenage son. I know about making babies."

"So you and Jillian *are* working on giving Mikey a little brother?"

"Mind your own business, Kincaid."

"Or maybe a little sister." Holden whistled through his teeth. "I'd hate to be the guy who tried to date her."

Alex easily pictured an image of Captain Michael Cutler, suited up in body armor, weapons and badge, greeting an already-nervous teenage boy at the front door. His daughter's unsuspecting date would probably pee his pants. Wisely, Alex buried his amusement by pulling the snacks away from Trip and helping himself to a bite before they were all gone. Only golden-boy Holden could get away with such teasing.

"You finished?" The captain arched an eyebrow as Holden's chuckle erupted into laughter.

"I can't hear myself think over here," Trip groused, giving Alex the evil eye as he easily reached across the table and pulled the pretzels back in front of him.

"You can think?" Holden snatched the book and the bowl from his hands before pointing to the booths behind Alex. "Read on your own time. Single women. Go."

Trip grabbed the book right back, but turned his focus to Cutler. "Permission to take him down, sir?"

The captain grimaced, looking very much like a babysitter who'd lost control of his charges. "Where are those beers?"

"Right here." Rafe Delgado had returned, seemingly even more grumpy than when he had left. He plopped the tray down, sending foam cascading over the top of the frosty pilsner glasses. "Help yourselves."

Wisely, each man kept his comments about the testy waiter to himself and reached for a beer.

Holden's phone vibrated on the tabletop just as the cell on Alex's belt buzzed. He set down his beer and wiped his hand on the leg of his jeans before answering. Trip and Sarge were opening their phones, too, as Captain Cutler's went off. The noise of the bar instantly muted and the tension around the table thickened as the captain picked up the call. Alex checked his watch. After 10:00 p.m. They'd been off the clock for more than an hour. A call summoning KCPD's premiere SWAT team at this time of night couldn't be good.

Alex was clearing the *Call Dispatch* message off his touch screen when the captain rejoined them at the table. "Got it. My men are still with me—I'll notify them. Cutler out." He disconnected the call and addressed the team. "Hold off on those drinks." He glanced at Holden. "Tell Liza the ice cream will have to wait."

"What's up, boss?" Alex asked.

"Looks like we're getting some overtime tonight. Rafe, I need you to head on back to HQ to get the van. We'll need all our equipment. We'll meet you at the Plaza address Dispatch gave and suit up there."

"Yes, sir." Rafe nodded, his surly mood hidden behind a face that was pure business. He grabbed his jacket and jogged out the door.

"Captain?" Holden prompted. They still didn't have an explanation for the off-duty call.

"Looks like we've got another Rich Girl murder. Banking family this time. The Cosgrove estate. They found Cosgrove's daughter strangled to death in her bedroom. Signs of torture." Cutler muttered a curse under his breath. "There was a party going on downstairs when they found her. Almost a hundred people on the scene with a dead woman upstairs."

"That's ballsy." Holden voiced what Alex was thinking. "Sounds as though this guy is trying to flaunt his crime."

"That's the second death with that kind of victim in just over a year, isn't it?" Trip asked, sliding a bookmark between the pages of his paperback and cramming it into the pocket of his jacket. "The first one's never been solved. I thought a task force had been set up to narrow down a suspect."

"Yeah." Alex frowned. They were men of action. Troubleshooters. Protectors. They weren't the cops who sifted through clues at crime scenes. "Why call us instead of homicide?"

"It's up to us to secure the scene so the detectives and CSI can get in and do their job."

"We're on crowd control?"

"Not exactly." The captain pulled his KCPD SWAT jacket from the back of his chair and shrugged into it. "The perp's upping his game. The party's no coincidence. This time he left a bomb threat with the body."

Chapter Two

Audrey Kline squinted against the swirling strobe effect of the four police cars and other official vehicles lined up on the street in front of the Cosgrove mansion as she climbed out of her Mercedes and tried to make sense of what was going on here. The scene outside the sprawling stone house resembled the aftermath of some kind of natural disaster, with people huddling under blankets, women wearing their escorts' suit jackets over designer dresses, one man sitting at the back of an ambulance with a blood pressure cuff around his arm, and many others silently weeping.

It was true. It hadn't been some cruel tabloid rumor that had blipped past on her local internet news site.

Gretchen was dead.

The certainty of it hit her like a punch to the gut and, for a moment, she sagged against the open door, her shocked breaths forming frosty clouds in the damp November air. How? Why?

Screeching brakes alerted her a split second before the glare of headlights spun around the corner half a block away, hitting her square in the face. A television news van. Audrey turned away and closed the car door, instinctively shielding her face from the unwelcome intrusion.

There was already a slew of other reporters here, searching for someone noteworthy from the wealthiest and most powerful of Kansas City society to give them a sound bite. And more of those underground bloggers who'd broken the news of the murder half an hour ago were probably mingling with the guests, texting away.

But Audrey was in no mood to be a media darling tonight. Gretchen's death was personal. Private. She needed answers. She needed this to make sense. This was the second friend she'd lost in the past two years. Her mother had died the year before that. Standing around and waiting with the others would only give her time to feel, to remember, to hurt. And to have that kind of weakness caught on tape and posted in the public eye would only make the grief that much tougher to deal with. If she ever wanted to be known as something more than Rupert Kline's little princess, then weakness wasn't something anyone here was going to get a chance to observe.

With newfound resolve giving her strength, Audrey buttoned up the front of her cashmere blazer, stuffed her keys into the pocket of her jeans and slipped through the suits and cocktail dresses of the party guests gathered outside the front gate. They parted like zombies, shocked and murmuring, as she made a beeline for the uniformed policeman standing by the driveway's wrought-iron gates. "Excuse me, officer? I'm a friend of the family."

Her father had taught her that standing as tall as her five feet five inches allowed and walking and talking with a purpose usually convinced people that she belonged wherever she wanted to be. But the young officer wasn't fooled. Leaving one arm resting on his belt beside his gun, he raised his hand to stop her. "I'm sorry, miss. No one's allowed to come inside the gate."

She tilted her chin to argue that she belonged here. "My father and Mr. Cosgrove went to Harvard together. I don't think he would mind…"

And then she saw the two detectives—one tall and light-haired, jotting notes, the other shorter and darker—talking to a pair of crime scene investigators, each wearing their reflective vests and holding their bulky kits in their hands. What were they doing outside the house? Had something happened on the grounds, as well? The blip she'd seen on her laptop said the victim had been found in her bedroom upstairs.

Why weren't they interviewing suspects? Taking pictures? Why were they just standing around? Didn't they know what a beautiful soul Gretchen had been? How much her parents and friends had loved her? Why weren't they tearing that house apart to find out who'd killed her?

Audrey took a deep breath to cool her frustration, wishing she'd taken the time to don a suit and high heels instead of quickly pulling on jeans and a jacket over her pajamas. She'd been up late working at home instead of attending Gretchen's party where she might have been able to do some good by kick-starting the investigation and putting these people to work. With no makeup and her hair hanging down to her shoulders in loose waves, she knew she looked more like a teenager than a grown woman. But she wasn't about to let her appearance stop her anymore than had the two red lights she'd run speeding across town to get here.

She'd known Gretchen Cosgrove since kindergarten. Their adult paths had taken them in different directions, but they saw each other at social functions like this one often enough to keep in touch. A friendship like that didn't die. A woman Audrey's own age shouldn't die.

"Please." She reached into her back pocket and looped the lanyard with her Office of the District Attorney identification badge around her neck. The job was new, her switch from private practice to public prosecutor a calculated bid to establish her independence beyond the shadow cast by her father. She hadn't had the opportunity to pull rank without her father's influence to back her up yet. But this was as good a time to try as any. "I'm an officer of the court. I'm sure there's something I can do to help."

"Sorry, ma'am," the officer apologized, "but my orders are strict. Nobody crosses the cordon tape until SWAT clears the scene, not even the commissioner herself."

"I don't understand. Wasn't the body found a couple hours ago? The crime scene is getting cold."

His gaze dropped down to her ID badge. Apparently, the judicial emblem held enough sway for him to lean in to whisper. "There may be a bomb inside."

"A bomb?"

He put a finger to his lips. "That's what the note with the body said. Captain Cutler said until we know more, we don't want to say or do anything that will cause a panic."

Cutler. She knew that name. That meant his SWAT team was on the premises, and that Gretchen's death might not be the only tragedy KCPD had to worry about. Audrey glanced around, recognizing many of the guests in attendance. There was the party planner Audrey had hired herself in the past, Clarice Darnell, along with her staff—servers, caterers, parking attendants. These were friends, colleagues, acquaintances Audrey had met at society events similar to this one. They were already traumatized by the news that their hostess tonight had been murdered. She didn't wish more trouble on any of them. "No. We wouldn't."

"You can check with me later," the policeman offered. "I'll let you in as soon as Captain Cutler gives the okay."

She nodded her thanks. "In the meantime, is there someone in charge I could speak with to get some details about what's happened? It's already on the internet. Rumors are going to fly if we don't contain this."

"Ma'am, all I've been told is to keep people back—"

"Never mind." She put up her hands, knowing she was pushing too hard, knowing he was just doing his job, knowing she wouldn't get her answers here. "Thank you."

"Audrey?"

She turned at the familiar voice and hurried to meet the tall blond man striding toward her. "Harper."

He wrapped his arms around her waist and lifted her clear off the ground, squeezing her tight as he wept against her neck. "She's gone, Audrey. Gretchen's gone." She held on tight and rocked back and forth with him. "I loved her, you know."

"I know. We all did."

He gulped in a shuddering breath and eased his grip enough so her toes could touch the ground. "We were always together at school—you, me, Gretchen, Charlotte, Donny, Val and the others."

Audrey rubbed circles at the collar of his gabardine suit, inhaling his familiar scents of tobacco and after-shave, sharing the loss with him. Their whole group of friends through high school had been tight, and though their lives and jobs had taken them in different directions after graduation, they'd found a way to keep in touch, trading calls and notes, coming together in times of tragedy like tonight.

"I used to think you were the one." Harper sighed, recalling the brief time they'd dated in high school. "But when I got back from law school, something about Gretch had changed. She was still as beautiful and fun and goofy as ever, but…"

"She grew up." She'd seen the new maturity in the once-capricious Gretchen, too.

"I asked her to marry me. We were going to announce it tonight."

That she didn't know. Tears welled up in Audrey's eyes, and she pulled back to touch his face. "Oh, Harper."

"I saw her tonight. In her bed. Before the cops chased us out." His red-rimmed eyes were dry now, and a brave smile creased his face. "You know she never gets any-where on time—she changes her mind about what she's wearing or can't find the right jewelry to match. But after the guests had been here for almost an hour, I got worried. I went upstairs to…" His smile faltered and Audrey's stomach clenched to receive the blow. "She looked so perfect lying there, like she was sleeping. But she… That bastard hurt her. Tortured her. There were marks around her wrists and neck. Her face was… I touched her and she…she was so cold."

Audrey looped her arms around his neck and hugged him again, hiding her own face against the starch of his collar. "I'm so sorry."

"It's just like Val all over again." They'd consoled each other the night Valeska Gordeeva Gallagher had been murdered, too. "Only, I never saw Val's body until the visitation at the funeral home. I saw Gretch—"

"Shh, Harp. Don't think of that. Let's remember how beautiful Gretchen and Val were."

"You're right. You're always right. I can count on you to say the right thing, can't I?" Someone jostled them in the crowd and Harper pulled away, straightening his tie, breathing deeply, tightening his jaw to keep the tears from falling again. "She's not coming back. I'll never see her smile or hear her laugh again."

With that grim pronouncement, the first tears spilled over onto Audrey's cheeks. She quickly swiped them away. "Harper—"

"I'd better get back to her parents. The press want them to say something. I've been running interference." He bent down to press a chaste kiss to her forehead. "They'll be glad to know you're here."

Another tear burned in the corner of her eye. She sniffed as her sinuses began to congest. Harper might have sucked it up, but she needed a minute to compose herself. "I'll be over to talk to them soon."

"Gotta go."

He walked away, leaving her shaking. She'd listened and offered comfort without realizing how much she needed it herself. They might not have been the closest of friends anymore, or else she would have known about the engagement—Gretchen had chosen a social path while Audrey had focused on her career—but she had been her oldest friend. And now there was a spot inside her, splitting open, emptying out, leaving grief and regret and helplessness in its place.

Audrey pressed a fist to her trembling lips and surveyed the crowd. She wasn't going to lose it here. The size of the gathering had nearly doubled with press and police, people who knew the Cosgroves and curious strangers. She couldn't expect to hold on to her anonymity much longer, yet she couldn't afford to be spotted as a bawling wreck—not if she wanted to impress her father and his old-school cronies, not if she intended to win the case she'd been assigned this afternoon and solidify her position in the D.A.'s office.

But the tears were burning for release. Hugging her arms in front of her, Audrey ducked her head and shuffled through the crowd, trying to draw as little attention as possible as she desperately sought out a private refuge. Her exposed skin would flush with every emotion she was feeling—a telltale, redheaded curse she'd endured her whole life—and there'd be no hiding the ache blooming inside her.

She shifted directions, deciding she should just get inside her car and drive away. But she stopped when she reached the curb. A camera crew was setting up a remote broadcast post on the opposite side of the street, and they'd recognize her as soon as she walked by.

Her throat raw from the constriction of emotions she held in check, Audrey turned and followed the sidewalk around the fringe of the gathering and just kept walking. Once she realized the voices from the crowd were fading, she stopped and raised her head, pulling her hair back from her face and tucking it behind her ears. She'd nearly reached the neighbor's house an eighth of a mile away.

There was her sanctuary. Not the house, but the red-leafed hedgerows and iron fencing that ran between the two properties. With the press and police focused at the front of the estate, the side yards were empty, shadowed and blessedly quiet. Audrey glanced behind her to Gretchen's house. They'd played hide-and-seek together on the massive grounds when they were children, and the memories of Gretchen's easy laugh and adventurous imagination reignited the grief that was set to consume her.

She needed to get out of here. Now.

She darted around the brick pillar at the corner of the Cosgroves' fence. *Oh, Lord.*

The security lights in the neighbor's front yard flashed on, reflecting off the white gold of her watch band. Reacting like the trespasser she was, Audrey tugged the sleeve of her jacket over her wrist and crouched down between the fence and hedge. The night was conspiring against her efforts to find a private moment to acknowledge her grief and center herself. Maybe she should just curl up in a ball here and let the tears flow.

But that would only add fuel to the paparazzi's rumor mill if they discovered an assistant district attorney huddled in the mud behind a burning bush shrub outside a crime scene.

"Why didn't I just stay home?" she muttered. Yet, as her jeans soaked up the chilly dampness from the ground beneath her knee, Audrey saw that she hadn't triggered the security lights, after all.

Instead, she got a clear look at the culprit. An armed

SWAT cop, wearing a flak vest over his black uniform, was lugging a large metal box to the back of the SWAT van parked in the driveway. Where had he come from? He was grinching to himself, maybe complaining about setting off the lights with his approach.

He set the box on the van's bumper with a heavy thunk, and the entire vehicle rocked, giving an indication as to the considerable weight he'd carried. The man unsnapped the strap beneath his chin and pulled off his helmet, dropping it to the concrete at his feet before scrubbing his black-gloved fingers over the top of his hair.

For a moment, Audrey forgot about the reporters and the mud and her grief. As he opened the back doors and hefted the box inside, his movements caught the lights in his short dark hair, revealing blue-black glints in the rumpled waves. Was he packing up? Did that mean the house had been cleared? The bomb discovered and dismantled?

He had the doors closed before she could think to move, and now she was forced to kneel there until the motion-detector lights went back off or the officer climbed inside the van. But he didn't appear to be in any hurry. With his rifle looped casually through the crook of his arm, he slowly turned, taking note of the vehicles in the street, the neighbors scurrying along the sidewalk to get a closer look at all the activity. Apparently oblivious to the approach of winter in the air, he unbuttoned the cuffs of his black shirt and rolled up the sleeves over a pair of muscular forearms. With a simple tilt of his head, he spoke into the microphone strapped to his Kevlar vest.

He was on guard, looking for something or someone,

scanning his surroundings, his dark gaze skimming past her hiding spot. Audrey hugged her arms closer to her body and made herself even smaller. Had he seen her? Sensed her presence? She could hide from friends and avoid the press, but something about the intensity of those watchful eyes warned her that it would be very hard to keep anything hidden from him.

Audrey held her breath. Waited. Tried to ignore the little tingles of awareness sparking beneath the emotions she held so tightly in check. He wasn't as tall as Harper or even her father. But he was all muscle, all alertness, all coiled energy. If the killer had planted a bomb inside the Cosgrove house, he looked like the type of man who could take care of it. He looked like the type of man who could have saved Gretchen's life in the first place.

Gretchen would have called him hot. She would have been introducing herself, flirting with him by now. She would have welcomed him as a friend and made him feel glad to be a part of her life long before Audrey even decided to admit he was handsome in an earthy, unpolished sort of way.

A tear leaked out, its hot moisture chapping her cheek in the cool breeze. Gretchen would have thought hiding in the shrubs to avoid the press and spy on hot guys was a grand adventure, but for Audrey this was pure torture. Another tear trailed along the same path, marking her skin. Grief could no longer wait for privacy and a sob squeezed through her throat in a muffled gasp.

Not here. Not now. The SWAT cop's gaze swung back around and she shoved her knuckles against her lips, stifling the breathy whimper of each sob while the tears streamed over her hand. She could read the headlines now—*Lawyer Can't Handle Crime Scene,*

Muddy Misstep for Kline's Daughter or *Newest A.D.A. Runs and Hides.* Just the kind of decorum and control that would inspire public confidence as she led the prosecution against gang-leader Demetrius Smith. Not.

But then a KCPD pickup pulled into the driveway behind the SWAT van and she had her chance to escape public scrutiny.

Audrey pushed to her feet, stumbling back against the iron fence, as that all-seeing cop walked up to meet the truck. Another uniformed officer—minus the armored vest and extra gear and weaponry of the first man—climbed out of the truck with a German shepherd bounding down behind him, to shake hands and trade greetings. By the time the SWAT cop had stooped down to wrestle the dog around its ears, Audrey was moving. Holding up her hand to shield her face from the prickly branches of the hedgerow, she jogged several yards along the fence until the bustle and bright lights from the front of the house could no longer be seen or heard.

She inhaled a lungful of the cool night air and exhaled on sobs that shook through her. Curling her fingers around the cold, unyielding iron of a fence post, she held on and let the grief overtake her.

Seconds passed, maybe a minute or two, as the pain knifed through her. With one hand braced on her knee and the other gripping the fence to keep from toppling over, she wept for Gretchen and for the void her death created in so many lives, including her own. She'd never learned Gretchen's gifts for spontaneity and handling stress and sharing joy, and now she never would. Kansas City had lost a generous and enthusiastic young benefactor. Harper Pierce had lost a fiancée. The Cosgroves had lost a daughter. Audrey had lost another friend.

Finally, the sobs became little gasps and hiccups as the worst of it passed. Audrey's diaphragm ached, her sinuses throbbed against her skull, her eyes felt puffy and hot. But she could think again. She could feel something beyond the pain—anger, perhaps, determination to honor Gretchen's memory and vindicate her murder.

And she could hear.

Footsteps.

Audrey snapped her attention to the soft, even rhythm of someone moving through the Cosgroves' backyard. Although muffled by the fallen leaves and dewy grass, there was no mistaking the tread of company cutting between the garden paths and towering oaks that shaded the yard on the other side of the fence.

The police officers she'd seen all carried flashlights. But this, this was something different. A noise in the dark. The whisper of stealth.

Pushing her hair away from her hot, sticky cheeks, Audrey peered between the iron bars to identify the source of the sound among the trees. Too big to be a squirrel or rabbit. Too real for her to feel safe. The breeze rustled through the hedge, sending a chill dancing along her spine. If that was a cop, where was his flashlight? And if it wasn't, how had he gotten past security inside the front gates?

She pressed her face against the bars, trying to spot the movement among the trees. But the footsteps had fallen silent. With no sound to listen for and nothing to see, her other senses took over. The breeze was damp and cool against her skin, and it carried the subtlest hint of cigarette smoke into her nose. Since when did cops smoke on the job?

Audrey straightened, her breath still coming in stuttering gasps, her legs willing her to back away. She dabbed at her nose with the back of her hand and brushed the moisture on her pant leg. Had he gone? Was that scent the whisper of a shadow that had moved on? Or was he standing there, waiting, watching from the darkness?

Watching her?

A beam of light hit the side of her face, blinding her. With a startled yelp, she raised her hand to block the light and turned. "Stop it!" She pointed through the fence. "Were you…? How…?" Her pulse raced faster than her thoughts could keep up. *Run.* No. Even as the instinct shot through her, she knew she had no place to go. *Game face, Audrey. Get your Rupert Kline, killer-in-the-courtroom game face on.* With a noisy sniffle, she pulled back her shoulders and lifted her chin. "Could you get that light out of my face, please?"

She was going for confidence, strength, with that order. But her bout of crying and uncertain fear made the tone husky, revealing she was far more rattled than she cared to admit.

"Audrey Kline?"

Oh, boy. Here it comes. "I don't have any statement to make at this time."

"Okay."

Okay? In a moment of confusion, her strength deflated. "The light?"

Thankfully, the man tilted the flashlight down to the ground. Not a reporter. Not a killer. He wasn't giving off a whiff of anything beyond leather and starch and

clean, musky man. She didn't need to see his face to
know from the width of his chest—and the assault rifle
pointed down to the ground at his side—that she'd been
discovered by the SWAT officer she'd been ogling only
minutes earlier. "Better come out of there, ma'am."

He pulled back the hedge where she'd been hiding.
No way had he just climbed that fence. She'd been so
busy sobbing and sniffling, then spying through the
trees, that she simply hadn't heard his approach from
the opposite direction. She pointed over her shoulder as
she stepped out. "There was someone over there. Maybe
just having a smoke, maybe something else."

"And you were checking it out?" He let the hedge
spring back into place and positioned himself between
her and the noise she'd heard. He pointed the beam
of his flashlight into the trees on the other side of the
fence.

"No, I…" Despite the warm, rich timbre of his voice,
she detected the tinge of sarcasm there. "How do you
know me?"

Apparently, he didn't see anything more than she
had, although he did pause a moment to touch the microphone at his shoulder and ask someone called Trip
to take another check through the Cosgroves' backyard.
"You're with the D.A.'s office."

Audrey struggled to wedge her defenses back into
place when he faced her with the abrupt pronouncement.
"I'm afraid you have me at a disadvantage."

"I saw you on the news earlier tonight. Besides," he
continued as he shone his flashlight on her chest, "I
can read your name tag." He swung the light to the
badge hanging from a chain around his own neck. "Alex
Taylor. I'm with KCPD."

Her gaze darted from his black vest to the handgun strapped to his right thigh, over to the ominous-looking rifle and back up to dark eyes that were nearly black in the shadows. "I figured out you were a cop for myself." Her throat grated as she coughed to clear it. But she managed a smile as she moved around him. "Nice to meet you. Excuse me."

"You can't go that way."

She shrugged off the gloved hand on her arm and gestured out to the street. "Well, I can't go *that* way. I'll just cut through the neighbor's yard and circle around to my car."

"No."

"No?" She uttered a sound somewhere between a sob and a curse. "I know it means nothing to you, but I have a reputation to uphold in this city. I have on no makeup and I've been crying my eyes out. If you recognized me, then those reporters who track my every move certainly will."

"Do you always hide in the bushes when you're upset?"

"Do I hide…? You…" Audrey clamped her mouth shut as her temper rekindled other emotions. She tipped her chin to look him in the eye. "I'm not trespassing on your crime scene. All I need is the chance to slip away undetected so I embarrass neither my family nor the D.A. You can't stop me."

He took a single step and blocked her path. "Yes, I can."

Oh, God. He was serious.

Temper. Grief. Frustration. Humiliation. Any one of those could have busted through her tenuous control of her emotions. Being hit by all four at once released the flood gates again. Audrey's eyes stung.

"Don't do this." She swiped away the first tear, chiding her own weakness.

"You don't cry pretty, do you?"

She croaked on a sound that was half laugh, half groan, and swiped at another tear, willing it to be her last. "Gee, thanks. Is that the best line you've got?"

"Never found the need to use lines. Here." He reached behind him and pulled a blue bandanna from his pocket. The hint of a smile eased the firm line of his mouth as he held out the cloth like a peace offering. "Was the woman inside a friend of yours?"

With an embarrassing snivel, Audrey nodded and snatched the gift from his fingers. She wiped her cheeks and nose, then pressed the soft cotton, still warm from the heat of his body, against her eyes. "Thank you."

"There's nothing pretty about losing an innocent life, is there?"

Although his hushed voice was as dark and soothing as the night around them, she got the faint impression that he was speaking about something personal rather than philosophical. Audrey shook her head. "No, there's not."

He shifted his stance, his eyes sweeping the area around them. "Look, I'm not trying to be a hard-ass when you're clearly dealing with something here. But KCPD has established a perimeter and wants to control the crowd for a reason."

"I heard about the bomb."

"We're thinking that was an empty threat—neither the dogs nor my team have found anything." He nodded his head toward the street. "But it got the perp the response he wanted. Detective Montgomery—he's in charge of the investigation—thinks the killer is getting off on all this attention. Chances are he's here somewhere, watching."

Audrey tensed and glanced over her shoulder, remembering the footsteps she'd heard.

"So you can see why it might not be too smart to wander off on your own."

She turned her gaze back to Alex Taylor's face, feeling more than a little unsettled by the possibility he was suggesting. "There has to be a hundred people involved with the party tonight. Double that if you count all the press and cops and curiosity seekers. You really think the killer is one of them?"

"I'm not the detective. But I do make sure everyone stays safe. Especially someone from the D.A.'s office who has a major trial coming up."

"What do you know about that?"

"Like I said, I watch the news. I'm one of the men who brought in Demetrius Smith. You cannot let that murderer walk."

"I'll do my best."

"I'd like it better if you said you were sure you could win. Or if D.A. Powers was handling the case himself."

Audrey bristled at the dig. It wasn't the first time someone had doubted her abilities because of her looks or her father's bank account or the fact she turned red in the face when she lost control of her emotions. "No one bought my law degree for me, Mr. Taylor. And I didn't just earn it—I was top of my class. I've worked as a defense attorney and now for the prosecution, so I know criminal law inside and out. I asked for this assignment, and Dwight Powers gave it to me because he knew I could handle it."

Did he just take an accusatory step toward her? "So you *are* trying to make a name for yourself with this trial."

Not in the glory-seeking way he was implying. Audrey tilted her chin and met the charges head-on. "I'm doing my job. I only got the case this afternoon. Just because I haven't had a chance to weigh all the options to develop a prosecution strategy yet doesn't mean I'm going to lose."

"He killed a ten-year-old boy today and didn't bat one eye of remorse. He's not going to be afraid of you."

Audrey saw the anger tighten his jaw, felt the pain radiating through the edge of his voice and regretted getting on her soapbox. It explained the "innocent life" remark he'd made earlier. Despite the sting of his doubts about her abilities, a keen understanding—a shared sympathy—passed between them. "I'm sorry. You were there, weren't you? When the boy died?"

For a split second, the intensity in those midnight-colored eyes wavered. "That bastard can't go back out on the streets."

"Then let's hope he underestimates me as much as you have tonight."

"Audrey, I… Hell. I shouldn't have opened my mouth." With a deep sigh, those broad shoulders lifted and relaxed a fraction. "You can hang here in the shadows for a minute to get it together, but then I really need you back out by the street."

Was that an apology? Or just a resignation to duty? Either way, after the charged intimacy of their argument, his unexpected capitulation surprised her. She found something calming about his breathing, slowing and evening out along with hers, something soothing in the way he altered his protective stance to stand between her and the world beyond this shadowy hedgerow. She touched the soft blue cotton to her eyes one more time. Even though it was just a bandanna, the old-fashioned gesture charmed her. "I didn't think men carried handkerchiefs anymore."

His soft chuckle warmed her. "You don't know my grandmother. There are rules to follow with the Taylors. Family dinner every Sunday. Men carry handkerchiefs in their pockets."

"Your grandmother tells a tough guy like you what to do?"

He winked, and Audrey felt like smiling, too. "She's my best girl. I do what she asks."

A check of his watch and Audrey suspected the minute to compose herself was up. She held out the bandanna. "Well then, thank her, too."

He wrapped his hand around it and her fingers, holding on longer than necessary to give her a sympathetic squeeze. She was startled by the heat emanating from his skin, even through the protective leather glove he wore. "Keep it. And you get Smith."

Audrey nodded, making a promise.

His grip suddenly tightened and he whirled around, pulling her behind him. A split second later, a camera flashed.

Alex Taylor was already on guard before her own defenses locked into place. "What the hell?"

Another light flashed. He took a menacing step forward.

An older, heavyset man slipped to the side, trying to

make eye contact with her. "Miss Kline, could we get a statement?"

Alex shifted his shoulder between her and the reporter, giving Audrey nothing but the large white SWAT letters on the back of his vest to look at. "Get back to the sidewalk, behind the yellow tape."

"Do you think this is the work of the Rich Girl Killer, Miss Kline?"

"The what?"

"I heard her throat was crushed like the other one."

"Oh, my God." The white letters blurred in front of her.

Alex Taylor was moving forward. "I said, back to the street."

She heard another reporter shouting from farther away. "It's Audrey Kline. Over here. Miss Kline, you fit the killer's victimology. Are you worried for your own safety?"

The whirs and clicks of flashing cameras crawled over her skin like an assault of mechanical spiders.

"This is a restricted area. If you don't leave, I'll have you arrested."

"Are you friends with Miss Kline, officer? Why were you holding hands? Is she in danger?"

"I said—"

"I'll handle this." Audrey blinked her vision clear. It was up to her and no one else to pull it together. She touched Alex's arm as she moved beside him, and gave him a squeeze of silent apology for getting dragged into her society-page world. His tricep was as hard and sinewed as his forearm, his skin as warm and reassuring as the grip of his hand had been. But it was time for her to be strong now. "I'll handle this," she repeated, pulling away.

His questioning gaze met hers over the jut of his shoulder. "You don't have to talk to them."

"Who knows what they'll say if I don't?" She stood in front of him, grateful for the wall of heat at her back as the vultures circled around them. "Officer Taylor is securing the scene of a crime. Please respect his orders and move back to the street so that KCPD can do their job and find Gretchen Cosgrove's killer."

"Do you think this death is related to Valeska Gallagher's unsolved murder? You knew both victims."

"No comment."

"Can you comment on the Demetrius Smith trial?" the heavyset reporter asked.

"Not tonight."

"Are you and—Officer Taylor, is it?—an item?"

That was the news they wanted to report? "One of my best friends was murdered tonight. My love life is not up for discussion."

Audrey startled at the broad hand at the small of her back and the hushed voice against her ear. "Don't let 'em rile you up, Red." And then Alex was reaching around her, moving the reporters back. "Miss Kline has no further comment at this—"

"What are you doing way over here?" The small crowd parted as Harper Pierce nudged his way to the front. Without so much as a nod of acknowledgment to her or Alex, he pulled her hand through the crook of his elbow. "I leave you alone for a few minutes and you get lost."

"Harper." Even in that teasing tone, it felt like a reprimand, as if she was a child.

"Take the help when you can get it," he whispered. He patted his hand over hers, pinning her fingers to his arm so that she couldn't pull away without making a scene and really giving the press something to talk about. "I need you. Gretch's parents want to know if you'd read a statement to the press for them."

"I appreciate the rescue, but I don't think I'm the best person for that right now." But Harper wasn't slowing down. He wasn't taking no for an answer. Maybe he just needed a friend at his side right now. Audrey set aside her own discomfort and summoned compassion. "Of course. Any way I can help."

Although he didn't seem to have the will to smile either, Harper paused with her to allow a picture of the two of them together before escorting her out to the sidewalk. Then his hand was blocking the next camera and they were striding on.

The number of people in the crowd was still growing, and Audrey couldn't help but glance at the technician by the news van, the parking attendant who was retrieving a car for one of the guests, the man in his bathrobe, pajamas and a pair of galoshes on the opposite sidewalk looking on. Alex Taylor said the police suspected that Gretchen's killer was here somewhere, watching the chaotic results of his gruesome handiwork. Had she just brushed past a killer? Been photographed by him? Looked him in the eye? Was it that man? That one there?

Audrey's gaze swept past two young black men, barely out of their teens, if that, lounging against a car at the fringe of the crowd. The shorter one, wearing a white ball cap twisted sideways on his head, leaned over to whisper something to the tall one in a black hoodie. The tall one laughed and looked right at her.

At her.

And then they both raised two fingers and pointed them at her, flicking their thumbs as if they were firing a gun.

"Oh, my God," Audrey gasped. She quickly turned away, missing a step and stumbling into Harper's side.

"Are you all right?" he asked, pausing a moment to help her regain her balance.

What was that about? Did they have something to do with Gretchen's murder? Did those boys know her? Or were they just taking delight in compounding the misery of an easy target?

"I'm fine," she lied, knowing her focus should be on Gretchen and Harper and whatever the Cosgroves needed from her tonight. "I'll be fine."

She looked over her shoulder to see Officer Taylor herding the reporters who'd found them back to the re-stricted area. He was watching the two young men who'd mimicked a shooting, too, and was already weaving through the crowd toward them. He looked up from whatever message he was relaying into the radio on his shoulder. She caught one last glimpse of those dark, watchful eyes focused on her before the crowd shifted and he was blocked from view.

Suddenly, she felt oddly alone, even attached to Harper's side in the midst of the crowd. The enormity of potential suspects—of one man, or maybe two— knowing, gloating, getting off on this chaos, closed in on her, constricting her breathing, making her skin crawl. She felt like a specimen under a microscope, completely at the mercy of unknown eyes.

Without really considering the significance of her actions, Audrey shoved the bandanna she still carried into her jeans. She kept her fingers in her pocket, clinging to the one true piece of comfort she'd had since hearing of Gretchen's murder.

Chapter Three

One Month Later

The strains of chamber music muted as Audrey closed the kitchen door behind her. The din of eager, friendly voices from all the polite conversations she'd endured tonight still seemed to echo in her ears, leaving her nearly deaf in the empty room as she breathed a sigh of relief. "That's what I needed."

After allowing herself a moment to savor the quiet, she kicked off her strappy Gucci heels and curled her aching toes against the cool tile, wishing she could shed the fitted gown with the stays that poked into her ribs, as well. But since hostess nudity wasn't the kind of buzz she wanted to generate with this holiday fundraising event, she settled for padding across the kitchen and opening the fridge in search of some caffeine. "Great." She scoped the shelves up and down. "Just great."

Not one diet cola to be found. Coffee? She closed the refrigerator and turned to the empty coffeemaker on the counter.

Out of luck. The only caffeine in the house was on the serving tables the caterers had set up, and she wasn't going back to the party any sooner than she had to. The whole point of sneaking off to the kitchen was to find ten minutes of silence where she could nurse her headache and maybe think a bit more about how she wanted to open her statement to the jury when Demetrius Smith's trial started in the morning.

She already had her arguments lined up. Her evidence was all in order, the witness list approved. Her boss, District Attorney Dwight Powers, had signed off on her strategy for putting away the reputed gang leader. Smith claimed he'd been an innocent bystander as the ten-year-old boy had been shot and killed in his backyard, thinking he could plead out to lesser charges. But Audrey intended to nail him to the wall for a list of crimes ranging from drug-dealing and witness intimidation to Calvin Chambers's murder.

As it did every time she read or thought about the ten-year-old's death, Audrey's memories went back to the night of Gretchen's murder—to the much more personal understanding she now had about violence and innocent lives so cruelly and callously taken. Inevitably, her thoughts of that night ended up at a shadowed hedgerow, where a dark-eyed, opinionated, compassionate cop had given her a few moments of respite from her grief.

You get Smith.

Alex Taylor had angered her, touched her heart, held her hand and handed down an edict.

Right. No pressure.

Apparently, the support of KCPD, as well as career success and personal independence, hinged on winning this trial.

No pressure whatsoever.

No wonder her head ached.

It was Audrey's first big case as a prosecutor. Her

chance to prove she was smart enough, gutsy enough and tough enough to win a case without the backing of her father's firm. Rupert Kline expected her to fail and was waiting to pick up the pieces with a hug and a told-you-so. He expected her to come to her senses and accept the lucrative partnership he'd offered in his firm. All his money and influence hadn't been able to save her mother from the cancer that had ravaged her body and ultimately silenced her beautiful spirit. So, by damn, he wasn't going to let anything happen to his little girl.

Even if all that love was smothering her.

So in the kindest, most reassuring way she knew how, Audrey was fighting to be her own woman, to create her own success story—to build her own life that included her father, but wasn't dominated by him. Her mind was more focused, her goals clearer now, than they'd ever been. She didn't need Daddy's money to get the job done. She didn't need his name to give her clout.

She didn't need lectures from some doubting Thomas of a cop, either. She could do this.

She had to do this.

Beyond getting a ruthless criminal off the streets, she needed to succeed in order to prove that, at twenty-seven, with a degree from Smith and a juris doctor from the University of Missouri, she was no longer Daddy's little girl. She was more than the pretty princess in the gilded Kline cage.

So why had she agreed to help her father host this fundraiser for a scholarship to honor Gretchen's memory on the night before the trial began?

Proof that she was her own woman, indeed.

Audrey pulled out a glass and filled it with water

from the tap, hating that vulnerable place in her heart. "Why can't I say no to you, Daddy?"

Probably because the arts and friendship were worthy causes. Probably because she was as fiercely protective of her father as he was of her. Audrey had moved back home those last few months when her mother had been ill—to take care of Rupert as much as her mother. Despite the tragedy, Audrey had finally understood what it felt like to be needed. Her. Not her family's money, not her father's name. Her parents had needed their daughter to be there, to love them, to be strong when they couldn't be.

Just like he needed her tonight.

But she really should be practicing her opening statement.

Taking a long drink of water, Audrey pulled out a stool from the counter and sat. Using the center island and the two ovens as her imaginary audience, she began. "Your Honor, ladies and gentlemen of the jury, I'm here today to prove that every citizen of Kansas City deserves justice. Every citizen deserves to feel safe, walking his own streets…" She groaned and shook her head. "Too pompous." She tunneled her fingers beneath the tendrils of hair loosely pinned at her nape and massaged the back of her neck. "No child should live in fear of walking home from school… What's this?"

Lowering her glass, Audrey picked up the sealed envelope lying on top of the basket of pledge cards on the counter. Recognizing the neat handwriting on the front, she smiled. "Charlotte."

Feeling as if she'd just gotten a hug, Audrey slit open the flap and pulled out a note card that was as smart and unassuming as the woman who'd sent it. Charlotte

Mayweather was another classmate who'd gone to the same private high school she, Gretchen and Harper Pierce had attended. Audrey tried to remember the last time she'd seen Charlotte—certainly not at Gretchen's funeral. And she hadn't been included on the guest list tonight because Audrey had known she wouldn't be able to come.

Still, as Audrey read the note, she wasn't surprised to see that Charlotte had enclosed a check for the scholarship fund. Somehow, Charlotte had known that they were honoring an old friend tonight. Although she'd never been the social butterfly Gretchen was, Charlotte had always been adamant about supporting the causes—and people—she cared about.

I wish I could be there

the note began.

Like you, Gretchen made a point to come visit me from time to time. She could always make me smile. Here's a token of my affection for her, and how much I miss her. Thanks for doing this for her, Aud.
Good luck with the trial. I'll be following you in the papers.
Charlotte

Good luck? Audrey sighed with a bit of melancholy as she tucked the note and check inside the envelope and dropped it back into the basket. Was there anyone in Kansas City who wasn't watching how she handled the Smith case?

And how many of them expected her to fail?

The swish of the kitchen door sweeping across the threshold gave her a split-second notice to paste a smile on her face before company joined her. "There you are."

Audrey turned to the distinguished man with the silvering, receding auburn hair and smiled. "Daddy."

"I wondered where you'd gotten off to." He picked up her sandals and carried them over to the counter where she sat. He pressed a kiss to her temple and dropped the shoes into her lap. "No fair skipping out if I can't. Our guests are starting to leave. Will you see them off at the door while I chat up another ten grand from the Bishops?"

"Of course." Pulling up the skirt of her gown, she pinched her feet back into the high heels. She inclined her head toward the basket on the counter. "We received a card with a check from Charlotte Mayweather, too."

"Charlotte? Now there's a name I haven't heard for a while." He pulled the card from the basket. "How is she doing?"

"I'm not sure," Audrey answered, fastening the delicate buckle at her ankle. "I haven't been to see her lately. But I know she misses Gretchen as much as I do."

"You had a wonderful idea with this scholarship. Gretchen was such a patroness of the arts, it's fitting that she be remembered this way." Audrey knew by his frown that he'd reached the end of Charlotte's note. "Even she knows about this unpleasantness with the Smith trial."

Audrey plucked the card from his hands and returned it to the basket. "That *unpleasantness* is my job. If I win,

I'll have the track record to be able to run for district attorney myself one day."

"And if you lose, you'll be vilified by the press. Why don't you come back to Kline, Galloway & Tucker?" *Where I can protect you.*

Where she'd never be anything more than Rupert Kline's daughter. Or wife to one of his partners, if he had his way. The unspoken arguments were clear and familiar.

But she needed to make her own decisions—captain her own victories and suffer her own mistakes without her father's money or influence to either make them happen or go away. Audrey needed him to know that she was smart enough, capable enough—that *she* was the necessary element to build her own career and find her own happiness, instead of accepting that her life was the result of whatever her father's doting yet misguided love for his only daughter allowed it to be.

Not wanting to tax what energy either of them had left tonight, Audrey wisely changed the subject. "So, are we a rousing success?"

Rupert pulled back the front of his tux and stuffed his hands into the pockets of his tailored wool trousers. "Everyone is interested in giving this time of year. I think Clarice earned her money with this event—pulling it together so quickly and bringing in a lot of donations. She knows how to throw a party."

Did she detect a hint of admiration when her father mentioned the event planner's name? Audrey felt a smile curve her own lips. Her father had been widowed for nearly three years now. If the right woman turned his eye, she wasn't against him seeing where things might lead. A new girlfriend might even distract him from his fixation on her. "Are you and Clarice planning on staying up late tonight to, um, go over some numbers after our guests leave?"

"I may have invited her to stay for a brandy to congratulate her." Rupert took her elbow and helped Audrey to her feet once she was cinched in and ready to report for duty again. He tapped the tip of her nose with his finger and smiled. "But you just put those match-making thoughts away, missy. We're only discussing business."

"Does Clarice know that?" As much as she hated the nickname he'd given her as a toddler, she loved her father even more, and let that argument slide, as well. She laid her palm over his heart, brushing over the bulge of his pacemaker to feel the strong beat of it beneath her hand. "I just want you to know, that if business turns to pleasure, I'll be locked up in my office upstairs, and I won't hear a thing that might go on in your study—or anywhere else on the first floor."

"You're wicked, missy." He scooted her out of the kitchen and Audrey was instantly assaulted by the noise and colors and pressure to be the perfect hostess again. As one of the tallest men in the room, it was easy to spot Harper Pierce when he excused himself from a conversation and headed into the foyer. Harper strode toward them, and Rupert whispered against her ear. "Speaking of matchmaking, I noticed Harper has been sticking close to your side all evening. He knows the board is considering him for a partnership at the firm. Do I give him credit for wanting to date you, or hold it against him?"

"Daddy!" Audrey swatted his arm for teasing her.

"Harper was engaged to Gretchen. Don't start throwing him at me before he's done mourning her loss."

He arched one of his silvery-red brows in a paternal warning. "Harper's an ambitious man. I don't know that he'd let grief stand in the way of getting what he wants."

"I don't care for him in that way anymore. He's just a friend—one who's co-hosting this evening's fundraiser with me. That's why he's been so attentive."

"Uh-huh."

"Seriously." Audrey reached up to straighten her father's bow tie. "I'm looking for a man who's a little more into me than he is my daddy's law firm or bank account."

He caught her hands in his and pressed a kiss to her fingers. "I want that for you, too."

Audrey grinned. "And he has to have a personality, support my career, be a good kisser and treat me like a princess."

Rupert laughed. "You don't ask for much, do you? Just promise me you won't be so hard on the boys and focused on success that you wind up all alone."

"That formula worked for you, didn't it?"

"Yes, I found success. But I also found someone to love. I married your mother and had a family."

"I will, too, Daddy." Audrey stretched up on tiptoe to kiss his cheek. "I promise."

As he excused himself to speak with the Bishops, Audrey turned and fixed a smile on her face for Harper's benefit.

"Were you and Rupert talking about me?" Harper asked, his lawyer's voice smooth and concise. Audrey hoped he couldn't feel the flinch that came with automatically steeling herself against the possessive touch around her waist. "I thought I heard something about marriage?"

"Don't flatter yourself, Romeo." Maybe her father was right. Was Harper rebounding from his relationship with Gretchen and setting his sights on becoming more than friends again? Their dates in high school seemed like a lifetime ago and, as far as Audrey was concerned, that was where any romance with him should stay—in the past. Subtly twisting to move his hand to a less intimate position, she pointed to the front door at the far end of the foyer. "I see the Hunts are leaving. I'd better go thank them and say good-night."

"I'll come with you."

Audrey endured a half hour of kisses and handshakes before the ache from her constant smile got a welcome relief from Jeffrey Beecher, the assistant who worked for tonight's event planner, Clarice Darnell.

"Audrey?" Pushing his way through the dwindling crowd, he hurried from the back of the house to join her. The earbud he wore, and wire running down the back of his collar, made her assume the interruption was related to the party. "Audrey, do you have a moment?"

"Sure." She worked the muscles on her face, trying to relax them. "Is there a problem?"

"Can't this wait, Beecher? And you're to address her as Miss Kline."

She stiffened at the unwanted and unnecessary defense on her behalf. "Audrey's fine. What is it?"

He reached inside his suit jacket and pulled out an envelope. "This just came for you."

"At this hour?" Audrey frowned and took the letter. "Maybe it's another donation."

"I don't think so," said Jeffrey. Harper *harumphed* at her side while the hired help monopolized her attention. "A courier delivered it to the service entrance—said to bring it to you immediately. I gave him a five-dollar tip."

Jeffrey pushed up his narrow-framed glasses onto the bridge of his nose and cleared his throat. That was when she realized he was waiting to be reimbursed.

Normally, Audrey would have given him the money herself, but with nothing on but gray silk and lace, and no cleavage to speak of, she had no purse or pockets or hiding place to stash any cash. She turned and rested her hand on Harper's sleeve, dredging up one more smile. "Do you mind?"

"Not for you." Although Harper's enthusiasm faded as soon as he turned his attention away from her, he pulled out his wallet and took Jeffrey aside.

For a delivery that sounded so urgent, the envelope was curiously devoid of red flags or clues as to what the contents might be. A glance through the guests gathering in the foyer indicated an easy exit to the kitchen was out of the question. Staying here meant she'd have Harper looking over her shoulder. Audrey opted for the quickest route to uninterrupted quiet by following the next couple to depart out the front door.

The night air instantly whipped through her hair, giving her senses a reviving shock and raising goose bumps along her arms. There was a dampness to the December breeze, hinting that they'd have a dusting of snow by morning. Perhaps taking a moment to find a wrap for her bare shoulders would have been a smarter move. But she was out here now, the porch was deserted, and the only sounds of company came from the music inside and the crunch of tires over bricks as the valet staff drove up with cars for guests waiting in the driveway below. Hunching her shoulders and shivering against the cold, Audrey moved beneath one of the brass lamps framing the entryway to study the envelope.

Jeffrey was right. It didn't look like any pledge card or personal note regarding tonight's scholarship benefit. There was just her name, typed and neatly centered, along with the address and the courier service logo. No return address, but that was probably included inside. Perhaps it was something from the defense attorney pertaining to Demetrius Smith's case, or a proof of some reporter's column about the pretrial buzz for the newspaper. Trading her society hat for her attorney persona, she opened the envelope and pulled out the enclosed letter to read it.

Her blood chilled.

Oh. My. God.

"You'll catch your death out here, ma'am."

Audrey jumped a mile inside her skin at the voice in the shadows. As the letter floated to the ground, she spun around to locate the balding man in a dark utility uniform climbing the steps onto the porch. Instinctively, she backed against the house at his approach. He was between her and the door now, and he just kept coming.

Her pulse thundered in her ears as she put up her hand. "Stop right there. Please."

That he did what she commanded surprised her even further. With an apologetic nod, he stopped and retreated a step, giving her a chance to calm her nerves and focus in on the name badge pinned to his dark gray parking valet's jacket.

"Bud." She called him by name, recognizing him now

as another employee of Clarice Darnell's event staff. "You startled me."

"Sorry about that, ma'am." Fear had given the dampness of the night a chance to sink beneath her skin and she was truly shivering now. "I just wondered if you'd forgotten your coat. I'd be happy to get it for you."

"I'm fine." Audrey rubbed her hands up and down her arms, completely aware that her words belied her actions. He could think her spoiled, an idiot or a liar—she didn't care. She just wanted him to leave. "I got overheated inside. The fresh air feels good." She pulled away from the chilled moisture of the limestone facade, standing straight and tilting her chin, determined to take control of her emotions. "That'll be all."

Bud, of the thinning brown hair and toothpick he rolled from side to side between his lips, stood beside the porch railing, staring—no, leisurely running his gaze from the goose bumps on her arms along her body right down to her polished toenails. Just when she thought the curious creep might never blink, he bent down and picked up the envelope and letter that had landed between them. "You dropped these."

Audrey snatched the papers from his fingers and tucked them against her stomach. "Thank you."

The tense seconds had stretched beyond uncomfortable when the front door opened beside her. Audrey nodded to the gray-haired couple who stepped outside before catching the door and giving Bud a succinct dismissal. "The Bishops will be needing their car."

"Yes, ma'am. You be careful now. And stay warm." After pushing the knot of his tie up to his collar, Bud took the ticket stub from Dr. Bishop and jogged down the steps onto the circular drive to retrieve their car.

Audrey's "Good night" was for anyone within listening range as she went inside and pushed the door shut behind her.

"Audrey?"

"Not now, Harper." She shrugged off the hand on her arm and marched straight up the carpeted grand staircase. At the top she turned and hurried all the way down the hallway to the circular tower where her bedroom suite and its adjoining office were located.

Even after pulling her dressing gown over her shoulders, she had a hard time feeling any warmer than she had outside. But this wasn't the time to worry about wintry temps or strange men who materialized from the shadows. She locked the bedroom door behind her, grabbed the tweezers from her manicure set to pick up the letter and envelope and went into her office.

Moving her purse from the office chair, Audrey sat and reached for the phone. She needed to call her boss, Dwight Powers, and tell him there'd been a new development in the Smith case. And then she needed to call KCPD.

But she was quickly on her feet again, pacing behind her desk while she punched in the numbers. When the D.A.'s home phone rang, she stopped and took a deep, calming breath. She'd better have her facts straight before she said anything.

Tucking the cordless phone between her shoulder and ear, Audrey flattened the letter on her cherry wood desk and read it again.

She hadn't been mistaken.

No law firm or newspaper logo.

No personal stationery stamp.

No return address.

No name.

Just a threat—as clear as it was anonymous.

*It's your turn, Audrey. The others didn't listen
to me, but you're a smart girl. Walk away from
this trial and go back to your tea parties.*

Do the right thing.

Or you'll die doing the wrong one.

"Come on, Dwight. Answer." Her boss had become a
family man with his marriage to his second wife and the
children that came with that union. Either they'd gone
to bed early or they were all out together for a family
night. But with each ring of the telephone, the tension
inside her wound tighter and tighter.

Who had sent that threat? Although it couldn't have
come from Demetrius Smith himself, even kept in isolation from other prisoners, it wouldn't be impossible for a
gang leader to get a message out to one of his lieutenants
or followers on the outside.

Ring.

Had it truly been a courier delivery? Or had one of
Smith's men disguised himself and come to her house?
Gotten past security? Been that close to her staff and
guests and father?

That close to her?

Was he watching her even now? Learning which bedroom was hers? Enjoying her shell-shocked reaction?

Ring. Ring.

Dwight Powers's voice mail clicked on and Audrey
suddenly felt disconnected. Isolated. Alone.

"Suck it up, woman," Audrey chided. She could not—

would not—leave a panicked, unprofessional message on her boss's phone.

And then she spotted the blue bandanna—washed and pressed and peeking out of her purse—waiting for a free moment for her to return it with a proper thank-you to its owner, Alex Taylor. She snatched it out of her bag and wrinkled it in her fist, hugging the soft swatch of cotton to her chest.

Alex Taylor's handkerchief had been a gift on one of the saddest nights of her life. His caring gesture—whether motivated by his personal stake in the Smith trial or something chivalrous his grandmother had taught him—had provided an unexpected anchor when she'd been buffeted by a storm of unwanted emotions.

Now she was holding on to it again, clinging to the strength and security it represented.

She wouldn't be scared off this case.

But she was scared.

So, ARROGANT, TOUGH-TALKING Audrey Kline—with all her preaching about being her own woman and setting the world on fire—ran for cover, just like the others.

She could be spooked.

He smiled as he stood in the darkness near the Kline's front gate, watching the imposing rock mansion with its historic architecture and air of refined taste and wealth. He enjoyed being a part of that world. But it was the fear he'd sensed when she'd run into the house that gave him real pleasure tonight.

He exhaled the smoke from his lungs with a deep, satisfied sigh as the lights filtering from her upstairs windows drew his attention. For a moment, he saw her slight figure silhouetted against the interior lights before she quickly moved away from the blinds—as if she knew he was out here—watching, wanting, relishing her distress.

He'd been right about her Achilles' heel. For one woman it had been about protecting her child. For the last one, he'd found it far too easy to prey upon her looks and her fear that once her beauty was gone, she'd have nothing but her money to offer to anyone who might care.

So he'd taken her beauty. He'd struck right at the heart of what terrified her most.

Now, he was free to toy with Audrey Kline. He knew what she wanted—independence, respect, professional success—and he knew how to take it from her.

He'd give her a chance to make things right. Perhaps the smile she'd given him tonight would prove more sincere than the others had been. Everyone deserved a chance.

But if she was playing him...

"I'm still here." He dropped his cigarette and ground it out in the leaves beneath his shoe, turning his attention to the impatient summons on his cell phone. "Yes, I've made all the necessary arrangements," he assured the simpleton who was paying to do his bidding. "I'll take care of everything."

"Is it safe?"

How tedious. "Blowing up anything is never completely safe. But if you follow my directions to the letter and you position yourself where I instructed, then you won't be hurt and you'll have the perfect alibi."

Just as he would.

"You're crazy, man. This better work or I'll be coming after you."

Crazy? His hand curled into a fist down at his side. Although it wasn't the first time he'd heard that word, he'd long ago learned to let the offensive misconception slide off his back. The man on the phone was the real fool if he thought insults or threats could hurt him.

The telltale buzzer of the Klines' security system warned him that the front gate was sliding open and one of the guest's cars was approaching. Forcing his fingers to relax, he backed into the shadows of the ancient oaks that lined the circular drive and blocked him from view of the estate's security cameras.

An unexpected snap froze him into place. It took a therapeutic mantra through his clenched jaw for him to ignore the twig jabbing at his shoulder and retreat another step.

The smooth hum of a finely tuned engine—a Bentley, by the sound of it—passed by before he responded to the nagging insistence of his caller.

"Will it work? Will this freaking plan of yours work?"

He ran his fingers along the broken twig, counting the dry brown leaves that had withered with the change of seasons. "You handle my problem, and I'll take care of yours."

He flipped the phone shut and slipped it into his slacks, pausing a moment before pulling out his pocket-knife.

In three strokes, he sawed away the fragmented wood and dropped it to the ground. With one more cut, he sliced off a leaf, leaving two on either side of the branch.

Something eased inside his brain at the symmetry of his handiwork, and he folded the knife and put it away.

Then he plucked his cigarette butt from the ground and stuffed it into his pocket. He straightened his jacket and tie and stepped onto the curving brick driveway, lengthening his stride as he headed to the house. The evening was winding down. It was time for him to get back to his duties before he was missed.

Chapter Four

Winter was in the air. So was something Alex couldn't quite put his finger on.

The powdering of snow that had fallen through the night was still clinging to the grass in the park across the street. Christmas was only three weeks away, but with all the freaks and crazies lined up outside the courthouse that morning, it felt more like Halloween.

Alex handed his gun over to the security guards just inside the lobby of the steel, glass and granite building. He wasn't surprised to see the reporters with their camera crews here to cover the opening day of Demetrius Smith's trial. A car with four of what he guessed were Broadway Bad Boys like Smith was parked beyond the blocked-off street in front of the courthouse. The uniformed officers pulling up in a black-and-white just behind them would check out their IDs and tell the teens and young twenty-somethings to move on.

What Alex didn't expect to see were all the motherly types, religious groups and activists in the park across from the courthouse, with signs of both support and damnation for the proceedings going on inside the building. Some wore colorful coats and banners draped across their chests to draw attention to their cause, he supposed. A few wore stocking masks to remain anonymous. The ghoul dressed up like the Grim Reaper was a little over-the-top, but the message was clear—an innocent child had fallen prey to gang violence, and the moms and grandmas and preachers and papas of Kansas City weren't going to stand for a scumbag like Demetrius Smith roaming their streets and terrorizing their families any longer.

The scar on his back where his Westside Warrior tat had once marked him burned with a mixture of suspicion and guilt. In his early teens, he'd been one of the thugs these people feared. He'd jacked a car once, had done his fair share of vandalism and had proved himself better than a kid should be in a fight. But with his birth mother providing a stellar example of drug abuse, he'd never used or sold the crap and he damn straight had never killed anyone—rival or innocent.

"Sixth floor," the guard instructed, returning Alex's badge.

"Thanks." Tucking the badge into the pocket of his jeans, Alex headed for the elevator. Those same street smarts that had kept him alive when he'd had no one at home to care about his next meal, much less his safety, hummed with an awareness of his surroundings. Something had him on edge. Something he'd seen walking in wasn't right.

Maybe it was just the beefed-up security around the building that made him hypersensitive to his surroundings. The guards monitoring the entrances and exits were routine. But when Alex got off the elevator, the extra uniforms positioned in the hallway and at the courtroom doors reinforced the sense that trouble was hiding someplace close by.

Had there been a threat? Usually, his team was put on notice, whether they were on the clock or not, if any warnings had been called in against the courthouse and its personnel, or if Homeland Security elevated its alert level. Since he was free to come watch the proceedings this afternoon, Alex had to assume that the extra security was simply a precaution with the highly publicized trial—a preemptive warning to dissuade any of those crazies or gangbangers from making a threat in the first place.

But that didn't keep him from wishing he still had his Glock on his belt as he shrugged out of his black leather jacket and showed his ID to the guard who let him in the courtroom's thick mahogany doors.

Once inside, Alex easily spotted Trip's wide shoulders and slipped into the aisle seat beside him.

"You're late, shrimp," the big man whispered.

"Told you I was moving some furniture out of storage for my grandparents this morning. I offered to let you help."

Trip grinned. "No, thanks. I thought somebody better keep an eye on Sarge today."

"I can hear you talking." Although Sergeant Delgado seemed to have taken Calvin Chambers's death especially hard, he wasn't above joining the sotto voce fray and putting his men in their places. "Shh."

Obeying the command, Alex took a minute to identify all the players in the room. Judge Grover Shanks was an imposing figure at the bench. Audrey Kline— pure class in her navy-blue suit, with her auburn hair pinned at her nape—stood at the table several rows in front of Alex. She was in a heated debate with Cade Shipley, a defense attorney he recognized as much from his press coverage as from Alex's few appearances in the courtroom. Shipley stood beside a seated black man wearing a charcoal pinstripe suit. Even from the back, there was no mistaking Demetrius Smith's shaved head, gold earring and bored slouch.

Alex's skin tingled with awareness. Smith looked more like a rap star at an awards show than the bleeding bastard they'd hauled out of his drug house in a black, skintight hoodie and handcuffs. Just one more thing that wasn't as it should be today.

Alex turned to Trip. "What's with all the uniforms in the building?"

"I'm not sure. Something's hinky, but I haven't heard anything official or seen anything out of place."

Good. So he wasn't the only one bothered by that intangible air of lurking danger. "How's it going?"

Sergeant Delgado offered a surly whisper. "The D.A.'s office is gettin' their butt kicked. Kline made a great opening statement, but it's been downhill ever since."

Alex leaned against the arm of his seat, giving himself a clear line of sight straight down the center aisle. The mention of butt kicking drew his focus to Audrey's sweet, round bottom.

Sucker. Why couldn't his unguarded thoughts this past month be filled with a woman who wasn't quite so far out of his league?

But no, he had to notice. As icily untouchable as the rest of her might be, there was an earthy sway about that backside that was as distracting in sedate navy-blue wool today as it had been in hip-hugging jeans that night at the Cosgrove estate.

More than once, he'd wondered how she'd dealt with

the intrusion of all those reporters that night. How was she coping with her grief? Burying it the way he'd seen her lock down control over her fears and vulnerability when the cameras had started flashing? Had the tall blond suit who'd claimed ownership over her given her a shoulder to cry on? Steered her away from the two thugs who'd pretended to shoot her? Alex ignored the little twinges of jealousy and contempt, and smiled inside. Did she ever find a powder puff to help her mask her pink-tipped nose and the all-too-human evidence of emotion that had reddened her eyes and splotched her cheeks? She'd been so self-conscious about him seeing her like that. Okay, so he'd gone looking for the trespasser he'd heard and found a frightened, upset woman instead. She'd argued with him and he'd pressured her about this trial. Still, remembering her with her guard completely stripped away like that—clinging to his hand, holding on to him—felt…intimate.

Dutifully ignoring the appreciative heat licking through his veins, Alex lifted his gaze to the defiant tilt of her head and tuned in to a voice that was much sharper than the raw huskiness he remembered. "Your Honor, my esteemed colleague, Mr. Shipley, seems to think he has an open-and-shut case."

"The burden of proof is on you, Miss Kline." Shipley's voice was nothing short of patronizing as he turned his dark eyes on Audrey. "While my client admits to being on the scene of the standoff with KCPD's SWAT team and drug task force, he, in fact, was an innocent bystander who was also injured."

Tanya Chambers's gasp echoed through the courtroom, drawing Alex's attention to the second row where she sat weeping, squeezing the arm of the older woman beside her. That took a lot of gall to compare Smith's flesh wound to the bullets that had killed a ten-year-old boy. A buzz of commentary instantly erupted among the crowd. Alex heard everything from words of sympathy for the boy's mother to accusations of, "Innocent, my ass" and a "Shut it" that identified where two young men from Demetrius's Broadway Bad Boy posse were sitting.

"Quiet!" Judge Shanks rapped his gavel on his bench. "This courtroom will be silent or it'll be empty. Do I make myself clear?"

As the comments quickly quieted, Audrey turned to give Tanya Chambers an apologetic smile. Whatever she was about to say died on her lips when those bright green eyes locked on Alex. Her pale cheeks flushed with color as he held her gaze. But before he could even offer a thumbs-up, she turned to face the judge again, quickly reaching into the briefcase on her chair and shoving something down inside.

That woman was a puzzle. Icy cool and smokin' hot. She wore her emotions on her skin yet denied feeling them with every tightly articulated word. "All I'm asking for is a short continuance to reinterview—"

"If Miss Kline's star witness is unable to testify—"

"The witness Mr. Shipley is referring to was found shot to death in his home this weekend, Your Honor." Alex could imagine the accusatory glare she turned on Cade Shipley and the defendant at his table. "If your client knows anything about Trace Vaughn's murder—"

"Objection." Demetrius shook his head while his lawyer defended the insinuation. "The prosecution is making a prejudicial statement about my client. Mr.

Vaughn was a known gang member. His unfortunate death is under investigation by KCPD, and no arrests have been made as of yet. Mr. Smith has been in a jail cell since his arrest, so he has an airtight alibi. He is not involved in that crime."

The ribbing chatter from the two thugs in attendance was quickly silenced with a look from the judge and the approach of one of the uniformed guards. Well, son of a gun. Did those two boys look familiar?

Audrey continued to argue her point. "Demetrius Smith also has an affiliation with the Broadway Bad Boys—"

"If that were the case, he'd hardly promote the shooting of one of his own people."

"He could order—"

Judge Shanks pounded his gavel. "The objection is sustained. Jurors will disregard any mention of the defendant's alleged knowledge of Vaughn's murder." He turned from the twelve people in the box at the front of the room to point his gavel at Audrey. "If you can prove a connection between Mr. Vaughn's death and the proceedings at hand, I'll reconsider your motion for a delay, Miss Kline. Until then, do you have enough evidence to proceed with the prosecution?"

Was Smith grinning? Alex sat up straight in his seat. He couldn't read the bastard's expression from this angle, but there was no mistaking that Demetrius was looking straight across the aisle at Audrey, no doubt daring her to make good on her promise to put him away. What the hell? He curled his fingers into his palm, fighting the urge to wipe that smirk off his face. Couldn't the judge see that?

Audrey apparently did. Whatever message had been

silently communicated, she shrugged it off, tilted her chin to that arrogant angle and faced the judge. "Yes, Your Honor. The D.A.'s office is ready to continue with its case against Demetrius Smith."

"Very well." The judge tucked his papers into a folder and closed it before striking his gavel one last time. "Court is recessed for this afternoon. We'll reconvene at 9:00 a.m. tomorrow. Bailiff, will you escort the jury out."

"All rise."

Alex stood with everyone else as the judge exited to his chambers and the jurors followed the bailiff through a door at the front of the room. With the sudden buzz of conversations and movement of people filing into the aisle, it was impossible to make out the exact words being exchanged up front. But Demetrius Smith was tall enough that Alex could see his focus on Audrey. And as two guards turned him and took him away, Alex saw the slight nod of his head out into the crowd. His two bros shouted something in return.

His body tensed and ready to spring, Alex stepped into the path of the two young gangbangers, reading their faces as they approached, trying to figure out what coded communication had just passed between them and Demetrius. Every gang had their own set of hidden signs, colors, words, symbols that could say anything from "I belong here" to "You're dead." But there were a few messages that remained universal between gangs and generations of gang members—even when they went on to become cops.

Alex widened his stance, breathed in deeply and claimed the path leading to the exit. Both boys were teens, maybe twenty. Both were taller, skinnier, than Alex. And both understood Alex's silent warning.

"What?" the first one said, stopping in his tracks, giving Alex his space. "You harassin' us, officer?"

So they did remember him chasing them away from the Gretchen Cosgrove murder scene.

"We ain't done nothin'," the second one said, pulling on a white ball cap before turning it to the side and tipping up the brim. "We's just here for a friend."

"What did Demetrius say to you?"

"Nothin'."

Alex wasn't playing games with these wise guys. "What did you say to him?"

If he stood there long enough, waited long enough, intimidated long enough, one of them would crack. The first one did. "We told D he was gonna get off."

"Any particular reason you'd say that?"

"Cuz there's this guy—"

"Shut up." The second teen took off his hat and whacked his buddy on the shoulder. So Hat Boy was the brains of the duo. He was smart enough to know when to cut and run, at least. "We ain't doin' nothin' wrong bein' here, officer."

"You're the boys I chased off that murder scene in Mission Hills. You wouldn't be stalking Miss Kline, would you? Intimidating the opposing counsel is a crime, you know."

The teen in the white cap put up his hands in mock surrender. "Hey. We's just here to support D. We ain't said nothin' to your lady friend. Are we free to go?"

With a nod, Alex stepped aside, knowing he wouldn't get anything else out of them now. "Be good," he warned.

Hat Boy slapped his friend in the back of the head, reprimanding him on their way out the door. Alex watched White Hat turn to the right, away from the elevators, as he pulled on his jacket.

He tapped on Trip's arm, interrupting his conversation with Sergeant Delgado. "Don't go anywhere for a while, okay?"

"You onto something, shrimp?"

"I want to check those two out. Sly and Twitch is how they introduced themselves last time. Call it in and see if you can get me their names. Turn on your phone and I'll keep you posted." Then he was weaving through the crowd, hurrying to follow the two members of Demetrius's crew through the closing steel door of the stairwell exit.

Alex caught the door and slipped inside onto the landing. He hugged the painted cinder-block wall, listening to the sounds of footsteps running down the stairs. Those boys would have been patted down for guns or knives before they even got past the front door. But that didn't mean they couldn't have found a way to stash something in the stairwell—not if there was some *guy* with a plan for them to make Smith a free man again. But the rhythm of their steps was even, continuous. They weren't stopping to arm themselves.

Alex took off down the stairs behind them, moving as quickly as he could without making a sound. Sly and Twitch were crossing the lobby when Alex came through the stairwell door behind them. They had no visible weapons, but Sly with the hat was on his cell phone before he even got out the door. They broke into a jog as soon as they were outside, skirting the crowd of reporters waiting on the sidewalk out front. Alex went to the glass and watched them run up to the corner, where a dark red Impala pulled up. The two got in and the car sped away. It was different from the car he'd seen on his way in. That was a lot of Triple Bs out of their neighborhood at one time. Could something be going down if they were all driving away?

He let his gaze slide across the street to the park. Maybe a third of the people there were wearing some sort of low-slung hat or mask—ostensibly to keep out the cold, but conveniently keeping them from being identified, as well. That'd be an easy enough way to gather enough numbers for an attack of some kind. But no, subterfuge wasn't a gang's way. They were about an in-your-face show of strength and violence.

Alex stood at the window a few moments longer, watching, thinking—wishing he could pinpoint exactly what felt out of place here. The protesters clamored behind the line where they were allowed to congregate. Some of them just wanted their moment on TV; others were taking a stand. Mothers armed with placards. Preachers having their say. The Grim Reaper.

Maybe it was just that guy's poor taste in attention-grabbing garb that made Alex think there was more than the usual trial hoopla going on here.

The elevator dinged on the far side of the lobby and when the doors opened, the noise level inside the building doubled. Audrey, wearing a green trench coat and carrying her leather shoulder attaché, stepped out. Her red hair seemed like a beacon that the security guard, Cade Shipley, a group of print reporters and others followed out. While another guard escorted Mrs. Chambers and her friend toward a quieter side exit, Audrey,

Shipley and the reporters all filed through the security gate at the front entrance.

The instant the front doors opened, the press contingency outside swarmed upon them. They split into two groups, some following Shipley's tall, dark, smooth-talking sales pitch, while others circled Audrey until she was hidden from view.

Hidden didn't sit well with Alex. So what if she was a striking, recognizable face from the Kansas City society page who could sell papers and give a cogent interview? Their eagerness to get a piece of Audrey's attention felt more like ganging up on her, as if she was trapped, as if they didn't give a damn about the invasion of her personal space or the job she was trying to do.

Even if that job didn't involve winning a case that was of personal importance to his team, every save-the-day instinct that had been drilled into him since the Taylors had adopted him and inspired him to protect and serve in the first place screamed at him to help out the lady. It took just over a minute for him to check out with the guard and collect his gun, and another thirty seconds to clip his badge on his belt and get through the door.

Catching up to Audrey's group was easy. Spotting her in the middle proved a little more difficult. What he wouldn't give for the eight inches Trip had on him in height right about now.

But what he couldn't see, he listened for. He tuned in to Audrey's voice and politely pushed his way toward the sound. "I got the jury I wanted picked this morning—more women than men. They should be sympathetic to our side of the case."

He almost grinned when he saw her red hair. She talked as if she was holding court, but there was nothing to smile about when he saw her effort to move forward, to get through them with little success. The uniformed officer who'd escorted her out kept the crowd at arm's length, but they weren't letting her pass.

A reporter who identified himself as Steve Lassen, an independent journalist, asked, "Did your office do anything to protect your witness, Trace Vaughn? Lining him up to testify against his former boss got him killed, don't you think?"

That was when Audrey's chin jerked up, a signal Alex was beginning to think meant someone had struck a nerve. "Mr. Vaughn wasn't the prosecution's only witness."

"But the fact you subpoenaed him to testify signed his death warrant, right? Any regrets over the deal you made with him?"

Audrey's steps stuttered to a halt. "I can't comment on an ongoing police investigation."

Alex gave up on being polite and pushed his way through to the center of the mikes and cameras encircling her. With a nod toward the officer beside her, he slipped an arm around her waist. At her startled gasp, he latched on to a handful of her coat and pulled her into the crowd. "Miss Kline has answered all the questions she can for now."

"What are you doing?" She tried to pry his fingers loose.

"Giving you a chance to breathe."

"Miss Kline…" Another round of questions bombarded them, and rethinking her resistance to his rescue, Audrey leaned her shoulder into his chest and hastened her stride to match his. His strong arm and stern look cleared a path for them and he got her through the crowd and onto the street.

"Thank you," she said, pulling away from Alex. She adjusted the strap of her bag on her shoulder, clutching it between them like some kind of shield. "I never used to be claustrophobic, but sometimes, when they're all shoving a camera in my face—"

"Keep moving."

One look at the throng of protesters and well-wishers waiting in the park on the opposite side of the street for their chance to be heard, and Alex claimed her waist again. Snugging her to his side, he angled their path up the hill to the intersection and empty sidewalk there. She fit nicely, just the right height for his five feet ten inches, even in those high heels that tapped across the pavement. But if she'd noticed the way her rounder hips butted against his harder angles, she wasn't savoring the contact the way he was.

Instead, she was fighting him. "I don't appreciate your caveman tactics, Mr. Taylor. Those reporters are just doing their job."

She wanted caveman? Alex stopped in his tracks, his left hand the only thing that kept her from pitching forward. His right hand settled on the opposite side of her waist and he turned her in his arms, letting her read the warning in his eyes. "And they're keeping you from doing yours."

"Yes, I'm very well aware that you and your friends were there to check up on me—to see if I could do my job or not." Her green eyes sparked and she flattened her palm against his chest, pushing some distance between them. Even through the jacket and knit shirt he wore, the unexpected touch singed his skin. Probably not the reaction she was going for. Not the one he needed to be feeling right now, when he was trying to maintain the upper hand and get her away from the crowd.

"Don't flatter yourself, Red. We weren't spying on you. But two of Smith's thugs were."

"What?"

"I thought so. The two thugs who threatened you at the Cosgrove murder scene?" Easily overpowering both her hand and that tongue, he tucked her back to his side and crested the hill, checking the crossroads in all four directions. The uniforms were keeping the protesters in the park. The lights kept the downtown traffic moving in a normal pattern. He nodded to the surface parking on one corner, and the parking garage on another. "Where's your car?"

"Two blocks down. At the D.A.'s office."

"Are you kidding? You're walking to your office?"

"*We're* walking the two blocks if you don't let me go."

Smart mouth.

"I always walk if the weather's nice. The snow has melted off the sidewalks—the wind isn't bad. The fresh air and exercise clear my head. Are you sure those were the same boys?"

So much for a quick escape, putting his conscience to rest and getting on with the rest of his life.

"Fine. Don't make this easy." He took her hand and veered south along the sidewalk, heading for the yellow limestone high-rise across the street from the far end of the park. She wanted to walk? Then she could hustle up those expensive shoes and keep pace with him before they got cornered by somebody else. "For your information, we were at the courthouse to support

Mrs. Chambers and Sergeant Delgado. Her son died in his arms, and he's not dealing with it very well. We're a team—we stick together. We're always there to back up the other. Frankly, you looked like you were fighting that battle all on your own."

Speaking of backup, he owed Trip a call or text message. Alex's instincts had been right about sensing trouble; it just hadn't come from the source he'd expected. But he wasn't about to tell Trip Jones that he was going toe-to-toe with a stubborn woman who was testing his patience. No, sir. An admission like that would only trigger another six months of giving the rookie grief.

"I know what I'm doing, Officer Taylor," Audrey insisted. "I'm not afraid of a fight."

"You prove that to me every time we meet."

She dug in her heels and jerked her hand from his grip. "Officer—"

"It's Alex." He spun around, sparing a glance beyond her shoulder to see a few members of the press sizing up this standoff between the police and the D.A.'s office to see if something newsworthy was about to happen. But it was hard to look away from pink creeping into Audrey's cheeks. "All I'm saying is that maybe you need to fight a little smarter. Maybe a little less guttin' it through on attitude, and using a little more common sense." The blush of temper faded and her gaze dropped to the base of his throat. He'd struck a nerve with that last observation. Hell. That hadn't been his intention. So all that high-and-mighty society arrogance *was* a defense mechanism. "I'm just making a point."

Her gaze shot back to his. "That I lack common sense?"

"That you're not as tough as you try to be." The breeze

whipped a tendril of fiery hair across her pale cheek. Alex caught it with his fingertip and brushed it back into place across her cool skin. He tucked the strand behind her ear, entranced by the warmth that colored her cheek beneath his touch. He exhaled a steadying breath, fighting the temptation to press his lips to the same spot to find out how responsively her skin would react.

But a flash of movement caught his eye at the same time she cleared her throat to break the tender mood. The protesters in the park were drifting this way, following Steve Lassen and his camera as the reporter decided there might be a story in trailing Audrey, after all. Although Lassen was twenty yards away and the protesters were following a parallel course through the park's walkways, they were getting entirely too close for Alex's liking.

He grabbed Audrey's hand and pulled her into step beside him. "C'mon."

This time he slowed his pace so it wouldn't look so much like they were running away. Audrey seemed to respond to the concession. She laced her gloved fingers through his and lengthened her stride to keep up. "Just because you've caught me at a couple of low moments in my life doesn't mean I lack the skills to be a good attorney who can make a difference in this city."

"I'm not knocking your skills, Red." He pulled his phone from his pocket and punched in Trip's number. "I just think you lack a backup plan."

"And you're it?"

He glanced across his shoulder at her sarcasm. "Did you want to be stuck in the middle of all that?"

"All right. Fine. Thank you," she conceded. "But this

is a one-time rescue. I'll be better prepared for all this chaos tomorrow. I wasn't expecting this kind of publicity. I'll just transfer everything I've learned about being in the spotlight with my personal life over to my work."

"I'm not talking about losing your temper and having it splashed all over the news, or getting claustrophobic in a crowd—I'm talking about your safety. If something happens to you, this trial gets delayed or dismissed."

"My safety? Did you not see the security at the courthouse?"

"Where is it now?" He swung his arm wide, gesturing to the entourage following them through the park. That Reaper creep with his painted face and hooded robe was moving along with the crowd, as well. That guy had some serious issues. Alex texted a message to Trip and pocketed his phone. "You've got dozens of people following you—"

"In broad daylight." She pointed to the two officers keeping the crowd in their designated area along the park paths. "Surrounded by cops. It's only two blocks from the courthouse to my office. What could anyone do?"

Was she serious? Open ground surrounded by tall buildings or crowded parking lots? Her bright auburn hair was as good as a target out here. And situations were almost impossible to control when there were this many people thrown into the mix. "Those cops are focused on the crowd, not you. Next time, you should arrange to have a car pick you up. And you definitely shouldn't make this walk on your own, not while the trial's going on."

"We're behind you, Audrey!" a voice yelled from the park.

Others joined in. "Keep our children safe!"

"We're counting on you!"

Audrey raised her hand to wave. Alex snatched it back down to her side and her smile for her fans turned into a scowl for him. "See? They know I work for them, not some high-priced law firm like Cade Shipley. They're on my side."

"Is that what this is about? Proving you're a woman of the people?" Alex kept walking. "You're giving the press and everyone in the park who are dying to have their voice heard a golden opportunity to question or harass you—or something worse."

"They have a right to be here. They're frightened for their children and their community. They want me to understand that message. They're supporting me."

"What if one of them thinks you're not doing the job the way they want? Or you're not doing it fast enough to suit them?"

"They're not…"

Alex heard the squeal of tires and instinctively put his hand on his gun and put himself between Audrey and the street. "Stay back."

Red car. Speeding toward them. Dark windows except for the one sliding down.

"Alex?" She tugged at his sleeve.

He pulled his weapon, steadied it between his hands. His finger brushed the trigger, but he lowered his gun at the last second. The car slowed as something sailed through the open window, but no one was shooting.

"You scared yet, bitch?"

Alex spun, reaching for her. But he was a split second too late. "Audrey!"

Something red and juicy struck her jaw and the side of her neck. A tomato.

She was stunned, but not hurt. The mess was dripping under her white collar and onto her coat, and she was pissed. She wiped the biggest glob of mushy pulp from her face and walked over to the trash can at the curb to flick it inside. "Are they kidding me with this?" She pulled a piece of the skin from her lapel. "Who throws tomatoes?"

"Are you hurt?" Alex didn't know whether to touch her or not. He ID'd the make of the car and read a partial plate before the first picture snapped. "You're gonna be front-page news if I don't get you out of here now." *Definitely touch her.* "Audrey?" Pointing his gun down at his side, he reached for her with his left hand. His eyes were scanning, assessing. Car gone, around the corner at the next block and out of sight. Uniforms closing in. Press closing in. Crowd... "We need to move, Red."

And then he heard the beep from the trash can.

"Get down!"

Alex picked her up around the waist and threw her to the ground across the sidewalk. He dove on top of her, shielding her with his body as the trash can exploded into shards of molten plastic and flying metal and rained down around them.

"Oh, my God. Oh, my God."

It took a few seconds for Alex's stunned hearing to adjust to the sound of Audrey's voice. He felt the throb of pain in his hand and the pinch of her fingers digging into his forearm through his jacket and sweater before he clearly heard the distress in her tone. The quick recovery time for his ears meant the bomb hadn't been that big, or else the concussive blast would have done more damage.

Nothing else on him was hurting beyond some bruised knuckles and a scrape above the band of his watch. He pushed himself up on his elbows, easing the crush of his body over hers. But he wasn't quite ready to free her. "Audrey, are you hurt?"

"Skinned my knee, maybe." She had a nice red welt on her cheek that was starting to ooze blood. But she didn't seem to notice her own injuries. Or care. "Is anyone else hurt?" She pushed at him with her hips, and he let her roll over and sit up while he knelt beside her. Like him, she surveyed the others, hunkered close to the ground—a few with some minor scrapes, one woman was holding her head—nothing that looked like a shrapnel wound, though. Some were in shock. "Is everyone okay?"

One officer was helping a woman to her feet. Another was on his radio. Good. Help was coming. As a police officer, he was supposed to be responsible for all these people, too. But his concern was focused solely on Audrey. Her hair had fallen loose from its pins and he brushed it away from her injured cheek. "Doesn't look like anything serious," he reassured her. "I'm sure backup and ambulances are already on their way."

She tilted her wide green eyes to his. "Is this my fault?"

"Don't go there." He holstered his gun as he turned to inspect the pattern of debris around what was left of the trash can. The blast area was small and localized, indicating that the goal of the explosion wasn't to do a lot of damage. It was meant to do *specific* damage. To a specific person? Alex looked back to Audrey, hating the suspicion pouring into his veins. "Whoever set that off is the one you should blame."

He heard the click of a camera and whirled around, on his feet, his hands curled into fists. "Get out of here, Lassen."

The heavyset man with a receding hairline and shrewd eyes shook his head. "Someone tries to kill Rupert Kline's daughter, and you don't think that's front-page news?"

Audrey's fingers pulled at Alex's, opening his fist as she pulled herself up beside him. "How much would it cost to buy that picture back, Mr. Lassen?"

"Are you kidding? This could get me back full-time at the paper, lady. No sale."

She wrapped her arm through Alex's and held on, although he wondered if she was shielding herself or sensing the tension roiling through him and keeping him in check. "You go have a nice career, Mr. Lassen. Just remember…" her tone was in full lawyer mode now "…you're trespassing on a crime scene. If you don't clear out of here right now, I'll have this fine officer arrest you."

Go, Red.

Lassen swore. Then swore again. "You big shots with all your money—you think you own this town. But you don't. I have every right to make my living, and you can't—"

"You really want to threaten her with me standing here, Lassen?" The instant the reporter took half a step forward, Alex planted himself squarely in his path.

"Are you the bodyguard or the boyfriend?" Was that going to be part of his story?

Alex faked a lunge forward. Lassen stumbled backward, cursing cocky cops and daddy's girls and life in general as he turned and stormed up the sidewalk.

Audrey wiped another swath of tomato juice from her neck. "You'd better brace yourself. We are so hitting the rumor mill tomorrow."

"That doesn't bother me." He picked up her attaché bag and handed it to her, steaming at the knowledge that that wasn't only juice trickling over her skin.

Just after the blast, the Reaper had been standing there in the park, watching. Now he was gone. That bothered him even more than the reporters who were finally on the scent of Lassen's story and hurrying along the sidewalk toward them. It bothered him more than the bomb.

"Should we go?" Audrey prompted.

The roar of a heavy-duty truck engine gunning down the hill was the best news Alex had had since leaving the courtroom. Backup had arrived. He hooked his fingers around her arm. "Yeah. Going is good."

Rafe zoomed up to the curb in his black pickup truck. Trip opened the passenger door and jumped out before they came to a complete stop. "We came as soon as we got your text and could get out of the garage. What the hell's going on?"

"Bomb in the trash can. More for effect than to do any real damage. Remote detonation. Could have been the kids in the car, could have been, hell…could have been anybody." Audrey tilted her chin up—way up—and sidled closer to Alex as he pulled her past Trip. "I need her out of here. Now."

Trip swung around at the approaching footsteps of a dozen curious onlookers and eager reporters. "I got this. Meet you back at HQ." He raised his badge in the air, his booming voice taking command of the scene. "KCPD. Stop right where you are. Everybody remain calm and do exactly what I say."

There wasn't a bigger wall between Audrey and potential danger than Trip Jones. But she braced her hand against the door frame and refused to climb in. "Wait a minute. I thought we were walking." They didn't have control of the scene yet and Alex wasn't in the mood to argue. He spanned his hands around her waist and lifted her into the cab, pitching her into the middle of the seat and climbing in behind her. "What are you doing? You're kidnapping me now? Who are you people?"

"SWAT Team One. That was Trip. This is Rafe." Alex pulled the door shut. "Go, Sarge. D.A.'s office. Unless you want to hit the emergency room first?" he asked her.

Audrey shook her head, sinking back into the seat between them as Rafe put the truck into gear and called Dispatch on the radio.

"I was in control of my life half an hour ago. What's happening?" She opened her attaché on her lap and pulled out a blue bandanna.

His blue bandanna.

After all this time she was still carrying that old rag with her?

As she pulled open her coat to clean some tomato drippings from her collar bone, Alex plucked the bandanna from her hand. He heard her soft gasp of breath and watched the self-conscious heat creep along her neck. When his eyes met hers, he tried to communicate that he had no problem with her holding on to his gift from that night of the murder.

Her eyes never left his as he pinched her chin between his thumb and forefinger, and angled her face to dab at her wound. He hoped she could read the same confusion in his eyes. He didn't get this connection between them, either, but it was there. Whether she wanted to argue or let him touch her gently like this, the connection was there.

The reality of knowing she could have been hurt so much worse by that bomb was there, too.

He held up the bandanna and let her see the blood. Her blood.

"I think somebody just made their voice heard."

Chapter Five

"Are you sure you're all right?"

Her blouse was ruined and the strawberry mark scraped across Audrey's cheek throbbed with every anxious beat of her pulse, but she hardly wanted to confess that to her boss. "I'm fine."

Dwight Powers stood behind his walnut desk, buttoning his suit coat and straightening his tie. "I'll take over the case."

That was exactly what she'd been afraid this meeting was about. "No." She shot up out of her chair and mirrored his stance across the desk. "That's what this person wants—to intimidate me right out of that courtroom." *You scared yet, bitch?* The words had gotten under her skin when she'd been crushed beneath Alex's body and the world had exploded all around them. But she couldn't let them get inside her head. "If I don't finish what I've started here, I'll never have authority over anything in this office again. No one in this city will trust me to protect them."

"An anonymous threat is one thing. Getting close enough to actually hurt you is something different." Dwight trailed a finger across the photo of his second wife and family framed on top of his desk before raising his probing gaze back to her. "I know what it's like to lose people you care about because of this job. No career is worth that."

Audrey fisted her hand on top of the desk. "Demetrius Smith is not going to get to me."

"He got to Trace Vaughn."

"We don't know that."

"Audrey—"

She threw up her hands and spun away, pacing around the guest chairs and collecting her thoughts before returning to the desk. "I realize that's the most likely scenario—the one KCPD is pursuing—that one of his Bad Boys took out Trace. But that has yet to be proved. Think about this logically. Think about Kansas City, not just me."

"I have to think about the people who work for me. You're my responsibility as much as the people we represent."

As tough and overprotective as her boss could be, she knew he could be reasoned with if her arguments were all in place.

With a deep sigh through his barrel chest, he pulled back the front of his suit jacket and propped his hands at his waist. "But I'm listening."

Audrey calmed her breathing, as if she was making a final summation to a jury. "I know you agreed to give me this assignment because the Kline name carries more legal clout than the other A.D.A.s can bring to the table. You considered the public relations message surrounding this case—city officials and the movers and shakers will see the Kline name and think you're bringing out the big guns to go up against gang violence in K.C."

"You *are* a 'big gun' in my office." Dwight folded his arms across his chest. "But your last name isn't the only reason I gave you this case."

"Exactly." Audrey had given up on her hair staying pinned into place, and had simply combed the waves down around her shoulders. Now she tucked it behind one ear and tilted her head, bringing the mark on her cheek into focus. "You're also counting on that intangible sympathy vote from the jury. If things are close, you're hoping they'll look at little ol' me—too skinny and too pale—standing up against a bully like Smith and his high-priced lawyer, and they'll vote for the underdog."

"That strategy won't do me any good if my *underdog* gets hurt and can't finish the trial."

"You're going to make my point for me, sir." Time to reel him in. "Any delays or a switch in counsel after today's opening statements makes our office look weak. A shark like Cade Shipley would jump all over that and sway the jury. If we're not ready to prove our case, if a rookie like me can't prove it—"

"You're too sharp to ever think like a rookie. Why do you think I hired you?"

"Thanks. But if you're going to believe in me, *believe* in me. Let me do this." Audrey was beat-up and tired, but she wouldn't reduce herself to begging. Yet she could tell he wasn't quite convinced that she could win—or maybe even survive—this case. "I have a ton of circumstantial evidence to present."

"That will convict him on lesser charges where he'll pay a fine and walk in a couple of years. I want that murder charge to stick."

"The lab can prove the bullet that killed Calvin Chambers came from the gun registered to Smith."

"Smith claims he couldn't find his gun that day, that it was stolen or one of his boys must have been using it. He had no GPR on him or his clothes. You need a witness to put that gun in his hand."

"Then I'll find one. I convinced Trace to turn on Smith for a reduced sentence. I'll find someone else to do the same."

"You know what you're saying, Audrey? You're talking about going into no-man's-land to meet with gang members on their turf—or sitting down in a room with them one-on-one. You're putting pressure on young thugs who'd rather chew you up and spit you out than cooperate." He swiped his palm across the top of his silver and blond hair and cursed. "And if you're not scared of Demetrius's threats, they will be."

"If this job was easy, I wouldn't have been interested in it." She could hear other attorneys and staff members outside Dwight's door closing down their offices and cubicles for the day. But she wasn't ready to quit on this. "I need to be in that courtroom tomorrow morning, Dwight. Please. Maybe if I show a little courage, I'll inspire a witness to show a little courage and come forth, too."

The D.A. scratched his head, frowned, cursed. But he knew she was right. "All right. You're still on the case."

"Thank you." The urge to run around the desk and hug him sparked through her muscles. But that would negate the image of strength she'd just sold him, so she settled for a grateful smile and headed for the door.

"But…"

Oh, the power of a single word. Relief curdled into frustration and made her wary. She slowly turned to find out what the catch was. Co-counsel? Direct supervision from the boss himself? "But?"

"I want you to have round-the-clock protection."

"We have a state-of-the-art Gallagher Security system installed at home. And there are guards all over the courthouse and this building."

"I'm talking about a bodyguard. Someone who's with you 24/7. From what I understand, that bomb went off when you were nowhere near a security team." He picked up the phone. "I'm calling KCPD."

A bodyguard? Now she'd really look like the spoiled rich girl who bought her own protection while the rest of the city—like those people in the park this afternoon, or Mrs. Chambers—had to face the dangers of this world on their own. She hurried to the desk and pushed the disconnect button. "The city can't afford that."

"It's not negotiable, Audrey. If Smith and his gang can get to someone from my office, that's the ultimate intimidation. This city will never feel safe again. And I won't stand for them hurting one of my people." He hung up the receiver and snapped his fingers, a man with a purpose striding out his office door. "I've got an idea."

Audrey followed him through the doorway, as curious as she was worried about the next kink someone else was going to throw into her life.

Dwight crossed straight past the empty cubicle stations to her tiny office. A compact, raven-haired man got up from the chair behind her desk and met them at the open door. A badge hung from a steel chain around his neck. The gun at his waist looked as dangerous as the broad stretch of his shoulders.

Oh, no. No, no, no. Audrey hurried to catch up.

Dwight extended his hand. "Officer...?"

"Taylor. Alex Taylor." The two men shook hands.

"You're the man who saved my A.D.A.'s life today?"

"I guess."

"Why are you still here?" Audrey quickly pressed her fingers to her mouth, embarrassed to hear her reactive thoughts spoken out loud.

His coffee-colored gaze flicked over her face, but he grinned at the unintended slight. "Good to see you again, too."

"I'm sorry. I just... You aren't supposed to be..." Damn. She dropped her hand into a fist at her side. She hated when her words got tangled up in her head like that. Taking a breath to buy herself a moment to articulate her thoughts, she tried again. "I thought you went back to the courthouse to get your truck."

"Already did. I'm parked out front."

Her boss, however, seemed to have no problem with this man making himself at home in her space. "You know Detective Josh Taylor? He's a good friend of mine."

"That'd be Uncle Josh."

"Chief Taylor over in the Fourth Precinct?"

"Mitch is another uncle. I'm Gideon's son."

"Chief investigator at KCFD." Dwight nodded, recognizing the name. "He broke that serial arsonist case a few years back."

Alex's pride was evident in his grin. "Ten years

ago. That was the year I met him and Mom. They adopted me."

"If you're a Taylor, then you're the kind of man I'm looking for. You on the clock?"

"Not tonight, sir."

Dwight glanced down at her before making a proposition to Alex. "Feel like volunteering for protection duty with the D.A.'s office?"

"Dwight—" Audrey protested, but these two were already bonding and planning the next few hours of her life for her.

"You want me to drive Audrey home?"

"And stay with her until I can get some kind of official protection detail arranged with the department."

"Yes, sir."

"What do you do with KCPD, Taylor?"

"I'm SWAT, sir."

Dwight touched Audrey's elbow and pulled her forward, as though one man was handing her off to the other. "Then you're in good hands. You focus on the case, and Taylor here will focus on keeping you safe. Now if you'll excuse me, I have a holiday program with my son and a bunch of first graders to get to." Audrey turned in the doorway, determined to make her own opinion heard. But Dwight's gray-green eyes seemed almost pained as he pointed to her cheek. "Be sure to have that looked at." Then he peered beyond her shoulder to Alex. "I'm counting on you."

"My pleasure, sir." Alex's hand settled at the small of her back and she bristled. The handoff was complete. "I won't let you down."

As soon as they were alone, Audrey shimmied away

from the warmth of his hand and stormed around her desk. "'My pleasure,'" she scoffed.

Wasn't the whole point of breaking away from her father's influence so that she'd have the ability to make her own decisions? So that she could have his respect as well as his love? So that he'd see her as a grown-up instead of forever his little missy?

And now, without so much as a consultation regarding her wishes, she had an armed escort driving her home. Either her father would think she couldn't handle herself on her own out in the big bad world and would jump in to make things right, or he'd be so worried that his health would start to decline the way it had when her mother had been ill.

Audrey opened her attaché and pulled out the folders which had gotten knocked around during the explosion and Alex's saving tackle, straightened the papers inside each one, and neatly tucked them back into her bag again. Pull. Straighten. Close. Insert. Maybe she couldn't do this. Maybe Dwight and her father were right to worry that she was in over her head. Straighten. Close. Insert.

"Try not to look so disappointed, counselor. It's hard on a man's ego."

Alex's teasing voice skittered across her eardrums, his tone a calm, patient contrast to her furious sorting and packing. She shot him an irritated look as he sauntered around the desk toward her. "Your ego isn't my concern."

"The D.A.'s right. After everything I've seen today, you need someone watching your back."

"I don't need a babysitter," she informed him. "Having you or anyone else dogging my every move makes it look like I can't do my job. I studied Demetrius Smith inside and out. I *know* he has a history of using intimidation tactics to get what he wants. I'm prepared for that. I won't give him the satisfaction of thinking he's gotten to me." She pointed a file out to the empty offices beyond her door. "Yet after just one day of this trial, my own boss thinks I can't take care of myself. I can't accept that."

Alex caught her hand and pulled the file from her fingers, interrupting her desperate need to maintain control of some aspect of her life.

"How about you accept a recon expert who can make sure all the people around you stay safe?"

"What?" The warmth of his touch was as unsettling as it was unexpected. But her gaze landed on the shredded hem of his sleeve and she couldn't seem to make her fingers pull away from his.

"Maybe you *are* invincible. But the people around you tend to get hurt."

"That's not funny." A quick glance up to his rugged face, which needed a shave and a few hours of sleep, told her the teasing had stopped. Had something else happened during her meeting with Dwight? "I thought your friend said no one in the park got hurt this afternoon— that it was mostly property damage."

"He said no one got seriously hurt."

A fist of guilt squeezed her gut as she took in the bruised and raw knuckles of the hand holding hers. She followed the snagged forearm of his sleeve up to the rip at his elbow. Her gaze moved higher and her pulse quickened. The black knit shirt hugged his biceps and shoulders, stirring some purposely guarded hormones. But her gaze came back to the drops of blood staining his sleeve and his scraped-up knuckles, waking something much deeper. She touched her fingertips to the frayed cotton.

He'd ruined his sweater saving her life. He'd gotten hurt protecting her. This wasn't how today was supposed to happen. She curled her fingers into her palm and raised her gaze to his, discovering just how deep and dark those brown eyes were. She was scared to think he could see that deeply into hers. "Are you all right?"

Alex leaned his hip against the corner of her desk and sat, tugging her half a step closer. Her thigh brushed against his, the soft wool of her skirt catching against his denim jeans and the hard muscle underneath. The shock of heat radiating from the frictive caress surprised her. One little brush and her emotions began to cloud her thinking. "I'm okay," he assured her. "I'm just as tough as I look." He reached up with one finger to brush her hair away from her cheek and tuck it behind her ear. "Have you looked in a mirror lately?"

Audrey jerked up her chin, fighting the instinct to turn her face into the gentle caress of his hand. "So I ruined a pair of panty hose and suffered a few bumps and bruises. I've had worse."

Alex pressed his lips into a tight line. "It could have been a *lot* worse. The D.A.'s right about a protection detail. Today was just about sending you a message."

The note she'd gotten during the party last night blipped into her mind, along with the creepy attention she'd gotten from Bud Preston. She had the feeling he'd been up to something far more sinister than parking cars. The message that someone meant to terrorize her was perfectly clear. But Alex's argument wasn't any comfort.

"A friend of yours was murdered a month ago. And now a bomb goes off when you've got the press and public hounding your every move. If you won't think about yourself, think about the rest of us. Trip said there were no serious injuries at the park this afternoon, but that might not be the case next time someone comes after you."

"Do you think this is about the Rich Girl murders? Not the Smith trial?"

"I don't know what to think. Yet." He adjusted his grip, sliding his fingers beneath the sleeve of her jacket. "But how many people have to get hurt before we do figure it out?"

"I didn't think about that. About them. What if he goes after my father? Or hurts a guard or sets off a bigger bomb or…" Frustration, confusion, guilt and fear all fought to find words inside her. But the calloused pad of his thumb, tracing slow circles at the pulse point of her wrist, seemed to short-circuit her usual eloquence. "I don't want anyone to get hurt because of me. But I won't quit this case, Alex. I can't."

"I don't want you to." Tiny bubbles of heat pooled in her blood where he touched her. "Smith doesn't get to win. I won't let him. I don't want you to let him, either."

Strange, how his words of support fueled the warmth seeping through her body. She hadn't realized how badly she needed to hear them. She never expected to feel this urge to turn her cheek against one of those shoulders and have Alex's strong arms and body wrap around hers. He could keep her safe. He could make her feel.

It wasn't until she saw her own hand, splayed at the middle of his chest, and felt herself leaning in, her legs butting for a more intimate position against his thigh, that she realized where her emotions were leading her. Clearing her throat, Audrey pulled away, breaking all contact with Alex's body. She picked up the file folder with both hands, keeping her fingers occupied and her desires on hold until she could get her thoughts back in order.

"Since I have an early morning in court, we should be going." She stuffed the folder into her attaché, saw there was nothing left to fiddle with on her desk and needlessly reached into the bag to check her phone and wallet and keys. Alex sat there, watching, his dark eyes barely blinking as she angled her chin and laid out her own expectations. "You can walk me to my car in the parking garage and follow me home."

"You're riding with me."

"I'll show you how the security system at home works, and you'll see how safe we are. I'd like to introduce you to my father before you leave, and tell him why you're there."

"I'm staying the night."

"He's probably already seen or heard something about this afternoon on the news."

"Audrey."

"I can call for a driver in the morning—or have a black-and-white follow me into the city."

"You forgot this." Alex slowly straightened beside her, holding up the blood-stained, wrinkled, faded blue bandanna he'd been sitting on.

Heat rushed into Audrey's cheeks and she plucked it from his fingers. It was so soft, still warm from the press of his body. "I didn't mean to keep it so long. I'll get this washed and ironed and returned to you. It was clean this afternoon before…" Right. It was blood-stained. She stuffed it inside her bag. "I'll buy you a new one."

"Stubborn, I understand. It matches the hair." She turned to get her coat from the stand beside the door, but Alex was there, blocking her path. Grinning. "But I never pictured you as the sentimental type."

When it became clear he wasn't going to move, Audrey tipped her chin to look him in the eye. "I am not sentimental. Don't read anything more into keeping your gift—your old bandanna—than the fact that I just got busy and forgot I had it. I'll replace it. Your sweater, too. And pay for any medical expenses. I suppose I'll have to pay the city to replace that trash can, also."

"Shh." He reached up and traced his fingertips along the line of her jaw.

Audrey shivered and pulled up. "I insist. You probably saved my life. The least I can do is buy you a—"

"I'm not interested in your money," he whispered, capturing the point of her chin between his thumb and fingers. He gave her chin the gentlest of tugs down. "I just don't want to see you hurt again. Not by violence or pressure or loss."

"Stop that." Was that husky gasp her own voice? And what was so damned mesmerizing about the supple articulation of Alex Taylor's lips?

"Stop what?"

Audrey opened her mouth, drew in a breath to speak. The scent of his skin filled her nose, distracting her from her argument. His dark eyes hooded and she watched in perplexed fascination as the distance between them vanished and he closed his mouth over hers.

It was a gentle kiss. An unexpected kiss. A very leisurely, thorough, thought-stopping kiss.

Alex pressed his lips to hers, warming her mouth. He touched his tongue to the bow of her mouth, tasted one corner, then the other. The lightest of stubble rubbed against the swell of her bottom lip, leaving it tender and achy and reaching out to hold on to his when he would have pulled away. His tongue stroked the seam of her lips and they parted to feel the warmth of his breath mingling with hers. She tasted the salt on his skin, the coffee he'd been drinking on his tongue. With a helpless moan, she opened more fully, seeking more, welcoming him.

He slid his fingers along her jawline and tunneled them beneath the hair at her nape. There was nothing connecting them beyond his fingers in her hair and his mouth moving over hers. And heat. Languid, silky, slow-moving heat that flowed from his touch into her skin, seeping through her blood, finding and filling a neglected well of doubt and need and want deep inside her.

Audrey's thoughts were cloudy, her skin feverish with a blush of desire when Alex finally pulled away. She felt his chest rise and fall beneath the clutch of her fingers balled in the front of his sweater. His breath washed over her cheek in a rhythm as deep and unsteady as her own. She saw the lines crinkling beside his beautiful eyes and knew he was smiling.

"Why did…? I can't…" she stuttered.

He brushed his thumb across her lips, sparking and soothing each nerve ending in its wake. "It's okay, Red. I feel this thing between us, too."

Audrey plucked her hand away and curled it against her stomach, but she couldn't come up with a single word to agree with or deny his hushed revelation.

"Nice." He stamped her with a quick peck on the lips, looped her bag over her shoulder and retrieved their coats from the hook beside the door. "I'll have to remember that trick next time I want to get a word in edgewise."

"Trick?" A knee-jerk instinct left Audrey fuming at the amusement at her expense. Whatever heat had dissipated flooded back into her cheeks. Kissing her into silence? Like she could fall prey to some Neanderthal tactic that short-circuited her poise, rerouted her goals and left her thinking only about him, about them, about the next time he might kiss her.

But she wisely turned her back and let him help her into her coat, keeping her sensitized lips pressed tightly together. She had no position to argue from when the man was only telling the truth.

HE SCRUBBED THE BABY WIPE over his face, cleaning off the last of the black makeup he'd worn with his costume. A satisfied smile looked back from his reflection in the mirror.

Audrey Kline had been scared—he'd read it in the shock that had blanched her skin. She'd been hurt—nothing serious, but enough to know he meant business. She'd been confused by the attack—and maybe that was the most delightful result of all. Confusion and uncertainty had to be particularly frightening for a woman who was used to power and control and having the last word.

Now *he* was the one in control.

He'd seen the way she'd looked at him. He knew her inside and out—what she cared about, what she feared.

She was afraid. She was fighting it. But he'd seen that fear. He'd smelled it on her.

She could throw her money and prestige around, and smile her pretty smile. Hell. Even he'd succumbed to it. But no more. She could steal the spotlight and have her pick of men and a career. But if she thought for one minute that she was better than him, that she could overlook him and not regret the slight, that she could keep him from achieving the success that was rightfully his, then she was woefully mistaken.

Audrey Kline had no power over him. No power. Nada. None.

He tossed the soiled cloth into the trash and carefully nestled the rectangular wipe dispenser box against the sink splash. He had to give his toothbrush and razor a nudge so that they lined up parallel to the dispenser, but the calming release he expected didn't come.

He pressed his fingertips to the knot of tension balling at his temple. Why did he always have to fix things? Why couldn't his world fall into place by itself? Now he had to turn his cell phone ninety degrees on the countertop so that it matched the pattern around the sink. The time flashing on the screen annoyed him further. Today had been a complete success, but the momentary balance in his world was already beginning to shift. He was running out of time to savor the memory of Audrey sprawled on the ground beside the sidewalk, bleeding and afraid—clinging to a stranger because she was too damn stubborn to let anyone besides her precious father into her life.

Hmm. That was a possibility. Rupert Kline was a harder target to reach, but he could certainly prove to be Audrey's Achilles' heel.

If he needed a Plan B.

He breathed in deeply, watching his nostrils flare in the mirror—seeing the intelligence and foresight that so many people missed reflected in his eyes. A slow smile crept across his mouth. He had yet to need a Plan B.

He released the breath he held and splashed some soap and water on his face. If he didn't get his butt in gear, he'd be late and he'd miss the opportunity to see the aftereffects of the explosion and threats with his own eyes. And that was a payoff he didn't want to miss.

Reaching for his clothes, he mentally fought to maintain the control that was slipping through his fingers. After dressing quickly, he went back to the mirror to pull on his jacket and smooth out the wrinkles in his lapels and collar. A tug here, a brush there—finally, he was satisfied that he looked the part expected of him. He'd see Audrey soon. Would she be distressed? Angry? Putting on a brave show for her father? It was too much to hope that she'd fall to pieces. Yet. But the opportunity to observe the results of his handiwork was a reward that hurried him out the door and into his vehicle.

He was speeding out of the city toward the posh suburb where the Klines lived like royalty when his phone rang. He read the number, cursed at the annoyance and pulled onto the interstate before answering the call. "What is it now?"

"The blast didn't kill her!"

This was getting tiresome. "It wasn't supposed to."

"This is your idea of a plan? We're the ones in there with the cops, risking *our* necks. We're the ones they're gonna come talk to—you know that."

"Don't worry."

"Don't worry?" The caller cursed. "We tried to kill

that hotshot lawyer today. The cops are gonna come straight to us."

That wasn't his concern. Still, his partners did offer a unique talent for violence and distraction that served his purpose, and he wasn't ready for them to go to jail. So he'd taken care of them. "Do you know how that bomb was put together?"

"No."

"Do you know who I am? Can you give the police my name or describe my face?"

"I can give them this phone number." Although the tone was menacing, it was an empty threat.

"This is a disposable cell—they won't be able to trace it. And since we've never met, you can't identify me." He paused long enough to signal his turn onto the exit ramp. "If you used a stolen car like I suggested and then disposed of it, the police won't be able to put you at the scene of the crime. And if they do, there's no way they can tie the bomb to you. You never touched it—you just happened to be in the wrong place at the wrong time— like your boss claims happened to him. The most they can get you for is throwing fruit at a pretty woman. I've given you plausible deniability."

"You've given me what?"

Idiot. He expelled an impatient breath as he pulled up to a stop light. Then he spelled it out in simple words. "I've taken care of everything. I took out your witness for you. You rattled the assistant D.A. for me. Events have been set into motion. There's no way she can win this case now."

But he'd enjoy watching every humiliating moment of the end of Audrey Kline's career. He'd revel in it.

Right up until the moment he had to kill her.

Chapter Six

"See?" Audrey said, her tone a mix of high-class attorney and told-you-so bravado. "My father paid a fortune for the best. State-of-the-art. You can only get through the gate if you have a pass card to swipe or you punch in the code—which changes daily."

Alex handed back her security card and waited for the tall wrought-iron gates at the end of her driveway to swing open. Despite the modern additions of technology, this place was like the castle keep out of some damned fairy tale. Tall granite and limestone walls covered in ivy faced the street, and the lights on the other side of those walls illuminated a stand of massive ancient oak trees and a long brick driveway leading up to...well, he couldn't quite make out anything through the skeletal branches beyond a three-story tower and a pair of porch lights. This place might be steeped in old money and architectural history, but it was built for privacy from the outside world, not security. "How many employees and family members have these cards?"

"There's just Dad and me. A cook, housekeeper, groundskeeper—although, they typically use the service entrance in the back."

That was already too many people with unrestricted access to the house.

"When they bring in extra staff, or we have guests, we make different security arrangements."

"By issuing extra cards?"

"Sometimes. Or—"

"—you leave the gate open. Hell." She wasn't going to make guarding her easy, was she? Alex squeezed the truck's steering wheel in his fist, guessing that another cautionary warning from him would lock Audrey firmly in independent ice princess mode, and rule one for a successful protection operation was to maintain the cooperation of the person he was protecting.

The forbidding rock walls that closed off the grounds from the rest of civilization might explain her desire to take the brisk, open-air walk from the courthouse to her office this afternoon. But the more he saw, the more he realized the sense of security Audrey lived with was false. True, Quinn Gallagher's security designs were the best in Kansas City, maybe even the country, and getting inside wouldn't be easy while the system was engaged. But if a perp ever did get beyond those gates, he'd have free rein to commit whatever crime and wreak whatever terror he wanted without anyone on this side of the walls knowing it before it was too late.

Alex pointed to the rotating cameras and motion sensors at either side of the gate as he drove inside. "Are the guards who handle the codes and equipment on-site?"

Audrey's weary sigh echoed across the cab of his pickup truck. But her posture stayed ramrod straight. She was withdrawing into prickly defensive mode again, a far cry from the soft, needy woman who had melted into his kiss less than an hour ago, and clung to him as if he was an anchor on the streets this afternoon. "Not unless Daddy hires extra security for certain events. Otherwise, the system is monitored at the Gallagher Security offices. We've never had a break-in at the house since it was installed, and the few times trespassers have gotten onto the property, Gallagher had someone here in a matter of minutes."

If a perp was bold enough, desperate enough or crazy enough, it only took a matter of seconds to attack or terrorize or kill. Shaking his head, Alex eyed the wide trunks of the trees lining the long brick driveway that still blocked a clear view of the house as they approached. The Chevy's headlights only emphasized the nooks and shadows where an army of bad guys who meant business could hide.

"The Cosgroves had a Gallagher Security system. Yet somebody got to your friend."

Audrey fingered the red mark staining her collar and, for a moment, those slender shoulders sagged. Alex reached across the seat, feeling like a jerk for having to resort to mentioning something so painful to make his point. But she curled her fingers into her collar and hugged her arms tightly around her, wanting no part of his apology or comfort.

He shifted his hand back to the steering wheel and propped his elbow out the open window. The cool breeze up his sleeve and on his face felt good. The subtle spicy scent off her skin and hair had filled the truck and gotten into his head. He needed the fresh air to remind him that he wasn't some overprotective boyfriend here. He was KCPD. He was SWAT. He was a Taylor. He wasn't chauffeuring Miss Fire and Ice because he wanted to uncover why she kept all that passion locked inside her, or to find out what it took to get those responsive lips and grasping fingers to cling to him again. He was strictly the hired help here, and no amount of fascination with a woman was going to change that. The D.A. had asked him to step up tonight because he was available, and because he knew how to keep someone safe. *So do the job, already.* Alex breathed in, blocking the frustration, curiosity and desire this woman triggered inside him with the scent of damp leaves and the terse words of his commander, Captain Cutler. "All the tech in the world can't replace a set of sharp eyes and surrounding yourself with people you trust."

"And who am I supposed to trust, Alex? You? Just because I let you kiss me—"

"Don't throw all that on me, sweetheart. You were right in there with me."

"So I lost control for a minute. You caught me at a weak moment."

"It was an honest moment." He was surprised at how her words stung. Like he went around taking advantage of vulnerable women. "Maybe your defenses were down, but that doesn't mean those weren't real desires and emotions passing between us."

"Fine." Even silhouetted across the seat from him, he could see the elegant point of that chin angling upward again. "So I…find you attractive. You're different from the men I know."

Good different? Or I've-strayed-to-the-dark-side-once-and-that-kiss-will-never-happen-again different? But she was on a roll now, her expression animated, her articulation sharp.

"And I'm grateful to you for…being there when I needed someone. More than once."

Uh-oh. There was a hesitation in that polished speech, a hitch that cut through his own defensive armor. Audrey might *want* to deny whatever was happening between them, but she wasn't denying that there was already some kind of bond between them.

"That doesn't mean I know you. Or trust you. Not enough to give up the things I do know and put my life in your hands."

"Some people you know better after ten minutes than you do after spending a lifetime with them. I knew my adoptive dad was a man I respected the first day I met him. I knew my mom understood where I came from, and loved me, anyway, the first time she hugged me. My birth parents?" Where was this coming from? He never talked about this crap. He tapped his fist against the truck's window frame and opened up the old wounds, anyway. "Tony Pitsaeli used to beat my mom when he was around. I'd hide in the closet or run away. When she came to, he'd tell her that he loved her. Never did understand that relationship. I tried to stop him one time, and he turned his belt on me. She took to drugs to escape the hell we lived in. I took to the streets. I wasn't even a part of their lives anymore by the time he went to prison."

"Alex."

Audrey's harsh gasp told him that he'd said enough to make his point. He slowed the truck and turned to her. She was facing him now. Her hands were still clasped in that protective hug, but even in the dimness of the dashboard lights he could see the color creeping up her neck. No wonder she fought so hard to guard her feelings—with that beautiful porcelain skin, she wore every emotion front and center for all the world to see.

Maybe he ought to be protecting that vulnerability as well as her life.

"Don't feel sorry for me, Red." This time he didn't hesitate to reach across the seat and touch her. He stroked the back of his fingers along her jaw, soothing the heat that colored her velvety skin. "I'm in a good place now. I'm my own man. But I've learned a thing or two about the world that may not be so easy to see from your ivory tower. Tony and Rae Pitsaeli were a part of my life for fifteen years, but I sure as hell didn't trust them. Gideon and Meghan Taylor had my loyalty and trust by the end of the first week they pulled me out of foster care."

He didn't take it personally when she checked the impulse to rub her cheek against his palm.

She leaned in, closed her eyes—but quickly snapped them open and pulled away. "So you're saying that we've known each other for only a month, but that, as annoying and presumptuous as you might be, we've shared enough for me to know I can trust you?"

Alex put both hands firmly on the steering wheel and laughed. "Something like that."

"I'll try. But just so you know, it's when I'm not in control of a situation that I feel the most insecure."

"Trust and control are two different issues. You can't always control a situation." Alex glanced over at her as the line of trees thinned and the driveway began to curve. "But you can always trust me."

With that, she settled back into her corner of the seat, her arms crossed, her gaze straight ahead. He could almost hear the wheels churning inside her head as she pondered his promise—no doubt lining up pro and con lists of arguments as to whether she should believe him or not.

Fine. Let her think. He tensed behind the wheel and went on full alert. As the driveway widened into a three-lane parking area, he could see he had plenty to worry about himself. "Is there a party going on here?"

He pulled into a space behind a white van, one of two parked out front, along with nearly a dozen cars and a dilapidated pickup. Could the Kline estate serve up any more places for someone or something unexpected to hide?

"More like the aftermath of one." Alex rolled up his window and shut off the engine while Audrey unhooked her seat belt. "We hosted a fundraiser for a fine arts scholarship in Gretchen Cosgrove's name last night. Clarice Darnell has her crew here packing up—probably while she's flirting with my dad." She nodded toward a red compact. "That's her car."

Alex recognized the Darnell name from the newspaper—not that he ever attended the type of pricey shindigs she put on. But apparently Kansas City's elite couldn't throw a party without Clarice at the helm. There was another niggling familiarity about the event planner's résumé, but Alex couldn't put his finger on it. Instead of playing detective, he'd do better to focus on getting Audrey safely inside. "Let's get in the house so I can familiarize myself with the setup there."

"You're my bodyguard only for tonight."

It could be only for one hour and it wouldn't change his training, or his determination to keep her beautiful, stubborn self safe. "Let's get inside the house."

After climbing out, Alex pulled back the front of his jacket to keep his badge in plain view and his Glock close at hand while he circled the front of the truck. The back of one van was open, but empty. The front door of the house was propped open while the brass lamps on either side were blazing.

By the time he reached the passenger door to hold it open and take her hand to balance her while she stepped from the running board down to the bricks, her skin had returned to a creamy shade of pale, indicating she had her emotions firmly back in check. "Did your grandmother teach you these manners, too?"

Alex grinned. "My commanding officer. He insists we stick close to the target we're protecting."

"There are more motion detectors and cameras installed around the house itself. With an alarm system we key in ourselves. Do you really think Demetrius Smith and his Broadway Bad Boys are smart enough to get past all the monitors and codes here or at the courthouse?"

Alex locked his truck and placed his hand at the small of Audrey's back, staying close to her side as he guided her through the rows of cars toward the front steps. "Maybe not—a direct, drive-by assault like this afternoon is more their style. But Smith has the money to hire someone who's smart enough to get in here. And you know he has a track record for doing whatever it takes to avoid prison time—witness intimidation, threatening the opposing counsel."

For a moment, she paused. Because of his grim words? Or did the hesitation in her step have something to do with the black Lexus that seemed to catch her attention as they passed it? In either case, she wasn't about to share. Her shoulders came back, her chin went up and Alex had to lengthen his stride to keep even as her heels clicked in a faster staccato up the steps.

He caught Audrey on either side of her waist when she jumped back at the edge of the porch. He felt the subtle tremor in her balance and held on as two workmen in coveralls barreled through the open front door, carrying a long folding table between them.

"Sorry, ma'am," the older of the two men said, pausing. "Didn't see you standing there."

Was Audrey inching back into him? Alex slid his arm around the front of her waist, shutting down his body's instant reaction to her firm bottom pressing against his groin and turning his attention to the man with the toothpick wedged at the corner of his mouth. "Move along, guys," he advised.

Toothpick man winked. "Glad to see you've got your coat tonight, ma'am. I was worried about you catching a chill last night."

Yep. She was definitely moving closer. Hackles that were more male than cop raised along the back of Alex's neck. "Move. Now."

It was an order.

With a friendly salute, the man with "Bud" embroidered above his front pocket nodded to his partner, and they carried the table on down the steps and loaded it into the back of the open van. While Alex tried to process what had spooked Audrey and why his blood was still pumping with a surge of adrenaline that went far beyond standard alertness, she pushed his arm away and stormed inside the house.

Alex dodged a second pair of men carrying another table outside, and hurried into the marble-tiled foyer behind her. Ah, hell. He'd worked the Plaza downtown on Thanksgiving night when the holiday crowds gathered to watch some official turn on the Christmas lights, and hadn't seen this many comings and goings in a confined space to contend with.

There were four more men, packing linens into laundry bags and tearing down tables in the first two rooms extending off either side of the foyer. Another man, this one wearing glasses and a suit and tie, was carrying a clipboard, jotting down notes and moving from room to room. He halted one man carrying a large silver bowl and pointed him back to a serving table, telling him to pack the bowl into a carrier before loading it. There were two women boxing up glasses and at least two more with cleaning supplies, wiping down furniture and vacuuming rugs.

For a split second, Alex lost sight of Audrey completely as she headed for a carpeted staircase. But he glared a worker out of his path and caught up with her as another man called her name. "Audrey?"

Her knuckles whitened as she squeezed the railing. But she was smiling as she turned to greet the red-haired man who dashed out of a walnut-framed doorway. "Daddy."

Alex retreated a step as she stretched up on tiptoe to trade a tight hug with her father. The older man framed her face between his hands as he pulled away, carefully studying the mark on Audrey's face, kissing her forehead and then wrapping her in another hug. "Don't you ever scare me like that again, missy. I saw it on the evening news. My God. An explosion?" He pulled away again, a loving reprimand stamped on his ruddy features. "And when you didn't answer your phone? It's a good thing Dwight Powers answered his. He told me what happened outside the courthouse."

She pushed some space between them, resting her

hand over her father's heart. "I'm sorry. It wasn't my intention to worry you. I left you a message that said I was okay."

"Uh-huh."

Clearly, Alex wasn't the only man in the room who disagreed with Audrey's idea of "okay." Then he felt himself popping to attention as Audrey's father turned to him and shook his hand.

"And you're the young man who saved her."

Audrey made the introductions. "Daddy, this is Alex Taylor of KCPD. My father, Rupert Kline."

"Good to meet you, sir."

Rupert Kline pumped Alex's hand between both of his. "It's good to meet you. Thank you. And don't tell me that you were just doing your job. Thank you."

Alex extricated his hand from the effusive greeting and glanced over at Audrey's slowly rising chin. Father and daughter shared the same coloring, but they were worlds apart when it came to expressing their feelings. He might have spent some time considering what would cause her to rein it all in, but the trio of other well-wishers joining their circle put him firmly back into protector mode.

"Aud. What a terrible thing."

The tall blond suit who'd claimed ownership that night at the Cosgrove murder swept past Rupert Kline and pulled Audrey into a hug. When he bent his head to give her a kiss, Audrey turned to give him her undamaged cheek. Alex could tell Blondie wasn't pleased with the friendly brush-off, and if she hadn't shrugged away his lingering grip, Alex would have answered the need to act buzzing through his veins and twisted the guy's grabby fingers from her arm for her.

"When Rupert told me about those gangbangers accosting you, I thought I'd lost you, too."

She chided him on a pinched breath. "Don't be so melodramatic. I'm fine. This is Harper Pierce. Jeffrey Beecher. Clarice Darnell."

But there was no shaking of hands.

The dark-haired man with the glasses and clipboard stopped her next. "Audrey?"

Pierce elbowed him back out of the circle. "Can't you see we're having a conversation here, Beecher?"

"Harper," Audrey chided.

Beecher adjusted his glasses on the bridge of his nose, his expression unfazed by Pierce's rudeness. He turned his smile to Audrey. "I just wanted to say that I'm glad you're okay. We've been trying to keep your father busy so that he wouldn't get too worried."

"Thanks, Jeffrey."

"Clarice?" Beecher turned to the slightly plump woman with unnaturally blond hair that was swept up and pinned with silk flowers on the top of her head. "Do you want to talk about the delivery options for the museum event?"

"In a minute." Alex cataloged names and faces and tried to gauge their relationship to Audrey. Family. Friend who didn't understand boundaries. Employees. The fiftyish Clarice had linked her arm through Rupert Kline's. The dart of Audrey's gaze indicated that she'd noted the other woman's connection to her father, but didn't seem to mind. "We're so pleased to see you in one piece, dear."

Jeffrey Beecher tapped the edge of his clipboard. "The vans are nearly full. We need a decision on storage versus delivery tonight."

Clarice shot him a killer glare and curled her fingers more tightly into Rupert's sleeve. So she didn't want to be considered one of the Kline's employees. Was there anyone here who wasn't getting on someone's nerves?

"I thought you were going to handle that," Clarice commented.

"Bud's ready to take the vans to either location. But you're the one who signs the checks, boss."

Audrey's gaze slid over to the handyman with the toothpick and the sudden tension in her mouth made Alex hate the commotion surrounding her here even more.

"Could you two discuss your work someplace else?" Pierce snapped.

Audrey's tone strained to remain polite. "I really do need to get upstairs and change out of these clothes."

Beecher moved over to Clarice to chat directly with her while Harper Pierce swung his attention back to Audrey. "But the Hunts offered to host something for the scholarship fund as well, and I think we should take them up on it. We can make the plans while the event planner is here."

"I told you I couldn't do any more of this until the trial was over. Besides, there's the holi—"

"But it's for Gretchen."

"Bud!" Clarice clapped her hands and Audrey jumped!

The tug at Alex's jacket sleeve was as clear as a cry for help.

Enough. Alex plucked his badge from his belt and held it high in the air. "I need everybody out of here. Now."

He shoved his arm in front of Audrey, blocking anyone else from getting to her.

"Alex—"

She better damn not try to pretend she wasn't overwhelmed by all the chaos here. "If you have a key card to the front gate, it needs to be checked in with me before you leave. I'll be changing the access codes immediately."

"How dare you." Clarice propped her hands on her ample hips. "I have every right to be here."

"We're not finished tearing down," Jeffrey protested.

"All of you. Out." Alex took a good look at Bud Preston's sneering grin and nodded toward the nearest exit before turning to Rupert. "Sir, I'm here to protect your daughter on D.A. Powers's orders. Audrey's my only concern. I need to secure this location and she needs her rest."

Thank God somebody here had his priorities straight. Rupert held up his hands, placating the gathering even as he ushered them toward the door. "Officer Taylor is right. It's been a long, difficult day for Audrey." He caught Clarice by the elbow and turned her with a kiss on the cheek. "Can we finish this tomorrow?"

The platinum blonde wasn't going peacefully. "Of course. But surrender my card? What about your invitation?"

"Not now."

"This will mean paying the crew for overtime," Jeffrey pointed out, using hand signals to get his staff to drop what they were doing and head outside.

Rupert whispered something to Clarice and she smiled. Erasing the affronted look she'd had for Alex, she broke away to come back to Audrey. "Some things are more important than money, Jeffrey." She reached for Audrey, but Alex wasn't budging. "I'm just so glad you weren't seriously hurt." Once she understood that she wasn't getting past Alex's protective arm, Clarice touched her own cheek, indicating Audrey's. "I have a great ointment you can put on that to keep it from scarring."

Witch.

Although the grip on his jacket eased, Audrey was still holding on. "I think a hot shower and some sleep are all I really need. Good night."

Rupert held out his arm and Clarice latched on while they retrieved her purse and he walked her to her car. Audrey's sigh of relief was audible before she turned back up the stairs. But this assault on her patience and composure—feeling every bit like the mob at the court-house that afternoon—wasn't quite over.

When Harper Pierce's foot hit the first step, Alex was there, his hand at the center of Pierce's chest, pushing him back down to the foyer. "You, too, buddy."

The tall man's blue blood was boiling. "Unlike you, Officer Taylor, I am a friend of the family—a good friend of Audrey's. Why don't you go sit out in your squad car and—"

"Harper, please," Audrey interrupted.

"No. I won't be talked to like this by some—"

"Get out of here, Harper." Audrey Kline might be down, but she was by no means out of fight. Once again, the stubborn redhead surprised Alex when she marched back down the stairs and slid her arm around his waist. "He's with me."

"I understand that the D.A. ordered a protection detail—"

"No, Harper." Audrey turned, the subtle swell of her breast branding Alex's chest as she lightly stroked her fingertips across the stubble of his jaw. His pulse raced beneath his skin, chasing the feel of her deliberate touch on him. She might be playing a game for Pierce's benefit, but the possessive, protective rightness of having Audrey pressed to his side felt real enough, and he slid his arm around her shoulders, completing the embrace. "Alex is with me. He's not leaving."

Pierce eyed the hand cupping Audrey's shoulder before throwing what sounded like an accusation at her. "So you're taking him to the Hunts' New Year's Eve reception?"

"Maybe. If I go."

"I thought we would attend together."

"When did you ask me? Has anyone even received an invitation?"

"Well, I never expected you'd take your boy toy instead."

That's it. Alex had Pierce by the back of his belt and his pretty starched collar and was dragging him across the foyer and out the door before he even got a threat about *suing his ass off* out of his mouth. Pierce was stumbling onto the porch when Alex slammed the door and threw the dead bolt.

Alex turned to face Audrey on the stairs, the sudden emptiness making the house seem even larger than before. He locked on to Audrey's emerald gaze as he strode silently back across the marble floor. She seemed smaller, even more vulnerable than before, framed by the grand staircase. "Your father has the key to get back in, doesn't he?"

Audrey nodded. "And he'll reset the alarm." Her soft smile was worth every curse being hurled at him from outside the door. "Harper *is* a talented attorney. He could take you to court."

"I'm a police officer carrying out my assigned duty. He's got no case against that, does he, counselor?"

"No." Alex halted two steps below her and watched her smile press into a flat line. "I'm going to bed. There are plenty of guest rooms in the east wing. Food in the kitchen—maybe even coffee. Make yourself at home. Good night."

She'd pulled off both shoes and unbuttoned her coat and blazer before she reached the top of the stairs and turned down the west hallway. The coat was sliding off her shoulders when Alex bounded the stairs behind her. By the time she pushed open a door near the end of the corridor, he'd caught up and slipped through the doorway behind her.

"What are you doing?" Weary as she was, there was nothing lagging about the sharpness of that tongue. He noted the length of the pale green sofa beneath the window in the curving tower room and two doors leading into a bathroom and an elegant bedroom of flower patterns and pastels. "Get out of here."

He watched as she tossed her coat and shoes onto the bed and followed him into an equally elegant, though decidedly less flowery office. "You said to make myself at home." He opened a door that led back into the hallway. "Does this lock?"

"Yes." He closed it, locked it. She followed him to the

window where he checked the lock and closed the drapes as well as the blinds. "I meant in a guest room."

Back in her bedroom, he checked each window lock and pulled the drapes, ensuring that no curious eyes could even see whether or not the lights were on. "You sleep in here, right?"

"Yes."

"Stay away from the windows. If anyone besides that crowd downstairs gets onto the grounds, I don't want them to be able to identify which rooms are yours." The walk-in closet and bathroom had no exterior exits and were easily secured. But Audrey was with him every step of the way as he learned the layout and identified the access points. A suite of four rooms—the same number of rooms he had in his entire apartment—were a lot easier to defend than the entire house and acreage outside. He returned to the sitting room and tossed his jacket onto the couch. "I can sack out here for the night."

She picked up the leather jacket, stuffed it back into his arms and tried to push him out the door. But her tongue was no match for his strength. "No, you can't. This is my home. These are my rooms, my space."

Which had been violated by at least twenty different people downstairs, and that didn't even take into account pushy reporters and bombs and Broadway Bad Boys. Alex saw the frustration—maybe even desperation—coloring her skin, making the strawberry on her cheek stand out in stark relief. "You expect me to guard you from the blind side of those rock walls and trees a quarter of a mile away?"

She almost said yes. Almost. Either he'd made his point or she'd grown too tired to argue.

Alex again laid his jacket across the couch, then gently took her by the shoulders and turned her back into the adjoining bedroom. "I won't let Demetrius Smith or his gang or anybody you don't want to see come near you tonight. Get some sleep. Be ready to kick some ass in court tomorrow morning. Close the door if you need some quiet time. Lord knows you deserve it."

Although he could have followed her right over to that queen-size bed, he released her and retreated to his side of the doorway, giving her the distance she wanted—the distance he needed. Something about this woman—everything about her—made him buzz with energy. He wanted when he was around her—he wanted to talk, to discover, to argue, to kiss, to touch, to protect—he probably wanted a lot more than he should.

She was hugging her arms around her waist when she turned to face him. He locked his feet inside his shoes, fighting how much he wanted to take her in his arms and shield the vulnerable beauty that was peeking out beneath her determined exterior. "How do I know you'll stay in there and not invade my privacy?"

"Lock the door if you still don't trust me. I'll knock it down if anything happens and I need to get to you."

Her chin jerked up. She studied him from shoulder to shoulder, noted his gun, his badge, his unblinking eyes. Finally, she resigned herself to the fact that he wasn't going anywhere. Not tonight. She clasped the door in both hands.

"Good night, Alex."

"Good night, Red."

Once she'd closed the door, Alex unhooked his belt and placed his Glock and its holster on the lamp table within arm's reach of the couch. He peeled off his tattered sweater and spread it over the throw pillows he stacked at one end. He turned off the lamp and settled onto the couch, getting accustomed to the sounds of the wind in the trees outside, and Rupert Kline coming back into the house and climbing the stairs. He heard Audrey moving in her bedroom, opening a drawer, crawling into bed.

And as clouds gathered outside and the house fell silent, he noted that, although the door between them was shut, Audrey had never locked it.

AUDREY STARTLED AWAKE at the clap of thunder that punctuated the explosion tearing through her in her nightmare.

Lightning flashed outside her window as she jolted up in bed, her mind racing, her heart thumping against the wall of her chest. She reached over to turn on the lamp beside her, centering herself in the familiarity of her own bedroom.

Seriously, a thunder-snow? While this type of weather wasn't unheard-of in the Midwest, as the seasons fought with each other to change, dumping a mix of rain, sleet and snow while the night sky rumbled overhead, the timing of the violent storm made Audrey wonder if this was still part of her nightmare.

But no, she was alive, she was awake and she was painfully alone.

As her breathing slowed to a healthier rate, she kicked off the covers that had twisted around her hips and tugged down the pant legs of the silk pajamas that had ridden up past her knees. The flashes of the storm peeked through the edges of her drapes, casting strobe-like shadows over the Monet hanging on her walls.

Matching sparks of adrenaline, remnants of the violent images that had haunted her dreams, coursed through her, making the idea of sleep as appealing as it was now elusive. Her one consolation as she grabbed a pillow and hugged it to her chest was that she must not have cried out or Alex Taylor would be in here already.

She'd seen the look in his eyes earlier—dark like the night, yet filled with such a light that she imagined he could see around corners and deep into her soul. Those eyes were as unsettling as they were handsome, and they'd left her with no doubt that, should he see fit, he'd bust down a door that had survived a fire, a tornado and hooch runners during Prohibition.

It was an idea that was equal parts frightening and reassuring and just a little bit exhilarating.

Why couldn't she have dreamed about that? Alex's hard, compact wrestler's body. That teasing grin. His gentle, drugging kisses. Those eyes.

But no—the rumble of thunder drummed along her spine and she shivered. The flashes of light and shadows creeping through her room transformed into the scattered images from her forgotten dreams. Speeding cars. Cold-eyed stares from a man she knew to be a killer. Grabbing hands. Exploding lights. *Are you scared yet? Do the right thing. Or die doing the wrong one.*

"Stop it." Audrey pulled her knees up and wrapped her whole body around the pillow, finding little comfort. Sitting here, wide awake, trembling in the dark, left her little to do but think.

It had taken forever to fall asleep. She was self-conscious about the man on the other side of her door, obsessing about the trial, remembering the threats, reliving the fear. Audrey looked over at the clock on the table beside her and groaned. Only an hour had passed since she'd last checked the time, shortly after midnight. That didn't bode well for a rested morning. She punched her pillow, lay back down and rolled onto her side. But the intermittent rumble of thunder and her own troubled thoughts kept her from falling back to sleep.

Out of all the craziness she'd gone through since Gretchen's murder, she could count on one hand the number of times she'd felt any real sense of calm or balance in her life. The first time, Alex Taylor had been offering her a handkerchief and holding her hand, another… She turned her lips into the cool cotton of her pillow case and remembered how warm and supple and completely seductive Alex's kiss had been.

There'd been one sane voice, one salvation through all of her waking nightmare of the threats and the trial—and he'd been talked down to by her friends and relegated to sleeping on a couch. Shamed by the way Alex had been treated by her guests downstairs, Audrey peeked over to see a dim light shining beneath the crack of her door.

Maybe she wasn't the only one who couldn't sleep tonight.

And maybe the need to offer an apology wasn't the only reason she slipped from beneath the covers and padded across the room.

When she quietly opened the door, Audrey wasn't surprised to see Alex sitting up in the next room.

"Did the storm wake you?" he asked, his voice a hushed echo of the thunder rumbling outside.

"My guilty conscience did. Couldn't you sleep, either?"

"I'm on guard duty, remember?"

The fractured images from her nightmare scattered into the recesses of her mind as something embarrassingly feminine and far too basic pumped into her blood at the sight of his half-naked body. He unfolded himself from the couch, creating ripples of awareness through the sitting room. There was much to appreciate about his sculpted pecs with their dusting of blue-black hair. His stomach was flat, his arms and shoulders heavily muscled. And the most intriguing thing was that, even though he stood only a few inches taller than she, everything about him was supremely masculine and perfectly balanced, from the leather bands on either wrist to the thin stripe of dark hair that disappeared behind the open snap of his jeans.

But she hadn't come out here to give her hormones a rush. She hugged her arms around her middle and rubbed her arms, the unexpected warmth firing inside her creating a chill along the surface of her skin. "I want to apologize for Harper's behavior."

"Why?" He tossed the magazine he'd been reading onto the couch. "You weren't the one throwing out the insults."

"He's not himself. He's still grieving over Gretchen's murder, and he's turned to me as a friend in need."

Alex propped his hands on his hips, refusing to accept her apology. "You're grieving, too. You've got your own problems to deal with. Who's taking care of you?"

"I take care of me." It was a valiant statement, but she wasn't even convincing herself.

"Why did you really come out here?" His eyes were fathomless in the shadows, his voice barely a whisper. Yet everything about Alex's words resonated deep in her bones. "What do you need tonight, Audrey?"

She ran through her list—polite apologies, thank-yous, fear of failing at the trial and letting Demetrius Smith and his lawyer make a mockery of her, fear that others around her would get hurt by her quest, guilt that a friend had died and she'd been too busy to be a very good friend to her at the end. But those dark, all-seeing eyes saw deeper inside. "I want to let down my guard for a few hours. I don't want to be responsible for anyone or anything. I just want to…be taken care of for a little while." The admission ended on half a laugh that just might be masking a few tears. She pressed her fingers to her mouth. "Oh, God, I do sound like a pampered princess, don't I?"

"You sound like an honest woman." He crossed the room with such purpose that Audrey instinctively backed away. But he caught her before she reached the doorway, tugged on her fingers and swung her up into his arms.

"Alex!" She tumbled against heat and strength and found herself not knowing exactly where to put her hands or even if she was pushing away or holding on. His chest hair tickled her palm. His bare skin was hot to the touch. A muscle flexed when she touched him there. He grinned when she touched him there. "Alex?"

"Shh. Around my neck is just fine."

She lightly wound her arms around his neck and held on as he carried her into her bedroom. Although certain traitorous parts of her had one idea in mind, Alex was taking her at her word, giving her what she'd asked for, what she needed. He laid her on the bed and tucked the covers up around her chin. After a gentle press of his fingertip to her lips, he left the room. Audrey had pushed herself up onto her elbows, wondering at his game, when he returned with his gun and badge. The edge of her bed sank beneath his weight as he leaned over to place his ID and weapon within easy reach.

But before he turned off the light, she saw the puckers of pale circular scars on the back of his right shoulder, like a spider's web standing out in harsh contrast against his olive skin. With her stomach clenching in knots of compassion, she reached up and brushed her fingers across the palm-size wound.

His skin jumped beneath her touch. And then Alex was turning, plucking her hand away and swinging his legs up on top of the covers beside her. "Easy, Red. You asked for comfort, and I'm doing my damnedest to be a good boy here."

"What happened to you?"

"Nothing too dramatic—laser surgery." He scooted down onto the pillows and rolled onto his side to face her. "I had a tattoo removed."

"A good-size one from the look of it. Did it hurt?"

"Not as much as when an old friend tried to cut it off me."

Audrey hissed at the horrid idea of the pain he must have suffered. She laid her fingers against his cheek, cupping his stubbled jaw. "Alex…"

He covered her hand with his. "It was a gang tat, Audrey. Westside Warriors. I may be the best qualified cop in KCPD to protect you against Smith. Because I grew up in a gang, too."

He didn't seem surprised when she freed her hand to clutch the sheet and comforter together at her chest between them. Maybe he thought she was judging him, but she was just…stunned. "Did you ever…?"

"Get into trouble?" He rolled onto his back and stared

at the ceiling. "Yeah. Not anything I'm proud of. All juvie stuff. I finally got out the year before the Taylors adopted me. They made me want to stay out."

"Don't gangs have some kind of violent...reverse initiation...if a member wants to leave?"

"Yeah."

He didn't elaborate and his stark response left Audrey imagining all kinds of horrible things—like peeling off a tattoo with a knife—and crawling out from under the covers to hug him tightly around his shoulders.

After a moment's hesitation, he folded his arms around her and pulled her squarely on top of him, holding her close for several timeless minutes. He buried his nose in her hair and breathed deeply. Audrey rode the rise and fall of his chest, settling more deeply, more intimately against him with every exhale.

But as his hands slid down toward her bottom, he muttered a curse and pushed her away. "You play hell with my best intentions, counselor."

Fine. Keep it friendly. Audrey tried to give him his space. But she didn't get far across the bed before he snaked his arm around her waist and pulled her back into the sheltering curve of his body, as though he, too, had a few needs that could only be assuaged by the closeness of another human being. He drew gentle, mindless circles across her belly as he spooned behind her, warming the silk and soothing something tight and needy deeper inside. "The point is, I know how Smith thinks. I know how a gang works. I know just how tough and ruthless they can be."

So he could be that tough and ruthless, too.

"Does that scare you?" he whispered against her ear.

Audrey laid her hand over his, lacing their fingers

together to still the errant caresses. "Having a former juvenile delinquent in bed with the assistant district attorney?"

His chuckle was a warm balm against her skin. "A headline like that couldn't be good for your reputation. A glory-seeker like Lassen would love to print that story."

"I only worry about headlines if they're a lie or they hurt my father."

"You're very protective of him."

"He's all I've got. I want him to know that I can take care of myself out in the world—that he doesn't always have to worry about me. When my mom was dying of cancer, the worries he had ate him up. They aggravated his heart condition."

"That explains a lot about your need to be independent. Striking out on your own and creating your individual success is your way of taking care of him."

"Yeah." He got it. She wasn't sure if that understanding surprised her or not. Alex Taylor seemed to intuit more about her than she even knew herself sometimes. It should have been a disquieting realization to know that someone had gotten so deep into her head. Instead, her body relaxed and she snuggled into the wall of heat at her back. "You're not exactly who I thought you'd be, Alex."

"I'm a different class of people than Pierce and your society friends, hmm?"

She shook her head. This wasn't about social standing. "You're more complex. When I expected you to be an ass, you gave me your handkerchief and stood up for me."

"That's Grandma's training."

She squeezed his hand at her waist and smiled. "I hear such love and unabashed gratitude every time you speak of your family. I never expected that, either. You fight with me—"

"They're discussions, Red."

"—yet you stand beside me when I need a friend." Or lie beside her. A tremor of awareness that had nothing to do with comfort and everything to do with sexual hunger rippled along every inch of her skin. "You're a little hard for me to figure out."

He misread her shiver as a sign she was feeling chilled, and tucked her beneath the covers again. He stretched out on top of the comforter and pulled her into his arms, facing him. "Oh, and that's eatin' you up inside, is it?"

She gave his shoulder a playful swat, followed almost immediately by an unexpected yawn. "Hard, I said, but not impossible. I won't quit trying."

Maybe he was feeling the same sexual tension, but he was determined to give her what she'd asked for. He traced relaxing lines up and down her back and continued the quiet conversation. "You're not what I expected, either."

"Daddy's society princess? That's one of the reasons I went to work for Dwight Powers—I want to prove I'm not that stereotype."

"Trust me, Red, you are too unique to fit into any stereotype I know of."

That comment gave her pause. "You know, that may well be the most meaningful compliment any man has ever given me."

"Who said it was a compliment?"

She giggled against the fragrant warmth of his skin.

But his strong arms and abundant heat and quiet conversation were working. Her eyelids had lead weights on them and it was getting harder and harder to focus. She nestled into the pillow of his shoulder with her hand resting at the middle of his chest. "Is there anything else you like about me, Alex?"

She felt his lips in her hair, felt the absolute security of his arms around her. He was taking care of her. In the tenderest way possible, he was giving her exactly what she needed.

"The list is too long to get into tonight. You need your sleep, and so do I."

Audrey wasn't sure when the darkness finally claimed her and she fell asleep. But she knew she wasn't alone. She was in a place where the nightmares couldn't reach her. She was calm, centered, secure in her dreams.

And for the first time in a long while, she believed that everything in her life might just turn out all right.

Chapter Seven

Audrey cracked one eye open as a narrow ribbon of light fell across her face. She put up her hand, wanting no part of pictures and reporters intruding on her blissful slumber this morning.

Slumber? Morning?

She rolled over to a cold spot and shivered. Both eyes snapped open. The bright line of light was peeking through the gap between her drapes. The storm had passed, the alarm clock was beeping and she was alone.

Alone.

She threw back the covers and scrambled out of bed. "Alex?"

The intimacy of holding each other through the night had passed. The doors were closed, the room was silent, his gun and badge were gone. How dare he? Not even a goodbye? He'd done his duty by her—he'd talked and shared and aroused and comforted and now he was gone? Or had something happened? Had his team been called out on a dangerous assignment? Had someone gotten onto the estate, after all? She went through confusion, anger, hurt and, finally, concern, as she ran to the sitting-room door and pulled it open.

"Alex!" She screamed when she saw the giant perched on the end of her couch and jumped back to cling to the door frame. "Who are you—? Where—?"

"Trip Jones, ma'am. Remember me from yesterday in the park? I'm a friend of Alex's from SWAT Team One. Didn't mean to startle you."

Now she saw the gun at his hip, the insulated SWAT jacket draped over the back of the couch. He set down his book and stood. And stood. And stood while she shrank back another step and estimated the distance to the hallway.

"Shrimp asked me to come over and keep an eye on things while he gets cleaned up."

Shrimp? She swiveled her head to the sound of running water and the door to the bathroom swinging open.

"Audrey!" Alex ran straight toward her, clutching a towel around his waist, dripping on her rug. With a muttered curse, he stopped and turned to the big man with the light brown hair. "You couldn't have announced yourself?"

"I didn't realize you hadn't told her that we were here. We were just getting acquainted."

"Wait a minute, *we?*" There were more armed police officers lurking around the house?

"Shrimp called for reinforcements." Trip grinned, never retreating one step from Alex's advance. "Now I can see why. You're sportin' a real tough-guy look there. Where are you hiding your gun?"

"You don't want to know." Alex slicked his fingers through his wet hair and glanced back at the bathroom. "Why don't you go outside and check the grounds?"

"Holden and Sarge are already on that. Captain Cutler

is on the phone with Quinn Gallagher's office, tracking down the security logs to find out everyone who's come and gone from the estate over the past month or so." He shrugged his black jacket onto his broad shoulders. "I called your brother like you asked. He's got his dog here to see if he can pick up any trace of intruders on the grounds."

"There's a dog?"

"K-9 unit, ma'am." Trip turned his warm hazel eyes to her before pulling a black KCPD ball cap over his super-short, military-cut hair. "Although I don't know if he'll be able to pick up much after all that sleet and snow we had last night."

With one hand holding tight to the towel that rode atop his hips, Alex gestured to the hallway door. "Why don't you track down Pike and see how he and Hans are doing?"

"Pike's the brother, Hans is the dog," Trip clarified, easily looking over Alex's shoulder to her before opening the door.

Alex's irritation was as evident as Trip's amusement as he shooed the replacement babysitter out. "I've got this covered in here, big guy. Go find the dog."

"You ain't got much covered." The door was closing in his face as Trip added, "Nice to see you again, ma'am."

Alex ducked into the bathroom to turn off the water and scrub a towel over his short, curling hair. He draped the second towel around his neck and apologized. "Sorry about that. When I called for backup this morning so I could get a couple hours of hard sleep, I didn't think my entire team would show up. You were zonked, so I thought I'd be done before you woke to warn you about the shift change."

Now that she recognized Trip Jones and understood why he was here, she remembered something Alex had said to her outside the courthouse yesterday. Yes, she'd been startled, but he had nothing to apologize for. She grabbed the ends of the towel hanging over his chest and tugged him closer. "Your team is here to back you up because you need them. We need them."

She tugged a little harder and angled his face down to hers to kiss him. His skin was steamy from the shower, his face clean-shaven and smooth. And his lips were just as warm and divine and wonderful as she remembered as he tunneled his fingers into her hair and deepened her *thank you* into a taste of a passionate *good morning.* Audrey curled her toes into the carpet, still holding on to the towel, as she forced herself to pull away.

"Thanks for last night. I guess I needed a little backup myself. You were right about me needing to realize that." She tickled her palm over the curls of hair on his chest. "But the reality of today is I have to return to the courthouse and face off against Cade Shipley and his client."

"Wait a minute. Rewind. I was right?" He slid his hands to the small of her back and pulled her flush against him, smiling against her mouth before he reclaimed it. "I have a feeling that's not something I'm going to hear too often."

Audrey squealed a token protest as the water from his wet skin soaked through her pajamas. It was like standing skin-to-skin, softness to hardness, need to need. Her pulse caught fire. Her nipples pearled beneath the friction of his chest moving against hers, shooting little tendrils of heat curling down inside her. Audrey wound her arms around his neck and pulled herself up on tiptoe, aligning her hips with his, recapturing the closeness they'd shared through the night, intensifying it.

Alex moaned deep in his throat and tore his mouth from hers a split second before the door opened and Trip walked back in. "Sorry. Don't mind the elephant in the room. Forgot my book. By the way, you aren't the only company here this morning. A Miss Darnell? Mr. Kline spoke to Captain Cutler and we cleared her. Otherwise, no one has been here except the paperboy and the morning staff. Just wanted you to know that some of us around here are doing our job, shrimp." He tipped his hat to Audrey and winked at Alex. "You two carry on."

"Get out of here!" Alex ordered.

Audrey landed flat on her feet as Alex released her and whirled around. The wad of towel that had been around his neck hit the closing door as Trip grinned all the way out.

She curled her arms around her waist, setting up a definite barrier as Alex reached for her to resume the kiss. His gaze narrowed and he settled for rubbing his hands up and down the silk on her arms. "Audrey?"

She backed away a step. She hadn't heard the knock on the door, or whatever had alerted him to Trip's return. He'd been on guard, as usual—aware of everything going on around him. He hadn't forgotten about the threats and his duty, while for the past few moments she'd forgotten about everything except getting that towel off his hips and getting even closer.

She'd forgotten about her duty. To the people of Kansas City.

"Don't be so hard on him." The interruption gave her the moment she needed to get her head screwed on straight. Burying those impulsive urges made her realize a bit of modesty was in order. She went to the door and picked up the towel to cover her now see-through pajamas. "I think the big guy's funny."

"Don't encourage him. *I'm* the guy on the team who gets picked on."

"He probably wasn't expecting us to move so fast into that…" Achy, raw, foolishly wanting to tumble back into bed and share the ultimate closeness feeling that was still reeling through her veins. "I'm sure he wasn't expecting…that."

"Apparently, you weren't, either."

Had she ever seen such an unreadable expression on Alex's face? "I'm sorry."

"Don't." He strode back into the bathroom and collected his jeans from the night before and a gym bag that Trip must have brought him. He tossed them onto the couch, pulled out a pair of black boxer-briefs, boldly dropped his towel and started dressing in front of her. Audrey shielded her eyes from that taut, head-to-toe physique and turned her head. "Don't apologize for acting on what you feel. Trust your gut. Don't over-analyze it and talk yourself out of what you want." He shook out a crisp pair of jeans and stepped into them. Audrey lowered her hand and faced him, knowing he was looking her way. "I don't know what the problem is that you have with us, Red—if it's where I come from, or if you're like Pierce and think I'm just the hired help—"

"No."

"—or if you just can't accept the idea that sometimes

things happen quickly between people." He left his jeans unfastened around his hips and crossed the room to her. "We fit, Audrey. You and me, like no other woman I've known before. I don't question it. I don't need time to weigh the whys or why nots, I just accept it."

"How do you know that?"

"I don't. I'm trusting my gut instincts. I feel something for you, you feel something for me. Why is that such a bad thing for you?"

Audrey hugged the towel more tightly in her arms. Alex Taylor's omniscient eyes really could see deep down inside her. No, she hadn't been expecting the intensity of her relationship with Alex to move so quickly. She hadn't been expecting any kind of relationship, period. She was a career woman with a life plan. Falling in love with him wasn't supposed to be on the agenda.

Falling in love?

Oh, Lord. Audrey pulled up the towel to her cheeks to hide the confusion and dismay and fear that his uncanny intuition about her was right on the money.

She did the cowardly thing and headed for the bathroom, plugging in her curling iron and retrieving her hair dryer, desperately needing to sort things out and regain some semblance of control over her life before continuing this conversation. "I have to be in court by 9:00 a.m."

An unexpected hand cupped the back of her neck and turned her. Alex stamped her mouth with a hard kiss and quickly released her. But those dark brown eyes ensnared her with something else. He wouldn't let her be a coward. "You think about it, Red—because I know you like to think. You think about giving us a chance, and I'll be with you all the way. I'll go as fast or slow as you like. But if you decide you just can't let yourself feel what you feel, do me the courtesy of letting me know, okay?"

Were those tears stinging her eyes? "I don't want to make a mistake. I don't want to hurt you."

"I know." He pulled the towel from her hands and dabbed at her eyes. "Maybe better than you do. But I'm worried that you're the one who'll really feel it if you don't give us a chance. Just think about it."

Yes. She definitely needed to think. No matter what karmic wisdom Alex shared about knowing his feelings for people so quickly, this was definitely moving a little fast for her—this needing, this wanting. Her life was changing too fast for her to process. Had she missed something more than companionship developing between her father and Clarice? And it was more than a little scary to think how quickly she was losing control of the professional relationship she should be maintaining with Alex. Right now, she needed to backtrack away from this crazy passion and emotional intimacy and return to A.D.A.-bodyguard mode for a while. She pushed him out the bathroom door with a shaky smile. "Work, Alex. We both have work to do. I'll have to deal with this—with us—later."

Alex's scent only intensified in the steamy room when she closed the door. But she couldn't be distracted by that right now. She shouldn't remember how secure she'd felt falling asleep in his embrace or how hurt she'd been thinking that he'd left her during the night. She couldn't think about kissing him and wanting him and feeling terrifyingly out of her comfort zone and perfectly in place each time he took her in his arms. Not right now.

Audrey stepped into the shower, turned her face into

the spray and let the pelting warmth of the water cleanse the distracting thoughts from her head. By the time she was drying her hair and putting on her makeup, she had the disturbing emotions triggered by Alex Taylor firmly under control. She was rejuvenated, reenergized and ready to take on whatever Judge Shanks, Cade Shipley and his menace-to-society client had to throw at her today.

She was buttoning her brown cashmere blazer over its matching skirt and coming down the stairs to grab a cup of coffee and a muffin when she heard the clatter of silverware on a plate and the sounds of distress coming from her father's office.

"Oh, my God."

Her father's voice.

"What are they doing to her? My little girl."

His pinched, gasping voice turned Audrey's walk into a run. "Daddy!"

"Mr. Kline!" the family cook, Mrs. Puente, called.

"Rupert? Oh, dear," Clarice said.

"Don't let her see this," Rupert demanded.

"Daddy? Alex!" she called to the trio of men and a big German shepherd huddled in a terse conversation just inside the front door.

Audrey dashed through the arched walnut door to find Mrs. Puente and Clarice Darnell hovering over her father in the leather chair behind his desk, trying to give him a glass of water and unbutton his shirt. Rupert Kline's narrowed gaze landed right on her as he clutched at his chest.

Heart attack.

"Daddy!" Audrey dashed to his side.

"It's okay, missy." He tried to smile. "Just a flutter. It'll kick back…into rhythm…in a minute."

She pulled the newspaper from his fist, focusing on his face.

"No!" Rupert wheezed.

She ignored him and tossed it onto the desk, snapping out the orders the doctors had trained her to do. "We need to stretch him out on the floor. Mrs. Puente, get the bottle of aspirin and a blanket. Clarice, call 9-1-1."

"Already done." Alex's voice was right behind her. He and Trip blew past her and lifted her father from his chair, nudging aside Clarice, who was still trying to unhook buttons. Audrey didn't have time to consider the implications of having the platinum blonde spending the night with her father. Alex thrust the phone into her hand. "I told Dispatch the address, you give them the details."

Whatever had happened between them upstairs, thank God, had been thrust aside to concentrate on her father. Alex and Trip were working like a smooth-running machine, asking her father questions and checking his pulse. Grateful for the help, Audrey turned her attention to the 9-1-1 dispatcher on the phone. "Rupert Kline. Yes, he wears a pacemaker. Dr. Trecha is his specialist."

Rosie Puente huddled against the floor-to-ceiling bookshelves, clasping her hands together in prayer. Tears filled her eyes. "I didn't mean to do this. I served him his egg whites and soy bacon and toast, and brought him his paper, just like I do every other morning of the week. And then he grabbed his chest. I didn't mean—"

"Get the aspirin, Rosie. You didn't do anything wrong." Audrey squeezed Mrs. Puente's hands and gave her a slight shake. There was no blame here, she just needed action. "Go." She turned her attention back to the dispatcher on the phone. "We're getting him an aspirin now."

Three more officers, including the sergeant who'd driven the pickup away from the courthouse yesterday, appeared. The oldest man of the group—clearly the one in charge—with dark salt-and-pepper hair, spoke in hushed tones. A tall blond man introduced himself to Clarice as Holden Kincaid and drew the older woman out of the room. Sergeant Delgado jogged out of the room after them, making a call on his own cell phone.

She completed her call to the 9-1-1 operator and knelt at her father's side next to Alex. She smoothed his silvery red hair away from the perspiration dotting his forehead. "It'll be okay, Daddy. The ambulance is on its way."

"It's just a palpitation, missy." He tapped his chest. "That's what the hardware's for. I'll be all right."

Sergeant Delgado came back in with a portable oxygen tank and mask. He handed it off to Trip. "We need to get this on you, sir."

"Just breathe, Daddy." Audrey handed the phone back to Alex, and didn't try to pretend she wasn't grateful for the quick squeeze of her fingers before he slipped the cell into his pocket.

She watched him press those same fingers to her father's thigh, checking his femoral pulse. The germ of a memory, the seed of something crucial to the Smith case she'd overlooked whispered through her mind. She murmured the thought out loud. "He was shot in the leg."

"Red?"

"Calvin Chambers was shot in the chest *and* the leg.

I think I just figured out how to win the trial. Since Plan A didn't work, and Plan B is… Never mind." She shook off the idea and focused on the most important issue at hand. "How is he?"

"We've just got basic medic training, but I don't think it's a full-on heart attack. Something must have given him a shock."

"He's still going to the hospital," Audrey insisted.

"I know, Red. I want a professional to check him out, too." Alex looked back down to her father. "Mr. Kline, can you tell me when this started?"

Rupert seemed to be breathing a little easier with the oxygen mask over his mouth and nose, but he was still alarmingly pale. "Reading that paper." He raised up slightly and grabbed hold of Alex's sleeve. "Don't let them hurt her. You keep her safe."

"Shh. Relax, sir." He eased her father back to the floor. "I'm not going anywhere."

Audrey smoothed her father's hair again and bent down to kiss his forehead, hiding her fear behind a smile. "Hang in there. Don't worry about me—I'm all grown up, remember?"

Rosie Puente huffed into the study, and they covered Rupert with a blanket and helped him swallow one of the aspirins. Within a matter of minutes, the real EMTs were at the house, rolling out her protesting father on a gurney, and assuring her that his heart rate was returning to normal and that the doctor would meet them at the hospital to conduct a thorough check of the patient.

Clarice had a hold of her father's hand and was hurrying alongside the gurney. "I'm so sorry, Rupert. Do you want to reschedule?"

When the EMTs paused at the front door, Audrey

glared Clarice away from her father and took his hand instead.

Clarice puffed up, her expression changing from concern to self-defense. "He invited me to breakfast."

Her father's fingers tightened around hers and he pulled the oxygen mask away from his face to give her a wry smile. "You're the one who encouraged me to start dating."

That she had. She'd even suggested Clarice as a candidate. So her campaign to prove to her father that she was a mature adult had just taken a serious setback. Was it because she subconsciously suspected Clarice Darnell was a gold digger? She herself had worked with her on several occasions, and had observed nothing but professional results. Or had she just seen another woman taking her place at her father's side and succumbed to a stab of jealousy? Emotions, right. She glanced over at Alex at the foot of the gurney then quickly turned away from his knowing gaze to replace the mask over Rupert's nose and mouth. "I'm sorry, Clarice." She straightened and faced the buxom woman. "You're welcome to join us at the hospital."

"No." Rupert snatched her hand again. "You have court this morning, and I know you just had a brainstorm that would do the Kline name proud. This trip to the hospital is just a precaution. You can come see me afterward."

"I'll call Judge Shanks. He'll understand an emergency and will grant me the delay."

"Absolutely not." Rupert Kline's killer-in-the-courtroom glare hardened his expression for a moment. "You have a job to do. You're my daughter. If this is what you want, you go get them."

"Daddy—"

"I'm trying to do the right thing here, missy." Fatigue and love softened his face with a paternal smile. "They brought this battle to our home, not once, but twice now. And as much as I want to protect you…" He took the deepest breath he had in the last twenty minutes. "Maybe it's time I handed over the reins and let you do your own fighting. If I was trying this case, I'd do everything in my power to make sure Smith and his thugs didn't win."

He believed in her. As much as he wanted to pamper and protect her, the great Rupert Kline believed she could win this case. Humbled and inspired and deeply grateful for his confidence in her, Audrey leaned down to kiss his cheek. "I'll get him, Daddy."

He winked at her before angling his gaze at Alex. "I'm counting on you, too, son. You watch her back."

"We need to go, ma'am," the EMT interjected.

Audrey nodded and stepped away. "Do you mind staying with him until I can get there, Clarice?"

"I'll take good care of him, hon."

"I love you, Daddy."

They were already wheeling him out the door. "Love you, too."

Once the ambulance pulled away, with an off-duty police escort, Alex shut and bolted the door. "What did Rupert mean, the battle has been here twice?"

Audrey marched into her father's office where Mrs. Puente had started to clear the tray from his desk. She thanked the cook and sent her off to the kitchen to take a break. Then Audrey went to her father's chair and picked up the newspaper. She frowned. "This isn't the *Journal*. Where did this scandal rag come from?"

She opened it to the second-page photo of her and Alex sprawled on the sidewalk in the middle of the debris field from the exploded trash can. There was tomato on her collar and a bloody mark on her cheek. Her knees nearly buckled. Her father had seen this?

Even more disturbing than the *Attack on A.D.A.* headline was the message drawn across the photo in black magic marker. *He can't save you from the inevitable, bitch!* Audrey felt the same sense of violation and fear as she'd felt yesterday at the park. But she curled her toes inside her pumps and stood tall as she handed the paper across the desk. "This isn't the first threat I've received."

Alex read the words and swore at the noose drawn around her neck. "This is Steve Lassen's work. Damn opportunist."

"The picture and article are his, at least. That doesn't mean he added the message."

Alex set down the paper and pushed it away as though the sight of it made him physically ill. "And you've gotten other crap like this? That might explain what Pike and his dog found outside."

A chill crept down her spine. "What's that?"

"A set of footprints in the slushy leaves out in your front yard forest, along with a handful of small branches that have been sliced off with some kind of knife."

"The groundskeeper wouldn't trim the trees until all the leaves are gone."

"And he wouldn't hack at it with a knife. Somebody's been here, watching you. Somebody who didn't want to be seen." He unlocked the holster on his belt and pulled out his gun. With a series of precise movements, he dumped the magazine, slammed it into place again, checked the sights and returned it to the back of his belt as if he was expecting a gunfight. *Not ill. Pissed off. Maybe too angry to feel.* Alex needed to *do*. "The D.A. wants me here. Your father wants me here. What about you?"

She met those unblinking dark eyes across the desk. She was ready to take action, too. "Have one of your buddies call the crime lab. See if they can get knife marks off those branches. Hopefully, the storm hasn't degraded the footprints too much. Dust this paper for prints. Make sure they take Clarice's."

"To eliminate her as a suspect?"

Maybe. She didn't see how her father's new girlfriend could possibly have a connection to Demetrius Smith, but Audrey was about facts, not taking chances. "This is a morning edition. Somebody had to bring it in here after you cleared the house last night."

"The Bad Boys could have cornered the paperboy and forced him to deliver it for them. They could have… waylaid him and made the delivery themselves." Forced? Waylaid? Was he speaking from experience? "Sergeant Delgado has already called the lab. Do you know the kid's name?"

Audrey's stomach turned at the idea of another innocent being harmed by the Broadway Bad Boys in their effort to get to her. "Mrs. Puente does."

"I'll have Sarge talk to her and get the info." Alex propped his hands at his waist and rephrased his question. "What do you want *me* to do?"

"Take me to the courthouse."

Chapter Eight

"Mac Taylor is the day shift commander of the KCPD crime lab, with twenty years of experience in the field. I think he knows what he's talking about." Audrey paced in front of the judge's bench, pointing to the man on the witness stand.

"Objection overruled. I don't think we need to debate the experience of this witness, Mr. Shipley, so sit down." Judge Shanks paused to take a sip of what had to be room-temp coffee by now. He might look tired, but there was no mistaking the pinpoint reprimand in his eyes. "But watch the sarcasm, Miss Kline."

Audrey thanked him with a deferential nod and turned her attention back to the forensic scientist with a scarred face, a blind eye and glasses, who'd remained completely cool and unflustered by Cade Shipley's groundless attack on his skills and the way he ran his office. "Mr. Taylor, back to my previous question. You found no trace of GPR—gun powder residue—on the clothes the defendant, Mr. Smith, was wearing when he was arrested."

"None."

She ignored Cade Shipley's snicker. Did he really think she was foolish enough to pursue this line of questioning if she thought it would prove his client's innocence? "But you said the jacket he was wearing had no bullet hole in it."

Mac Taylor leaned forward to speak directly into the microphone. "Correct. The jacket had his blood on it. Part of the zipper had been broken and ripped out, as though it had gotten caught on something, or he'd gotten frustrated with it when he was putting it on."

"Relevance, your honor?" Shipley protested. "It's after four o'clock and I'm interested in eating dinner sometime tonight."

Audrey bit down on what she thought Shipley could do with his dinner if he kept on interrupting her. She thought it a wiser move to smile at Judge Shanks. "I have a point to make, Your Honor, I promise."

"Then get to it."

She returned to the witness. "So there was no bullet hole in the jacket Demetrius Smith was wearing, yet Mr. Smith's medical records clearly show that he'd been shot in the arm. What conclusion did your lab reach, based on that evidence?"

"That Smith wasn't wearing that jacket when he was shot."

"Now Captain Cutler of the responding SWAT team on the scene has already testified that they stormed the house within a minute of hearing Mr. Smith yelling that he'd been shot and wanted to surrender." She looked out into the gallery watching the trial, reminding the jury of the tall, salt-and-pepper-haired man in his black KCPD SWAT uniform who'd been on the stand earlier. Her gaze skimmed over Alex, sitting beside him. It shouldn't give her that little rush of confidence that he was out there supporting her, protecting her. But those dark eyes watching her did make her think that she could do this. She brought her gaze back to Mac Taylor's sighted eye. "Your lab also processed a jacket worn by another suspect at the scene, Tyrell Sampson. Would you tell the court what you found on Mr. Sampson's jacket?"

Mac nodded. "A bullet hole in the right sleeve. Blood. GPR on the right cuff. And traces of gun oil with minute metal filings that match the gun registered to Demetrius Smith."

"The gun that killed Calvin Chambers?"

"Yes."

"Had Mr. Sampson been shot?"

"Not according to the police report."

From the corner of her eye, Audrey saw Demetrius lean over and whisper something to his attorney. Seconds later, Cade Shipley was on his feet again. "Your Honor, if you recall, in that same police report, the interview with Tyrell Sampson stated that he was already in the system as the victim of a gunshot wound. An accident with a friend who was cleaning his gun, I believe."

Judge Shanks scratched at his curly black beard and sighed into his hand. "So noted. Miss Kline? Your point?"

Audrey cleared her throat to keep from smiling. *Keep going, Shipley. Help me win this case.*

She wrapped her fingers around the railing in front of the witness box and asked a simple question. "Was the blood on Tyrell Sampson's jacket his?"

"No. It was Demetrius Smith's."

Audrey let the grumbling through the courtroom gallery subside before she spoke again. "So is it feasible to assume that Demetrius Smith changed jackets with

Mr. Sampson in the minute between him being shot and being handcuffed by SWAT?"

"A quick-change artist could do it, yes."

Cade Shipley quickly objected. "Your Honor. Speculation."

"Withdrawn." Audrey quickly responded before looking up at Judge Shanks. "I have no further questions for this witness, Your Honor."

"Thank you, Mr. Taylor. You're dismissed."

Audrey returned to her seat, stealing a sly look at the jury as she walked by. She could see by their reactions that she'd successfully put the possibility into their minds that Demetrius had indeed shot and killed Calvin Chambers, and then switched the jacket that held the incriminating evidence as soon as he realized he was going to be captured.

It wasn't a fact she could win a case on. But if she could find one Broadway Bad Boy who'd been on the scene to say he'd seen Demetrius switch jackets, then she didn't need to put the gun in his hand. The forensic evidence would put it there for her.

"All rise."

Audrey checked her watch as the courtroom was dismissed. If the fates were with her, she could wrap up a conviction in a matter of days rather than dragging this out over the holidays or settling for reduced charges against Smith. Alex had put in a call to his uncle Josh, one of the detectives working the Chambers shooting, and he and his partner were rounding up Tyrell Sampson for her to reinterview before the end of the day. Maybe she couldn't get him to state that he saw Demetrius fire the kill shot, but she might be able to get him to say something about changing clothes—unless he wanted to say the jacket with all the evidence was his, and take the rap for killing Calvin Chambers himself.

She tucked her notes into her attaché bag and looped it over her shoulder.

If the fates were…

When she turned to leave the prosecution table, Demetrius Smith was looking right at her. Staring at her. No, damning her. Yes, he was in handcuffs. Yes, he was listening to whatever Shipley was saying to him. But this silent conversation was all about him and her.

You scared yet, bitch?

Audrey couldn't seem to catch her breath. Her hand fisted around the strap of her bag. She couldn't seem to look away from the vile promise in his eyes, either.

And then she heard, "Turn around, Smith."

Her breath rushed out in a gasp of relief as Alex pushed through the gate and inserted himself between Audrey and the defense table. She hadn't noticed it when she'd seen him earlier, but he must be back on the clock because at some time during the day, he'd changed into his SWAT uniform—long-sleeved black shirt over a turtleneck, black pants tucked into black army-grade boots, his sidearm strapped to his muscular thigh. Even from this view, he looked as imposing and official as the night she'd first met him.

Demetrius licked his lips and smiled. "I'm just enjoying the scenery, officer. There aren't any pretty girls where I'm at right now."

Tension sparked off every corded muscle. "Shipley, corral your client, or I will."

Shipley said something that displeased his client, but the courtroom officers were already pulling Demetrius away from the table. Alex stood fast, blocking

Audrey between the table and the railing until Demetrius had been removed and Shipley was packing up his briefcase.

Only then did he turn. "You okay?"

His hand came up, but quickly dropped to his side. She couldn't tell whether it was the protocol taboo of keeping his hands off the A.D.A. in court, or their prickly argument this morning about giving her time to think through her feelings that made him limit his concern to the dark expression in his eyes.

Audrey nodded, wondering at her own wistful response to the fact that he *hadn't* touched her. She tilted her chin and pretended her nerves weren't still rattling. "I must be making pretty good progress on my case for him to think he has to scare me back into my place like that."

"Do you think it'd cost me my badge if I punched him out for leering at you that way?"

Screw protocol. She reached over and grazed her fingers against his. He needed to take a step back from his gangbanger instincts, and she needed…she just needed to touch him. She needed that inexplicable anchor she felt whenever she connected with him in some way. It was just a simple brushing of fingertips, down low between them where only someone who was looking for the forbidden contact might see. But it was enough to regroup and feel grounded again. "Take the advice of an attorney, Alex. I'm okay. Just walk me to my car. I want to get to the police station and talk to Demetrius's friend Tyrell."

"Uncle Mac set the stage for you to wrap up this trial, didn't he?"

"Are you related to every cop at KCPD?"

"About half of them, it seems." With a nod to Trip, who quickly exited the back of the room, Alex pushed open the gate for her and followed her out of the near-empty courtroom. "He'll pick us up at the side entrance so you don't have to run the gauntlet of reporters today."

"I have to say something to them."

"No, you don't. Do you know how hard it is to spot a threat in a crowd like that?"

"They'll hound me all evening if I don't at least give them a statement."

He stopped her at the elevator and indicated to others that they go on so that she and Alex could ride down in a car alone. "Fine. Make a statement. But no questions. I'll alert Trip."

By the time she hit the chilly sunshine on the sidewalk in front of the courthouse, Audrey wished she'd taken Alex up on his offer to sneak her out the side entrance. *Gauntlet* was right. When she exited the glass doors, enough lights flashed to temporarily blind her. The assault of questions was equally unnerving. She barely got a look at the bundled-up onlookers and protest signs across the street in the park when the cameras and reporters swarmed around her. The salt that had been put down to melt the sleet and snow crunched beneath her boots as she took an instinctive step of retreat.

She bumped into Alex's hand at her back and was reminded she wasn't facing this alone. Raising her chin to a level of authority and control she didn't quite feel, she quieted them long enough to make her statement.

"The prosecution's case against Demetrius Smith is proceeding according to the strategy the district attorney's office has mapped out. We have strong circumstantial evidence and a timeline of events that shows—"

"But you can't get any witnesses to testify against him, can you?" someone shouted.

"Do you think Trace Vaughn's murder silenced any hope of getting someone to come forward?"

She felt Alex shift behind her. "Just a statement, Red."

Audrey cleared her throat and continued. "We have more expert testimony scheduled for tomorrow, including a representative from the drug enforcement task force to detail Mr. Smith's criminal record."

"He's going to get away with killing that little boy, isn't he?" She turned to the other side to face the new accusation. "Cade Shipley says you can't prove murder."

"Mr. Shipley is welcome to say whatever he wants. Of course, he's going to come out in support of his client."

She recognized Steve Lassen pushing his way to the front of the crowd and braced herself before he ever spoke. "He's got you running scared, doesn't he, Miss Kline?"

Alex's arm tightened around her waist, pulling her forward. "We're done here."

You scared yet?

Audrey planted her feet and faced Lassen's chubby red nose. "I didn't appreciate your article in the paper this morning, Mr. Lassen. It'd be nice if you'd stick to the facts instead of sensationalizing a tragic event."

He had the audacity to smile. "Which tragic event would that be? That kid's murder—?"

"That 'kid' is Calvin Chambers."

"—yesterday's bombing? Or your father's heart attack this morning?"

"How did you…? How dare you!" Every blood cell in Audrey's body swelled with fury. "My personal life doesn't have a damn thing to do with your story."

"Audrey." Alex strong-armed his way through the crowd, dragging Audrey along with him, forcing her into a trot to keep up. "He's baiting you. Now isn't the time to let those emotions go."

But Steve Lassen and a barrage of questions dogged their every step out to the street.

"Is Rupert Kline still alive?"

"What hospital is he in?"

"Any time now, Trip," Alex muttered, pulling Audrey into his arms and spinning her away from the crowd.

"Have you received any more threats from Demetrius Smith's crew?" Lassen prodded.

"Don't answer that."

Audrey twisted against Alex's grip. How did Lassen know these details? Did he really think his tabloid tactics were going to get him a regular assignment back at a legitimate newspaper? Or was he privy to inside information?

"Do you think you're going to live to see the end of this trial?"

Audrey felt the unwanted hand on her arm, urging her to turn. She saw Lassen's camera flash to capture her open-mouthed shock.

"Get your hands off her!"

In a matter of milliseconds, Lassen's grip on her arm popped open and Alex was shoving the bastard's face down to the pavement. Tires screeched to a halt on the pavement behind her and Alex raised his fist.

"Alex!"

A woman screamed. Cameras flashed.

"Taylor!" Trip called out.

Audrey yanked on Alex's shirt. But he'd already frozen at the sharp command.

"You—cuff this guy." Trip Jones ran up beside them, ordering the reporters back, summoning the uniformed officers nearby. He closed his big hands over Audrey's shoulders and pulled her back. "Into the truck, ma'am. Let's go, Taylor."

Steve Lassen spat out blood and cursed Alex for breaking his camera as two officers locked his wrists behind him and pulled him up. Alex rolled to his feet, his shoulders still heaving with every steadying breath, his eyes never leaving the reporter who'd gotten to her.

"Book this guy on assault and confiscate that camera as potential evidence," Trip ordered.

"What about my rights?" Lassen argued.

"What about *her* rights?" Alex crept forward. "You think terrorizing her makes a good story?"

"So I was right. The Society Princess has received another threat." Lassen made a terrible mistake. He smiled.

"Alex!" Audrey dove out of the truck to stop him from attacking the loathsome reporter. She grabbed on to his belt and tried to pull him away.

But Trip was there first, one big hand on Alex's shoulder, warning him back—the other hand pointed at Lassen's face. For a big man with a booming voice, Trip's hushed words sounded far more dangerous. "Let me tell you one thing, Lassen. I may be twice this guy's size, but I'm not the one you want to be pickin' a fight with. Now you go quietly with these officers, or I'll add resisting arrest to the assault charge and trespassing in a restricted area without your press credentials."

The two officers pulled Lassen away from the scene, but the washed-up reporter kept right on talking. "You know, one of these days I'll get my regular job back at the *Journal,* and I'll be writing such an exposé about police brutality and how the rich girls in this town get to call the shots and the poor jerks like me have to bow down to whatever you say. I'm going to change things. You wait and see."

"Rich girls?" Audrey released a breath she didn't know she'd been holding. "He blames me for him getting fired at the *Journal?*"

Lassen was locked inside a black-and-white cruiser before Trip released his hold on Alex. "He's an old drunk who can't keep a job, so he's trying to prolong his fifteen minutes of fame. Don't let him get to you."

Alex shoved his fingers through his hair, leaving a rumpled wake. "I let him get to Audrey."

"No, you kept him from hurting her, from exploiting her."

Finally, Alex took his eyes off Lassen and glanced up at Trip. "Semantics, big guy. Now's the time when you should be giving me the lecture about the rookie forgetting procedure and losing his cool."

"If somebody I cared about was being mobbed like that…?" Trip thumbed over his shoulder. "Get in the truck."

As the crowd dispersed and the legitimate reporters got on their phones and in their cars to call in their stories, Audrey climbed up into the truck between the two men and they headed toward KCPD headquarters just a few blocks away.

Alex glanced over and touched the smudge of dirt Lassen had left on the sleeve of her coat. "The next time I give you grief about checking your emotions, tell me to shut up."

"He's not allowed to touch her, Taylor." Trip stopped at a light. He checked the intersection in every direction, even using the mirrors to see behind them. "You did your job."

Did Alex notice that Trip had refrained from using his "shrimp" nickname? Alex's friend was backing him up. Understanding.

"Yeah. Just doing my job. Maybe I haven't outgrown my street background as much as I thought."

"Alex…" Audrey began. Maybe Alex didn't hear the distinction Trip had made. He fisted his hand in his lap, seething in uncharacteristic silence beside her. She reached over and curled her fingers around his hand. "I was scared back there. It felt so personal, like it didn't have anything to do with the trial."

He instantly opened his fist and turned his hand to match his palm to hers and lace their fingers together. "I wouldn't have let him hurt you."

She squeezed his hand, believing his promise, thanking him. "I was scared you were going to get yourself into trouble. But mostly I was scared by how much I wanted to see you punch his lights out." His dark eyes narrowed quizzically and she shrugged. "Not very high-brow or politically correct of me, is it? He knew Dad was in the hospital. He knew about the threats. He said 'rich girl.'" Her hand shook inside Alex's grip. "I've lost two friends, Val Gallagher and Gretchen Cosgrove, to somebody the police are calling the Rich Girl Killer."

Alex brushed a tendril of hair off her cheek and

tucked it behind her ear. "Sweetheart, he was pushing your buttons, that's all."

"He didn't give a damn that I might be upset or afraid. I wanted you to hit him, to shut him up." She paused as Trip moved into traffic again, waiting for the implication to set in. "See what happens when I get emotional? I don't cry pretty, my face turns pink and I want to hit something. And here I thought I'd been raised to be a lady. Does that make me 'street,' too?"

Trip threw back his head and laughed. She felt the tension in Alex finally relax. He lifted her hand to his mouth and kissed her fingers. He was grinning. "Audrey Kline, you've got so much class running through your blood that you couldn't be 'street' if I tattooed it on your ass." He leaned over and kissed her mouth. "But you're learning. Now let's go convince some Bad Boys to turn on Big D."

Audrey latched on to his hand with both of hers and rested her cheek against his shoulder. Maybe, just maybe, she could learn to live with her heart wide open the way Alex Taylor did.

If nobody killed her first.

Chapter Nine

Promising that she wouldn't leave her office until Alex came to escort her to the courthouse after their lunch-time recess the following day, Audrey finally got her first private moment since that morning. Pulling her gaze from the well-formed back of Alex's uniform as he strode across to Dwight Powers's office to make a requested report on her safety, she darted around to the chair behind her desk and picked up her phone to call Clarice Darnell's number.

Her father answered on the first ring. "Yes, missy?"

"Daddy? Why didn't Clarice answer? Isn't she there?" She stood up as quickly as she'd sat down. "I thought the whole point of you staying at Clarice's was so someone could be with you around the clock. Mrs. Puente can take care of you during the day and I'll be home tonight if you want to move back to the house. And what about the protection detail? Are they there?"

Rupert Kline's warm chuckle sounded perfectly normal. "You sound like an old mother hen. A police cruiser is parked right across the street, keeping an eye on things. Clarice is fixing me a sandwich. I was sitting right by the phone and saw your number so I picked up. You don't have to call me every two hours to make sure that I'm all right."

Audrey took a calming breath, forcing herself to remember that her father was as much of an adult as she
was. "Are you sure this is a good idea? The doctor said
that you didn't suffer a full-fledged heart attack, but…"
That didn't mean she wasn't worried about him running
across a subsequent threat and succumbing to the real
thing. Getting away from the house, from her, might
be another benefit to staying with his new lady friend.
"You sound tired."

"The nurses kept waking me up throughout the night,
checking my pulse and who knows what else. I swear
I don't know how anyone can rest up in a hospital.
Frankly, I'm glad to be here."

"Is she taking good care of you? Making sure you
rest?"

"She turned all her work over to her assistant, Jeffrey,
and is devoting her entire day to me."

"And tonight?"

Her father was chuckling again. "Are you worried
we're going to sleep in the same bed?"

"Dad!" Oh, Lord, she hadn't gone there yet. Clarice's
offer to care for her father after his release from the hospital this morning was a generous gift, and should have
eased some of Audrey's concern. But she knew where
her thoughts had been when Alex had tenderly held her
through the night again. And she was no more ready to
admit that her father might be falling in love when she
was barely able to get her head around the idea that she
herself was falling for someone she never would have
imagined herself with.

"You still there, missy?"

"I'm here." Audrey pulled her thoughts back to the

conversation. "I guess I'm just not used to sharing you with another woman."

"Don't worry, dear. We're not talking about anything permanent yet. And if we do get there, you know that no one writes a better prenup agreement than I do." His words took the edge of her concern. "You're still the number one woman in my book. How's the trial going?"

In other words, change the topic already. Rupert Kline was a successful man and certainly no fool. *Duly noted.* Although the lawyer in her still wanted to question Clarice Darnell's motives for being so attentive to her father, Audrey was beginning to understand how insulated and lonely they'd become since her mother's death. If her father was willing to embrace a new relationship, maybe she should support his decision—and consider doing the same with Alex.

Audrey cleared her throat, tucked a stray tendril of hair into the bun at her nape and answered. "Technical stuff this morning, mostly. Cade Shipley seemed to have an answer to rebut almost all of the expert witness testimony I presented."

"Shipley is more interested in headlines than in justice. Just keep your head about you—you'll get the job done." He cleared his throat, changing his tone. "Have there been any more threats since that newspaper? Do the police have any leads?"

"They're working on it. The lab didn't find any usable prints on the paper, and a Detective Fensom talked to the paperboy—he said a black man paid him twenty dollars to deliver that paper instead of the *Journal*." Audrey hugged her arm across her waist to ease the tension gathering inside her. If her father hadn't heard about her run-in with Steve Lassen yesterday afternoon, she wasn't about to tell him. "Thank goodness the boy wasn't hurt. I don't know if I could handle any more collateral damage because of Demetrius Smith."

"So KCPD thinks one of Smith's gang sent the threat?"

"I suppose." She pressed her lips together to keep any mention of the Rich Girl Killer from accidentally popping out. Audrey was sure the threats were all trial-related, but now that Lassen had thrown the idea out there that Val's and Gretchen's murders—and the threats against her—might be the work of a serial killer who targeted wealthy women, she was having a hard time getting the possibility out of her head. But no way was she going to repeat that sensationalized suggestion to her father.

"Is Officer Taylor keeping you safe? I warned him to keep a close eye on you since I can't be there to do it myself. He's screening your mail? Your calls?"

Despite her quest for independence, she was a little bit glad that in some ways she would always be her daddy's little girl. The love she heard in his overprotective words gave her the strength she needed to summon a smile. "He has me on a short leash, Dad. I haven't been anywhere without Alex or someone on his team keeping me company."

"Good. If they're not doing their job, I'll put in a personal call to Police Commissioner Masterson."

"Daddy—" A firm knock at the door made Audrey's pulse race for a moment, but the anticipation quickly diffused when she saw a tall blond in a suit and tie instead of a uniformed cop with blue-black hair. "I have to go, Dad. Harper's here."

"Tell him hello."

"I will. I love you, Dad."

"Love you."

Harper Pierce invited himself into her office as she hung up the phone. "How's Rupert?" he asked.

Audrey tucked her phone into her attaché. "The doctor says he'll be just fine. The pacemaker did its job. He needs his rest, of course, for a few days."

"Glad to hear that." His smile transformed into something closer to a scowl. "So you're not taking my phone calls now?"

With a guilty start, Audrey punched the buttons on her phone and discovered five missed calls from his number. She apologized with a shrug. "I'm sorry, Harper. It's been crazy the past few days. With Dad. And I've been in court—"

"Were you in court last night? The night before that?"

"What?" So much for idle chitchat.

"We need to talk. I figured in person was the only way I could get your full attention and make you listen to reason." He thumbed over his shoulder. "I waited until your shadow disappeared into Dwight's office."

Not this conversation again. Pulling back the sleeve of her jacket, Audrey made a point of letting Harper see her checking her watch. "Can we schedule another time to catch up? Lunch this weekend, maybe. I know you were upset when you left the house the other night, and I want to clarify any misunderstanding between us, but I do have to be at the courthouse in thirty minutes. With the press and traffic—"

"This can't wait." He took another step inside and closed the door behind him. His face was lined with concern when he turned to face her. "I'm worried about you. I heard about the bomb. That crazy reporter at the courthouse. I saw the picture in the paper."

"No serious harm done." She tapped the fading bruise on her cheek. "I have a bodyguard, Harper. I'm taking precautions."

"I'm worried about your feelings as much as your safety."

"My feelings?"

"You're vulnerable right now, Audrey. God knows you're attractive and a catch that any man with an eye to his future would want."

Not the smoothest of compliments, but she already understood where this friendly warning was going and bristled beneath the silky fabric of her blouse.

"When you're under stress, when you're frightened, it's natural to turn to the people closest to you. I thought you'd have the sense to turn to someone you know you can trust."

"Like you?"

"Yes. You're pushing away the people you've known for years and leaning on a man you barely know."

Audrey looped the strap of her attaché over her shoulder and circled around her desk. "I'm not leaning on anyone. I stand on my own two feet."

Harper's subtle step to the side blocked her exit. His handsome face wore an apologetic expression—the hand on her arm was gently familiar. "You're getting defensive already. I can tell you think you care about Taylor."

Think? She'd been doing nothing but for the past forty-eight hours. "Thanks for caring, but my relationship with Alex is my business, not yours."

Harper's fingers tightened around her wrist. And there was nothing handsome about the accusation in his eyes. "You're screwing him, aren't you?"

Audrey tugged her arm from his grip. "I beg your pardon?"

"He's not good enough for you."

Audrey's chin shot up. "He's a better man than you are. He'd never talk to me like this, like I'm still some impulsive teenage girl who doesn't know her own mind. This isn't the kind of support I need from you right now."

"I checked him out. You know Taylor's adopted?"

"Yes."

"And his real dad is in prison?"

Audrey pushed him aside and reached for the doorknob. "I don't know you anymore. This conversation is over."

He pulled her hand off the knob and turned her around. "I thought you and I had something special, Aud."

"So did I. A friendship." Was that hurt? Confusion? Anger she read in his eyes? "You keep insulting Alex Taylor and my intelligence and I'm not so sure we have even that."

As quickly as he'd grabbed her, Harper let her go. His posture sagged as he retreated a step. "After all we've been through together, you'd pick him over me?"

In a heartbeat. That was her gut answering. But how much of what she was feeling for Alex was gratitude? The way he made her feel so protected? Or even an honest amount of lust? Tamping down those unresolved questions, she reached behind her and opened the door. "I've tried to give you some leeway because I expect you're still grieving over Gretchen, and maybe you think I can take her place in your life. I can't. I'm not interested in doing that. Now I have to get to court. My escort is waiting."

She knew by scent and heat—and the shift of Harper's contemptuous gaze—that Alex was there. Right behind her. Backing her up.

"Is there a problem?" Alex asked.

"No. I'd like to go now."

"Yes, ma'am."

Audrey grabbed her coat and, with Alex's arm around her waist—between her and the friend she no longer knew—left the office without looking back, giving her parting words a double meaning. "Goodbye, Harper."

AUDREY'S STOMACH GROWLED loudly enough for Alex to hear it across the cab of his truck. He turned on his headlights and drove out of the KCPD parking garage into the last hurrah of rush-hour traffic. "Hungry?"

"What was your first clue?" She leaned back against the headrest and closed her eyes. "I guess between the trial and Dad, interviewing gangbangers who are too terrified or too loyal to say anything against Demetrius, and that run-in with Harper, I forgot about eating."

He liked seeing her kick off her high-heeled boots and wiggle her toes. While he'd keep his opinion of that bullying snob Pierce to himself, he understood that she'd been dumbfounded by whatever they'd argued about, and was probably mourning the loss of the relationship they'd once shared. Her devotion to her father and her dedication to her work were admirable traits, but sometimes she got wound up so tight that he didn't think she knew how to relax or have fun.

"Can I take you to dinner?" he asked.

"Are you asking me out on a date, officer?"

"Well, you saw for yourself after court today that your dad and Ms. Darnell have settled in for an evening of popcorn and DVDs while the sarge keeps an eye on them." He checked his watch, hoping it wasn't too late and his idea wasn't too lame for a woman like Audrey. "It won't be Brennan's on the Plaza, but I could rustle up some chow."

Her giggle was a lovely sound in her throat. He hadn't heard it often enough. "I'm not as high-maintenance as you think, Taylor. As long as it involves a cup of hot tea, I'm in."

Good. Then he had a plan. Someplace intimate, away from any crowds, where the service was stellar and the food even better. He turned north toward the City Market and pulled out his phone to make a reservation. Another set of headlights turned north about half a block behind him, and while he always took note of his surroundings, he also realized that they weren't the only people heading home for dinner.

Audrey was dozing as they neared their destination. Three cars were still with him as he turned into the working-class neighborhood where the best food in Kansas City was located. The headlights from downtown were still there, two cars back. He was aware, but not alarmed yet.

He wasn't sure his choice of dining would meet with Audrey's approval, but he knew it was where he needed to go tonight. He'd followed her to bed last night like some kind of eager adolescent. And with her tucked up against him, she'd slept while he lay awake for most of the night, content to simply be close yet wanting to be inside her all at the same time. He'd lost track of the hours he lay there, breathing in her sweet jasmine scent and wondering if he was as low-rent as Pierce seemed to think, believing that a man like him and a woman like her could be together—*should* be together. After damn near impulsively confessing his love and watching her throw on her armor and deny her emotions yesterday, and then reverting to his beat-down-the-enemy tactics he'd used on Steve Lassen, he needed a good dose of grounding, of familiarity, to get his head screwed on straight. He couldn't do his job, he couldn't do right by Audrey if he couldn't get himself centered again. So yeah, this dinner was about what *he* needed.

Still, he'd better wake her up and give her a chance to put on a little bit of that armor before they arrived. "We're almost there. Your father seemed to think you have a pretty good strategy lined up to take down Demetrius Smith."

"It is if we can keep Tyrell Sampson alive until he testifies."

"He's under protective custody with Holden and Trip watching over him. You can't get any safer than that."

She glanced over at him. "I might debate that."

Right. Like he hadn't blown his protection duty yesterday afternoon when he'd put the beat-down on Lassen. The majority of his SWAT training had taught him that the best security was about planning, controlling every possible variable and being aware of his surroundings—not violence after the fact. Although he'd been trained to carry out the necessary violence, it was supposed to be a last resort, not a gut reaction to some creep putting his hands on Audrey.

He vowed to do better by her next time. Alex turned

onto his grandparents' street. "Do you think Tyrell will stick to his word and say what you need him to up on the stand?"

She hummed as she stretched out her arms and legs. "He will if he doesn't want to go to prison for Calvin Chambers's murder. Because right now, all the evidence points to him as the shooter." She reached down to wedge her feet back into her boots. "Did you see how skinny he is?"

"Probably from the meth he uses."

"I'm half tempted to have Demetrius try on the jacket he claims is his as a visual aid for the jury. There's DNA from both Demetrius and Tyrell on both jackets. But no way does that medium-size hoodie fit him."

"Uncle Mac did say the zipper ripped."

"They had to have switched clothes after the shooting." She pulled down the visor in front of her, turned on the lighted mirror and combed her fingers through her hair. "And if that doesn't work, I guess I'll just have to get Big D to confess."

"If anybody can talk a man into confessing…"

"That better be a compliment."

They were both smiling when he pulled into a parking space at the curb.

"Taylor's Butcher Shop." She read the darkened sign over the closed shop. "Where's the restaurant?"

"Upstairs."

Now she got it. "Alex, I don't think I'm up to meeting your family tonight. I'm wrinkled and tired—"

"And they'll love you. It's just Grandma and Grandpa. They live over the shop. They're retired and he's leasing it to someone else—but I promise you, you can kick off your shoes when you're inside, and Grandma will have a cup of tea."

She thought about it for a moment, then smiled. "Okay. I want to meet this lady who taught you all those old-school manners and whipped you into shape."

"If you still have that bandanna on you, it'll make her cry." Audrey's face blanched. He saw her glance down to the attaché at her feet. His heart flip-flopped inside his chest. "Seriously?"

"I meant to take it to the cleaners. That's all. You know how busy we were today. I just didn't get it done." She reached for the door handle. "I'll leave it here."

"Hold on." He caught her wrist and stopped her from opening the door, keeping an eye on his side-view mirror.

"What is it?"

The car that had been following them all the way from downtown slowed down, but drove on past. Alex memorized the model and make of the sleek black car, but noted, "No license plate." He didn't like that. He released Audrey and pulled out his phone. "Give me a sec."

"Should I be worried?"

"I'm not sure. Yeah, this is Alex Taylor." He spoke into the phone, gave his ID number and reported the suspicious car. The car disappeared two corners down and Alex quickly got out and circled around to open the door for Audrey. He locked the door and tucked her under his arm, keeping his body between her and the street as he walked her through the door and up the stairs to his grandparents' apartment. "Thanks. Keep me posted." He clipped the phone back onto his belt. "They'll see if they can get a black-and-white to track it down. See if it's stolen. You didn't recognize it, did you?"

"To be honest, I wasn't looking. Do you think it's the Broadway Bad Boys?"

He wasn't convinced. The car might be stolen, which was definitely a trademark of the gang, but it was too nice a vehicle not to be stripped for parts yet, and it hadn't been souped up enough to meet the gang's need for speed and power. That left…? Hell, what did that leave—something to do with Audrey's suspicion about a link to the Rich Girl murders? Like that was a better option for being followed than a bunch of gangbangers who wanted to frighten her into losing the trial?

"Let's just get inside." He knocked on the apartment door.

A moment later it opened to a robust, gray-haired man who still sported a military cut and posture despite the arthritic bend to his knees. "Come in, come in."

"Grandpa." He pulled Audrey inside and closed the door before trading a hug that included a couple slaps on the back.

"Alex." Their host extended one of his gnarled hands to Audrey. "I'm Sid Taylor, Alex's grandpa. Welcome to our home."

"I'm Audrey. Thank you, sir. It's a pleasure to meet you."

Martha Taylor came hurrying from the kitchen, wiping her hands on her apron before opening her arms wide. "And who is this handsome young man in uniform?" Alex traded kisses and a tight hug before she pulled away and beamed a beautiful smile at him. "Whenever I see you dressed in your work clothes, it makes me think of the first time I met your grandfather.

He was in uniform, too. Such a handsome man." She cupped Alex's cheek before turning to Audrey. "Introduce me to your beautiful new friend."

Audrey extended her hand, her cheeks turning rosy with a blush. "Audrey Kline. Nice to meet you."

Martha clapped her hands together. "The famous lawyer from the newspapers. Well, this is an honor. Sid, you should have warned me. If I'd known we had a celebrity coming, I'd have fixed something besides leftover meat loaf." She arched one silvery-blond brow in apology. "But I do have a pie."

"What kind?" Audrey asked.

"Apple."

"Do you have a slice of cheddar cheese to go with it?"

"I think so."

"Oh, I am so going off my diet tonight. Hot tea and apple pie with cheese sounds like heaven to me."

Martha linked arms with Audrey and invited her into the kitchen. "It's a recipe I got from my mother. I get carried away with baking this time of year…"

Sid nodded his approval to Alex as they followed them in to dinner. "A woman with real class has class in any situation, even when she's served leftovers."

"I love Gran's meat loaf." Alex followed Martha's standing orders and stopped at the credenza outside the kitchen, removing his service weapon and setting it safely out of the way before sitting down at the table.

"So do I. That one's a real lady, son. Just like your grandma."

"You think I've got enough class to match up with that? For the long haul?"

His grandparents' home was more than a haven where

Alex could relax for a couple hours. Sid understood that he'd come for a little friendly advice, too. He clasped his hand over Alex's shoulder. "The real question is, do you have enough love?"

"I've only known her for a few days. It's crazy how fast I thought I knew, but…I don't know."

"Could you stand to lose her?"

That took him aback. Alex looked up into Sid's eyes, eyes that were dark enough to make them look like blood relations. Maybe he should trust his instincts with Audrey. But could he convince her to trust hers? It was an all too important debate that he'd file away for later. "I'm hungry, Grandpa. Let's eat."

AUDREY WAS EMBARRASSINGLY full, totally exhausted yet curiously content after spending the evening with Alex and his grandparents. It made the trip home to an empty house seem a little less daunting, her father staying the night with his new lady friend a little less worrisome, and her feelings for Alex Taylor a little less frightening to admit.

To herself.

Alex had backpedaled a long way from his *We fit* and *I don't question it* lecture. Last night, although his actions had been tender, he'd been curiously quiet—and she'd been too exhausted to restart the debate. Maybe he'd begun to rethink his belief that some people could know each other, love each other—if they were the right two people—after a short period of time, just as she was beginning to consider it a real possibility.

He seemed to have a very special bond with his adoptive grandparents—and they clearly adored him—and seemed to have enjoyed their evening together. Martha

Taylor had shared a lovely romantic story about meeting Sid for the first time, and how quickly she'd discovered that he was the man for her—for almost fifty years now.

But Alex had continued to be unusually quiet on the ride home. Not that he'd been rude—he'd answered every question she'd asked, and had cut short the phone call that told him KCPD had had no luck finding the car he suspected had been following them. Audrey stole a glance out the side-view mirror to see if she could spot any mysterious black car trailing after them as Alex swiped the key card and opened the front gates. He waited until the gates had locked securely behind them before turning his lights on high beam and following the long drive to the house.

When they cleared the trees and began to curve around the circle, Audrey was reminded of growing up here. "When I was little and we'd drive to the house at night—when the windows were dark like they are now—I always thought this big, stern facade looked like a multi-eyed monster's head." She pointed to the corner tower where her rooms were located. "I imagined the house was a creature with one horn, frozen in stone by some powerful wizard."

"That's a little fanciful for you, isn't it?" He said just enough to keep the conversation going. "It'd make a great Halloween house, though."

"Not that we ever had any trick-or-treaters." But despite the isolation, Audrey had plenty of good memories here. "I used to have parties here when I was a kid. We'd play hide-and-seek for hours. Charlotte had the best imagination—we'd find her up trees or in the root cellar or hiding between floors on the dumbwaiter. Harper—"

"—probably was more interested in winning than anything else."

"You do get to know people quickly, don't you? His favorite game was tag—mostly because he could outrun the rest of us. I wish…" She paused with a heavy sigh that sounded like pure sorrow. "I wish I'd seen that coming today. Somehow his feelings for Gretchen must have gotten all twisted up with what he used to feel for me—back in high school. I haven't felt anything romantic toward him since then. It's not his place to be so possessive or to assume any kind of relationship. I made that clear, didn't I?"

"If you didn't, I will."

She was smiling again as he pulled the truck to the bottom of the porch steps. "You can park in the garage out back if you want."

He shook his head as he killed the engine. "Too far away from the main house, and I know the entrances and exits on this side of the house better, in case we need to get out quickly."

Her amusement at his own possessive impulse quickly vanished. "Are you expecting trouble?"

"I want to be prepared so that nothing catches me by surprise." His smile tried to reassure her. "It's just a precaution. With Holden and Trip babysitting Tyrell tonight, I don't have the same backup I did last night. Captain Cutler ordered some extra patrols to swing by the house. He said to call if I needed anything else. In the meantime, all you've got is me."

She reached across the seat to take his hand. "Then I'll be just fine."

Audrey reset the alarm system as soon as Alex bolted the front door behind them. She dropped off her attaché bag in her father's office, gave herself a moment to absorb his lingering presence, and really feel that he was going to be all right and back home in the morning. Then she peeled off her coat, kicked off her shoes and headed upstairs while Alex made a sweep of the house.

She was curled up in her peach silk pajamas, sitting on top of the flowered comforter in her bedroom, when she heard Alex enter the sitting room on the other side of the door. "The house is secure, Red," he called out. "Pleasant dreams."

But she couldn't get an answering "good-night" past her lips. As weary as she'd been after leaving the police station and Clarice's, their visit with his grandparents had revitalized her. Her brain was running ninety miles a minute, going over everything she was feeling, thinking of the words she should say. Why had Alex's demeanor changed since that takedown of Steve Lassen at the courthouse? Had her admission about wanting to clobber the guy herself shocked him? Changed his opinion of her? Had Sid or Martha said something that put him in this distant state? Or was he simply concerned about her security—so focused on that that he had no room for anything else in his head right now?

In the end, she took a page from Alex's own book. Quit overanalyzing everything. Don't muddy up her wants and needs with too many words. If she had a feeling about something—or someone—she should trust her gut and *do* something about it.

Audrey inhaled a steadying breath and slipped out of bed. Time to do.

She soundlessly opened the connecting door and found him hanging his Kevlar vest over his black uniform shirt on the back of a chair. He peeled off his black turtleneck with the white SWAT letters embroidered at the neck, and tossed it onto a stack of pillows at the end of the couch.

"Did you need something?"

His back was to her and she'd barely breathed, yet he knew she was there behind him. She took another step into the room. "Are you psychic?"

He glanced over his bare shoulder and grinned. "I smelled you. Jasmine or lilacs—some delicate perfume that clings to your hair."

The compliment danced along her skin and fluttered inside her. "Sounds like my shampoo."

The man was a poet in the most basic of ways. Her eyes were instantly drawn to the scar on the back of his shoulder. Whatever hard edges and insights into people he'd learned on the streets growing up, the Taylors had fine-tuned into something beautiful. Alex was the best of both worlds—smart and observant, tough, funny, caring and kind. And freaking hot when he moved around without a shirt like that.

Audrey cleared her throat, feeling the heat creeping up her neck as she tried not to notice every flex of muscle along his arms and back as he sat to untie his boots. "I think your grandmother may be a little psychic. Apple pie is my favorite dessert. Mom and I used to spend a lot of time in the kitchen—she went to culinary school and loved to cook. I've tried several times since she's been gone to make her pie, but I can't get the crust quite right. Martha said she'd share her recipe."

Alex dropped the second boot and pulled off his

socks. "That's like opening up the vault at Fort Knox. She must like you."

"I know. I'm practically a stranger. That's so generous of her. I think maybe she sensed that I was missing my mother—"

"You know, you're talking a whole hell of a lot for a woman I thought was coming in to say good-night." Alex stood and crossed the room to stand right in front of her.

She closed her eyes and trembled, savoring his gentle touch as he traced the pattern of heat coloring her neck and jaw.

"So what's this blush really saying?"

Audrey blinked her eyes open to the whisper of Alex's warm breath caressing her sensitive skin. His eyes were so close, so deep, so beautiful—his jaw needed a shave—and his lips…she couldn't seem to look away from his strong, supple mouth.

"Talk to me, Red."

She followed the movement of his lips and felt something warm and wicked clench and release deep inside her.

"I wanted to say…" *Don't overthink this, Audrey. Do it.* She touched her fingertips to his stubbled jaw and lifted her gaze to his. "Are you sleeping in here tonight?" She walked her fingers to the nape of his neck and slid them up against the silky midnight of his hair. "I don't want you to."

His hands settled at the nip of her waist, branding her through the thin layers of silk. His nostrils flared as he inhaled a deep breath. "I may not be the gentleman you think I am, Red."

Just the words she needed to hear. Whatever was

troubling Alex, it wasn't that he regretted admitting he had feelings for her.

She wound her free arm up behind his neck and re-treated a step, pulling him with her through her bedroom door. "Maybe I don't want you to come in here and be a gentleman." His eyes never left hers as he dutifully followed. "Maybe I want you to tell me some more of those wonderful stories about your family." She ran her palms along the column of his neck and out across his shoulders, then down the hard cords of his arms, setting her hands on fire with the friction created by every hill and hollow of warm, male skin she explored. She caught her breath on a stutter and reversed the path, pulling herself closer, breathing harder, wanting more, until she had her fingers lost in the silky curls on top of his head. "We could make some stories…of our own." She angled his face down toward hers, caught her breath as the pebbled tips of her breasts brushed across his chest. "Last night, together, and the night before…that was really spec—"

"Shut up, Red." Alex planted his mouth over hers, sliding his arms behind her waist and pulling her onto her toes, crushing her breasts against the wall of his chest as he plundered her mouth.

Audrey fisted her fingers in his hair and held on as her toes left the floor entirely and he walked her backward until her thighs hit the edge of the bed. His hands roamed at will over her back and buttocks, the silk offering little barrier to every calloused caress. Audrey was no longer aware of breathing as he buried his fingers in her hair to guide her mouth this way, and then another—plunging in, supping, seducing with each kiss. He groaned deep in his chest as Audrey mimicked his demands, pulling him impossibly closer and thrusting her tongue between his lips to taste the moist fiery heat that threatened to consume her. She grazed her lips along his jaw, delighting in the sandpapery abrasion against her feverish bruised mouth.

Alex opened his hot, wet mouth over the throbbing pulse at the base of her neck and she gasped. The graphic heat she knew colored her skin responded to his every touch, sending matching ribbons of heat deep beneath the surface, making her small breasts feel molten and heavy, and intensifying the aching weight building between her legs.

Audrey gasped against his skin when he flicked his thumb over the painful nub of one breast. "I don't really want to tell stories."

"I get the picture," he rasped against her ear. "You're sure about this?"

In answer, Audrey leaned back against the cradle of his arms. Her fingers were shaky, she couldn't quite catch her breath, but she knew her own mind.

She unhooked the first button of her pajama top, and then the second, and then Alex grabbed it by the hem and pulled it off over her head.

Audrey reclaimed his mouth and held on as he laid her on the bed and followed her down. His sure hands that handled guns and grandmothers and bad guys with equal ease made quick work of their remaining clothes. She bucked beneath him as he closed his mouth over an aching breast and suckled her into a mindless puddle of want and need.

"Oh, baby, it goes all the way down. You're so beautiful." Her telegraphic skin betrayed every bit of emotion and desire—he was tracing a line from her neck. "So beautiful." Over one breast. "So, so beautiful." Down her stomach to—

"Al…ex—I…I…" She couldn't catch her breath, couldn't find the words. She clawed at his shoulders, snatched at his hair, tugged his face back to hers and silently pleaded.

He looked down into her eyes and grinned. "It's okay, Red. You don't have to talk."

He entered her on one long stroke and Audrey flew apart in his arms. She buried her face against his shoulder and cried out in pleasure against his skin. Then she simply held on as he moved inside her, lifting her to another crest before they both tumbled over the precipice together.

Afterward, Alex pulled back the covers and wrapped his arms and body around her, sealing her in warmth and contentment, sheltering her with whispered praises and quiet strength.

Audrey drifted off to sleep in his arms. He was right. She didn't need words for this. She didn't need more time to know.

She loved Alex Taylor.

Chapter Ten

There was something about waking with a woman's warm, beautiful breast pillowed against his side that made Alex reluctant to tune in to what his other senses were trying to tell him.

It was especially hard when that woman was Audrey Kline, the icy, overanalytical, career-focused heiress who turned out to be a passionate, uninhibited, uniquely adorable lover who'd charmed his grandparents, welcomed him into her bed and opened up her mind to the possibility that the two of them could work. A gangbanger from the streets romancing Rupert Kline's only daughter wasn't a match that would make the society page of the *Journal,* but it was a match that he hoped Audrey would still want to pursue once the Smith trial was over.

She didn't make him feel as if he was just a bodyguard or a boy toy as that crass Harper Pierce had suggested. When she cuddled up in a ball beside him and snored softly against his chest, Alex felt as if she was his woman, as if they were equals. When she cried her eyes out or admitted she had a temper or rolled over in the middle of the night with a drowsy *Can we do that again?*, he felt as if they could truly communicate on a level that most couples—no matter what class they came from—rarely achieved.

He'd certainly never had a woman get so deep inside his head and heart before that his grandfather's words had made him shudder as if he'd already been robbed of his soul. *Could you stand to lose her?*

Alex dipped his head and pressed a kiss to the crown of Audrey's hair, fearing that if he hugged her as tightly as he wanted to at that moment, he'd frighten her awake.

Even with the thin strip of moonlight sneaking into her room between the drapes and blinds, he could admire the porcelain beauty of her body exposed above the covers that had caught at their waists. And he didn't need any light to still know the smell of her on his skin, the taste of her in his mouth, the sounds of her earthy cries of pleasure in his head.

She made him stop and think.

He made her stop and feel.

This was exactly where he was supposed to be. Right here beside Audrey.

The problem was convincing her that was still the case outside of this bedroom. He needed Audrey's skills in arguing to persuade her that not only was a future together with him an option, but that he believed it was the only option for the two of them to be happy and find the balance they needed.

There. He had heard something. Alex stilled his breathing and angled his ear toward the window. *Thup. Thup.* The muffled sounds jerked through his muscles, honing his senses, alerting him to the threat of danger in the distance. Metal on metal. Car doors closing.

He untangled his legs from Audrey's and slid out

of bed. He pulled on his shorts and black pants and grabbed his weapon off the bedside table. He crept to the window without disturbing the drapes and lined up his eyes with the thin beam of moonlight, scouting the trees out front for movement while he tossed aside his holster and cocked a round into the gun's firing chamber.

The click-clack of sound, or his absence from the bed, elicited a murmur from Audrey. She was stirring. Waking, but not yet aware.

He heard another car door slam and swung his eyes back outside. Damn those trees! He squinted, peering through the shadows. Was that movement down at the gate?

Son of a bitch. Alex snatched his phone off the bedside table and punched in a number. The battle had come to him. And there wasn't anything standing between the multiple attackers skulking through the darkness outside the gate and Audrey, snug in her bed, except for him, his gun and the survival instincts that had kept him alive on the streets and forged him into the cop—into the man—he'd become.

When Michael Cutler's clipped voice answered, Alex didn't apologize for waking him. "Captain. It's going down. Kline estate. I need backup. Now."

He didn't need to clarify or wait for a response before hanging up. The clock was ticking. On silent bare feet he went back to the bed and covered Audrey's mouth. Her eyes instantly popped open, wild and afraid. "Shh. It's me, Red."

She nodded her recognition and he released her. Her gaze darted down to the gun in his other hand. "What is it? What's wrong?"

She sat up and scooted off the edge of the bed as he

returned to the window. "I need you to get dressed. As fast as you can. Shoes you can run in."

"Alex?" She darted to her closet and grabbed the first pair of jeans and T-shirt she could find.

"We've got company."

She shoved her bare feet into a pair of sneakers. "Should I call 9-1-1?"

"We'll need all the help we can get." He plucked his cell from his pocket and tossed it to her across the room. She caught it and flipped it open with one hand, punching in the numbers while she zipped up her jeans. A woman with no undies who could catch like a center fielder would have been mind-numbingly hot if he wasn't so caught up in trying to figure out... "What the hell?"

He counted one, two, three—four unknown perps running *away* from the front gates. They crossed through the light from a streetlamp and disappeared into the trees several yards beyond the great stone fence. Gallagher Security better be picking up all that movement and sending over a fleet of squad cars—

Alex jerked his head away and cursed at the flash of light that blinded him a split second before a concussive blast rent the air and rattled the windows. They were too far from the gate to sustain any damage up here, but that wasn't the point.

"What was that?" Audrey asked, crouching near the bed.

The explosion at the gate had triggered the alarms. He had to give Gallagher credit for putting on a show big enough to deter most intruders. Floodlights outside turned the shadowed trees into a daylit forest. Emergency lights flashed on and off in Audrey's bedroom and under the hallway door. A siren pulsed, shrieking its warning and forcing him to shout.

"Come with me!" He grabbed Audrey's wrist and ran into the sitting room while engines revved and tires squealed through the night outside. He pulled the Kevlar off the chair and slipped it over her head. "Strap this on."

She tried to pull the vest back up. "We're under attack! You can't face them without any protection. You don't even have any shoes on!"

He tugged it back down and fastened the first Velcro strap beneath her arm. "I'm not asking you, sweetheart. Put it on."

Thankfully, she batted his hand away and took over. Alex didn't waste any time. The one good thing about a gang fight was that he could always hear the enemy coming—even over the blare of the alarm. He could hear the two cars speeding across the bricks with their music blasting and their souped-up mufflers roaring like doomsday.

"Where are we going?"

Alex squinted against the flashing lights and ran as fast as Audrey could keep up. "Your father's study." Leading with his gun, he took the stairs two at a time and circled around at the bottom. "It's the one room in this house that has no windows. And only one door. I want you to go inside and lock it—"

"Aren't you coming?"

"—and get underneath the heaviest piece of furniture you can find."

"Alex!"

"Smith's Bad Boys are here." He couldn't wait for the cavalry. He needed to get out to his truck and try to reach his Benelli shotgun and spare cache of ammunition. "That means guns and lots of bullets flying."

She clung to his free hand with both of hers. "What about you?"

"This is my job, sweetheart." He pushed her inside. *No, Grandpa, I couldn't stand to lose her.* "I love you. Lock it."

He pulled the door shut, said a prayer and ran outside to meet the enemy.

THE BULLET RIPPED THROUGH Alex's shoulder like a red hot poker as the first car spun out on the driveway's frozen slush and careened into an unbending oak. He had no time to do more than grunt at the searing pain as he flattened his back against the side of his truck and dropped the semiautomatic shotgun at his feet. The weapon would be useless to him now that the muscles on his left side were shocky with the wound and he'd be unable to steady his aim or control the recoil with one good arm.

But his second shot had taken out the driver and bought him a few seconds to expel the spent magazine from his Glock and reload the gun with the spare mag from his glove compartment. He sucked in a lungful of cold air, letting the winter dampness cool his body and clear his head. Fifteen bullets. Another car coming. One target down, two scrambling out of the wrecked car—he must have wounded another of Smith's Broadway Bad Boys when he'd returned fire on the approaching vehicle because he'd counted three passengers when he'd first spotted the back window going down and the semiautomatic coming out. And who knew how many more with how many weapons were zooming up the drive with one intent?

To take him out.

"KCPD!" Alex shouted. The bright security lights and patchwork shadows among the trees were wreaking havoc with his 20/20 vision. He couldn't make a clean shot. "You're firing on a police officer! Drop your weapons!"

"You can't take all of us!" one of them shouted, peppering the opposite side of his truck with another spray of bullets. Alex crouched down, cocked his weapon.

"You're dead!" another shouted. More bullets. Speeding car. "And then the bitch is dead, too!"

Like hell. Nobody was getting to Audrey as long as he was alive.

With the revving engine roaring in his ears, Alex swung around, bracing his arm between the open door and hood of his truck, and returned fire. Fifteen. Fourteen. Thirteen. One kid went down, grabbing his leg and rolling.

On foot, Alex was evenly matched, but the car racing toward him gave his attackers an advantage he couldn't hope to defeat on his own. Two more shots forced the last kid to the ground. Twelve. Eleven. Windows going down. Guns coming out.

Don't react. Think. Do your job, Taylor.

Where the hell was backup?

Alex shifted behind the door and emptied six shots into the speeding Impala. Ten. Nine. The windshield cracked. Eight. Seven. A tire went out and the driver slammed on the brakes. Six. The windshield splintered. Five. The front-seat passenger dropped his gun to the bricks and jerked back inside the car.

Another shot pinged off the hood of the truck and he ducked back behind the door. "Come on!" he yelled to the fates, knowing the odds were shifting, and not necessarily in his favor.

He was up, aiming. Four. Three. Two. The kid on the ground wasn't getting up again.

A siren wailed in his ears, battling with the strident pulsation of the estate's security alarm. A car screeched its tires on the wet bricks, its engine bellowing like two massive storm systems charging closer and closer on a collision course. Two? Another vehicle was coming?

One bullet left. One freaking bullet.

He was outmanned. Outgunned. The kiss of death in any gang fight.

Alex glanced up at the mansion's front door. His heart was pouring out with every pulse beat of blood that throbbed from his shoulder. "Audrey…"

Bam! The thunderous crash jolted through Alex.

But he wasn't hurt. He hadn't been hit.

He pulled up behind the truck's door. "Hell, yeah!" The cavalry had arrived.

Sergeant Delgado had rammed his big truck into the Impala's back fender and was shoving it across the bricks until the screeching friction of the Impala's tires ended with a crumpling smash against the porch's brick foundation. Even before the gang's car was wedged in tight, Trip Jones jumped out of the truck, his PSD rifle already aimed through the car's back window.

"Taylor!" Trip shouted. "Report!"

Until Trip and Rafe had the guns secured from the gangbangers inside the Impala, Alex stayed hunkered down behind the protection of his vehicle. "SWAT is in the building," he muttered to himself, almost light-

headed with relief as he checked his weapon, verifying
the last bullet. Inhaling a deep breath, he realized that
the light-headedness might have something to do with
all the blood dripping down his left arm.

"Taylor!"

Alex exhaled a cloudy breath into the chilled air and
raised his voice. "I'm here. Ammo's about gone. I'm hit.
But it's not bad. I'm not dying today, big guy."

"Better not, shrimp." Alex slowly straightened as
he listened to Trip and Rafe shout orders to the perps
inside the car. Two were already facedown in the slush
with their hands cuffed behind their backs when Alex
peeked through the windshield. Rafe had a third teen
by the arm and was putting him down on the ground
beside the others while Trip pulled the passenger Alex
had wounded out of the front seat. It took a matter of
seconds to trade a few curses, assess that the wound was
superficial and put that one down on the ground, too.

Trip and Rafe exchanged nods before the sergeant
called out. "Clear!" He pointed his gun over the four
perps and motioned Trip over to Alex's position. "Check
him out."

"Got it."

"How many targets do we need to account for?" Captain Cutler's voice buzzed over the radio inside Alex's
truck. With the team on-site, providing backup, Alex
finally ventured from his hiding place to see the captain marching one handcuffed perp out of the trees. He
nodded toward Alex. "You're out of uniform, son."

"Yes, sir." They all were. Underneath their vests and
gear, everyone was in off-duty clothes. But they'd all
shown up. For him. For Audrey.

Alex was part of a team. He was part of *this* team.

"I made four perps in each car." Alex gritted his teeth and grunted a curse as Trip probed his wound.

"And Miss Kline?"

"Inside."

"It's through and through." Trip pulled off a black glove and wrapped his hand around Alex's forearm, checking his clammy skin and halting him from mounting up the porch to get Audrey out of hiding. "What's your body temp, frosty?"

"Good enough that you don't need to baby me." He pulled away from Trip's first-aid efforts and headed for the front door of the Kline estate. His gun hung at his side from his good hand. "I need to make sure Audrey's okay."

"Wait a minute," Rafe warned, his grousing tone echoing over the radio and from just a few yards away. "Eight perps?" He pointed to the ground where Captain Cutler was placing the teenager he'd escorted from the woods. "We've got five here."

Holden Kincaid strode up with the strap of his sniper rifle secured over his shoulder. In one smooth motion, he pulled it down into his hands, arming himself. "Driver and one on the ground are dead out in the trees. Didn't spot any other movement out there."

Alex's gut twisted into a knot. "There's another one."

Each man instantly positioned his gun in a defensive stance. While Rafe kept the prisoners under control, the captain, Holden and Trip faced away from the vehicles, securing a circle, scanning the grounds. Captain Cutler was on his radio, calling in a fugitive alert to the KCPD cars they could hear approaching in the distance.

But Alex's instincts—a gut-deep dread—was already pushing him up toward the front door.

"Alex?"

He halted in his tracks at Audrey's hushed greeting from the open doorway.

He read the threat in the stark pale cast of her beautiful skin even before he saw the white-capped gangbanger walking through the front door behind her—with his gun boring into the base of her skull.

His old buddy Sly from the courthouse—the slick-talking twenty-something who'd denied exchanging any kind of message with Demetrius Smith—had Audrey in his grasp and a gun to her head. And the bastard thought he could bargain with Audrey's life. "Now you fine officers put your guns down and get the hell out of my way. I'm taking your truck and I'm driving out of here. Or she dies."

AUDREY SHIVERED WITH the chill that shook her from the inside out. But the cold steel pressed against her scalp didn't scare her half as much as seeing all the blood staining Alex's bare chest and arm. He was only a few yards away, just a couple of steps below the edge of the porch. But with the lights flashing and the alarm blaring and a frightened, angry man holding her in front of him like a shield, Audrey couldn't reach out. She couldn't run to Alex. She couldn't help.

He was bleeding, maybe dying. Because of her.

No. Because Demetrius Smith and his thugs didn't understand anything but power and intimidation. They didn't understand compassion. They didn't understand healthy communication. They didn't understand caring.

But she did. Because of Alex Taylor, she did. A thought blossomed inside her head, even as Sly urged her forward, daring the five armed warriors facing him to back away.

Alex was breathing hard, his deep, rhythmic breaths forming white clouds in the air. But nothing could hide the rage and pain that darkened his eyes, or the deadly stillness that held every exposed muscle of his body tense and rigid. "Don't do this, Sly. Let her go."

She flinched as Sly poked the gun against her neck. "Shut up! I said put down your weapons. You—toss it in the bushes." When Alex didn't immediately comply, he jabbed her again. "Toss it!"

"I'm doing it." Alex tossed his gun into the hedge beside the steps. And though he motioned with his un-injured hand for the others to lay down their weapons at their feet, his eyes never left hers.

At the edges of her hearing, she heard Rafe Delgado mutter something like, "Don't even try it." A handcuffed man on the ground reconsidered his decision to get up.

This standoff wasn't going to end well. When the shooting had ended and she'd heard the crash, Audrey had climbed out from beneath the desk in her father's study and hurried out to see if Alex was dead. If her heart would be crushed. But she'd run into a desperate Sly instead. His crooked white cap so at odds with the deadly intent of this attack.

"Now back up!" Sly ordered.

Alex didn't budge.

"You're going to kill me, anyway," Audrey pointed out, knowing that if she made it to that truck, her life would be over as soon as Sly drove her away. She looked straight at Alex, letting her fear and anger and desperate effort to be understood register on her face. "Isn't that what you said inside, Sly? My head was the trophy that would secure your position as Big D's number one lieutenant?"

"Shut up." Her pushed her another step closer to Alex.

"You'll never get out of here alive, kid," Alex warned.

Sly wouldn't listen. "Give me your keys."

"Well...you weren't nearly so eloquent, but I got the message. Kill me and Big D walks. And you'll have earned his everlasting gratitude."

"Red..."

Alex's gaze darted to Sly and the gun and back to her before she continued. "I talked to Gallagher Security Services while I was hiding. I hear the sirens now. I asked them to send several ambulances—and all the backup they could spare. But I don't need any more backup, do I? You can take him out, can't you?"

"I'll kill you first, bitch."

Alex's dark eyes narrowed.

Understand me, sweetheart. Please understand. "You know, it's not politically correct, but...I'd really love to see someone put Smith and his Bad Boys in their place."

"Shut up."

Captain Cutler took a step forward. "Son, this is going to end badly for you. Put down your gun. There are five of us."

"And one of her." Audrey grimaced as the gun ground into her scalp. "Now back up." Alex's commander retreated a step as Sly turned his focus back to the more immediate threat. "Give me your damn keys or I'll do her right in front of you."

"Alex?" Audrey heard the spooky calm in her own voice and braced herself. "Give him the keys."

ALEX NODDED, HATING WHAT she was asking of him—and loving Audrey Kline for being smart enough, brave enough and trusting enough to ask it.

Could you stand to lose her?

He reached into his pocket for his key ring. "My grandpa says a class act is a class act in any situation. You're all class, Red."

"What?" Sly frowned. The bastard didn't know it yet, but he was doomed.

"Take my keys."

Alex tossed them. In the split second it took for Sly to release his grip on Audrey to catch them was all the time it took for Alex to attack. He charged up the stairs, lowered his shoulder and rammed Sly in the gut, taking him down to the porch as Audrey jumped to the side. Sly kicked. He punched. Alex grabbed at the wrist that held the gun, and managed to hold on, cursing as the kid rolled over on his wounded shoulder.

But Alex was too fired up to really comprehend the pain. This sicko had threatened Audrey, maybe hurt her, frightened her. Two people were dead in her front yard because this jackass thought he had the right to take down the woman he loved. No way. No. Freaking. Way.

With a surge of pure adrenaline to fuel his strength, Alex called on every fighting skill he'd ever learned—on the street and at the police academy. In a matter of seconds, he had the advantage. He was on top. Sly was unarmed. And when he tried to rise up to hit Alex's wounded shoulder, Alex finished it.

One punch. Down and out. The white cap went flying and Sly collapsed onto the porch, his eyes woozy, the fight knocked right out of him.

Spent, chilled, breathing heavy, feeling every ache of the past few minutes, Alex pushed himself up to his hands and knees and then wearily rolled to his feet. He turned, stumbled forward—seeking one face, one reassurance.

Holden and Captain Cutler had Audrey secured behind them, but she was already pushing her way through. Trip was kneeling beside Sly and rolling him onto his stomach so he could put handcuffs on him.

Alex held out his right arm and pulled Audrey as tight against him as he could hold her. Her arms anchored themselves behind his waist as he pressed a kiss to her temple and whispered against her ear. "You're right, Red. That did feel good."

THE POLICE CARS AND ambulances were wheeling through the gates as the men of SWAT Team One finished securing the scene.

Alex was trying to brush the hair off Audrey's face, find her mouth, find out if she was okay. "I'm so sorry. I didn't want this to happen this way. I told you to stay in that room. You're not supposed to be in the middle of my—"

"Your world?" She pulled Alex down to the step beside her and reached into her pocket.

Ah, hell. Either the shock from getting shot was wearing off, or he was getting sentimental himself, but he was grinning like an idiot when she pulled out *his* bandanna and pressed it against his wound. He jerked at the stabbing pressure, but his eyes never blinked, never wavered from hers.

"This is my world, too, Alex. But we're going to make it better. Together—we can make it better."

She leaned over and kissed him gently on the mouth. He moved his lips against hers and she kissed him again.

"You earned your keep this time, shrimp," Trip intervened, pausing as he walked Sly down to the driveway to razz Alex one last time. "You think he's one of us now?"

Rafe Delgado joined in. "Let's see. He took out five perps before we got here and he's got a bullet hole in him—I think he's passed initiation."

"Welcome to the team, Taylor." Trip made some sort of snorting noise that Alex barely heard as he leaned in to kiss Audrey again. "Oh, now he's gonna go and spoil the moment by getting all mushy with his girl."

Alex tunneled his fingers into Audrey's hair, touching her, verifying with his own hand that she was alive and safe. And his. "Damn straight."

Chapter Eleven

Messy. Messy. Messy.

He pounded on his steering wheel with both fists, wailing his fury against the black steering wheel until his fingers went numb.

How could Smith's men be so stupid? He had everything under control, everything in place to get Demetrius released after serving just a few months on a minor drug charge. Audrey Kline would have looked like a fool trying to pin that kid's murder on him. Like a pitiful, pretty little girl playing grown-up in a courtroom she could never hope to command. She wouldn't be able to save her own skin, much less the world if they'd let him destroy her the way he'd wanted.

He killed Trace Vaughn for them. After following Audrey and her bodyguard boyfriend from the Fourth Precinct station to that drab neighborhood where shopkeepers sold groceries and souvenirs to other working-class clods, he'd prepped an explosive for Tyrell Sampson's car. Yes, he was under police protection, but he'd be released after testifying. And all Demetrius had asked him for this time was retribution. Kill any Triple B who betrayed him, scare the others back into

line so that they'd carry out his wishes even if he went
to prison.

But tonight those idiot Bad Boys had taken the bomb
and used it to go after Audrey themselves.

Idiots. Idiots. Idiots.

He spied the pack of cigarettes lying on the seat
beside him and picked it up, tapping it on his hand three
times and pulling one out. As he slipped the filter between his lips, he noticed one cigarette still sticking
out of the pack. He pushed it down, taking an easier
breath once the symmetry of the rectangular package
had returned.

But it was only one easy breath. He felt the agita-
tion growing inside him again as he watched from the
shadows of his parking space. He lit his cigarette and
counted the parade of police cars and the coroner's van
driving in and out of the Kline estate. He didn't care
how many Bad Boys were dead, how many went out in
ambulances. He didn't care if the cops rounded up the
ones who got away.

What he cared about was that Audrey could have
gotten hurt. She could have been killed in that blitz
attack.

And it wasn't their place to kill her. That was supposed to be his prize.

He inhaled a deep drag off the cigarette and tried to
think. He wasn't done toying with Audrey, but the police
would be all over her now—not just that pint-size cop
and his SWAT buddies. It would be harder to get the
messages to her. Harder to be there to watch her suffer.
It would be damn near impossible for her to lose that
trial now—if nothing else, after such a blatant, violent

attempt on her life, she'd win the jury's sympathy vote. And the press's.

He took another hit off the cigarette. He could see it now—she'd be in all the papers again, but this time as a hero.

All he'd asked for was a little patience, the opportunity to carry out the plan in his way. But Demetrius's buffoons had ruined everything. He needed to end his ill-advised alliance with the Broadway Bad Boys and come up with a new plan.

Yes, that was it.

Audrey Kline wasn't the only woman who'd lied to him. Who'd led him on. Who'd wronged him. Let her have her moment of glory. There were easier targets who could give him just as much satisfaction. Maybe even more.

He knew countless ways to make his enemies suffer.

He pulled out the ashtray, snuffed out his cigarette and smiled.

He'd move on to the next victim.

AUDREY SAW THE BEADS OF perspiration dotting Demetrius Smith's upper lip and squelched the urge to smile. She set down her notes, took a deep breath and strolled back to the witness stand.

"So you admit that Tyrell Sampson was telling the truth."

"'I told that fool to change jackets with me and keep his mouth shut. And then none of us would get taken in." Demetrius smacked his hand against his thigh. "But I only shot that kid in the leg. The most you can get me for is assault. Tyrell's the one who put that bullet in his chest."

"Your Honor…" Cade Shipley rose to his feet, slowly buttoning his suit coat, acting as if he wasn't worried that his client was destroying the defense he'd so carefully put together. "My client is charged with murder. That's the crime Miss Kline should be trying. All she's doing with this line of questioning is confusing the jury as to the legalities—"

"Is there an objection in there somewhere, Mr. Shipley, or are you just making a speech?" Judge Shanks groused. "I didn't think so. Miss Kline, continue."

"Thank you, Your Honor." She turned to Demetrius once more. "So you admit to shooting Calvin Chambers in the leg?"

"Tyrell said there were a couple of Warriors running through my yard, spying on us. In *my* territory. We shot a couple of times into the air to scare 'em off."

"But you didn't hit the two Westside Warriors on the scene."

"No, they were already gone. I didn't know that kid was there."

"The one you shot in the leg."

"Demetrius!" Shipley warned.

"What? I said it. I shot him in the leg." He scowled at Audrey. "Book me on that, sister."

Audrey smiled right back. "Your Honor, may we approach?"

Judge Shanks waved Cade and Audrey to his bench.

"Your Honor," Cade began, "opposing counsel is badgering my client."

The judge shushed him and pointed at Audrey. "She gets to talk right now. Miss Kline?"

"Your Honor, I just wanted to give Mr. Shipley a heads-up. If you recall the details of the medical examiner's report, Calvin Chambers was wounded in the chest. But that wasn't the kill shot. He bled to death—from a gunshot wound to his femoral artery." She turned to Cade. "Your client just confessed to murder."

ALEX WAITED A HALF HOUR for Audrey to accept her last handshake and for the courtroom to clear before he stood up from his seat in the back. "Congratulations, counselor."

"I won."

"That's right, Red. You did it."

"I won." Her cheeks bloomed a bright pink as she shook off her staid, proper, public demeanor and shot her arms up into the air. "I won!"

Reveling in her emotions, fists pumping, she ran through the gate, straight down the aisle and leaped into Alex's chest, hugging him tight around the neck as he swung her around. It wasn't the easiest thing to hold on to her with his left arm tied up in a sling, but he'd damn well do whatever he had to to keep this woman close to him. Forever.

"I have to call Dad at his office and tell him the good news. I think he'll be proud of me. I'm proud of me."

"Add me to the list, too." When his shoulder started to ache, he set her down, but he couldn't let her go. He brushed aside the auburn tendril that had fallen across her cheek and pressed his lips to the warm spot there. "I bet if you come with me to the Shamrock Bar tonight, you'll find a whole room full of cops who'll want to shake your hand and buy you a drink. I know of at least five SWAT cops who'd like to drink a toast to you for getting Demetrius Smith off the streets and pretty much decimating what's left of one of the most dangerous gangs in town."

"I couldn't have done it without you, Alex. And the rest of SWAT Team One."

Yeah. He owed a lot to Trip, Rafe, Holden and Captain Cutler.

"Not just to keep me alive or to keep the press at bay or to keep my father from worrying himself sick about me—but I needed you to believe in me. I needed you to help me understand that I could do this."

"I never had any doubts."

"Yes, you did."

"Audrey." So she'd proved him wrong. She'd shown him that first impressions weren't always the right impression. And he'd be forever grateful for that lesson. He leaned in to kiss her. "You're right. Point taken."

"Wait." She pressed her fingers against his lips and pushed him away. "I'm not done talking."

"I conceded the argument. You're sure you don't want me to kiss you?"

"Alex." Her fingers trembled against his mouth with a gentle, tempting caress.

She was probably remembering where the last few kisses between them had led, and the courtroom probably wasn't the best place for *that* kind of interpersonal communication. With a reluctant sigh, he pulled her hand down and laced their fingers together to walk her to the front of the courtroom and collect her things. "Come on. We can continue this discussion at home. Trip's waiting outside to drive us. If the Rich Girl Killer had anything to do with this nightmare, I'm not taking any chances. I asked the guys to help me keep an eye on you until I'm back at a hundred percent."

She pulled her hand from his. Planted her feet. "No. I mean, yes, that's really generous of them and I can never thank them enough for all they've done. But I have something private to say that can't wait any longer."

She tilted her chin to that vulnerable angle that had first tempted him to take her in his arms. But he listened. Audrey Kline had something to say, so he listened.

"I love you. Just in case it isn't perfectly clear. Just in case you think you're the only one who can say it or I don't know how to say it or I'm afraid to say it—I just want you to know that I love you, Alex Taylor."

He smiled. "Trip can wait. Now can I kiss you?"

She smiled. She wound her arms around his neck and pulled his mouth down to hers. "I'm done talking. It's time to do."

* * * * *

BEAR CLAW CONSPIRACY

BY
JESSICA ANDERSEN

DID YOU PURCHASE THIS BOOK WITHOUT A COVER?
If you did, you should be aware it is **stolen property** as it was reported
unsold and destroyed by a retailer. Neither the author nor the publisher
has received any payment for this book.

All the characters in this book have no existence outside the imagination of
the author, and have no relation whatsoever to anyone bearing the same name
or names. They are not even distantly inspired by any individual known or
unknown to the author, and all the incidents are pure invention.

All Rights Reserved including the right of reproduction in whole or in
part in any form. This edition is published by arrangement with Harlequin
Enterprises II B.V./S.à.r.l. The text of this publication or any part thereof may
not be reproduced or transmitted in any form or by any means, electronic or
mechanical, including photocopying, recording, storage in an information
retrieval system, or otherwise, without the written permission of the publisher.

This book is sold subject to the condition that it shall not, by way of trade or
otherwise, be lent, resold, hired out or otherwise circulated without the prior
consent of the publisher in any form of binding or cover other than that in
which it is published and without a similar condition including this condition
being imposed on the subsequent purchaser.

® and ™ are trademarks owned and used by the trademark owner and/or its
licensee. Trademarks marked with ® are registered with the United Kingdom
Patent Office and/or the Office for Harmonisation in the Internal Market and
in other countries.

First published in Great Britain 2011
by Mills & Boon, an imprint of Harlequin (UK) Limited,
Eton House, 18-24 Paradise Road, Richmond, Surrey TW9 1SR

© Dr Jessica S Andersen 2011

ISBN: 978 0 263 88567 5

46-1211

Harlequin (UK) policy is to use papers that are natural, renewable and
recyclable products and made from wood grown in sustainable forests. The
logging and manufacturing processes conform to the legal environmental
regulations of the country of origin.

Printed and bound in Spain
by Blackprint CPI, Barcelona

Jessica Andersen has worked as a geneticist, scientific editor, animal trainer and landscaper...but she's happiest when she's combining all of her many interests into writing romantic adventures that always have a twist of the unusual to them. Born and raised in the Boston area (Go, Sox!), Jessica can usually be found somewhere in New England, hard at work on her next happily ever after. For more on Jessica and her books, please check out www.JessicaAndersen.com and www.JessicaAndersenIntrigues.com.

Chapter One

"Help! Help... She's... I need help!"

The shout came from outside Ranger Station Fourteen, followed seconds later by the sound of someone running flat out, skidding on the loose gravel of the trailhead.

Matt Blackthorn bit off his briefing mid-sentence and strode from his office, his pulse kicking and then leveling off as he went into crisis mode: six feet and two inches worth of black-haired, green-eyed competence, laced with the determination of his part-Cherokee forebears and the killer instincts that had once been his trademark.

Grizzled park service veteran Bert Grainger was right behind him, while young charmer Jim Feeney veered off to put the dispatcher on standby in case they needed outside help. The station's fourth ranger, a clever brunette named Tanya Dawes, was already out in the field. Hopefully, they wouldn't need her.

As Matt headed through the station's front room, he mentally reviewed the hikers who'd checked in at Station Fourteen—the most remote and isolated of the Bear Claw Canyon ranger stations—over the past few days. He fixed on the newlyweds who had come through earlier that morning. They had been too busy mooning over each other—and their new city-bought hiking gear—to really pay attention to his spiel on backcountry safety precautions.

Muttering a curse, he stiff-armed the door leading outside. *Damn it, I told them to head back down toward Bear Claw.* Station Three, with its brightly marked trails and pre-planned walking tour, would've been a better fit for those two. Fourteen was no place for city softies.

They hadn't listened, though. And sure enough, Mr. Newlywed—Cockleburr? Cockson? It was cock-something, anyway—was pelting toward him across the dirt parking lot, eyes frantic enough to have Matt's gut twisting.

"Oh, thank God you're here." Newlywed's words tumbled over each other as he staggered to a halt and sucked in a ragged breath. "She's hurt, unconscious, and—"

"Stop!" Matt said firmly, using his cut-through-the-panic voice. When Cochran—that was it, Cochran—quit babbling, Matt said, "What happened to your wife? Did she fall?" The trails were dry as hell and starting to crumble in places.

But Cochran shook his head furiously. "Tracy's fine. The woman we found is one of yours."

"One of—" Matt's stomach did a nosedive. "A *ranger?*"

Cochran patted his chest, near where the men and women who oversaw Bear Claw Canyon State Park wore their badgelike name tags. "Tanya. Her name's Tanya."

"Jim!" Bert bellowed back toward the station. "Get out here!"

"That's—" *Impossible,* Matt started to say, but then bit off the word. Arguing was a waste of time.

His mind locked on Tanya as he'd seen her last— pretending to ignore pretty-boy Jim while blowing a kiss to divorced, old-enough-to-be-her-father Bert as she headed out to one of the Jeeps. Her dark hair had been tied back, her dark eyes laughing as she had joked with the two men: one her self-proclaimed partner in meaningless flirtation, the other her friend.

Matt hadn't been part of the bunkhouse horseplay that morning or any other time. He had his own place beyond the station house and kept to himself. But Tanya was definitely one of his.

His ranger. His responsibility.

There was a commotion behind him as Jim thud-ded down the steps and Bert relayed the bad news. Jim blanched and surged forward, but Bert grabbed him by the arm and held him in check.

Matt focused on Cochran. His mind raced through scenarios from fixable to fatal. *Please let it be fixable.* "Where is she?"

Cochran gestured northward. "At the bottom of a shallow wash, that way, about forty-five, fifty minutes from here. We saw her when we were hiking up to this cave mouth that's shaped like a heart."

"That's right by Candle Rock!" Bert burst out. The distinctive formation was part of his patrol area, not Tanya's.

Matt bit off a curse. Candle Rock was difficult to reach, with too many river crossings for vehicles to get all the way in. And what the hell was Tanya doing over by Candle Rock? *Later,* he told himself. He'd worry about the whys later. "She's unconscious?"

Cochran nodded. "Looks like she slipped and fell. She had a knot on her head. There was a little blood, and she was cool to the touch, but her breathing and pulse both seemed steady. Trace stayed to try and warm her up."

"Good," Matt said gruffly. "Okay, then." He was starting to think the Cochrans weren't as much of a lost cause as he had initially pegged them for. And for Tanya's sake, he hoped to hell that was the case.

He turned to Jim. "Get an emergency medical chopper en route. Bert and I are going to drive in as far as we can and hike the rest of the way. We should get there about the same time as the chopper. I want you back here coordinating things."

Jim's face clouded. "But—"

"I could stay—" Bert began.

"Not open for discussion," Matt broke in. He gestured to Bert. "Get one of the first-aid duffels and our climbing gear." To Jim, he said in a low voice, "Let us take this one. You can see her later." When the kid—okay, he was twenty-five, but as far as Matt was concerned, still very much a kid—started to protest, Matt fixed him with a look. "That's an order."

Jim hesitated, then nodded reluctantly. They both knew that although Matt didn't pull rank often, he meant it when he did.

And in this case, he meant it in spades. He knew all too well that there was no room for emotion during a crisis…and when things went bad out in the backcountry, they could go very, very bad.

Tanya was an expert climber, though. What the hell had happened? And why was she out of her territory? Those questions clouded his concern for the young ranger as he drove his Jeep out toward Candle Rock, with Bert and Cochran following in a second vehicle.

Despite the rangers' best efforts to educate the hikers who had the chops to handle the backcountry and discourage the ones who didn't, the treacherous terrain, wildfires, poisonous snakes, and drought-starved predators had combined to take their toll. In his almost six years as head of Station Fourteen, he had led eight search parties and arranged transport of three bodies. His sector—which included the park's most remote territory—averaged an airlift a month, and two or three times that many hikers had to be driven straight to the E.R. Do not pass go. Do not collect two hundred dollars.

He hoped to hell this would be one of the easy ones, requiring little more than a couple of ibuprofen and a day or two off. If Tanya had been unconscious for an extended period, though, that didn't seem likely.

At the thought, he hit the gas and sent the Jeep lunging forward. Then, when the wheels shuddered, he made himself ease up and breathe. Panic didn't solve anything.

They made it most of the way to Candle Rock in the vehicles after all—the drought that had contributed to the wildfires currently devastating Sectors Five and Six was a backhanded blessing now, drying up the two rivers that usually blocked the route.

When their luck ran out at the base of a steep hill, they parked, shouldered their gear, and hiked in the rest of the way, jogging along a narrow game trail that crested a rocky, tree-lined ridge near the cave.

Matt brought up the rear, carrying his shotgun. If Tanya was bleeding, there would be scavengers in the area, maybe even one or more of the bigger predators.

"Up here!" Cochran ran forward, cresting the ridge as he called, "Trace? We're back!"

"Hurry!" a woman's voice responded immediately. "She's in shock, and I don't like how low her heart rate is getting."

Matt cursed and lunged up the last stretch and down the other side, partly jumping from one rock to another, partly skidding along the loose, crumbling gravel. "Get the ropes anchored," he said to Bert, waving the older man back as he reached the edge of the deep wash.

"Will do. You should wait until—"

"No time." Matt yanked the straps of his knapsack tighter, checked his shotgun, and jumped over the edge of the wash right behind Cochran.

He dropped nearly a dozen feet and his boots hit the ground hard, but he barely noticed the impact; his focus was locked on where Cochran had one arm around his wife. Their heads were tipped together, their bodies leaning into each other.

But even as that image burned itself inexplicably into Matt's brain, he looked past them where Tanya lay sprawled in the gravel. She was covered with two brightly colored jackets, and other pieces of the Cochrans' clothing were tucked around her. Her eyes were closed and a slender blood trail tracked across her cheek. Her supposedly shockproof radio lay smashed nearby, in a scuffed spot below the crumbled ledge.

Something jarred faintly wrong, but that was quickly blotted out by a twist of guilt. She looked so damn young lying there…and he had sent her out alone. Which was protocol, but still.

"Hey, Tanya," he said as he crouched down beside her. "It's Matt." Had she ever called him by his first name? He couldn't remember. "Bert's here, too. We're going to get you out of here."

Her pupils were unequal, her vitals too damn low across the board. Yeah, she was shocky all right. Concussed, too, and maybe suffering from internal injuries. It wasn't that much of a fall, but she must have landed exactly wrong.

Grabbing the radio off his belt, he toggled it to send. "Jim?"

There was a hiss and a squawk. "Did you find her?"

"Got her. How are we doing on that chopper?"

"Should be there any minute. How is she?"

"Banged up." The faint noise of rotor-thwack saved him from having to elaborate. "Chopper's here. Patch me through will you?"

As he was talking options with the pilot, a trio of climbing ropes sailed over the edge and slithered down, followed moments later by Bert. Raising his voice over the increasing noise of the helicopter, the grizzled ranger called, "They going to stay in the air and drop a basket?"

Matt shook his head. "The pilot thinks she can land on that flat section beyond the wash. We'll use the ropes to bring Tanya up and out." It felt good to have a plan, better to know she would soon be getting the medical help she needed. Turning back to the injured ranger, he gentled his voice and said, "The chopper's almost here. They'll get you down to the city, and—" He broke off when her eyelids fluttered. "Tanya? Can you hear me?"

She shifted uncomfortably and frowned, then lashed out with a fisted hand as though trying to physically fight off unconsciousness. Cochran and his wife made soothing noises but stayed back, yielding to Matt. He caught her flailing fist. "Easy, killer. You fell off the ledge and banged yourself up a bit, but the med techs are on their way."

Her lips moved. "Didn't…fall."

He blew out a relieved breath that she was making sense. "You hit your head. It'll come back." Maybe. Maybe not. At least she was talking.

But she shook her head, wincing at the pain brought by the move. "No fall. Ambushed."

His blood chilled, but it didn't make any sense. Ambushes were for narrow alleys and drug dealers, not wide-open skies and park rangers. Hallucination? Maybe. He didn't know. Leaning closer, he said urgently, "What happened?"

Her eyes opened to slits as she tried to focus on him. "Two men grabbed me…wanted…" She struggled to say something more, but then her body went lax as she lost her brief grip on consciousness.

"Wait!" He surged up onto his knees and bent over her, gripping her fisted hand in his. "What men?" The controlled crisis mode he'd long ago perfected lost out to anger at the thought of someone doing this to one of his people, on his territory, his watch. "Tanya, *what men?*"

"Matt." Bert gripped his shoulder. "She's out."

Damn it. He subsided, loosening his grip on her hand. When he did, something fell free and floated to the ground.

Cochran leaned in. "What's that?"

Catching the small, colorful scrap between his thumb and forefinger, Matt lifted it. "A feather."

The shaft was thin and curved, and the barbs ran a wild-colored gamut from white-and-black at the top to a deep reddish orange in the middle, then back to black at the base. He frowned at it, but there was no time to really get a good look, because right then the rotor noise increased to a roar and the chopper appeared overhead.

It paused, spun, and then dropped in for a more-haste-than-grace landing. Moments later, shouts and the sound of thudding footfalls up above announced the arrival of the med team.

Matt stuck the feather in his breast pocket and buttoned it in for safekeeping.

The next few minutes were ordered chaos as the medical team rappelled down and hustled to get Tanya stabilized for transport, with a rapid yet thorough triage, warming blankets and an IV line of fluids to combat the shock. The techs didn't say it, but he could see from their faces that they didn't like her continued unconsciousness any more than he did. Working quickly and efficiently, they strapped her down and okayed her for travel.

Working together, Matt, Bert, the Cochrans and the

med team hauled her out of the wash and loaded her onto the chopper.

Matt heard the copilot radioing ahead to let the hospital know they had a serious head injury on the way. He wanted somebody to look at her and say that she'd be fine, but it didn't happen.

He slid the door closed, then ducked out of range as the rotors screamed and the chopper lifted up and away, heading for the city. He was relieved to have Tanya in the care of professionals, but there wasn't any time to stand around congratulating himself on a job well done...especially when he hadn't done his job well at all.

It was his responsibility to make Sector Fourteen as safe as he possibly could. His mind churned. Two men, she had said. What men? What had happened, and why was she out of her normal range? Had she followed them and been discovered, or had they brought her all this way and dumped her? And what was the deal with the feather? Was it important, or just something she'd been carrying when she was ambushed?

He winced as phantom pain sliced through his lower left abdomen, where a gnarled scar and low-grade ulcer formed a pointed reminder that it wasn't his job to be asking those questions. Hadn't been for a long time.

As the rotor noise dimmed, he pulled Bert aside, out of the Cochrans' earshot. "Take those two back to the station and keep them there."

The other man darted a look at the hikers. "You think they hurt Tanya?"

"No. But they may have seen something and not even realized it."

Bert craned around, eyes widening as he followed Matt's thought process. "You think the guys who got Tanya are still around?"

Probably, said Matt's instincts. "Just get back to the station and put them in separate rooms so they can't compare stories any more than they already have. Then you can relieve Jim on the radio so he can go to the hospital. If he balks, make it an order."

He didn't think the younger man would give even a token protest. Jim and Tanya had been circling around each other for the past six months, ever since she transferred up from Station Seven, and the fear and emotion in the younger man's face had been real. While that kind of romantic connection didn't work for Matt, he wasn't about to make the choice for someone else. He had sworn off trying to run other people's lives.

"Aren't you coming back with us?" Bert asked, still looking around, searching for monsters in the shadows. But that was the thing about monsters. Most of the time, you couldn't see them until the damage was already done.

"I'm going to stay and look around, scare off any scavengers who might be interested in the scene." Human or otherwise. Matt tapped the butt of the shotgun riding over his shoulder. "I'll be fine."

Bert looked unconvinced, but there was enough of an enlisted man still left in him that he followed orders without further argument, collecting the Cochrans and getting them moving back toward the Jeeps.

When they were gone, Matt was left alone beneath a brilliantly blue sky, warmed by the summer sun. But the beauty and isolation didn't settle him like they normally did. Instead, there was a heavy weight on his chest as he lifted his radio. "Jim, you reading me?"

"Here, boss. She get away okay?"

"Yeah. They're en route. You can go down to the city as soon as Bert gets there. Right now, though, I need you to patch me through to Tucker McDermott." This wasn't a case for Homicide, really, but Tucker was a friend. One of his very few.

There was a beat of silence. "I thought she fell."

"It looks like it wasn't an accident."

"*What?*"

"Just put me through to Tucker, okay? Bert will fill you in when he gets there."

The patch-through from radio to telephone took a minute, but was necessary. There was no cell coverage in the back of beyond, and even satellite phones were hit-or-miss. So the rangers often relied on radios, especially for the more out-of-the-way sectors: Seven and Eight on the eastern side, Thirteen and Fourteen on the western side, and good old Sector Nine, which formed the bridge between the two lobes of the huge park... where the crime usually ran to vandalism and careless fires, not attempted murder.

Matt took a long look at the scuffed-up sidewall of the gulley and the three ropes that snaked from a big boulder and disappeared over the edge. He didn't need to glance down there to know that the bottom of the wash was churned up and littered with scraps from the med techs' sterile packaging. The scene was seriously contaminated, and it was going to take a hell of an analyst to make anything out of it. Fortunately, the Bear Claw P.D.'s crime lab was staffed by a group of

talented analysts who were the ultimate professionals…
with one glaring, purple-booted, on-loan-from-Denver
exception.

Matt grimaced at the intrusive image of sparkling
gray eyes in a sharp face framed by sleek dark hair. Gigi
Lynd. Even her name sounded expensive and citified, not
like anything that belonged out in the backcountry.

He would tell Tucker to send anyone but her. Hell,
Station Two's nature trail would be a stretch for someone like her…and the last thing he needed to be doing
right now was babysitting some city-slicker analyst who
dressed like she was looking for trouble.

Chapter Two

Gigi nailed three bad-guy targets, skipped the little old lady cutout, tagged the last two baddies and slapped her Beretta on the counter with a flourish that might not have been strictly necessary, but damn, she was on a roll.

Granted, the firing range's offerings were pretty basic, but still.

She slipped off her headphones and turned, just catching the tail end of her friend Alyssa's impressed whistle. The heavily pregnant blonde's eyes glittered with appreciation behind her tinted safety glasses, but she faked a pained look. "Please tell me you didn't just pick that up for the test, like you did the computer stuff you showed me."

Gigi grinned and slicked her dark, asymmetrically bobbed hair behind her ears before pulling her clip, clearing the chamber, and giving the weapon a quick, practiced wipe down. "I shot my first rifle when I was nine, started with handguns when I was thirteen."

"Thank God. I was starting to get seriously depressed, thinking that you'd only been shooting for the past six months or so."

"Nope. More like the past two decades. And you don't look the slightest bit depressed." In fact, the head of the Bear Claw P.D.'s Forensics Division looked amazing—rosy cheeked and curvy, with the mysterious "I know something you don't" look that Gigi associated with her sisters' first pregnancies. "I take it you're feeling better?"

"Incredible." Alyssa smoothed her palm across the top of her protruding belly. "After the past three weeks of abject almost-time-to-pop yuckiness, I woke up this morning feeling amazing." A smile touched her lips with an entirely different sort of knowing look. "Tucker did, too, much to his surprise and delight."

"Ouch." Gigi exaggerated the wince. "Taunting the celibate again, are we?"

Alyssa twinkled at her. "A girl who looks like you and shoots like that doesn't need to be celibate."

"Right. Because guys perform best at gunpoint." When Alyssa gave her a "yeah, right" look, Gigi lifted a shoulder. "I guess I'm not a casual sex kind of girl."

Her friend's blue eyes narrowed. "I never thought you were."

Maybe not, but plenty of guys looked at the outside packaging and thought they knew what was going on inside it. If she mentioned that, though, Alyssa would bring up the *m* word again—makeover—and that wasn't happening. What might look a little too glittery in Bear Claw played just fine in Denver, and Gigi liked her personal style. There was nothing wrong with being different.

So as they crossed the parking lot toward her borrowed SUV, she went with a second, equally honest answer. "I'm not going to be here for much longer, which would make any sort of hookup, for entertaining sex or otherwise, casual by definition. No offense, but when the call comes, I'm out of here."

The Denver P.D. was piloting an accelerated SWAT/ critical response training program that would leapfrog a few select forensic analysts straight into existing hazardous response teams—HRTs—where they would act as both technical support and boots on the ground. Although the TV shows made it seem like every CSI was a badge-wearing, gun-carrying cop, that was far from the case in most jurisdictions, where the cops were cops and the lab rats were…well, lab rats.

Going from the lab straight to hazardous response was a heck of a leap, but the members of Gigi's family were anything but conventional when it came to their ambitions. Whatever the Lynds did, they did it full throttle.

Alyssa glanced away. "I know you've only been here a few months, and we're just really getting to know each other. And it's not like I don't have other friends. Good friends. But…I like how you bring a new perspective to things around here. I wish—selfishly, I admit—that I had the budget to hire you away from Denver and keep you here in the lab. Thanks to Mayor Tightwad, I don't, so I have to think outside the box. If that means hunting down a few eligible bachelors…"

"Aw." Throat tightening, Gigi nudged the other woman gently with an elbow. "Thanks. But let's be realistic—I'm focusing on my career, which means you can't tempt me with a guy." The members of her family paired off in their mid-thirties, once they had a degree or two and a tenure track. She might not have inherited the Lynds' love of academia, but she had gotten their ambition in spades. "Besides it's not like I'm going to Mars or Timbuktu or something. I'll visit."

Alyssa shot her an "it won't be the same" look. "Are you sure—" Her phone rang with the plain digital ringtone that said it was official business. Immediately straightening away from Gigi's SUV, Alyssa pulled the phone and answered with a clipped, professional "Mc-Dermott, Forensics." But then her face softened. "Hello, McDermott, Homicide. What's up?"

Gigi started to wander off and give Alyssa privacy to talk to her husband. Baby McDermott's arrival was so imminent that most of the couple's business conversations inevitably turned personal, which made Gigi… Well, better to give them privacy.

"Station Fourteen?" Alyssa said, voice going worried. "Matt's station?"

The name stopped Gigi in her tracks.

Matt. As in Matt Blackthorn, head ranger of the state park's most remote outpost. The one guy she *had* noticed in Bear Claw, and not necessarily in a good way.

Her first impression had been positive—how could it not be? Blackthorn looked like one of the guys on the glossy brochures put out by the tourism bureau—edgy and gorgeous, with subtle bronzing and hard, commanding features that fit with his rumored Cherokee heritage. But unlike the professional models in the brochures, Blackthorn carried a rugged, purposeful energy and seemed to bring the mountain air down to the city with him—not the tame air of the ski slopes, but that of the wilderness, uncivilized and predatory.

The first moment she'd laid eyes on the big ranger, she had actually caught her breath.

They'd both been in the hallway outside of Tucker's office, her coming in, Blackthorn going out. And for a moment, something had sparked between them. At first, she had thought it was mutual attraction—the heated flash in the depths of his dark green eyes had resonated with the "hell, yeah" her hormones had been chorusing.

Then his gaze had shifted as he took in the rest of her, and his expression had tightened, killing the light of interest. Zap. Gone.

She didn't know what he had or hadn't seen in her, or what it had meant to him. She only knew that he'd touched the brim of the black felt hat he wore over his dark hair, and kept going. And the next time they'd crossed paths, when she'd done a briefing on a rash of parking-lot break-ins at several trailheads leading to the backcountry, Blackthorn had cut the conversation short enough to earn them a couple of raised eyebrows from the other cops and rangers involved in the meeting.

After that, she had avoided him. Not because he made her uncomfortable—she didn't give anyone that power—but because it didn't matter whether or not the head ranger of Station Fourteen liked her. She was there to work evidence for the Bear Claw City P.D. and prove to her bosses back home that she could fit herself seamlessly into an existing team like the BCCPD's crime lab. Blackthorn wasn't part of that world.

Unless there was a crime scene up at Station Fourteen. Then he was very much a part of her world—at least for the duration of the case.

Alyssa frowned. "Cassie's going to be tied up for the next few hours and there's no way I'm driving up to the middle of nowhere, never mind hiking to the site. Gigi can—" She broke off and glanced in Gigi's direction. "Okay. I can switch some stuff around and send Cassie, I guess. Tell him she'll be coming in behind the officers, and will need really good directions or a lead-in. We're shorthanded as it is. It won't do us any good to lose an analyst to the Forgotten."

Gigi barely heard the last part. She was too busy seething at the realization that Blackthorn had told Tucker—a former member of the Denver P.D. who had a direct pipeline to her bosses—that he didn't want her on the case.

"That backstabbing—" She bit off the snarl as Alyssa clicked her phone shut and regarded her curiously.

"What on earth is the problem between you and Matt?"

Taking a deep breath, Gigi slapped a layer of professionalism over her other emotions. "As far as I'm concerned, there's no problem. We met a couple of times, I was pleasant, he wasn't. End of story." At least it had been. Now she wanted a piece of him for trying to torpedo her. What had she ever done to him?

Nothing, that was what. Judgmental idiot.

"There's got to be more to it than that," Alyssa said. "It's not like him to be a jerk to anyone, especially a woman, never mind leaning on Tucker for something like this."

Gigi said through her teeth, "I've barely spoken to the man. If he took one look at me and decided he didn't like what he saw, that's his problem."

Alyssa's look went speculative, but she said only, "He told Tucker he didn't think you could handle the backcountry, that he'd rather wait for someone he didn't have to babysit."

"He…" Gigi counted to ten and reminded herself that it didn't matter what Blackthorn thought of her. Tucker was a fair guy and a top-notch cop, which meant he cared about results. "Fine, let's give Ranger Surly what he wants. I'll take over for Cassie and she can deal with his parking lot smash-and-grab."

But Alyssa shook her head, expression clouding. "It's way more than that. A few hours ago, two men attacked and injured one of his rangers—a woman named Tanya Dawes. They just airlifted her out."

"Oh." *Oh, damn.* Gigi exhaled in a rush, knowing full well that aggravated assault trumped any personal issues that might or might not exist between her and Blackthorn. "Is she going to be okay?"

"It looks like she took a serious blow to the head and may have some internal injuries. I guess she came around just long enough to tell Matt that two men had ambushed her."

"Sexual assault?"

"No sign of it, which is good. But the head injury… that's not good."

"Did she give Blackthorn any sort of description?"

"Nothing."

"Damn." Which meant that the crime scene analysis could be critical. "How do you want to handle it?"

Alyssa thought for a few seconds, then said, "I want you to head out to Station Fourteen. According to Matt, the scene took a beating when they airlifted her out,

which makes you the better choice. Cassie is hell on
wheels with the tech stuff, but you've got more experience with contaminated scenes. And if the problem
between you and Matt is strictly an oil-and-water sort
of thing, you'll deal with it. Right?"

Gigi nodded, already mentally reviewing the field kit
she had with her, looking for gaps. "Of course. I've taken
static on crime scenes before. I can handle myself."

More importantly, this wasn't about her and it sure
wasn't about Blackthorn. She was there to do a job and
she didn't intend to let anyone get in her way...espe-
cially not a park ranger with a great body and a nasty
judgmental streak.

WHEN THE FIRST BCCPD vehicle churned into view in
a cloud of dust, Matt was surprised to see Jack Williams
at the wheel.

Williams, who topped six feet and had early salt in
his chestnut hair though he was just on the downside of
thirty, was one of the top detectives in Homicide. Born
and raised in Bear Claw, Jack was the latest in a long
line of Williamses to serve the BCCPD, and Matt's gut
had long ago put the guy in the "solid cop" category.

As Williams climbed from the SUV, Matt headed
over, hands in his pockets, still wearing his shotgun and
knapsack over his shoulder. "I'll have to thank Tucker,"
he said to Williams. "This isn't exactly a case for Homicide, but I'm damn glad to see you."

The detective gave him a nod. "We take care of our
own."

Matt didn't think he was talking about the close
connection that had evolved between the P.D. and park

service in Bear Claw, but didn't want to go down that road, so he said simply, "Thanks." He glanced over as a second cop got out of the SUV—a younger uniformed officer with a startling shock of white-blond hair and pale eyes that together made him look washed out beneath the late-summer sun. "New partner?"

"Billy Doran," Williams said by way of introduction. "Thanks to Mayor Cheapskate's latest round of cuts, we're down to under a dozen detectives trying to cover the whole damn city. Rather than partnering detectives, Tucker's got some of us teaming up with uniforms."

Despite his one-time interest in politics, Matt had stayed well clear of Bear Claw's issues, just as he largely avoided the city itself. He hadn't moved to Station Fourteen to get involved in city stuff, after all. Even so, he knew that Mayor Percy Proudfoot had been taking some serious hacks at the budget in an effort to turn around a huge budget deficit. The P.D. in particular was having to get creative.

He sent the kid a nod. "Doran." Turning back to Williams, he said, "I'll lead you guys in, then come back down for Cassie when she gets here." He hesitated. "There's something I didn't get a chance to tell Tucker." He told them about the feather, patted his buttoned pocket. "You guys want it?"

"Keep it until Cass gets here," Williams said. "It's probably better not to move it around more than necessary. But don't be surprised if she wants your shirt, too, in case there's transfer." He grinned. "Just watch what you say if she does. Last guy who made a sexist joke about the crime scene girls got the rough side of Alyssa's tongue, and then spent some quality time directing traffic for a sewer repair crew, courtesy of Chief Mendoza."

"I'll keep that in mind." Actually, it didn't matter to him whether the Bear Claw analysts were women or Martians, as long as they got the job done.

"Grab the gear," Williams said to Doran. To Matt, he said, "Lead on and let's see what these bastards left us."

"Not much that I could see. The scene is pretty torn up."

Sure enough, once he got them up there, Williams shook his head. "You weren't kidding. What isn't bare rock is a frigging mess." He sent Doran to take pictures and notes, but didn't look optimistic. "I have a feeling our best bet is going to be talking to Tanya when she wakes up."

Matt nodded, partly in thanks for the word choice. *When* she woke up. Not if. When.

The detective said, "Want to run me through what you saw? Maybe being up here will kick loose something new."

"Of course." Matt started right from the moment he heard Cochran's first shout, but it was becoming rote. And, really, he hadn't been there when it counted.

By the time Doran was done, Williams was ready to head back down to the station and question the Cochrans, so Matt led them back to the vehicles.

On the way, he radioed Bert for an update and got confirmation that Tanya's injuries were from an attack rather than a fall, along with the grim news that she was still unconscious and the early scan results weren't good. *Damn it.*

Forcing his emotions down where they belonged, Matt asked, "How about the CSI? Did she come through the station yet?" If Tanya wasn't waking up, they needed to get moving on the scene. Every minute they wasted was another minute the perps were using to get away… or plan another attack.

"Yeah. She should be there any minute."

Sure enough, the cops were loading up their SUV when the radio on his hip squalled a broken transmission. All he caught was a woman's voice and the words "almost there."

The dust kicked up by Williams's departing SUV was just clearing when a new cloud took shape and a nearly identical vehicle appeared coming the other way.

Matt checked his watch and was surprised to see that even though it felt like days had passed, it had only been five or six hours of real time. That meant they had a couple of hours of daylight left.

They would need it, too. It wouldn't be easy to truck in lights, and there wasn't much chance of an airdrop. Tucker had already given him the heads up that the P.D. was getting pressure from higher up the food chain— aka Mayor Proudfoot's office—to keep Tanya's assault on the down low and not over-commit resources.

The official line was that the attack wasn't all that different from an in-city mugging, and while Tanya would get some preference as a ranger, the P.D. shouldn't go overboard. The real rationale, though, was even simpler: Bear Claw City was hurting for money and couldn't afford to lose any tourists.

Matt hated the equation, the politics.

The SUV cruised in going too fast and kicked up

dust, suggesting that Cassie, too, knew they were racing the sun. Grit hazed things as the door swung open and she got out, hauling a heavy-looking tackle box with her.

He headed over, extending a hand. "Let me grab that for…" He trailed off, stopping dead as his gut fisted on a surge of heat mixed with dismay.

The woman coming toward him wasn't the business-like blonde he'd been expecting.

Not even close.

A sizzle shot through him at the sight of a sharp, tri-angular face beneath a crooked cap of shiny dark hair. He told himself the sensation was dismay, because he sure as hell shouldn't be feeling anything else toward a woman like Gigi Lynd.

Gigi. It sounded like it should come with a French label and an import tariff. And from her trendy haircut and unbalanced ear piercings—one on the right, three on the left—to the silver-gilded tips of her gleaming lizard-skin boots—black today rather than the purple she had been wearing before, but equally as impracti-cal—she didn't belong anywhere near the backcountry. Or him.

His pulse raced. He was going to kill Tucker.

Her white button-down was open just low enough to show a hint of cleavage, and the black belt that rode below her narrow waist had a gleam of silver that drew the eye.

"No," he said without preamble as she squared off opposite him. "I want one of the others."

Her smoky gray eyes narrowed. "You made that clear when you trashed me to McDermott."

"I didn't—" He broke off, guilt stinging because he hadn't exactly trashed her, but he'd made it clear he didn't think she had the backcountry experience or analytical chops to handle the case. "Look, it's nothing personal."

"Bull. You took one look at me and decided that I was incompetent based on, what? Some eyeliner and a little bling?" She flicked the more heavily pierced of her earlobes. "Fine, whatever, that's your problem not mine. But you're one-hundred percent right that this *shouldn't* be personal. You don't have to like me. Just get out of my way and let me do my job."

The guilt twisted harder because she was right. He'd snap judged her, hard, which was so far from his usual style it was practically alien.

That didn't mean she was the right analyst for the job, though.

He glanced up the trail. "Look, I'm sorry about the attitude. It's just… Believe it or not, I don't doubt your competence—McDermott wouldn't have leaned on his contacts in Denver to get you if you weren't the best crime scene analyst available. But you're a long way from home, and the backcountry isn't anything like the city. Alyssa, Cassie and Maya have all worked scenes out here before. You haven't."

She pierced him with a cool look. "Yet they sent me, even after you told Tucker not to. Want to take a guess as to why?"

"I don't want to… Damn it." He jammed both hands in his pockets, knowing he was beaten. And what was more, he was dead wrong. She hadn't done a damn thing to deserve his suspicion. It wasn't her fault that she was the first woman in a long time to make him want to stop and take a second, longer look. Maybe a taste.

And that so wasn't happening.

He didn't know what she saw in his face, but her expression softened. "I'm sorry about what happened to Tanya. And under the circumstances, I'm even sorry that my being here bothers you. But back in Denver I was the analyst of choice for badly contaminated scenes. Right before I left, I worked a murder scene at the edge of an eroded riverbank the day after a downpour. And yes, we got the guy." She paused. "You want to get the two men who hurt your ranger? Then take me to your scene… and make it fast, because we're burning daylight."

Matt wasn't sure which was worse: having been so thoroughly set down…or knowing that he was going to have to stick right with her. Because he'd be damned if anyone else got hurt on his watch.

"Okay," he said. "Okay, yeah." Mind already skimming ahead to what he was going to need out of the Jeep, he whipped off his shirt and held it out. "You're going to want this."

It wasn't until she gave a strangled gasp, eyes going wide, that he realized he was standing there bare-chested, and she had no clue why he'd just stripped down.

Heat washed through him. Oh, hell. That was so not cool.

"There's evidence in the front pocket," he said quickly. "A feather Tanya was holding when I got to her. Williams said you would want the shirt, too, for transfer." He started to apologize, would have except for one thing:

She was staring at his chest.

He stilled, watching a faint flush climb her throat and work its way to her face as she swallowed. Then she jerked her eyes to his, and the blush hit hard.

Electricity raced over his skin, tightening his body as they stared at each other for a three count.

She recovered first, with a gulp and a small shiver that he felt deep in his gut. "Um," she said, voice huskier than it had been a moment earlier, "hold that thought."

When she put down the tackle box that contained her field kit, he thought…hell, he didn't know what he thought. His brain was gone, melted by whatever had just telegraphed between them. So when she rummaged and came up with a large evidence bag, he just stared at it for a second.

Then reality returned and his brain reassembled itself.

Tanya. Evidence. The crime scene.

What the hell was he doing?

Without a word, he folded the shirt and tucked it into the bag, watched her seal it and scrawl her name on the first line of the evidence chain. Then he turned away and headed for his Jeep, saying over his shoulder, "Let me grab my jacket and we can hit the trail."

And as he led her up to Candle Rock, he worked like hell to get his head screwed back on straight. Because he couldn't afford to let himself get distracted in a crisis situation. Bad things happened when he did.

Chapter Three

Wow. That was all Gigi's brain could formulate as she followed Blackthorn along a narrow game trail that led up a sharply rocky incline.

Wow, he had a seriously fine body beneath that drab, tan-and-green park service uniform. His sleek bronze skin covered sculpted muscles, its perfection marred by two scars, one high on his shoulder, the other wrapping around his waistline.

Wow, that had been the hottest stand-and-stare moment of her life. Her blood was still humming, her coordination slightly off as her body focused inward.

And wow, this was way outside her comfort zone.

It had been a while since she had made the time or effort, but she'd had her share of relationships, all based on affection, attraction, and the freedom to move on when the time came.

Those relationships had been fun. Satisfying. And not once, not even in the bedroom, had any of those guys lit her up the way she had just ignited from nothing more than seeing Blackthorn's chest.

Even now, as she scanned the rocks and scrub for

scuff marks, the image of his naked torso seemed burned onto her retinas.

Temporary insanity. That was all it was. They'd both had their tempers up, and his adrenaline had probably been pumping for hours. More, she had been disarmed by the way he had backed down, owning his bad behavior when she called him on it.

In her experience, that wasn't the way real jerks operated. Which meant…well, it didn't matter what it meant. Her gut said he was complicated, and she didn't have any room in her life for personal complications. She was there to do her job…which was about evidence, not ogling.

Deliberately, she forced her mind back on track.

The bagged shirt was tucked in the bottom of her field kit. She would process the feather back in the lab, where she could keep absolute track of the environment. But she already knew some of the assessments she would need to make: Was it real or fake? Where had it come from? Why had Tanya been clutching it?

The last question wasn't really part of an analyst's job—it was up to the cops and attorneys to turn the data into a story.

But then again, she lived outside the box.

When Blackthorn hit the top of the high ridge, he paused and turned back to her. Surprise flickered when he saw that she was only a few paces behind him and not even breathing particularly hard.

She grinned. "When I was in my early teens, my parents went on a survivalist kick and decided all four of us kids needed to know how to take care of ourselves, no matter what. Our family vacations turned into something out of *Survivor* for a few years. Yosemite, the Sonoran Desert, Alaska... Some of it seemed like torture at the time, but looking back, it wasn't. It's just the way my family operates."

"As survivalists?"

"As the best at whatever we choose to do. Usually it's academics. In my case, crime scene analysis."

He held her eyes for a moment, then nodded slowly. "Point taken."

"Then let's get to work." She gestured around them. "How are you at tracking?"

"Fair to good, but when we came up this way the first time, I was looking more for four-legged predators than two-legged tracks. I can't swear to it, but I don't think there were any fresh footprints other than Cochran's at that point, and even those were pretty faint. I took a closer look around once Tanya had been airlifted out, but nothing jumped out at me." He grimaced. "Frankly, given the rock, hardpan and loose gravel, we're not looking good for tracks."

"Hopefully I'll have better luck."

"It's a mess down there."

"So I heard." But as she moved up beside him at the crest of the ridge, she sucked in a breath. "Okay. Yeah. That's a mess."

Their vantage point overlooked an oblong flattened bowl that fell away into a dry riverbed on one side. There was a brushed-clean spot where the helicopter had come and gone; ropes snaking across the shale, which was gouged where they had been moved and dragged; and a scattering of detritus in the bottom of the wash.

Although she gave Blackthorn points for not cleaning

up the med techs' leftovers after Tanya was airlifted, the overall effect was not encouraging.

He shot her a look from beneath lowered brows. "Tell me you can do something with it."

"I've seen entire cases hinge on a few strands of hair or a fingernail scraping," she said. Which wasn't quite an answer, so she added, "I've worked under worse conditions. At least here I won't have to waste time going through a ton of alley garbage that has zero relevance to the case."

"Small blessings."

"In this job, you take what you can get." *And you'd better watch it, we seem to be having a semi-normal conversation,* she thought but didn't say. Instead, she nodded to the shotgun he carried slung over his shoulder. "I'm going to be pretty involved for the next couple of hours. You'll keep lookout?"

Something shifted in the dark green depths of his eyes, and he nodded. "Nobody else is getting hurt on my watch."

Sensing he didn't want to hear that he wasn't responsible for what had happened to Tanya, she gripped his forearm briefly. "Thanks."

As she moved past him, she felt his surprise just as clearly as she had felt his leashed strength through the thin layer of his windbreaker. She wasn't sure if his shock had come from the touch or the fact that they were getting along, but she would take it.

She had a feeling she would be better to have him a little off balance around her, not vice versa.

When she was halfway down the incline, he called, "Hey. Gigi."

He gave it the softer pronunciation, as though they were in Paris rather than the middle of nowhere.

She turned back and found him backlit by the afternoon sun, a solitary figure on the ridgeline. She had to clear her throat before she said, "Yeah?"

"I'm sorry I was a jerk to you back in the city. You're okay."

"Be still my heart." But she grinned when she said it. "And my name is Gigi," she corrected, giving it the harder sound. "It's short for Greta Grace, so you don't need to get fancy with it. Or with me."

He didn't say anything, just gave her a slow nod, but she felt his eyes follow her the rest of the way down.

Then she tuned him out and got to work.

The next ninety minutes were a focused blur of photographs, sample bags and jars, and a whole lot of frustration at the lack of what she thought of as "big foam finger evidence"—the kind that pointed straight to an answer, or at least a new set of questions.

Granted, that was the exception rather than the norm, but still, she had been hoping for a quick break in the case.

By the time the sun dipped behind the mountains and the sky went pink around the edges, she was finishing up her preliminary round of collection. She locked her kit, and hauled its now considerable weight back up the ridgeline, where Blackthorn stood guard, silhouetted against the dusk.

He gave her a long, unreadable look. "All set?"

"With the first step, anyway. Now it's time for me to put in some serious lab hours."

He took the case from her without asking, his fingers brushing against hers. "But you're not hopeful."

"I'm always hopeful," she corrected, telling herself it was impossible to get a whole-body tingle from that small contact. "But in this case, I'm not very optimistic. I didn't see anything I could link straight to Tanya's attackers. Between that and the beating her radio took, it was like she was dropped…" She trailed off, sudden excitement sparking. "Wait a second. Let me see your radio."

He unclipped it from his belt and handed it over. "Bert can hook you up if you need a patch-through back to the lab or something."

"That won't be necessary."

She took the sturdy unit, which, aside from being bright yellow rather than matte black, was very like the ones used by the HRTs back home, with long-range capabilities, GPS, a digital display…and a hinged faceplate that usually broke off within the first few weeks of use. It was the one design flaw in an otherwise solid piece of equipment.

Blackthorn's still had its faceplate in place, though, and had a couple of upgrades she hadn't seen before. "Is this new?" she asked.

"They arrived last week."

Damn it, she had assumed Tanya's faceplate was long gone—and because she had made an assumption, she almost missed the evidence…or lack thereof. "Do all of your rangers carry the same model?"

"Yeah, they're interchangeable. We just grab one off the charger in my office. Why?"

She looked up at him, pulse kicking. "Did hers still have its faceplate when she left this morning?"

He thought for a second, then nodded. "Yeah, I'm sure it did." He looked back down to the scene, making the connection. "It could've bounced pretty far. Even given that some of her injuries came from an attack, she still hit hard when she fell."

"Or we were meant to think she did."

He went very still, eyes darkening as he slowly looked down, then back at her. "Damn. I saw it."

"The faceplate?"

He shook his head. "No, that there was a problem with the way she and the radio had fallen." His expression went distant as he replayed the scene in his head. "She was lying flat on her back, kind of sprawled, with the radio a few feet away. There weren't any impact marks…but there was a smoothed-flat place." He refocused, met her eyes. "Like someone had been there, swept his tracks, and then tossed the radio down after the fact."

"All we're going to have on that is your statement," she cautioned, "and my not finding the faceplate doesn't necessarily mean it wasn't there. I can't use a negative to prove a positive." But they were onto something. She was sure of it. "We're going to need more."

His expression firmed. "Then we'll find it." He paused. "You think this is a secondary scene. A dump site."

She nodded. "That's how it reads to me. And it's consistent with her Jeep not being right in this area." The vehicle's GPS wasn't registering and it hadn't been sighted along what should have been Tanya's morning route, either.

"So we have another crime scene to find."

With another man she might've told him to stay out of the way and let the cops do their job. Given that he was the local expert, though, and the P.D. was spread very thin, she said, "The faceplate is going to be a needle in a really large haystack, and there's no telling whether the Jeep is even still in the park. Take your pick."

A muscle ticked at the corner of his jaw. "The Jeep would be an easier target, obviously, but an air search is going to be difficult to pull off, if not impossible. All the working birds are tied up fighting the wildfires, and a bunch are down for repairs. We've put out feelers to other parks, other options, but so far we haven't come up with much." His head came up and his shoulders squared. "So we go old school."

"A foot search?" She looked around, unable to imagine any search being able to cover the vast, varied terrain that made up the state park.

"Yeah. I'll line up off-duty rangers, any of the on-duty rangers who can be spared, maybe even some expert hikers." He gestured down the ridge toward their vehicles. They went down together, side by side. "I'll get the search organized for first light tomorrow. We'll start with her sector and work out from there." He shot her a look. "You want in?"

"Absolutely." The invitation kicked a warm buzz through her, not just because he was admitting she could handle the backcountry, but because it felt good to be planning something rather than just gathering data. That was a big part of why she wanted to make the jump from lab rat to HRT—she wanted to do both.

Within minutes, Blackthorn was on the radio with three other station heads, getting their cooperation and coordinating the mobilization.

As they neared the parking area, she shot him a side-long look, struck by the change in him. His face was animated, his green eyes fierce and intense. More, his voice now carried a heavy weight of command that had the heads of the other stations practically snapping to attention.

She remembered the scars on his shoulder and waist, belatedly recognizing them as bullet strikes. *Ex-military,* she thought, and pegged him as an officer. But if he had that kind of background, why had he buried himself out in the middle of nowhere?

New interest stirred, not just for the sexy package, but for the man inside it. *He's complicated,* she reminded herself. But this time she found herself thinking that maybe she could handle some complications for the few more weeks she would be in Bear Claw.

Especially if those complications looked—and sounded—like Ranger Blackthorn in get-it-done mode.

"Thanks, Harvey. I'll be in touch," he said into the radio, then clicked it off and returned it to his belt. They had reached their vehicles, which were dark shapes in the gathering dusk. His shadow merged with that of his Jeep, and his voice seemed to come from the darkness when he said, "The cops collected the hikers' clothes and stuff, said they would log it all into evidence for you. And Williams suggested you take a look around the station house, particularly Tanya's room."

"I've done some work in profiling and victimology, and have helped Jack out on a couple of cases. He's hoping I'll see something that could point toward a motive."

"You don't think this was random?" His voice carried a new edge. "What aren't you telling me?"

Suddenly reminded that he wasn't technically part of the investigation, she said, "There's nothing to tell yet. We're still exploring options."

He moved in closer and dropped his voice an octave. "Hiding behind the official line, Gigi?"

Nerves stirred low in her belly, coiling her tight, but she met his eyes and said levelly, "I'm just trying to do my job, Blackthorn, so don't crowd me. And don't make the mistake of thinking you're something you're not." He wasn't a cop, couldn't expect her to keep him fully in the loop unless he cleared it with the higher-ups.

He growled something under his breath, but eased back a step. He tried the door of her SUV, found it locked, and set her field kit on the ground. "You'll want to follow me back to the station. Wouldn't want you getting lost."

He headed for his Jeep with long-legged strides, un-slinging his shotgun and knapsack as he went.

Gigi watched him go, trying not to be fascinated. He held himself apart but felt responsible, knew how to lead but had buried himself far from any troops, respected competence but wanted to be calling the shots…and was attracted and didn't want to be.

No, she had definitely been right the first time around.

She didn't have the mental energy to deal with him right now, not even for some short-term fun.

Too bad, she thought, remembering the gleam of bronze skin, the pucker of two bullet scars, one high, one low. Then she shook her head, climbed into her ride, and focused on the puzzle of two attackers, one missing faceplate…and a gut feeling that said there was far more to this case than anyone suspected.

Chapter Four

Matt kept it under warp speed as he led the way to the station house, but he was tempted to hit the gas and see if he could outrun his anger and frustration.

The case and the woman had him badly off-kilter, leaving him raw and reactive…and those were two things that didn't belong anywhere near an investigation like this one. If he didn't pull it together, he wasn't going to be any use to his rangers, the cops, or Gigi. And the fact that his mind slotted her into a category of her own just proved that he was badly out of whack. He didn't prioritize like that. Ever.

The radio crackled. "Hey, boss, you out there?"

"Yeah, Bert. What's up?"

"We're up to five stations sending rangers for the search, and three others are pending. We're going to be ready to roll at first light."

"Good." He would run it past Tucker, but couldn't imagine there would be a problem. The searchers all had training, and it wouldn't cost the city a dime. "How's Tanya?"

"No change."

"Damn." The station lights came into view, piercing the darkness up ahead. "We're here."

He parked the Jeep in its usual spot, while Gigi unknowingly took Tanya's.

She locked her field kit in a strongbox in the back of her SUV, pocketed the key and turned for the station. She hesitated when she saw him standing there, watching her, then met his stare, unspeaking, as if to say, "Here I am. What are you going to do about it?"

That was the question, wasn't it?

As before, heat laced the air between them. This time, though, there was a softer layer, one that came from the realization that she was smart and dedicated, and was busting her ass to help find Tanya's attackers.

He wasn't looking to get involved, hadn't been for a long time, but there she was.

And he was in serious trouble.

"Bert!" he shouted, louder and sharper than he'd intended.

Boots thudded and the older ranger appeared in the screened doorway of the faux log cabin. "Boss?"

"I need you to show Ms. Lynd around the station for me."

He needed some space, and he needed it now.

GIGI WATCHED HIM GO, trying to suppress a twinge of what should have been irritation but felt more like hurt. She had thought they had called a truce of sorts out at the scene. Apparently not.

"Please excuse Matt," Bert said blandly. "He was raised by a grizzly."

She glanced over at the older ranger, who had silver-shot hair and laugh lines at the corners of his weathered eyes. "Not wolves?"

He shook his head. "Nope, too social. We're pretty sure it was a single bachelor grizzly of the pissed-off variety—the kind that snarls when cornered." He toed open the screen door and held it for her. "Come on up. I'll show you Tanya's room and whatever else you want to see. Anything that'll help."

"Thanks." Forcing her mind off Blackthorn's Dr. Jekyll and Ranger Surly routine, she followed Bert into the station.

The building was T-shaped, with the main entrance—the public area—centered on the crossbars.

They entered a long, narrow room that was divided roughly in half by a waist-high counter, with bathrooms on either side: men on the left, women on the right. A door centered on the back wall led to the longer bunk-house wing that finished the T-shape.

The walls of the front room were lined with maps, brochures and copies of the fliers the park service put out each year, complete with instructions on bear avoidance, trail safety and what to do in the event of an emergency. On the other side of the counter—the rangers' side—the papers hung on the walls and office cubbies leaned more toward emergency numbers and scrawled notes.

Bert waved her through a flip-up pass in the counter, then gestured to a small desk. "That's Tanya's. So are the pictures."

A row of sketches were tacked along the wall to the right of the desk. Tanya had captured dozens of moments: a stark, barren landscape of rocks and stunted trees; a doe and fawn silhouetted atop a sparsely forested ridgeline; ghostly wisps of mist rising off the surface of a pond as a coyote paused to drink; the curl of a fern, so mundane until seen through eyes that found something beautiful in it; a hawk's flight, sketched so sparsely as to be mere suggestions of line and motion, except for the creature's head and its bright, fierce eyes.

But Gigi's attention was immediately drawn to a deft caricature off to one side. In it, a handsome young man—presumably Jim Feeney—and Bert were horsing around together there in the station. There was a hint of a Stetson-shadow just visible through a doorway, putting Blackthorn in the picture. Sort of.

"She's talented," Gigi commented past the sudden tightening of her throat.

Bert reached out to brush his thumb across the bold *T* at the bottom of the caricature. "She hasn't woken up yet."

There was guilt beneath the pain, just like with Matt. It made Gigi think that maybe rangers weren't as different from cops as she had thought—both protected their people and their territories, and took it very seriously when one of their own went down in the line.

"Tell me about her," she said.

"She's a good kid, a good ranger, and practically has eyes in the back of her head. Whoever these guys are, they would've had to know the backcountry to get the drop on her."

Which narrowed things down, but not by much. "Does she have any enemies you know about? Anyone who would want to hurt her?" Williams would have asked the standard questions, but it didn't hurt to repeat them.

He shook his head. "No way. She wasn't that kind of person."

"How about a boyfriend?"

"She and Jim flirted, but I don't think it was serious, at least not on her part. And before you ask, no, he wasn't mad about it, and yes, he was here all morning. He's at the hospital right now, driving himself nuts— just like we all are—wondering if there was something he could've done to prevent this and hoping to hell she wakes up soon." His voice had sharpened, but before she could say something to bring things down a notch, his shoulders slumped. "Sorry. This really sucks."

"Yeah. It does." She touched his arm in sympathy. "I'm sorry to make you go through it again."

"Don't be. I'll do whatever I can to help. It's just…" He paused, then said slowly, "The rangers who work the outer stations tend to be out here for a reason. Some because they need space, others because they plain don't like being around other people. Tanya is one of the first kind, or at least she was when she got here. Lately, though, she's gone from this—" he tapped one of the lonely, barren landscapes "—to this—" his finger moved to the doe and her fawn "—to this." He touched the caricature.

"She was healing from something?" Maybe something that had made enemies?

"That'd be my take. She didn't talk about it, though, at least not with me. Just said she had made mistakes and wanted to move on. Recently, though, she seemed to be coming out of her shell."

"Because of her relationship with Jim?" Or was there something else going on?

"Maybe. Or maybe it was just time. Who knows?" He straightened away from the pictures. "Come on. I'll show you her room."

Gigi followed him through to the bunkhouse wing, where a wide hallway was flanked on either side by rows of closed doors. The hall ended in a set of double doors leading out, their windows showing the pitch black of night beyond.

"That's the boss's office," Bert said, jerking a thumb at the first on the left. "The rest are all dorm-type rooms from back when this was a research station. Matt's house was the old observatory. He converted it when he came out here five, six years ago."

"You don't seem like the kind of guy who has trouble being around people."

He shot her a look that said he knew exactly what she was asking. "My wife and I separated a couple of years ago, which made the 'getting away' part attractive. This is the perfect setup—close enough to the city that I can visit my one kid who stayed local for college and see the other two when they come back to town. Not to mention that room and board is included, which helps when you're scraping to pay three tuitions."

"And Jim?"

"Won't last out here much longer. He came for the hiking and stayed because he was enjoying himself—and maybe a bit to see how things would go with Tanya— but I doubt he'll be here come winter. He doesn't need it the way the rest of us do." A muted crackle of static had his head whipping around. "I need to get that." He pointed to the end of the hall. "Her room is the last door on your right. It's not locked."

She watched him disappear through the door to the main room, wishing she had asked about Blackthorn just then. He had been there six years, and…what? Stalled? Healed? Found exactly what he was looking for?

As she headed for Tanya's room, a faint shiver touched her nape. Under other circumstances, she would have thought it was her instincts telling her to watch her back, but she was safe in the station, and she knew darn well the threat wasn't coming from outside.

She was on the borderline of a major crush.

And she needed to stop it.

"Okay. I'm stopping." Blanking her mind of the lingering images of Blackthorn standing guard, silhouetted against the setting sun, she took a deep breath and pushed through into Tanya's room.

Since it wasn't a crime scene, she didn't need to print the doorknob or wear protective gear. She just closed the door behind her, flipped the light switch, and stood there for a moment.

The room was maybe twice the width of the twin-size bed that sat along one wall beneath a colorful quilt. A desk and short chest of drawers took up the other wall, leaving only a narrow runway down the center of the space. The door was centered on one end, a window on the other.

The small space might have resembled a cell if it weren't for the warm colors and bold textures decorating it, and the profusion of sketches tacked to the walls.

The pictures were similar to the ones out in the main station—mostly nature scenes, with a few caricatures of the other rangers, done on newer paper and layered atop the others. There was also a detailed sketch of blond, good-looking Jim, posed casually and looking at the artist with a seriously devilish glint that practically screamed "let's get out of here and have some fun."

Heart tugging for the victim, Gigi took another, longer look around the room, trying to get a sense of Tanya—or, more importantly, what she had been trying to escape.

Most everything in the room seemed to belong to her present incarnation: hiking and climbing equipment, sturdy clothes, trail maps, a few field guides on local plants and animals, a couple of paperbacks and a cache of chocolate bars. There was winter gear under the bed… and behind it, a set of high-end downhill skis, boots and other equipment, carefully wrapped in worn-looking plastic, as if they had been stored away for longer than just the summer. Gigi filed the observation and moved on.

There was a laptop on the small bureau, but it was wearing a layer of folded laundry, suggesting it wasn't used all that often. Making a mental note to see if Jack wanted her to bring it down to the P.D. for the techies to look at, she took a quick rifle through Tanya's bathroom stuff and then flipped through the books.

A folded piece of paper fluttered from one of the field guides, slipping from between a couple of pages at the back before she could catch it, or see what it had marked.

It proved to be another sketch: a quick pencil study of a dark-haired man in his mid-twenties, long-nosed and serious-eyed, sitting on an oblong boulder that jutted out across the impressive backdrop of a huge waterfall. The paper was soft with age and worn along the fold line, and the man looked oddly familiar, though she couldn't immediately place him.

Did he look like someone a girl would disappear into the backcountry to forget?

Instincts humming, she secured the picture in one of the evidence bags she had brought with her, and tucked it into an inner pocket of her windbreaker. She thought about bagging the field guide, but decided to come back for it later if the picture turned out to be important. Tanya's things weren't going anywhere, and for all she knew, the guy was a family member, the waterfall far away.

That was the tricky part about victimology: it wasn't always clear how the puzzle fit together until long after the fact, if at all.

And there weren't any big-foam-finger clues here, at least not that she could tell at this point. Which meant it was time to head back down to the city and hit the lab.

Letting herself out of Tanya's room, she stepped into the hallway. She heard radio traffic from the main room, and raised her voice to call, "Hey Bert, can you—"

Movement flashed in her peripheral vision and a heavy blow slammed into her from behind, driving her to her knees. *Ambush!*

Panic flared at the sight of a man dressed in dark clothes standing over her, his face obscured by shadows.

Part of her recorded details—*six foot, shaved head, athletic*—while another had her shouting, "Help! They're in the station!"

Her body reacting more from training than thought,

she tucked and rolled, then lashed out with a foot. She connected and her attacker fell back with a curse. But before she could follow up, the lights went out, plunging the hallway into pitch darkness.

"Come on!" a voice called from farther down the hall. "Forget about the stuff. The fire'll take care of these two, along with everything else."

Fire? Heart hammering with new terror, Gigi screamed, "Bert? Help!"

It was a mistake; her attacker oriented and slammed her aside. She swung another kick, but didn't connect with anything, and moments later feet pounded away from her.

A door slammed, and then there were two dull thuds. Seconds later, she heard the crash of breaking glass on either side of her, behind several of the closed bunkroom doors, one of them Tanya's.

Then there was an ominous *whoomping* sound that had her instincts sparking with terror as she identified the sounds: the man had thrown Molotov cocktails into the dorm rooms!

Worse, she could see the orange glow through the exit-door windows, smell it on the thickening air.

Atavistic fear flared and she froze in place, blanking on everything except the insidious crackle and yellow-orange glow. Her brain jammed, and all she could think was: *impossible*. This wasn't happening, couldn't be happening.

Except it was.

"Help! Fire!" She screamed it so loud that her throat went instantly raw. The pain snapped her back to reality, adrenaline cleared her head, and the two together got her moving, fast.

She remembered seeing extinguishers, didn't know where they were, remembered seeing smoke alarms and sprinklers, didn't know why they weren't going off.

She lunged for the doors that led outside, but they didn't budge, not even when she twisted the deadbolt back and forth. They were jammed from the other side.

Forget about the stuff. The fire'll take care of these two, along with everything else.

Her stomach roiled. Oh, God. They were trapped, and she had missed something important. Something the men—there had to be more than two—would kill to protect.

The air was heavy with smoke, making her cough.

Her mind was jumbled with half-memorized crisis response protocols, terror, and the drive that made her one of the best at her job. She reeled back to Tanya's room and banged open the door, noticing too late that the knob burned her palm.

Flames roared greedily, leaping at her, and a wall of heat sent her staggering backward. Instead of providing an exit, the broken window fed oxygen to the flames that engulfed the bed and desk, curling the sketches to blackness and then racing toward her.

"No!" She reeled back and slammed the door. A rasping moan brought her whipping around. "Bert!"

With no light except for the unearthly glow of the fire that was spreading outside, along the building's too-dry exterior, she stumbled in the darkness, feeling her way to the door that led to the front room. The knob was warm but not scalding, so she pushed through, coughing when she tried to breathe the hot, smoke-laden air.

There were emergency lights on in the main room, but the fire outside was worse, licking past the level of the windows. She saw Bert sprawled in the corner near the men's room, but raced across the room and tried the front door first. It was locked.

Her pulse thudding so loudly it almost drowned out the fire's insidious crackle, she crouched over the older ranger, breathing the thinner air near the floor. He stirred and groaned, but wasn't fully conscious.

She checked his pulse; his skin was baking in the increasing burn of the air around them, but his heartbeat was sure and steady. "Bert? It's Gigi. It's going to be okay. You're going to be okay. I'm going to get us out of here." But how?

He stirred weakly, rolled onto his side, and started struggling to rise, but was clearly out of it, wobbly and incoherent, coughing wretchedly in the smoky air. She took off her windbreaker, draped it over his head and ordered, "Stay down."

She lurched to her feet and stumbled to the nearest window and wept when it didn't budge.

Heart hammering, fear jamming a hard lump in her throat, she felt along the counter, searching for a radio, an extinguisher, something—anything—that would help.

The air scorched her skin, and the roaring sound coming from behind her suggested that the bunkhouse was fully ablaze.

Her fingers brushed something fastened beneath the counter, and she nearly sobbed in relief when she recognized the butt of a shotgun, secured out of public sight but ready if needed. Her hands shook so badly that it took her several tries to yank it free, but she finally got it.

Staying low, she pumped it, took aim, and fired both barrels through the window.

The blasts deafened her, but she raced to the window, stuck her head through and screamed, "Blackthorn, help! *Fire!*"

Chapter Five

The gunshots and distant scream rang in Matt's ears like a nightmare. *Fire!*

He broke off in the middle of saying something to Tucker on the phone and spun toward the far window of the living room in his house, which was a short hike from the station.

His gut fisted at the sight of a sickly glow where the station's lights should have been.

In the split second it took him to process the shock, a dark figure streaked past in silhouette, brake lights flashed from a rolling vehicle he damn well hadn't heard pull up, and gravel spat as the culprits accelerated away. "Son of a *bitch!*"

"What's wrong?"

"Get whatever eyes you can on the access road and send men up here to Fourteen, a fire chopper if you can get one. Someone just lit the station and took off!"

Gigi's scream echoed in Matt's head as he jammed his radio on his belt and took off at a dead run.

As he skidded down the short path between his quarters and the station house, the ranger in him noted the wind strength and direction and hoped to hell the flames wouldn't jump to the nearby trees. The rest of him just saw a damned inferno where a T-shaped building should've been.

Flames shot up from the bunkhouse windows and roof, eating through the too-dry wood like it was fresh newspaper. The front wasn't yet fully consumed, but fiery fingers of yellow-orange twined along the logs and licked at the pitched roof.

For a second, Matt thought that he was too damn late. Then he caught movement at one of the windows and—*thank God*—heard Gigi call, "Blackthorn!"

He bolted for the spot just as a figure came through the broken window, movements slow and uncoordinated, body too big to be Gigi. Bert.

Matt surged forward to help, his mind locking on the awful knowledge that the bastards had lit his station and he hadn't been there to stop it.

"Grab him!" Gigi's voice was raspy, her eyes wet and afraid, but she was wholly focused on getting a woozy Bert out first. "Watch the glass. I had to shoot it out."

The window was shattered and jagged, the frame wedged shut by a narrow chunk of wood shoved into the top.

Murderous rage boiled through him, but he held himself in check as he helped Bert down, then tucked a shoulder under his arm to prop him up. "Come on," he said to her, holding out his free hand. "Jump down."

The air was barely breathable, the heat unbearable. It seared through his clothes and crisped his skin. Small cinders were starting to break loose and sail up into the sky.

Gigi slithered through the window in a practiced,

feet-first rush, but when she landed, staggered a few steps and went down on one knee, coughing.

He caught her by the arm and hauled her up, then started half-dragging, half-carrying both of them away from the blaze.

She leaned into him, gasping for air, trying to get out information between her ragged breaths. "White guy, maybe six foot, one-eighty...said something about 'the stuff'...evidence..." She stopped dead and yanked away with a gasp, eyes going wide in shock. "The *picture!*"

"Who—" He broke off when she whirled and ran back toward the station. Blood congealing, Matt bellowed, "Gigi, damn it, *no!*"

"I know who he is!" She vaulted back through the window.

"Gigi!"

"Go." Bert pulled away from him and stood swaying. "You go get her. I'll call it in."

"I already did." Matt yanked his radio off his belt and handed it over. "Tucker's probably still on the channel." Then he took off, running back into the fire after a crazy woman.

He was still a dozen paces away when something crashed inside, and flames exploded through the broken window. The fire had spread to the main room.

"Gigi!" He didn't stop to think or plan, just boosted himself through the window feet-first like she had, managing to avoid the worst of the jagged points in a practiced move from another lifetime.

"Matt! Over here!"

He landed, crouched low and cursed viciously when he saw that she was down, pinned beneath a chunk of counter that had shifted when part of the roof caved in. The fire hadn't yet reached that far, leaving her in a small pocket of safety.

A small and rapidly diminishing pocket.

His mind spun and panic threatened, but he pushed through it and bolted for her, dodging a burning beam and stretching over the tilted counter to yank a small extinguisher from its wall rack.

"Cover your eyes!" When she complied, he hit several small hot spots near her with short blasts of the extinguisher, adding powdery clouds and more smoke to the already foul air.

Coughing, he wedged his shoulder under the edge of the counter and levered it up a few inches. "Go!" He had to bite back a groan when something ripped low down in his left side, where the scar tissue was thick and uncompromising. It burned like hell.

"I'm out!" She dragged herself up, clutching something to her chest.

"Come on!" They staggered toward the window. He boosted her out first. "Run. I'm right behind you."

Of course she didn't go anywhere, damn her, just turned back and reached for him as he came through. Not willing to take any more chances with her, he caught her by the waist, slung her over his shoulder and headed away from the fire.

Her wadded jacket—she went back for her freaking *windbreaker?*—was caught between them as she squirmed and thumped his lower back with her fists, making him wince.

Pissed off and running on way more adrenaline than he wanted to admit, he growled, "Quit it."

"Let me down!"

There was no sign of Bert, but he had moved her vehicle and the three remaining park service Jeeps well out of the range of the fire.

Matt headed toward the cars, dumped her next to her SUV and loomed over her. "What in the *hell* were you thinking, going in there like that?"

She glared right back and opened her mouth to snarl something at him, but he didn't give her a chance. He couldn't listen to an explanation he knew he wouldn't like, couldn't stand the fear and anger, the raging emotions he hadn't felt in years, hadn't ever wanted to feel again.

Overwhelmed with relief that she was okay and fury that she was making him feel things when all he wanted was to be left alone, he closed in on her, used his body to push her up against the SUV. And kissed the hell out of her.

GIGI'S SMARTER SELF would have ducked the kiss, but her smarter self also wouldn't have gone back into a burning building after a piece of evidence.

She almost hadn't made it out.

Blackthorn had saved her life.

Oh, God.

Reaction would set in later, she knew. For now there was only the heat of relief and the pounding burn of adrenaline, which redirected itself the instant his lips touched hers.

The spark that had ignited the first moment she saw him detonated in an instant, decimating her self-control. She gave in to her primal instincts and kissed him back.

He groaned approval and took it deeper.

His mouth seared hers with flames that had nothing to do with arson. He pressed her back against the door of her ride so she felt him, hard and hot and male, with every inch of her body.

Sizzles raced along her skin and beneath it; electricity flowed in her veins and gathered at the points where their bodies aligned.

She gripped his forearms and felt his anger, slid her hands to his shoulders and felt his control slipping. Hers was long gone. She was reckless, wanton, only peripherally aware of the world around them.

The kiss went on and on, until her pulse throbbed and her blood roared in her ears, sounding like the race of an engine.

An engine.

They jerked apart just as headlights speared through the darkness, jolting crazily when the driver gunned the SUV over a hummock.

The vehicle caught air, bounced hard, and swerved into the parking area with a spray of gravel, coming to a rest with its headlights pinned on Gigi. The engine wasn't even fully dead before the doors flew open. Tucker sprang out and rushed toward them with Jack Williams right behind him.

She wasn't sure which was worse: that she had been kissing Blackthorn in the middle of a crisis, or that she resented the interruption. But who would have guessed that Ranger Surly could kiss like that?

Her senses boiled and desire bounded through her with the thick, heavy beat of her heart. She could have died.

Which she hadn't, thanks to him.

The detectives advanced on Blackthorn, who squared off to meet them. He was sweaty and soot-streaked, and his uniform shirt was torn and burned along one side, the skin beneath abraded and angry. And he had lost his hat. Without it, he stopped looking like a cowboy throwback and started looking more like a security professional. Which, she supposed, he was in a way.

"Everyone's out," the ranger reported, voice rasping. Behind him, the station was fully ablaze, sending a thick column of dark smoke into the sky.

Tucker's eyes fixed on Gigi, dark with concern. "You okay?"

She was still pressed flat against her vehicle, and hoped to hell she didn't look as thoroughly kissed as she felt.

Taking a deep breath that did very little to settle the churning in her stomach, she pushed away from the SUV and tried to find some semblance of her professional self.

Looking down, she said, "Well, I think these pants are shot, but the rest of me should be salvageable."

Tucker relaxed a little. "Good to hear. Alyssa made me promise to bring you back down to the city in one piece."

"Then take her with you now and keep her there," Blackthorn said tightly. "She went back into the damn building for her coat."

She rounded on him, arousal souring at the sight of

his face set in hard, uncompromising lines. He was only a few paces away, but it suddenly felt like miles.

And he was trying to get her off the scene. Off the case.

She bristled. "I needed—"

Two low-flying planes roared suddenly overhead, drowning her out. The surrounding rock had shielded their approach, but now amplified the propeller noise as the planes skimmed low and dropped their payloads of gritty reddish fire suppressant.

The first load hit the station, dousing a large portion of the flames. The second painted a barrier line between the fire and the trees immediately downwind, snuffing the few small fires that had been started by flying sparks.

Radio static echoed, and a stocky figure stepped into the distant reaches of the headlight wash to wave at the planes. "Right on target," Bert said into his radio. "Thanks for making the detour."

His voice echoed strangely, coming from the receiver in Tucker's vehicle, but Gigi was reassured by the sound.

They were all out, all okay. That was what mattered. Not the kiss, how much faster Blackthorn had recovered, or the fact that he was trying to get rid of her now.

"Okay, it was a stupid move," she admitted. "But I think you'll agree that the payoff was worth it." Turning to Tucker and Jack, she said, "The guy who knocked me down said something about the fire taking care of 'everything,' which suggests that Tanya got her hands on something they want to keep off the radar. And when I was in her room, I found this hidden in a book."

She scooped her windbreaker up off the ground, dug in the pocket and pulled out the evidence bag holding Tanya's worn sketch. Both the bag and the sketch were worse for wear, but she could still make out the guy sitting in front of the waterfall.

She offered the evidence to Tucker. "Call me crazy, but that looks like Jerry Osage to me."

Osage had been killed during a jailbreak a few years earlier…one that had freed terrorist mastermind al-Jihad and sparked a flurry of terrorist activity in Bear Claw City. Although Osage had seemed to be an innocent by-stander, the new rash of attacks could mean otherwise… And if that was the case, they weren't just dealing with aggravated assault. They might be looking for a terrorist cell.

Chapter Six

Matt cursed under his breath as Tucker took the evidence bag and stared at the sketch, brows drawn together.

Jack looked over his shoulder and whistled. "I'd say Gigi-girl did some serious homework on old cases in Bear Claw."

His too-familiar tone got under Matt's skin the same way Gigi had, leaving him stirred up and pissed off.

Kissing her had been an impulsive move, an effort to burn off some of the fear and frustration that had been riding too high in his bloodstream, but he was the one who'd wound up burned. Her sharp, enticing flavor was branded on his neurons, the feel of her imprinted on every part of his body that had come into contact with hers.

Instead of leveling him off, kissing her had only made things worse.

"It's Osage," Tucker confirmed. "I'd put money on it. If I remember the story right, he moved out here to be with his girlfriend, who was a competitive skier of some sort. We never followed up on her because he looked like collateral damage." He glanced at Gigi. "Impressive."

Her eyes lit a little, but she stayed on task. "Bert

mentioned how most of the rangers who request isolated postings are trying to get away from something."

She walked the detectives through her thought process, but Matt was only half listening, his mind hung up on what Bert had said. Not just because he wondered whether she had asked about him—and, if so, what Bert might have said—but because he wasn't sure he knew the answer anymore.

For a long time, he had believed he came out to Fourteen because out in the backcountry he could contribute without being on the front lines. And because he didn't need anybody but himself.

Over the past few months, though, he had found himself making the trip down into the city more and more often. And feeling restless, edgy, the way he used to get when his subconscious was trying to tell him that he had missed an important connection.

But although he didn't know what he was looking for these days, or what it meant, he knew for damn sure that it wasn't an overly impulsive crime-scene analyst who seemed to want to play cop.

"Good work." Jack gave her a one-armed hug. "I mean it. Seriously impressive."

Matt had to fight not to growl. Or think that the detective would look better without that arm.

She returned the friendly embrace. "The profile was your idea. If you hadn't suggested it, I might've just gone straight home from the crime scene."

If she had, Matt thought, he would have been in the station when the arsonists showed up, and she never would have been endangered. But they also wouldn't have known about the Osage connection, which could prove to be a critical break in the case.

Damn it.

"You going to put together a task force?" Jack asked Tucker.

"That's the chief's call, but we should definitely hit up Fairfax and his people. They're the ones who rooted out the embedded terrorists within the ARX Prison and the Bear Claw P.D. If there's a connection to Osage, they'll find it."

Gigi said, "I'd like to be in on the task force, if there winds up being one."

Jack nodded. "You can ride with me."

Matt's gut churned, especially when Tucker didn't immediately turn down the offer. He cleared his throat. "No offense, but I don't think that's such a good idea."

She flicked him a cool glance. "Prefacing that with 'no offense' doesn't make it any less insulting. Lucky for me, you don't get a vote here."

The fact that he even *wanted* a damn vote went to show how off-track he'd gotten. He turned to Tucker. "You can't seriously be considering this. She's just an analyst."

Jack snorted. "She's also a sniper-level marksman, a seriously dirty street fighter, and a better than decent security-system hacker. She's been doing a couple of ride alongs per week with me, sometimes more."

A pit opened up in Matt's gut. He looked down at her, eyes narrowing. "You've got a badge?"

"Not yet, but I'm working on it." There was a flash of pride beneath her answer. "Denver's piloting an accelerated crisis response program aimed at analysts. I'm in line for one of the first slots."

Crisis response. He wasn't sure if he said the words aloud, or just thought them, but either way they sounded like a curse, and put a nasty, slippery knot in his gut. "You're kidding."

Anger blazed in her eyes, but beneath it, he thought he caught a look of hurt. "I can take care of myself. And what do you care, anyway?"

He didn't. He shouldn't.

"You're right. Sorry." He touched the air near his temple—where the brim of his hat would have been if he hadn't lost it in the fire—and said, "I'll let you guys do the cop thing. Give a shout if you need anything."

Then he turned and headed for where Bert was organizing the volunteers into teams to search the surrounding scrub for hot spots.

They all had jobs to do, and he had come out to Station Fourteen precisely to avoid conversations—and frustrations—like this.

GIGI WOKE UP THE NEXT morning with the bedclothes tangled around her legs, her lips tingling and her mind awash in half-remembered dreams of glittering green eyes.

Banishing the memories—and the warm churn they brought—she blinked at her surroundings. The short-term rental had come furnished in Early Ski Bum, complete with old wooden poles tacked on the wall. Some days she woke up, looked around and thought, *What am I doing here?*

Today was one of those days. She liked Bear Claw well enough, but she wasn't much of a skier.

Unlike Tanya, she thought, who appeared to have quit after Jerry Osage's death.

That was enough to get her up and moving. But it also got her thinking again about the fire. And Blackthorn.

She had held herself together until she got home last night and then let herself have a good cry, needing to get the fear and the shakes out of her system so she would be clear-headed today.

In the light of day, though, it was even more patently obvious that she had been dumb.

Yeah, she'd gained major points with the cops by making the Jerry Osage connection, but that didn't change the fact that she had been reckless, maybe even showing off a bit. And she could have died. Probably would have if Blackthorn hadn't come after her.

The idea of being killed in the line wasn't a new concept. She wasn't stupid; she knew what she was getting into in fighting for a place in hazardous response.

But on a response team, she would be working with the best available information and wearing serious protective gear. And, most importantly, she wouldn't be working solo. She would have a team surrounding her, or at the very least a partner to watch her back.

A partner would have been scouting the bunkhouse while she went through Tanya's room; a partner would have noticed the men outside and sounded the alarm, and the fire never would've gotten started.

And a partner wouldn't have pinned her against her ride and kissed her to the point that her priorities flew right out of her head.

Which she so couldn't think about right now.

Instead, she headed for the P.D. and let herself into the basement complex that housed Bear Claw's crime lab.

She was early enough that she had assumed she would be the first one in, but Alyssa was already in the outer office, hammering away at one of the computer stations.

Bear Claw's head analyst scowled. "I thought I told you to take the day off. Go home."

Gigi returned the frown. "I thought I came here to fill in for Maya so you could take it easy while Baby McDermott gestates. Go home yourself."

"I'm not the one who nearly got crispy crittered yesterday."

"I…" Realizing she wasn't as steady as she had thought, Gigi held up a hand. "Give me a couple of hours before we talk about it, okay? I need some time to process."

Process evidence. Process events. Think about that damned kiss.

She traded her light, subtly studded blazer for her lab coat and headed for the inner lab door. And she felt Alyssa's worried eyes follow her as she pushed through into the first of the lab's interconnected rooms.

The main space housed workbenches, hulking machines, and a row of evidence lockers. On the far side, an airlocked door led to the "clean" rooms, where the more technical procedures—DNA testing, chromatography and other assays—were carried out under negative pressure, fume hoods and other fail-safes.

The whole place was well-lit, painted a creamy white,

and hung with brightly colored posters and prints that ranged from the ridiculous to the macabre. But as far as Gigi was concerned, it still felt like a basement. And for a second, she really, really wanted to be back in her Denver lab, with its wide windows and view of the mountain-flanked city.

Or, better yet, on a deserted tropical island with a lifetime supply of Twix, Caesar salads with full-fat dressing and movies on demand.

Might have to rethink Bert's whole "get away from the world" theory. She was a social creature by nature, but certain topics made her want to head for unoccupied territory. Having people worried about her was one of them.

She got that caring for someone and worrying about them went together. Her mom was six years cancer-free, but Gigi still got nervous when recheck time came around. And she'd found herself watching Alyssa too closely at times over the past few weeks, her instincts pinging a warning every time she thought the mother-to-be might be overexerting herself.

When it came to her work, though, friends and family worrying about her too often made her feel like they didn't think she was good enough to do the job. She had worked her butt off learning to fight harder and shoot better than the other people in the running for the accelerated program, but her family thought it was a phase, and a good chunk of her coworkers still looked at her and saw a lab rat who dressed with a bit of flair.

Or, as in Blackthorn's case, a city slicker who didn't belong anywhere near the backcountry. Even once she'd proved to him that she could hold her own, he'd wanted to shut her out of the action.

She looked around and scowled at the realization that she was exactly where he wanted her—shut up in the lab while he and his rangers searched the foothills. But logically, she could be more use here than there. For the moment, anyway.

So she got to work.

Cassie had collected physical evidence from Tanya at the hospital and started running it last night—the rape kit didn't show any evidence of sexual assault, but there had been some skin under the ranger's fingernails, and she'd had a few defensive wounds. The DNA was processing and Cassie had printed out photos of Tanya—mostly close-ups of her injuries—and stuck them on the magnetic wipe board, where they joined a copy of the Jerry Osage sketch and some earlier, candid photos of Tanya.

Gigi took a long look at Tanya's face in the hospital photos—still pretty and patrician beneath the narrow bruise running along her jaw and the gash on her opposite temple. Then her hands, which were bruised along the knuckles, and splinted at one thumb. Her nails were short and neat, practical. And she had fought back.

That resonated. But it was the last picture in the line that had Gigi pausing. It was a middle-distance shot taken through the door into Tanya's hospital room. A uniformed officer sat by the door, but it was the man inside the room who was the focus of the shot. Cassie had caught Jim Feeney perched on the edge of a visitor's chair, with most of his body angled over Tanya as he held her hand in both of his. Although his face was partly turned away from the camera, the edge of his profile read "grief" and the set of his jaw conveyed "I'm going to stay for as long as it takes"…but the weary lines of his rangy body said he wasn't sure his being there was going to make a difference.

Gigi touched the picture and swallowed to loosen her too-tight throat.

Initially, she had been committed to the case because she was committed to every case that came through her hands, especially when it was a violent crime. More, the victim was a woman close to her age, working in a male-dominated field. There was kinship there. Sympathy.

Another layer had been added when she tangled with Blackthorn, making her determined to show him what she was capable of.

Now, though, she shifted all the way onto the treacherous footing of involvement…which could either help or hinder an analyst.

Usually, with her, it helped.

"So get to work," she told herself.

In the evidence locker, she hesitated over the pencil sketch of Jerry Osage, but decided to wait on processing it. Copies had been sent around, and the rangers were going to check out a couple of the depleted waterfalls in their sectors and see if they could match the background, but she had a feeling they had gotten what they were going to get out of the sketch.

Tanya's clothing was bagged and tagged, as were the hikers' duds, but Tanya had been moved around so much that trace was likely to be a nightmare, and the hikers were incidental. Of the stuff Gigi herself had collected at the scene, there were really only two things that sparked her instincts: the feather and the radio.

She started with the radio, on the theory that if Tanya had been attacked somewhere else, the radio smashed there, then her attackers had probably been the ones to move it. Which might mean they had handled it, maybe even left a print or two.

An hour later, though, she didn't have much. She had gotten three smudged partials that matched Tanya's prints, a couple of hits for each of the other rangers— which was consistent with what Blackthorn had said about the radios being up for grabs—and one really smeared thumb print that didn't belong to any of them, but had retained almost zero detail. She could make out part of one whorl and guess at a couple of the other landmarks, but it wouldn't hold up to any sort of database search.

That was usually the score when it came to crime-scene analysis: five percent big foam fingers, ninety-five percent packing peanuts.

"Let's see if the tech-heads can make anything out of you," she said to the smashed radio. "Maybe they can resuscitate you and get your GPS to cough up something interesting." She rebagged it, put her name on the next line down, and logged it back into the evidence locker.

Then she went for the bag with Blackthorn's shirt in it. And caught herself hesitating.

For crap's sake, Lynd, it's just a shirt. You can process it without picturing him naked. Half naked. Whatever.

She did her best, anyway. It helped that Blackthorn

had ended the evening by trying to run her off the case again. It was really too bad the fates had matched such a truly excellent body with that superior—and totally annoying—attitude.

Remembering his look of horror when he'd heard she wanted to be a critical response cop made it easier to pull the uniform shirt out of the bag, spread it out and start going over it, working her way toward the chest pocket.

His name tag was still in place, the engraved letters spelling out *Matthew H. Blackthorn*. She spent way too much effort not staring at it and wondering about the *H*. Under other circumstances, it would have made her nervous to realize how much she was thinking about him. As it was, she gave herself a pass and called it what it was: a defense mechanism.

If she was thinking about Blackthorn's great ass and borderline personality, she didn't have to think about the fire…or worry about how she was going to smooth things over with Alyssa.

They were good friends and clicked on a level that Gigi didn't connect with many other people on, but now they were heading square into an argument they had skirted around once or twice before, knowing they weren't going to agree.

She was just teasing the feather out of the shirt pocket when the door swung open and Alyssa came through, expression set. She was moving slowly in the final week or so of her pregnancy, but that only added to the impression that she was, in her own way, as much of an immovable force as her husband.

Gigi could be a solid wall when she needed to,

though. And if her family hadn't managed to get her to stick with the lower-risk analyst's position, her new best friend didn't have a prayer.

Alyssa lowered herself to a swivel chair, put her feet on the waist-high desk that ran the perimeter of the room, folded her hands atop the curve of her belly...and fixed Gigi with a look. "Officially, I'm impressed with the drive and dedication you showed last night. That will go in your file. Unofficially, though, I've decided that being your friend isn't for the faint of heart." She paused, and a crack of hurt and concern showed through. "What were you *thinking*, Gigi? You could've died."

"I know that." She met Alyssa's baffled stare. "But right then, all I was thinking about was getting that sketch. It was evidence, and my job is to collect the evidence, period. Not to mention that 'identify the goal and go for it' is pretty much a family motto." She tried a smile. "I think it got cribbed by a sneaker company in edited form: *Just do it.*"

"This isn't a joke, damn it. How do you think I felt, sitting down here while Tucker blasted up into the park, with no clue whether you were okay or not? And then to find out what you *did* do? God." She knotted her fingers together. "I was up half the night thinking about what it would've been like to have you lying in a hospital bed like Tanya, or worse."

"Sorry." The word was an automatic knee-jerk response, but Gigi followed it up with, "Seriously, I'm sorry. I know you care, and I..." She was going to say "I appreciate your concern," but that was a total brush-off line and Alyssa deserved better. The thing was, she *did* appreciate the concern...but it also made her feel squirrelly and trapped, made the basement walls seem suddenly closer than they had been last week, or even an hour ago.

"You can't promise to stay out of trouble," Alyssa finished for her, "because you're hardwired to play hero."

"I'm not playing anything," she said, trying to make her friend understand. "This is my *life* we're talking about—not just the safety part of it, but the living part of it, too. If I compromise on this, I'm giving up part of what makes me...*me*."

"I just want you to be a little more careful. You admit that going back into the station was stupid, right?"

"Now? Yes. But that doesn't happen often." And there had been extenuating circumstances. Distractions in the form of one Matthew H. Blackthorn. She didn't say that, though, partly because she didn't want to go there, and partly because it was no excuse. There would always be distractions during a crisis. "The thing is, I can't promise that I won't make the same mistake again." She paused, trying to choose words that would get across to Alyssa something she hadn't yet gotten even her family to understand. "If I get picked for the program and make it through the training—"

"You mean 'when.' Because if you're not at the top of the list, your bosses in Denver are a bunch of idiots."

"Okay, 'when' I get on a team, my teammates are going to be depending on me to react appropriately, no matter what's going on around me. And although there's lots more sitting-and-waiting-and-planning than you'd think, there will also be times that I'm going to need to prioritize the job over my own safety. I'm not stupid and I'm not suicidal…but I can't be as cautious as the people who care about me want me to be."

People like Alyssa and her other analyst friends, who didn't get why she needed to escape from pure after-the-fact labwork. And like her mother and sisters, who still sent her job listings from their universities, somehow thinking that teaching and doing were the same thing.

"Are you sure the program is going to be right for you?"

"Of course."

"Why?"

"What do you mean, 'why?'" Gigi would have rolled her eyes, but she didn't want to minimize Alyssa's concerns—she just wanted to get at something. Choosing her words carefully, she said, "I want to get into the program because the members of the hazardous response teams are the ultimate cops, and their work is the ultimate adrenaline rush." Which wasn't far off from the answer she had given the selection committee during her interview. More, it was the truth. Her parents had given her every opportunity to excel, and she intended to do exactly that. Maybe not the way they had intended, but still.

"And you're happiest when you're the ultimate?"

"It's not about being happy or unhappy, it's about establishing myself. Once I've done that, then I can think about the other stuff in life—a husband, family, that sort of thing." But that rang false, and honesty forced her to add, "Not that I'm likely to do the family thing if I'm with HRT. Not many guys can deal with having a wife who's right out on the front lines."

"Especially one who'd jump back into a burning

building because she forgot her jacket." But Alyssa paused, then shook her head. "I think you'd be surprised. More guys than you might imagine are okay with stuff like that. Or at least some of them can get themselves square with it if that's what it takes to make things work." She sent a speculative look. "Tucker said Matt was pissed about you going back in there."

"I can't totally blame him. He was the one who had to carry me out."

Whether thanks to hormones or a shared desire not to turn this into a friendship-leveling fight, Alyssa let herself be diverted. Unfortunately, she veered in a direction Gigi had been hoping to avoid. "He *carried* you?"

Gigi flushed and focused on the feather, dropping it into the bottom half of a plastic Petri dish and slipping it into position beneath the bright field of a light microscope. "He was probably just making sure I didn't double back again."

But Alyssa wasn't buying it. "Tucker said there were vibes. What's going on with you two?"

"Me and Tucker? Nothing, I swear."

"Ha ha. Very funny. Spill."

"There's nothing *to* spill." At least nothing she was ready to talk about. "Blackthorn is rude, temperamental, arrogant, cynical and…" She trailed off because that wasn't fair. He was all of those things, yes, but he was also tough, capable and fiercely committed to his job and the people who worked for him.

"And?"

"And I'm not interested." Gigi made a few notes, switched the scope from 100x to 400x and looked again. No big foam finger yet.

"There's a difference between 'not interested' and 'don't want to be interested.'"

"Fine. I don't want to be interested. Aside from the know-it-all attitude, the guy's got some pretty serious layers, and I'm not into layers. I prefer men where what you see is what you get."

Alyssa made a "no kidding" face, but then sobered. "I could tell you about a couple of those layers if you want."

She hesitated, but shook her head. "No. Don't." She had her path charted, her goals set. A pleasant detour was one thing. A cross-country trip on dirt roads without a map or GPS was another. The first one was fun. The second could go really wrong.

Increasing the magnification another notch, she got up close and personal with some little alien-type creatures that were crawling on the feather. *Ew.*

Alyssa pressed further. "Look, Tucker has known Matt a long time, and says he's never seen him act the way he was acting last night over you. And maybe I haven't known you all that long, but I've never seen you do the verbal duck-and-weave like this before. That tells me there's something there…or could be."

"No." Gigi shook her head. "I'm sorry, but no. The timing is…well, it's wrong. That's all."

"You're the one who pointed out that moving back to Denver wasn't the same as taking a trip to Mars."

"It's not the logistics, it's…" Everything. She made another note, caught herself looking at the shiny name tag again. "You know how I've told you about how my family lives life full blast? Well, the same thing goes in the relationship department. It's all or nothing.

Consuming. The emotions…there's no room left for anything else except the emotions. And when it crashes, the debris field goes on for miles." She couldn't risk something like that. Not when she was so close to nailing a slot in the accelerated program.

Alyssa narrowed her eyes. "Who was he?"

"What are you, an analyst or something?" But Gigi lifted a shoulder. "It doesn't matter. It was a long time ago." She could barely picture him now, in fact. All she knew was that for one glorious, tumultuous summer during college, he had been her whole universe. And when he left, she had crashed hard, nearly washing out of her senior year in the process. She had graduated, but had been the only one of her four sisters to miss getting summa cum laude honors. "What matters is that I let everything else around me take a backseat to a guy, and I can't afford to do that right now."

Maybe not ever. Miserable wasn't a good color on her.

"I think first love is supposed to be awful like that," Alyssa pointed out. "You're all grown up now. It'll feel different."

"Yeah. It's worse. After Matt kissed me—" She broke off.

"Hel-lo. He *kissed* you?" Alyssa's feet thumped to the floor. "Was this before or after he carried you out of a burning building?"

Gigi pressed a gloved hand to her lab-coat-covered stomach in a gesture that did zilch to settle the jitters. "After. I dreamed about him last night."

What was it about him? He wasn't anything like the men she usually gravitated toward. *Opposites might attract,* her grandmother liked to say, *but they don't stick for the long haul.* Was this some sort of belated teenaged rebellion on the part of her subconscious? Had her hormones latched on to him because, like her job choices, he went against the grain? She didn't have a clue.

All she knew was that even though he had done his Ranger Surly routine last night, the thought of him still sent hot and cold shivers racing through her body. And that, more than anything, warned her that there wasn't any sort of compromise to be had. She couldn't get involved with him partway, couldn't have the sort of "just having fun" interlude that had once been as natural to her as breathing.

"I can't go there," she said, more to herself than to Alyssa. "I'm on the verge of my big break. I need to concentrate on that. Besides, even if I were inclined to get involved with someone right now—which I'm not—I need someone who respects my career choices. Which he doesn't. He made that perfectly clear last night."

"About that—" Alyssa began, but the ring of the lab's landline interrupted her. She checked the display, and her expression softened as she answered, "Hello, Mc-Dermott, Homicide. What's the word?" She listened for a second before her expression shifted. "Really? Wow. Okay. Come on down."

Gigi went on alert. "What's going on?"

"The P.D. is forming a new task force, and I've been officially asked to release you to them for the time being. You and your new partner will both be deputized for the duration."

The words banged around in Gigi's head for a

moment, refusing to compute. She was thrilled about being tapped for the task force, but… "What do you mean, deputized? And what new partner? I ride with Jack."

"Not anymore you don't," an all-too-familiar voice said from the doorway behind her.

She froze. Oh, no. Tucker hadn't. He wouldn't.

Would he?

The look Alyssa sent her—part sympathy, part dare—said that he would, and he had.

Gigi's body washed hot, then cold, then back to hot again. She turned slowly, not ready to face Blackthorn, especially not now, when her usual defenses were gone, stripped away by girl talk.

But there he was, and she was going to have to deal with him. And with the way her body lit up at the sight of him filling the doorway. His presence seemed larger somehow down here in the rapidly shrinking confines of the basement.

Heat speared through her, tempting and tantalizing, and making her think of hot sheets and waking with his taste on her lips.

Maybe her awareness was so thoroughly heightened because she knew him now, had kissed him, been kissed by him. Or maybe it was the jeans and short-sleeved white button-down he wore in place of his tan-and-green uniform, making him look different, somehow less aloof.

But then he shifted away from the doorframe, and her eyes zeroed in on his worn leather belt. Or, rather, on the badge and holster that rode together on his left hip.

Deputized, Alyssa had said, which accounted for the

badge, with its familiar Bear Claw P.D. insignia. But that didn't explain why the holster bore LAPD markings… or why, when he saw her staring, his expression went brittle and he looked away.

Gigi's instincts fired in all directions, telling her something big was going on, but not what, or how she was supposed to handle it.

In the end, she said, stupidly, "But you're a ranger."

He looked back at her, one corner of his sculpted mouth kicking up with zero amusement. "I am now. Before that, I had a decade on the job. Now I guess I'm doing an encore, thanks to budget cuts and the fact that Tucker knew I was going to be working this case with or without sanction." But his expression said that was only half of the story.

She had a feeling she knew the rest. "I don't need a babysitter."

"Nobody said you did. And speaking of babies…" He looked past her to Alyssa and mock-glared. "I thought you were supposed to be taking it easy."

Hello, subject change. Gigi didn't know what to make of that, what to make of any of it. But she couldn't take her eyes off his weapon, which was an older Sig Sauer, a warhorse of an automatic.

"My darling wife is *supposed* to be on her way home," Tucker said, coming up behind Blackthorn to shoot Alyssa a stern look.

"I'm sitting," she said primly, but with a "don't push me" look in her eyes. "So catch me up. Where do we stand on the Jerry Osage connection?"

Gigi only half listened as Tucker summarized what his contacts had come up with so far, which was that yes,

Jerry's murder had been the catalyst for Tanya packing up her skis and becoming a ranger, but no, there didn't seem to be any connection between the two cases. "Nobody's taking any bets, though," he said, "which is why we're mobilizing a joint task force with the park service, including our newest deputies." He raised an eyebrow in Gigi's direction. "You on board? Ready to get deputized so you and your partner can head out?"

Deputized. Partner. This wasn't happening.

Was it?

Her better sense screamed for her to take a second to think it through, turn it down. There was no way in hell she and Blackthorn would survive being partnered up. He was going to try to rein her in, marginalize her, and she was going to be tempted to be twice as reckless as usual just to prove she could.

But she nodded to Tucker. "Lay it on me."

Because, really, there was no way she could turn down the opportunity. It meant she would be working the case on an official basis while shadowing a ten-year veteran of the LAPD. It was going to look great on her résumé. As for the rest of it…well, she would deal. She was a Lynd, she could handle anything.

Besides, maybe she would get lucky. Maybe he'd be such a jerk that her blossoming crush would wither and die.

"Here. Catch." Tucker tossed her a badge like the one Blackthorn wore on his belt: a Bear Claw P.D. shield with the serial number blank.

She snagged it on the fly, and took a deep breath to settle the sudden churn of excitement in her belly as Tucker led her through an abbreviated swearing-in and ran through what she could and couldn't do out in the field. "As for the rest of it," he finished, "just ask Captain Blackthorn here, former leader of SWAT Team Four out of East L.A."

Gigi's heart *thudda-thudded* and the bottom dropped out of her stomach, as though she had suddenly jumped onto an elevator headed straight up into the stratosphere. She stared at Blackthorn as a whole lot of clues suddenly lined up.

Blackthorn was SWAT, or had been. Not only that, he had been a team leader. The best of the best.

His face darkened. "Seriously, McDermott, don't call me that. And if you value your face, you won't get anyone *else* doing it, either." He glanced over at Gigi, though she couldn't read much in his expression.

She sucked in a shaky breath. "Blackthorn, I—"

"Call me Matt already," he interrupted. "Not Blackthorn. Not ranger. And not captain anything. Just Matt. Got it?"

She nodded, but wasn't capable of coherent speech as her brain finally assembled the four critical new facts and entered them into evidence:

Fact one: Blackthorn—or, rather, Matt—was a former über-cop.

Fact two: he outranked her. Even if she aced the accelerated program, it would be years before she could shoot for captain. And although logic said his old rank shouldn't matter here and now, it did.

Fact three: he looked incredible in street clothes, and he wore his gun and badge like they were a part of him that had been missing.

Fact four: she was in serious trouble. Because if there

was one thing a Lynd woman liked better than being the best at what she did, it was meeting a man who was even better.

Chapter Seven

Within about a minute of walking into the lab, Matt had decided that if Gigi at full throttle had put a serious scare in him, she was even more terrifying when shocked into silence. Worse, she was staring at him like he'd just grown a second head…or thrown a cape over his shoulders and whipped off his shirt again, this time to reveal superhero spandex.

Ah, crap. He hadn't seen this one coming. Maybe he should have, but he was seriously rusty on the man-woman stuff. And Gigi was…well, she wasn't like anyone else he'd ever met. Or kissed.

And, yeah, the kiss was going to be a problem; it had been since the moment he'd moved in, his body overriding his usual survival instincts. He didn't know how much further it would have gone if Tucker hadn't shown up, but the simple kiss had made him all too aware of how damn long it had been for him. She was hot—if unconventional—and he was horny, and he had decided that was a bad combination even before Tucker called to float the idea of them working together.

His first response had been a flat-out "No way in hell!" But Tucker had promised him that Gigi would be gone in thirteen days. The word from her home base was that they would need her one way or the other: either she would be heading for the academy or she would be covering for someone who was.

That was why sometime during the long hours Matt had spent staring at the ceiling of his bedroom, far too aware of Bert tossing and turning on the couch in the main room of his quarters, he had talked himself into going along with Tucker's plan. He had told himself that being deputized would get him smack in the loop, and it would mean he'd be stepping on fewer toes.

Really, though, there was only one real reason he was doing it: to keep Gigi from getting herself killed.

He had sworn off trying to fix people's lives, it was true. But given all the stuff that had gone down in the past twenty-four hours, and the fact that he knew damn well that she was going to keep herself square in the middle of the case, he hadn't been able to walk away. Not from her. Not from Tanya. And not from whatever was going on in his sector.

He could handle himself around Gigi for a couple of weeks. Or so he'd thought. But that was before he'd strapped the gun and badge back on, and things had gotten even weirder.

The moment he'd felt those familiar weights, old feelings came flooding back: the responsibility and connectedness; the knowledge that the whole damn world was riding right over his shoulder, breathing down on him…and the low-grade acid churn that said no matter how good he was, how much he planned things out, plugged gaps and covered contingencies, the odds were that he'd lose someone.

Worse, now Gigi was staring at him like she expected him to leap tall buildings and shoot laser beams from his eyes. Oh, she was trying to hide it, of course, but it was there.

This was a bad idea. He should back out now, head up to the mountains where he belonged, and join one of the search parties.

Or, better yet, go search on his own.

But if he did that, she'd be riding along with Jack Williams, who thought she'd make a hell of a cop.

At the thought, the churn got worse.

"How is this going to work?" she asked him, a reasonable question that put him back in the too-familiar role of calling the shots. He didn't kid himself, though. Soon enough the shock would wear off and the loose cannon would return.

"Security here in the P.D. is going to be ramped up until we know one way or another about the terrorist connection." That was a no-brainer, given that the building itself had been infiltrated once before. "But any time you want to be out in the field, you'll hit me up and we'll make arrangements to meet."

Her eyes narrowed. "News flash. You're supposed to be my partner, not my bodyguard."

"I'm the one with the gun." He patted his hip, wishing he had his damn shotgun instead. And wishing that the Sig didn't feel like such an old friend.

She rolled her eyes. "Hello? Sharpshooter here. My ACP is in my locker and I'm licensed to carry concealed."

"Hell." This just got better and better.

"If I could interject?" Alyssa said drily.

"Only if you're going to tell her not to go out without backup."

Gigi's expression went smug. "She's seen me shoot. The only time I hit the granny cutout was when I meant to. And I called it first."

"Which isn't the same thing as taking down another human being. Especially one that's shooting back and aiming to kill."

She didn't have a comeback for that one, just scowled at him.

"He's right," Alyssa said, "and what's more, you know it. Or you would if you took a breath and chilled for a second." Gigi transferred her glare, but Alyssa just blinked unperturbed, and continued, "Regardless of whether or not Tanya's attack and the arson were committed by al-Jihad's people, the cases are clearly connected to each other."

Tucker stepped in. "Gigi's attacker wanted to destroy something. Maybe there's a drug connection? There's been some buzz lately about a new product on the streets, and there have been a couple of really weird ODs." He paused. "And let's not forget about all those break-ins up at the upper-level ranger stations over the past few months. They could fit in somehow, too."

"Huh," Matt said. He hadn't gone there, but Tucker was right. It played.

"Whoever these guys are, and whatever they're after," Tucker continued, "the one Gigi saw has got to be seriously stressed."

Gigi scowled. "Having Alyssa do a detailed sketch of the back of his head isn't going to get us anywhere."

"He doesn't know that's all you saw, and the fire

made it on the news, so they probably know that you survived. Are you willing to bet they're not going to come after you to finish the job?"

"We could use me to lure—"

"Like hell," Matt growled over Tucker's calmer "Let's hold off on that."

Gigi drew breath to argue, but Alyssa lurched to her feet, getting their attention in a hurry. To Gigi, she said, "I want you to promise me you'll let the P.D. protect you. No sneaking off, and no ditching your backup. If you don't want to work with Matt, I'm sure Jack will trade."

"Hold on a minute—" Matt began.

"No, you hold on." To his surprise, Alyssa rounded on him, eyes stormy. "I don't care what you and Tucker cooked up. Gigi is my analyst, and she's right, I've seen her shoot. She's good. Better than good. In fact, she's good at just about everything she tries. She's also one of the most intuitive analysts I've ever worked with. Which means she doesn't need a babysitter—she needs someone who'll give her room to do her job. If you can't do that, whether because of your history, or because of what is or isn't going on between the two of you, then you need to step aside. I will *not* run the risk of someone getting hurt because you're wrangling when you should be watching out for each other."

Gigi's wince was almost comical. Almost.

Matt gritted his teeth, but Alyssa was right, he was riding on adrenaline and emotion, and that wasn't going to do any of them any good. He needed to get a freaking grip, and he needed to do it now. Because handing

Gigi off to Williams might make sense, but he couldn't do it.

"You don't have to worry about me," he said, flinching when he heard the words come out in his crisis-mode voice: calm and level, a total lie that covered up the other stuff inside. "Your call, Greta Grace."

He saw Alyssa mouth, *Greta Grace?* but kept his eyes locked on Gigi.

She made a face. "You call me that again, and I'll 'Captain Blackthorn' you so fast it'll make your head spin."

"Noted." But something inside him uncoiled a notch. "So we're good? Partners?" He thought about holding out a hand to shake, but stuck his thumbs in his belt loops instead.

"I don't know if I'd call us 'good,'" she said, voice going wry, "but yeah, partners. Largely because I need a bird expert, and I'd probably have to ask you for an intro anyway. You being a ranger and all."

"I already gave a buddy over at the university a heads up that we'd be there right after lunch." At her look, he shrugged. "The feather was in *my* shirt." And he'd been planning on working the case with or without a badge. Or a partner.

"Fine. Ready when you are." Gigi avoided his eyes as she moved past him to grab a fresh evidence bag and tweeze the feather into it.

"And you promise not to ditch him?" Alyssa pressed. When Gigi hesitated, she made big, mournful eyes. "You wouldn't want your oh-so-pregnant friend to spend another sleepless night worrying about you, right?"

Gigi winced. "No fair."

"I mean it."

"Okay. I swear. Pinkie swear, even." She sealed and signed the evidence bag, then slanted a look in Matt's direction. "Aren't you going to make him promise?"

"I'm not worried about him."

Maybe you should be, he thought. Not because he would ditch his partner, but because he wasn't in the zone anymore. And even when he had been, he'd failed, badly. But there was no point in bringing that up now, so he tipped his head toward the door. "Come on, partner. Let's go see a man about a feather."

She hooked the badge on her belt, tucked away the evidence bag, exchanged a few words with Alyssa about other pieces of evidence, and headed for what looked like a break room, calling over her shoulder, "Let me just grab my gun and we can go."

He winced, but didn't argue.

PARTNERS, GIGI THOUGHT, fighting not to hang on to the door handle as Matt sent his Jeep hurtling through the city like a madman.

A day ago, she would've thought he was driving like he was in the backcountry, heedless of traffic and signs. Now, though, she knew better: he was driving like he had a siren and wig-wag lights going, and he was hustling his team to a crisis call.

His jaw was set, his knuckles white, his bearing screamed *cop*…and her stomach was knotted with a mix of nerves and desire.

This was the guy she had seen last night when he was organizing the search, the one who blew her away, turned her on. Where Ranger Blackthorn had tried to lose himself in isolation, Captain Blackthorn was right there with her. And he was hurting.

He had fled to the backcountry to escape something that happened while he was on the job, she realized now. More than the scars, this was the unhealed wound.

"So," she said when he seemed content with silence. "What made you leave L.A.?"

He cut her a dark look. "Could we not do this right now?"

She knew she could run a Google search for it, but she wanted to hear it from him. Not just because it would be coming from the perspective of a team leader—a goal she hadn't yet even really admitted to herself—but because…well, because. "When, then?"

"Later."

"Which really means never."

"It means later. I say what I mean."

She thought about it, realized he'd withheld information, but never actually lied to her, at least not that she knew. "Fair enough. I can be patient."

He snorted, but the air lightened between them. A few blocks later, he unbent enough to say, "The arson investigators confirmed that they used Molotov cocktails in the bedrooms and kitchen, and gas around the exterior."

Her stomach gave a low-grade twinge, but she said only, "I keep trying to figure out what they were trying to get rid of. Whatever it was, either Tanya hid it well, or it wasn't in her bedroom."

"If it was in the station, it's gone now." He paused. "Maybe they just wanted to wipe out her connection to Jerry."

Which brought them back to the terrorists. "How would they know to look for that sketch? And why now?"

"No clue. And given that the search hasn't turned up Tanya's Jeep, never mind any radio parts, we probably won't know unless she wakes up." He took a corner so fast that the outside edge of the Jeep got light. Cursing under his breath, he got the vehicle back in line, and eased off on the gas. "Sorry."

Her fingers dug into the door handle, but she kept her voice mild. "Just get us there alive and without collateral damage, and we'll call it even."

She didn't blame him for being angry, would've respected him less if he hadn't been. And she already respected him far too much.

He fell silent, but kept the Jeep within ten of the legal limit for the rest of the drive out to the sprawling U.C. Bear Claw campus, where he weaved through interconnecting roads, bumped the vehicle up onto the curb in front of a big stone building and killed the engine in a No Parking zone.

His slanted look dared her to comment, but she just climbed out, plenty used to city cops in "get it done" mode. And as they headed up the stone steps of a big, museum-like building, walking shoulder-to-shoulder, she realized she was relating to him better on that level than she had as a ranger.

Up in the backcountry, he had stared off into the distance as he had watched over her, standing motionless on the ridgeline. Here at the outskirts of the city, he watched the corners and shadows and stayed on the move. His energy was different now—edgy and restless.

"Tell me about your bird guy," she said as they passed beneath a sign that read "Absalom Center of Environmental Studies" and went into the building.

"Ian Scott. He's a friend."

He said it simply, but she had a feeling there weren't many people he considered friends. Tucker, maybe. "Did you meet him rangering?"

"In college." He ignored her sidelong look and turned down a wide, waxed hallway that was weekend-empty, though the building had the faint vibe of life that said it wasn't totally deserted. "We had some classes together back in the day."

"Was he why you picked Bear Claw?"

"No. Maybe. I don't know." He pushed open a glass door with "Ornithology" stenciled in black. "What matters right now is that he's our best bet for a quick ID on that feather."

It all matters, she thought as she preceded him into an open office space that had a seemingly random assortment of cubicles, bird posters on the walls and the distinctive airlock door that led to a working lab.

The tall spider of a man who unfolded from behind a cluttered desk surprised Gigi. He wore jeans, rope sandals and a T-shirt with a picture of a big black bird, wings outstretched, that invited her to "hang with a cormorant," whatever that meant. His mid-brown hair brushed his shoulders and he had an abstract tribal tattoo encircling his throat.

Gigi liked him at first sight.

"Blackie!" He came toward them, arms outstretched

to first pump Matt's hand and then enfold him in a back-thumping hug. "It's about time you came down off that mountain of yours."

To her surprise, Matt returned a couple of shoulder slaps before he drew away. "Hey. I like my mountain."

"Not enough birds." As the ornithologist pulled back, he looked past Matt's shoulder and saw her, and his dark blue eyes lit appreciatively. "But who needs a flock when one will do nicely?" He held out a hand, as much inviting her into their familiar circle of two as he was offering to shake. "Dr. Ian Scott, at your service. But you'll call me Ian, of course."

"Gigi Lynd, CSI." She took his hand, let his fingers enfold hers and draw her closer.

"Sit, please." He scooped a pile of books off a visitor's chair with one hand, keeping hold of her with the other. "You're a crime scene analyst? Fascinating. I love the shows, you know."

She sat, perversely enjoying Matt's low growl. "Don't believe everything you see on TV. Those shows are more fiction than fact sometimes. Given the level of specialization required in the lab these days, lots of analysts are hired for their science backgrounds, not because they're cops. The TV shows tend to combine real jobs to make things more interesting."

"Of course," he said cheerfully. "Just like movie science. Total crap, but entertaining despite—and sometimes because of—the fact." Leaving Matt to roll his own chair from behind a computer workstation on the other side of the room, Ian sat back down at his desk opposite her, eyes gleaming. "So. Blackie said you have a feather?"

"Yes. How much has, um, Blackie told you?"

Matt put his chair beside hers, sat too close and leaned in to say under his breath, "You sure you want to go there, *Greta?*"

Resisting the organic, almost animalistic temptation to lean into him, she made herself straighten away instead. But her blood hummed and her skin prickled, brought alive by his nearness. Which was so not cool.

Ian answered, "He told me that you needed help IDing some evidence. Because I don't shut myself up in the middle of nowhere, and therefore have some knowledge of current affairs, I assume it has something to do with the ranger who was attacked, and the subsequent torching of Matt's station."

Despite the quips she saw the underlying concern, the quick shift of his eyes toward Matt and away, as if making sure he was really there, really okay.

How long had it been since they had last seen each other? Had Matt left behind not just his career in L.A., but his family and friends, as well? How many more layers were there?

"The ranger who was attacked was clutching the thing when she was found. I know my bird basics, but I didn't recognize it." Matt glanced at her. "Did you get anything off it?"

She reached into the inner pocket of her jacket for the flat carrying case. "There wasn't any obvious trace or transfer, and so far, all I've come up with is that it's not synthetic, hasn't been sterilized for commercial use and probably came from a living bird relatively recently. The mites I saw under magnification were still alive, at any rate." She slid the evidence bag across the table.

Ian waggled his finger. "Mites are resilient buggers. They can go for weeks, months, even years on just—" He broke off with a strangled noise, face draining of color. Almost hesitantly, he used one finger to pull the bag closer, then leaned in to inspect the strangely striped feather. "Holy. Crap."

Gigi's heart thudded in her chest and she nearly shot to her feet and punched the air. Finally, it looked like they had caught a break!

"Where was your ranger found?" Ian's voice was cathedral-hushed.

Matt had gone very still, his expression wary, as if he didn't want to get ahead of himself over something that might be nothing. "About an hour northwest of the station house. I take it we've got something here?"

"I'll say." Ian tapped the edge of the bag, well away from the feather itself. "This is...wow. Unexpected. It's from a barred eagle."

"They're rare?" Gigi pressed.

Ian shook his head and met her eyes, expression lit with wonder. "No, not rare. Completely extinct."

Chapter Eight

Gigi sat back in her chair, stunned. "Extinct?"

"Well, as it's technically defined, anyway. There's no real way to prove that something doesn't exist, you know. The last known breeding population died out in the sixties. At the time, the naturalists blamed pesticides, but the barred eagles stuck to really barren areas at fairly high altitudes, which weren't exactly farming hot spots. The current theory is that they suffered from heavy-metal poisoning. The darn things were attracted to ore sites, mines, that sort of thing, which meant they were probably overexposed to the metals." He paused. "There have been sightings off and on up in the backcountry, but no evidence." He looked back down at the feather, and said softly, "Until now."

"Barred eagles?" Matt muttered. "What is going on? What do they have to do with Tanya?"

"Beats me. I'm just following the evidence." Gigi stared at the bagged feather. How had they gone from terrorists to an extinct species?

She had the sneaking suspicion that this particular piece of evidence could lead them off on a tangent. And even if it was relevant, how could the information possibly help them? It was one thing for the feather to belong to a rare bird that had only a few nesting grounds, thus narrowing down the search for a primary crime scene. It was another thing entirely to go goose-chasing after an ecological ghost.

Matt said, "What if the al-Jihad connection is just a coincidence, and this is the real motive?"

"What, you think Tanya could have crossed paths with someone who wanted to make sure he was the first person to 'rediscover' the barred eagle?" She shook her head. "I don't see the guys who torched your station as ornithologists."

But a glance at Ian made her wonder. He seemed lost in exuberant thought, his eyes gleaming as he muttered to himself, "We need to get in there and confirm, see what we can do about conservation." His hands spasmed, as if he wanted to yank the plume out of the evidence bag, but was holding himself back.

Matt, too, was watching him. "The whole 'publish or perish, you have to be number one or you're nothing' thing can be a powerful motivator."

An inner quiver shook Gigi because that hit close to the bone, but she tried to think it through. Ian had been legitimately shocked at seeing the feather; there was no way he was involved in anything underhanded there. Still, his passion was evident. In another man, it might look a lot like fanaticism…and from there it was often a short fall to violence.

She shook her head. "I don't see this as a battle over who gets bragging rights. For one thing, we're dealing with a whole bunch of guys." Jack and Tucker estimated that it would've taken at least four to lock down the station house so quickly. "And while there have been cases of academic murder…" She shook her head. "It doesn't feel right. But then again, my job is working the evidence. The story is up to the cops and lawyers."

"Yeah, well, today you're on story duty, too."

"An hour northwest of the station house, you said?" Ian asked, seeming to remember they were there.

"Not so fast." Matt held up a hand. "Listen to me, okay? You can't go running off with this feather and start calling in the barred eagle experts, okay? We need to take this slowly."

"Huh? What's wro— Oh." Ian stared at them, his eyes clearing as he refocused, then darkening with understanding. "The feather is still evidence."

Gigi added, "Not only that, but we were hoping it would help lead us to the place where she was attacked." Instead it looked like they were going to have to find the place some other way, and in the process maybe lead Ian to the eagles.

"Can you give us any specifics on where we should be looking?" Matt asked. "High altitudes, you said. How high? And what kinds of ore? I don't know of any copper mines or deposits up near Fourteen, but we could check for surveys."

"Good point," Gigi said. Maybe the evidence wasn't quite played out yet, after all. "What do they eat?"

"I think… Let me see." Ian spun his chair and rolled it to a stuffed-full bookcase along the wall. "Where is… Aha. There you are." Gigi's stomach took a long, slow roll as he pulled out a thin volume. *"Ferrier's Guide to the Flora and Fauna of the Colorado Mountains,"* he announced. "It was the definitive guide back in the day.

Comprehensive, though the organization is seriously wonky. It may take me a minute to find our eagle."

"Look near the back," she said softly. "About three-quarters of the way through."

He shot her a curious look, but complied, then flipped a few more pages and stopped, eyebrows raised. "Well, hello. I guess you didn't need me after all, did you?"

"I didn't know the bird. I knew the book." She met Matt's eyes. "Let's add a waterfall to our list of things to look for." Because the sketch of Jerry Osage sitting in front of a waterfall had been stuck between the pages near the entry for the barred eagle.

Matt leaned in. "What else is listed near there?"

"This is the end of the birds." Ian flipped a few pages. "Then we get into the 'flora' part. Which, for some reason, starts with trees. Specifically those weird pines that grow up near the Forgotten."

Gigi frowned. That was the second time in as many days she'd heard the name. Alyssa had said something about it yesterday. "I assumed that was a ghost story or something. You mean it's a real place?"

"It's both," Matt said. "It's this grim chunk of wasteland that runs along the edge of the park's northwest corner—except for a couple of rivers, it's too dry to support anything but some real scrubby trees and a few coyotes, too far away to be a real tourist draw, and not challenging enough to interest the more extreme hikers. Question is: Would it be barred eagle country?"

Ian shook his head. "Unless they've done some major adapting over the past fifty or so years, the elevation is too high. And there wouldn't be much in the way of food. The place is pretty deserted."

"Is it part of the park?" Gigi asked, trying to figure out where the Forgotten belonged in the puzzle, if at all.

"It's federal land," Matt answered, "but the feds'll never do anything with it, which makes it a perfect buffer for Sector Fourteen."

"Actually, the city bought it from the feds," Ian corrected. "Last I heard, the mayor had nearly managed to pawn it off on a private buyer to help offset budget problems, but there was some holdup over the paperwork. Something about impact statements, I think."

"How long has this been going on?" Matt snapped.

"Six months maybe." Ian sent him a look. "I assumed you knew. As it is, I think it's pretty much a done deal at this point. Just needs the last few rubber stamps."

"Son of a—" Matt broke off, gritting his teeth. "Proudfoot must've made sure word didn't reach me. Probably a deal of some sort with the Park Service so they wouldn't fuss. But Sector Fourteen needs those rivers. Hell, that whole damn side of the park does. If some private buyer starts mucking around up there and screws with the water, the west side will go as dry as the east and it'll all burn."

Gigi said, "If there are already problems with the impact statements, maybe there's still time to make some noise."

Ian shook his head and said, "Proudfoot has it all tied up." He glanced at Matt. "Too bad nobody legitimate stepped up and ran against him, even after the mess he made as acting mayor." His voice was mild, but there was something very far from mild in his expression, and in the way tension suddenly snapped into the air between the two men.

Matt glared at him. "Leave it alone."

"But you could have—"

"Leave. It. Alone."

Gigi did a double take as the conversation veered from the Forgotten to something else entirely. "Wait. What did I just miss?"

"Nothing." Matt tugged on her arm to bring her with him, and said in a suddenly formal, cop-to-civilian expert voice, "Thanks for the help with the feather. We'll let you know if we see the eagle, and if not, when it's safe for your people to come in and search."

Ian rose and came around the desk to put himself between them and the door, eyes firing. "I'm just saying it would've been nice if there had been someone else to vote for. Someone who has a political science degree and used to say he was going to put in his twenty on the force and run for governor, because if an actor could do it, why not a cop?"

Matt's fingers closed tighter on her arm, almost to the point of pain. His face, though, had gone hard and distant. "You should've taken the hint when I ducked all your calls. I'm not that guy anymore. I haven't been in a long time."

"You don't need to be anybody but who you are right now, today," Ian insisted. "The last mayor resigned in the middle of a sex scandal, and Proudfoot is well on his way to running the city into the ground. If someone like you could bring integrity back to the office, it would go a long way to healing—"

"Fine," Matt snapped. "If that's your plan then go

and find someone like me. Because I'm not interested, and I'm not available." He dropped Gigi's arm and headed for the door, leaving her standing there, brain spinning.

This wasn't the ranger's detachment or the cop's intensity she was seeing—this was anger overlain with a deep, restless frustration that was as powerful as it was unfocused.

Ian followed them to the door. "Okay, you're not interested or available. So what are you? Because you sure as hell don't look happy."

Matt stopped and spun back, expression dark. "I'm in the middle of the case from hell. It's not murder yet, but it's only a matter of time before they get brave enough, desperate enough. I've got a ranger in the hospital, another one sleeping on my couch, and I'm wearing a damn badge. So forgive me if I'm not in a very happy place at the moment."

"I'm not talking about right this second and you damn well know it," Ian pressed. "Are you doing what you really want, or is it just easier this way? Tell me you're happy, Blackie, and I'll leave you alone."

Gigi wanted to slip out and let them argue in private, but she couldn't move. Her pulse thudded in her ears.

"I *was* happy, damn it. Forty-eight hours ago, I was just fine. I had air, sunshine, privacy and three good rangers in charge of keeping the hikers from killing themselves. And I'll get back to that peace and quiet when this case is over and life goes back to normal. A week, thirteen days on the outside, and, yeah, I'll be happy again." His voice went harsh. "I just want to be left alone. Is that so damn much to ask?"

"Not if that's what you really want."

"I just said it was, didn't I? Ian, let it go already. And don't call us, we'll call you." Cutting a black look in Gigi's direction, Matt snapped, "Come on. We're leaving." He yanked open the door and stormed out, boots thudding angry beats on the waxed marble, the sound cutting off as the glass door eased shut in his wake.

She didn't follow, just stood staring after him for a moment, stomach roiling in such tight knots that she didn't know whether she wanted to scream, cry or shoot something. Or all of the above.

A gentle touch on her elbow startled her so badly that she jolted and spun, fists raised.

Ian jerked back, hands up, evidence bag dangling from one. "Whoa. It's just me. And despite what you probably think right now, I come in peace. It's just that peace doesn't always start out that way with him. Never did."

She uncoiled, swallowing past the aching tightness in her throat. "Sorry."

"No. I'm the one who's sorry." He shot a telling look at the door. "I thought from seeing the way he was when he came in, and the way he was with you, that he was... well. I thought he was in a different place, that's all."

"It's not like that." But the heavy weight pressing on her heart said that deep down inside, part of her had hoped.

Not if all he wanted was to be left alone, though. Not if he wanted to be the ranger, the loner, the closed off man who didn't need anything except space and didn't offer anything in return.

He had said he would have his peace and quiet back

in thirteen days, and he hadn't picked the number at random. In thirteen days, the academy assignments were being announced and personnel shifted around. Which meant Tucker had used the information to talk Matt into teaming up with her...and he was looking forward to her departure.

Well, screw him. She could take care of that part right now.

She pulled out her phone, bypassed the first McDermott number and speed-dialed the second.

"McDermott, Homicide."

"It's Gigi. I want to trade in my cop. He's broken."

MATT MADE IT HALFWAY down the hall before he spun and slammed his shoulder into the wall. Pain flared at the point of impact and lower down in his gut, but he deserved all of it and more.

Sagging, he leaned back against the wall, which felt far steadier than he did just now.

One second he and Ian had been doing okay, and then the next...damn it. They'd been back at it like they'd seen each other four days ago, not four years.

And Gigi had been right in the line of fire.

He had caught a glimpse of her face as he stormed out, and the dark-eyed mixture of sharp hurt and dull resignation was singed into his brain. He deserved that, too, because he had insisted that he was the best one to watch her back when really he was about the worst possible choice to protect her.

Which he had just proven in spades.

His emotional control was gone, incinerated the moment their lips touched. Or maybe it had happened

before then, somewhere between the first sizzle of seeing
her in the hallway outside Tucker's office and the second
his brain had kicked back into gear and warned him that
she was trouble. That she was the first person he'd met
in a very long time who had the potential to mess with
his head.

Only she wasn't trying to mess with anything—she
was just trying to do her job. He was the mess—what
had just happened back there had nothing to do with her
and everything to do with old scars, even older dreams,
and a friend who knew how to push his buttons.

Damn Ian for going there. Damn Proudfoot for whor-
ing out part of Bear Claw Canyon because he couldn't
handle his finances.

And damn him for not being the man he should have
been.

Behind him, a door opened and Ian's voice became
audible, saying, "…any time, day or night, seriously."

"I may just take you up on that." She sounded as if
she really meant it, too, which put a nasty twist in Matt's
gut, even though he knew he didn't have the right to
feel anything even remotely approaching jealousy right
now.

In college, Matt had been the charming jock, Ian the
poet, and they'd both had their share of conquests. Later,
though, their lives had diverged. Ian had gone to grad
school, flourished, and emerged both poet and charmer,
while Matt had worked long hours in uniform, trying
to make everything okay when it couldn't possibly be.
And now Ian was still charming, while Matt was…hell,
he didn't know what he was, but it wasn't good.

Ian and Gigi exchanged a few more pleasantries that

had him grinding his teeth, then she headed in his direction, her silver-toed boots clicking like a ticked-off metronome.

She wore a studded black blazer, beige pants that clung to every dip and curve, and a purple shirt that did more than hint at her cleavage. But where yesterday he would have looked at her and seen a city slicker, now he just saw *her*.

He pushed away from the wall as she neared him, stuck his hands in his pockets when they wanted to reach for her. "I know it's not nearly good enough, but I'm sorry. Ian and I…well, he's always been able to get into me like that, just keeps going until I snap."

"He's worried about you."

So am I. It had never been like this for him before, all rage and mood swings, with him feeling like he was barely hanging on. "Give it five minutes and he'll be back to worrying about tracking down those supposed barred eagles. Which is what we should be doing." Not wasting time arguing politics and impossibilities.

She stared at him for a long moment, her hair falling in angles across her face like war paint, making her look in that moment both wholly feminine and terrifyingly capable. "Okay," she said softly. "Let's hit the road."

He had the feeling he had just failed a test he hadn't even known he was taking.

As they rolled away from the U.C. Bear Claw campus, she called the lab, gave a brief report on the eagles, and had Alyssa send a bunch of altitude maps and ore surveys to her phone. When he tapped the brakes at the main road, she broke off her conversation to say, "Head for Station Fourteen. Jack's waiting for me up at your place."

Matt winced at the continued invasion of his private space, but he headed north out of the city without comment. She called someone else, got a different map sent and studied the information on her phone's tiny display, frowning.

He glanced over. "I know you're mad at me—and with good reason—but that's my territory. Talk to me. I can help narrow down the search."

"I'm not mad at you. I'm thinking."

And the thing was, she didn't really look mad. She looked sad and resigned, and the two together tugged at something inside him. "What did Jack find?"

She glanced at him, brows furrowed. "Nothing that I'm aware of. Why?"

"I thought you were going to go over some new— Oh." The detective wasn't waiting to show her evidence. He was picking her up and taking her away.

"You said you wanted your peace and quiet back." She was focused on her maps, or at least staring at them. "You saved my life. Giving you yours back seemed like the least I could do."

"I didn't…" He trailed off as a heavy weight settled on his chest at the realization that she was right that they should split up. Williams had his head on straight. He would do a better job of protecting her, because there wouldn't be any emotion in the mix beyond friendship and respect.

"This is what you want, right?"

For a second the air between them went tight with anticipation; he had a feeling she was waiting for him to argue. When he didn't, she gave a soft sigh and looked out the window.

He told himself to leave it alone, that it was better this way. Instead, after a moment he said, "Have you ever slept wrong on your gun hand, and woke up with it totally numb and useless?"

"I shoot okay lefty." But the corner of her mouth softened a little, and she nodded, still staring out the window as they headed up into the foothills. "Yeah. I know the feeling. And I know how much it hurts when everything starts waking up again, how you just want to stand there and scream, or maybe hit something, because of the pain. But at the same time, you know you have to get through it or you won't be able to shoot properly."

How was it that she could see so clearly something he was just starting to get to himself?

"I thought I put myself back together the best I could. Now, though, I think maybe I've been sleepwalking for the past six years, and this case, meeting you…I'm starting to wake up."

She looked at him then, expression unreadable. "And that back there was what, emotional pins and needles?"

"Whatever it was, it wasn't me. Or not the guy I want to be. Especially not around you."

A flush touched her cheeks, but she looked down and fiddled with her phone. "I'm just passing through. Another thirteen days and I'm out of here, either to the academy or to fill in for someone who's gotten the call."

"Caught that, did you? Yeah, Tucker got word this

morning. I wasn't supposed to say anything until he knew one way or the other. Sorry."

"Don't be. It's a reality. Just like it's a reality that I don't have time for a new complication right now, even a short-term one."

He turned on to the winding route that led alongside brittle, dry Sector Nine to the western half of the back-country. They were alone on the familiar road, so he put the pedal down.

He didn't know whether she had meant to make him think about short-term, no-harm-no-foul sex between them, but he was suddenly filled with her flavor as if he had just kissed her, was warmed by her skin as if he had just touched her. Although his body was on board for short-term anything, logic said she would be far better off riding with Williams. He might be waking back up, but he was far from leveled off.

"Okay," he said quietly. "Yeah. Okay." He glanced up in the rearview mirror to see if he could catch her expression, some glimpse of what she was feeling.

Instead, he saw a truck that hadn't been behind them a minute ago.

It was big and black, with tinted windows. And it was catching up fast.

Chapter Nine

Matt's pulse accelerated and his knuckles went white on the steering wheel. "Hang on," he ordered grimly, "we've got company."

"What?" Gigi craned her head to see out the back just as the rearview mirror caught a flash of metal coming out the passenger's-side window of the vehicle.

"Down!" Matt caught her shirt and dragged her aside a split second before a machine pistol chattered. Cracks spiderwebbed the rear window, radiating from a quartet of bullet holes.

Gigi screamed and flattened herself. More slugs punched through, one whining way too close past Matt's ear.

Cursing, he swerved as much as he dared on the curvy road, trying to stay away from where a guardrail blocked a hell of a drop on their left.

"Call it in!" he snapped. "Tucker first." McDermott wasn't the chief, but he was the one Matt trusted.

Hitting the gas, he sent the Jeep lunging up the steady incline, accelerating away from the heavier truck.

He hugged the high side as much as he dared, blood chilling with the realization that these guys—whoever they were and whatever they wanted—were finished with leaving their victims to die. They were going to make sure they got the job done this time.

Not on my watch, he vowed grimly. And not with Gigi there. If he had been alone he might've tried to turn the tables and get his hands on the bastards chasing him. As it was, all he wanted to do was get the hell out of there, fast.

More bullets came spraying through the back window. Air screamed into the cabin, turning the world to a roar.

When the road straightened out, he concentrated on getting ahead of the truck, out of range.

Gigi was talking into the phone, making her report in a shaky voice. "I don't know," she said, "we're—hang on." She punched her phone to speaker and held it up to him. "Where are we, exactly?"

"West access road, near mile marker ten, in that snaky section with the drop-off."

"Christ," Tucker said. "Okay, cars are on the way, and I'll get a bird in the air. Somehow. Just hang on."

"Planning on it. You're looking for a black truck, late model Dodge half-ton, no front plate."

"On it."

Matt clenched his teeth as he gunned it around a sharp curve going way too freaking fast, and had to hit the brakes. Rubber chirped and the Jeep threatened to tip. But they were still three car lengths or so ahead of the truck.

Gigi braced herself, pocketed her phone, and went for the radio. Her hands were shaking, her eyes stark in her bloodless face, but she was holding it together like a warrior. A cop.

In another lifetime, he would've been proud to have her on his team. In this one, he didn't want her anywhere near the action. He had seen too much, lost too much. But when she racked the radio and pulled her Beretta, he knew the choice was out of his hands. There was no way to keep her out of the action now. He glanced over, met her eyes, and nodded. "Go for the tires on the right." That would send the bastards into the wall, giving him half a chance of getting a witness out of the crash.

They hit a straightaway that flattened and then descended. The truck picked up speed, caught up and the guns came back out.

Gigi found a decent vantage, took aim and fired.

"Headlight," she reported, then cried, "Hang on!"

Matt had seen them coming, but wasn't braced nearly enough for the shuddering impact that ripped through the lighter Jeep when the truck rammed them. He cursed viciously, but the sound was lost beneath the crunch of impact and the scream of tires as the Jeep half-spun and slid sideways, being pushed along by the truck.

That put the two cabs practically on top of each other. Through the heavily tinted windows, he glimpsed the driver's panicked surprise, the passenger's scramble as he tried to clear a jammed clip. The men were strangers, average-looking white guys who were trying to kill him and Gigi.

Acting on fury and instinct, blood going crisis-cold, Matt pulled out his Sig and fired into the tint, aware that Gigi was doing the same with her Beretta. The truck's front windshield cracked and blood splashed inside the cab.

One of them was wounded, but would it be enough?

Then momentum swung the vehicles another ninety degrees, slingshotting the truck ahead of the Jeep just as the road curved. The truck flung free, fishtailing as it headed for the curve.

The Jeep kept sliding sideways, totally at the mercy of momentum.

"Take this!" Matt shoved his gun at Gigi and grabbed the wheel, fighting the top-heavy vehicle when it listed and tried to spin out. A tire blew on the left side, making the drag worse.

The truck's brake lights flashed as the vehicle disappeared around the curve.

But the Jeep wasn't turning fast enough; inertia was dragging it toward the far side of the road, where there was a low guardrail and freefall plunge. Pulse hammering, Matt fought the skid, trying to regain control.

They weren't going to make it.

"Son of a— Hang on!" Giving in, knowing it was the only way, he cut the wheel the other way, hit the brakes, and sent them into a hard spin in the other direction. They whipped around once, twice, then headed for the rock wall.

Letting go of the wheel, he lunged against the restraints of his seat belt and wrapped his arms around Gigi as best he could, shielding her. "Keep your head down!"

They slammed sideways into the wall with a rending *crunch* of metal and a crash from what was left of the glass, the *whumps* of three of the four airbags, and Gigi's soft scream, which was buried in his chest.

His belt burned his hips and shoulder; glass and other fragments pelted him where he was curled around her. But as the Jeep rocked back on its opposite tires and shuddered to crippled stillness, he became aware of a protected strip across the back of his neck and one shoulder, where she had wrapped her free arm around him and spread her hand to cover as much of him as she could reach.

Not daring to name the strange, soft feeling that moved through him, he pulled away from her. But he didn't let go all the way. He couldn't.

As he eased back, her hand slid along the side of his neck and down to flatten on his chest, over his heart, which was beating fast.

Her eyes were wide and dark, her hair an angular slash across her forehead, and the four diamond studs she wore, three and one, twinkled like stars. He realized that all the things that had initially warned him off her had become part of him now, because they were part of what made her uniquely *her.* And somehow, in the space of a day, she had wormed her way inside his heart.

She straightened a little and unwrapped the arm she'd held clutched tightly to her chest between them. In it, she held two guns: his and hers. Which was some seriously quick thinking, because if there was anything worse than spinning a Jeep and slamming it sideways into a big-ass rock, it was doing all that with a couple of pistols bouncing around.

She was a natural.

Any praise he might have given her jammed in his

throat because he didn't know what to say, how to tell her that her instincts and talent impressed him as much as her guts and reckless disregard for her own safety terrified him.

Then they heard the low thump of rotors and the building wail of sirens, and it was too late for him to say anything.

She drew away with a small smile that didn't reach all the way to her eyes, and handed him his Sig. "Nice driving, hotshot. I guess that's two rescues I owe you."

"Let's call it even. Your shooting kept them too busy to take out our tires."

Beyond the drop-off, an unfamiliar stealth-painted chopper suddenly swung up from below the guardrail to hover. It was heavily armed but none of the guns were pointed in their direction, and as Matt watched, the pilot gave them a dip-wiggle that signaled "we're on your side." Where the hell had Tucker dug *that* up?

"Okay. We're even." Without another word, she booted free of the airbag and headed toward the chopper, holstering her gun as she walked…and leaving him kicking himself for missing a moment that suddenly felt like it could have been very important, even if he didn't know what to say.

It's better this way, he told himself. *No complications.* But as he climbed out of the Jeep, his blood was doing a slow burn…not because the bastards in the truck had gotten away from him, but because Gigi was about to.

RIGHT AFTER THE CHOPPER'S arrival, three P.D. vehicles came around the corner and hit the brakes. Within fifteen minutes, Gigi was at the center of a law-enforcement huddle that her competitors for the academy slots would have killed for.

In addition to Tucker, Jack and the seven other Bear Claw cops that had converged on the remote stretch of road, the sleek chopper—whose tail numbers looked suspiciously magnetic—had dropped off Cassie and her husband, FBI analyst Seth Varitek, along with two people Gigi had heard about but never met: Jonah Fairfax and his wife, Chelsea, formerly one of Bear Claw's medical examiners. The two had been instrumental in foiling al-Jihad's terrorist plot, and now worked as partners in an unnamed government agency.

Based on the stories, Gigi had been expecting a pair of glossy superspies like something out of the movies. But while Fairfax—aka Fax—was killer handsome, with ice-blue eyes that instantly seemed to look through her, Chelsea was lovely in a honey-haired, girl-next-door sort of way. The two were clearly very much a part of the Bear Claw gang, fitting seamlessly with Tucker, Cassie and Seth, and razzing Alyssa, who was attending the meeting by speakerphone and was trying not to be too cranky about being left out.

In contrast, Matt stood well apart from the group near the guardrail, staring into the abyss.

A couple of times Gigi started to call him over, but stopped herself. He was a grown-up; he could join or not, his choice.

Besides, even though for a second there she had thought that he might finally be seeing her for who and what she really was, the evidence said otherwise. He was in a weird headspace right now, and if he needed to get away from the crowd, it was the least she could do for him. She owed him her life. Again.

He might think they were even, but she knew better. And a Lynd always paid her debts. So she bought him the room he seemed to need by briefing the others on the attack and describing—as best she could, anyway— the truck and its occupants, who seemed to have disappeared into thin air.

"They're down a headlight and windshield," she finished, "and the driver took at least one bullet." She was pleased that her voice sounded level and businesslike. That was no small feat given that she was holding on to her cool by force of will, along with the inner promise that she could have the shakes later, in private, for as long as she needed to.

"Was either of them the guy who knocked you down during the fire?" Jack asked.

She thought about it, tried to picture it, but shook her head. "I barely saw him." The whole shoot-out was a blur of fear and the ping-whine of ricochets. And she didn't want to admit it, but Matt had been right—shooting was different when the cardboard cutout wasn't cardboard, and it was shooting back.

"I'll check the hospitals for any gunshot victims coming in over the next few hours," Alyssa said from the speakerphone, "then see what I can do on the truck."

"Seth and I can process the Jeep and the rest of the scene," Cassie said, eyeing the crumpled vehicle and the trail of tire marks and glass that stretched around the far turn. "That should keep us busy for a while."

Gigi's body sang with bruises that hadn't yet formed. She couldn't believe it was barely noon, but she manned up. "I'll help."

"The hell you will," Tucker said mildly, though there

was steel in his eyes. "You're out of here until tomorrow morning at the earliest. Both of you."

"But—"

"Take some downtime. We'll call you if something breaks."

She drew breath to argue, then realized she didn't want to. Letting out a long sigh, she nodded. "Okay, yeah. Thanks." Glancing at the Jeep, she said, "I think I'm going to need a ride back to the city, though."

Tucker and Jack both started to protest, but Matt's voice overrode them. "Not the city." He pushed through the crowd and stopped facing her, ignoring the others. "And not alone. Those guys came after us specifically… and they were shooting to kill. Not all that well, which, along with the expression on the driver's face when he got a close-up of my pistol, tells me they're not pros. But that doesn't make them any less dangerous. They missed, and one of them is hurt, but if we're right about there being a bunch of them, those two will be calling in reinforcements."

"They… Right." Gigi pressed a hand to her stomach as it went suddenly raw. "Of course, you're right." He was standing way too close, his strength making her want to lean, despite everything.

"The break room at the lab should be safe," Cassie suggested.

"We can do better than that," Chelsea said. She glanced at Fax, got a nod of assent. "We've got a little place outside the city, part getaway spot, part safe house. It's tight as a tick, so if you want, you can lock yourself in and forget about the world without needing any additional manpower." She crouched for a second, fiddled with what looked like a high-tech ankle holster and came up with a keyless fob, which she held out.

"That sounds like heaven," Gigi said fervently. "I'm in."

"*We're* in," Matt corrected, and snagged the fob.

Something sparked deep inside her, feeling suddenly very different from the near-tears of moments earlier. She wanted it to be irritation. "I'm riding with Jack from now on, remember?"

He cursed under his breath. "Fine. Then he stays in the safe house, too. I don't want you going it alone."

She drew breath to snarl, then stopped when her mind played back Ian's parting words to her: *Blackie's coming back from a really dark place. I'd rather he didn't have to go it alone.*

She hadn't been able to give Ian the reassurance he'd been looking for. Now, though, empathy tugged when she saw echoes of her own fatigue and stress in Matt's expression. He acted as if she shouldn't trust him, but then he'd been there each and every time she'd needed him.

He hadn't asked her to give him a chance…but Ian had. And, oddly, she trusted the ornithologist when she wasn't sure she trusted herself anymore.

So, finally, she nodded. "It makes more sense for the two of us to stay together than for me to tie up Jack's time." She needed to take a break someplace safe…and maybe she didn't want to go it alone after all.

THE SMALL LOG CABIN, which was ninety minutes or so on the other side of the city from the crash, was made of some sort of impenetrable composite and boasted a warren of tunnels that led to concealed doorways sprinkled across the ten-acre property, several of which were outfitted with go bags and getaway vehicles.

As Matt rolled the rented Blazer into the attached garage, and blast doors glided into place behind the vehicle, he noted three different levels of security, figured he had probably missed several others and decided he felt good about the setup.

He wasn't so sanguine about the situation, though. The part of him that needed to be there with Gigi, to know she was safe and taking care of herself, was offset by the part of him that said it was a really bad idea for the two of them to spend the night under the same roof.

Then again, safe houses weren't exactly known for their ambience. The handful he'd been in over the years had all been boxy and practical, with enough bedrooms for the protectee and several marshals or cops. He should be able to stay close, yet keep his distance.

"You coming in or staying out here?" she asked. She stood at an inner door that led from the garage to the main cabin, holding the keyless fob, one eyebrow raised.

"Coming in." He joined her as she used the fob and a security code to open the reinforced door, and they stepped through together.

And stopped dead. Because this was no safe house. It was a freaking armor-plated love nest.

Chapter Ten

Gigi swallowed hard. "Um. This is…cozy."

What had looked like a modest two stories from the outside proved to be a single main room with a vaulted cathedral ceiling, decorated in warm neutrals with splashes of local art. A small kitchen took up one of the short walls and a huge fieldstone fireplace spanned the other.

But her attention was fixed on the wide stone-veneered platform that began at the hearth, took up half of the main room…and housed a sunken hot tub approximately the size of her apartment's bedroom. There were multiple connected pools, some deep and jetted, others shallow and smooth. And some were just the size of two bodies intertwined.

Bolsters were scattered around, bright colors against the composite surface. And there was a console that would have done the Enterprise proud controlling the tub and fireplace, along with an entertainment center she suspected was also jacked into the security cameras.

The other half of the main room offered a sunken living room furnished with a wide, plush couch that was practically a bed itself, and a thick, plush carpet strewn

with pillows. There were two doors on the long wall,
one leading to a bathroom, the other a bedroom.

The hot tub was dry and drained; a discreet placard
on the wall described the eco-friendly solar heating,
scrubbing and recycling protocols, and listed the number
of the maid service that had been cleared onto the property. A panel beside the door they had come through
offered a second security hub along with a touch screen
computer that, once they used the log-in sequences Fax
had given them, would provide full data access as well as
information on the cabin's defenses and escape routes.

But those stark practicalities did nothing to lessen
the sudden suggestive intimacy of the space.

"What," Matt said drily, "no bearskin rug?"

Her face heated. "I'm sure they figured that would
be over the top."

"Like this isn't?" But he notched the go bag he'd
rescued from the wrecked Jeep a little higher on one
shoulder. "You want the first shower?"

For a moment, she just stared at the tub and felt every
bone in her body ache. Then she nodded and headed for
the bathroom, allowing herself a harmless tug of envy
for Chelsea, who had not only found herself an über-spy,
she held her own against him. They worked together,
functioned together as a team. And, apparently, enjoyed
their getaway time.

Gigi didn't let herself look back at Matt, didn't let
herself wish for things that weren't going to happen.
Instead, she went into the bathroom, closed the door,
turned the luxurious shower to its highest settings,
stripped down and climbed in. Then she curled herself

into a ball in the corner, pressed her face into her knees and waited for the storm.

It didn't come.

Always before, in the aftermath of terror had come the tears, the emotional outpouring that had, oddly, made her feel normal, as if it said "yes, you're a woman, not a robot." She wasn't fearless, wasn't nearly as brave as others thought her. But she was good at setting the doubts aside for a few hours, even days, and just dealing.

At the age of eleven, she had spent three days alone, lost on the Appalachian Trail when a freak storm had separated her from the rest of her family. She had dealt, she had survived and she had eventually found her way back to the main trail. And she hadn't shed a single tear until she saw her parents and sisters rushing toward her—at which point she had sat down in the dirt and howled.

It had been like that ever since: she subsumed the fear and did what needed to be done, then weathered the weepy aftermath.

Only now there weren't any tears. There was only a hollow, tired ache and the sense that this was the first of the many chases, many adrenaline rushes that would come with being on a crisis response team.

Which was what she wanted.

Right?

But just as she couldn't summon the emotional release that usually helped her clear her head after she made it through a dangerous situation, she didn't have an immediate answer to that question.

She tried to tell herself she was tired, strung out and

pent up. Only she didn't feel all that tired, and she didn't feel like crying. Instead, she felt alive and alert, and intensely aware of her surroundings. The water was warm, the tiles cool, slick and not very comfortable.

Finally giving up on the idea of a good crying jag— maybe she just couldn't let down her guard all the way knowing Matt was out in the other room—she dragged herself upright and finished showering, feeling restless and dissatisfied.

Too late, she remembered Chelsea's offer of spare clothes in the bedroom. But there were clean robes folded on a rack, and she couldn't face putting back on an outfit that stank of fear. Hesitating only briefly, she pulled on one of the robes, belted it firmly, and headed out into the main room, expecting to step from the shower's fog into cool, dry air.

She got warm humidity instead, along with the smell of grilled cheese from the kitchen. She stalled at the sight of the filled hot tub under turned-low lights and the flickering illumination of a small fire that provided more ambience than warmth. Motor noise hummed a soothing monotone, jets and bubbles did their thing, frothing the surface of the water, and a Bose radio was tuned to something low and jazzy. There was no sign of Matt, and the bedroom door was closed.

He had set the scene for luxurious pleasure…and then shut himself away.

The message was clear: *You've got your space, I've got mine.*

Instead of turning her off or making her angry, it made the gesture that much more poignant. It made her feel cared for, tended to. And it made her ache for him.

She let out a soft sigh. "He's right. It's better this way."

She was already in danger of falling hard for the complications and losing sight of what mattered. And he was in a weird place, not yet sure if he wanted to be his old self, some new incarnation, or the loner who disappeared into the backcountry, shutting out the people who wanted to care about him.

Yeah, the closed door was the right call. But as she headed for the kitchen and found the plate he had fixed for her, along with a cooling cup of herbal tea, she caught herself eyeing the door, wondering if it was locked. And wondering, too, what would happen if she knocked.

Don't go there.

She didn't let herself stand near the door and listen, picturing him on the other side doing the same thing. Instead, she took her meal up to the hot tub, debating only briefly before she slipped off her robe and climbed in. The warmth surrounded her instantly with cheerful bubbles that burst against her skin, easing the sting of the day.

She lay back, closed her eyes and thought about the fading ache of bruises, the noise the crash had made, and the way he had hung on to her at the last minute and shielded her with his body.

She thought about her condo back in Denver, and how it would feel to be there alone after a day like today.

She pictured Chelsea and Fax winging through the air in the sleek black helicopter, laughing as they agreed that yes, a bearskin rug would definitely be too much for the safe house.

She heard the soft cadence of Alyssa's voice as she

and Tucker did the "Hello, McDermott, Forensics, this is McDermott, Homicide," thing.

And, finally knowing what she needed to do, she reached for the phone handset that rested near the hot tub's controls, and used the secure landline to dial out.

When the call went live, she took a deep breath and said, "Mom? It's Gigi. I need a reality check."

MATT PACED THE BIG bedroom like a cougar behind a chain-link fence: restless, edgy and angry. It was tempting to pretend the frustration came entirely from him wanting to be out there working the case, but he knew damn well that if he was out there he would've been wishing himself right back inside the safe house.

He wanted to be there with her, for her, wanted to watch over her, protect her. But that was the lie cops told themselves, that it was possible for one human being to ensure the safety of another. It was a comforting illusion, one that gave them purpose and kept them going when knives flashed and bullets flew. But it was just an illusion.

Accidents happened. Crimes happened. People died because they were in the wrong place at the wrong time.

Aware that he had his Sig in his hand and was methodically dropping the clip and slapping it home, over and over again in a jittery tic he had conquered by his second month on the job, he set the weapon aside and reached for the phone. Line one was lit, so he punched the second line and went through the motions of getting himself patched into the radio up at his house, resigned to the fact that someone would be there.

Sure enough, there was an answer right away. "Station Fourteen."

So much had happened over the past few days that it took him a few seconds to place the voice. "Jim?"

"Hey, boss." Anticipating the question, the younger ranger said, "No, she's not awake yet. But she's stable, and her parents flew in, so I figured I'd come back up and put in some hours."

Hearing fatigue in the other man's voice, Matt said, "I hope some of those hours are bunk time. Or I guess couch time."

"I can sleep later, once we've got these bastards," Jim said, voice low and fervent. He didn't really sound like a kid anymore.

"Yeah. I know how you feel. What's the latest?"

"Nothing and more nothing." The answer was laden with disgust. "There's no sign of her Jeep anywhere in Sector Fourteen—at least as far as we can tell with the really sketchy air-search time Bert has managed to beg, borrow and steal."

"Her attackers must've driven it out."

"Or stuck it in a cave. Either way, it doesn't look like that's going to lead us anywhere."

"How about focusing on places you might expect to see a barred eagle?"

"Your bird guy says we're looking at only two places in Sector Fourteen—we're pretty low on copper ore—and a few more in Twelve and Thirteen. Bert is checking them out."

"Alone?"

"Hell, no. The place is crawling with volunteers. The parking lot has gone tent city."

Oddly, the thought brought only dull surprise—and gratitude—at the way the ranger crews had banded together and volunteered their time. "Make sure nobody goes off alone."

"Yeah." Jim hesitated. "Is this about Tanya's old boyfriend, do you think?"

Matt's attention sharpened away from the window, where he'd been blindly staring out at the treeline as the late afternoon edged toward dusk. "Maybe. Why? What do you know about him?"

"She told me how he died in that jailbreak a couple of years ago. She never said it in so many words, but it seemed to me that she felt like it was her fault, because he wouldn't have been in Bear Claw if it weren't for her. I guess he asked her to stay with him back east, even get married, but she wanted to keep skiing and wasn't sure about the marriage thing, so she came here instead. A couple of months later, he got a job in the ME's office and followed her. I think she figures that if she hadn't wanted to ski so badly, they both would've stayed back east and he wouldn't have died." He paused, then added, "At least not that way."

Definitely not a kid anymore.

"The cops aren't sure whether or not the murder is connected to what's going on right now," Matt said, "but regardless, I want you watching your back, okay?" And even though he was out of the business of managing other people's lives, he added, "Don't feel like you have to stay up there, either. It sounds like Bert's got plenty of help, so you should take all the time you want down at the hospital."

"Count on it. I'm planning on being the first thing she sees when she wakes back up. I want her to know how I feel about her right away, and that I'll be there for her, no matter what."

"Okay." A heavy weight pressed on Matt's chest. "Good. That's good."

"I spent too much time waiting for her to get over the ex and making sure I knew what I was feeling, and... well. I'm not going to make that mistake again. Just because the timing isn't perfect doesn't change the way we feel about each other."

Matt tried to tell himself that wouldn't sound nearly so profound if he weren't closed in an armored bedroom, elementally aware of the woman on the other side of the door, and the fact that they felt something for each other despite being at completely different places in their lives.

He cleared his throat. "Okay, kid. Stay safe. And tell Tanya's family that we're all pulling for her."

"Will do." Jim signed off and the airwaves went blank, hissing with static. But that was nothing compared to the thoughts buzzing in Matt's mind as he stood alone in the bedroom, barefoot and wearing the worn black cargo pants and plain white T-shirt he kept in his go bag.

He didn't feel like the ranger, or even the cop. It was like those other pieces of him had been temporarily emptied out so he could be someone else for a few hours—maybe even the man he would have become if things had been different.

But that man also knew he was coming down off an adrenaline high and working on zero sleep. And he couldn't tell if that was making things more or less clear.

He wanted Gigi like he wanted his next breath, and he knew that the chemistry went both ways, but the timing was just plain wrong. Her life was poised to explode in new, exciting directions. His life was…well, he didn't know anymore what it was doing, or where he wanted it to go next, and that was a large part of the problem.

She was burning up the pavement while he'd been standing still. Even if he got moving now, he wouldn't be able to catch up and might not be going in the same direction. They might collide, but he didn't see how they could get in step together.

Was there a workable solution? Damned if he knew. But one thing was certain: he wasn't going to last much longer in that bedroom. She was too close, his memories of the chase too fresh. He could be sitting looking down at her lying in a hospital bed like Tanya. Or worse, a casket.

But they had survived unscathed and for now, at least, they were safe.

More, Jim's words about not wanting to wait too long kept colliding with the pins-and-needles sensation that had been chasing Matt ever since he kissed Gigi, the two together letting him know that sometimes it wasn't possible to wait for the perfect moment, the perfect plan. Hell, he didn't have a plan, didn't know what he was expecting. All he knew was that he couldn't sit in that bedroom alone another minute if there was any chance she was feeling half of what he was.

Already moving before he was consciously aware of having made the decision, he crossed to the door. He cracked it and heard her voice, opened it all the way and saw her reclining in the hot tub, mostly submerged in bubbles, with her wet hair slicked back from her face, her eyes closed, and her head tipped back against the curving wall of the faux stone surround.

With the fire in the background, candles around the edges and music carrying just over the water's burble, the space was a warm, comforting fantasy that put him instantly on edge and told him this wasn't a good idea, that it was as much an illusion as his peace and quiet had turned out to be.

He took a big step back and reached for the door. But then he hesitated, empathy tugging when he realized that Gigi might be surrounded by soft luxury, but she didn't look comforted. She looked stark.

A woman's voice emerged from a hidden speaker. "We're keeping our fingers crossed for you, baby. Call us the minute you hear anything, okay?"

"I will," she said softly. "'Bye, Mom. I love you."

"We love you, too, sweetie."

Those simple, profound words cut through him and left him aching for the things he'd lost. But at the same time, there was a dullness in Gigi's voice, a sense that she was deeply disappointed.

The line went dead, but it was a long moment before she sighed and stirred, reaching across to cut the call.

"She doesn't know what's happening out here, does she?" he asked.

She stiffened, but didn't do the jerk-gasp-squeak routine he would have expected from so many other women.

Instead, she slowly opened her eyes. "How long have you been standing there?"

He suspected that she meant to glare, but the effect was ruined by an air of quiet unhappiness. It tugged at him, drew him closer, until he was standing at the edge of the hot-tub platform. He was all too aware that her robe was draped nearby, her skin pink beneath the swirling, bubbling water. "Just through the goodbyes. Did you tell her about the fire and the crash?"

For a second he didn't think she was going to answer. Then she looked away and sank a little deeper, so the water covered her shoulders. "I was going to—that's why I called her. I was going to tell her everything, ask her what she thought about…well, all of it. But then she started asking about the academy, all excited for me, and I just couldn't. It's taken this long for her to stop asking 'are you okay?' right off the bat every time I call. I just…"

She shrugged, the movement causing ripples in the restless water. "She doesn't need to worry about me. I can take care of myself." She paused, lips quirking. "And now you're going to tell me that someone sure as hell needs to worry about my reckless butt, and how I don't take care of myself nearly as well as I'd like to think."

He might have, but he was caught up in the sudden realization that even though she was surrounded by friends and intimately connected to her family, at the same time she was, in her own way, very isolated.

Maybe because of that realization, or the strange emptiness inside him and the things Jim had been saying about the dangers of waiting too long, he found that it wasn't all that hard for him to say what he'd been meaning to say. "You know how I said I would tell you later why I left L.A.?"

She nodded slowly, eyes sharpening on him.

"Well, it's later." He paused. "That is, if you still want to hear the story."

Her lips parted in surprise. She hesitated, and for a second he thought she was going to be the smarter, saner one by turning him down. But then she reached over to dial up more bubbles, obscuring his glimpses of pink skin beneath the water, and patted the soft faux stone beside her.

"Come and put your feet in, at least," she said softly. "The water helps."

And so, he realized, did the feeling of moving toward something for a change, rather than walking away.

Chapter Eleven

Gigi made herself keep breathing as he levered himself easily up onto the platform and padded toward her, barefoot. His faded black pants had slipped below his hipbones and his white T-shirt clung, dampening in the humid air.

With any of the fun, insubstantial men she had spent time with over the years, she would have stripped those last few pieces of clothing off him and pulled him, laughing, into the hot tub with her. More, a small, panicked part of her brain said that would be safer than peeling back this layer. Not because she feared she wouldn't like the man beneath, but because she was badly afraid she would, and she wasn't sure she could afford it.

That scared part of her said to run. Instead, she stayed put as he rolled up his pants to reveal masculine, muscular calves and the hint of a small surgical scar below one knee.

His eyes followed hers and a corner of his mouth kicked up. "I tore my ACL trying to get around this tall, obnoxious guy during a pickup basketball game my freshman year of college. Ian busted me up back then, and he's been doing it ever since."

It was the kind of small detail she had never cared about with other men. Now she stored the information away as he sat beside her, let his feet drop into the water, and braced himself on his palms.

His entry sent new currents brushing along her body, touching her breasts and thighs. Not that she needed anything to heighten the churning burn of desire. It had taken root the moment she saw him in the bedroom doorway, eyes dark with an emotion she couldn't name. Didn't dare.

Okay, this so wasn't going to work. "Close your eyes," she ordered. "And no peeking."

When she was pretty sure he had obeyed, she grabbed the robe and climbed out of the hot tub, wrapping the garment around her.

Then, feeling better armored with a layer of white terry cloth around her rather than bubbles, she sat beside him, slipped her feet into the water beside his, and said, "Okay. Start talking."

He didn't say anything at first, which made her think the moment had come and gone.

But then, without looking at her, he said, "The summer before my senior year in college, my father's chopper went down during a National Guard training exercise. When my mother heard that he was being rushed to a trauma center about an hour away, she and my fifteen-year-old sister Lena jumped in the car and took off." His voice was almost inflectionless, as though time or repetition had robbed the story of its emotion. "They ran a red light a couple of miles from home and got T-boned by a furniture truck. They both died instantly."

Oh, she thought. *Oh, no.* A soft sound escaped her.

She had heard the stories the cops told at Shakey's after shift—about families devastated by multiple blows at once, wretched coincidences where even the survivors were victims. But she couldn't imagine—didn't *want* to imagine—the pain.

He continued: "Ian and I were in France, spending a month before school started back up. It took the authorities two days to track us down, took me another day and a half to get home. They had been dead four days before I made it back."

Gigi nearly closed her eyes to block out his pain. But then, knowing that was the coward's way out, she instead reached out to him. He didn't offer a hand, didn't offer anything, just stayed braced back on his palms, staring into the bubbling water. She wrapped her fingers around his wrist and squeezed, feeling his pulse beneath her fingers. "I'm sorry."

"It was a long time ago."

"Not for you."

"Yeah." He unbent a little, shifted and took her hand. He twined his fingers through hers so gently that tears prickled behind her eyes, though she didn't let him see.

"Afterward, the whole political science thing seemed...pointless, like it was just people sitting around and arguing about stuff most of them would never need to worry about. I wanted to make an immediate difference in peoples' lives, make things safer for them, better."

"So you became a cop."

He paused, mouth twisting in a humorless smile. "I lost my father because of a freak mechanical problem, my mother and sister because of distracted driving and bad timing, not any sort of crime. But yeah. I became a cop. Within a few years I was the guy they called on for the tricky stuff, the one who always went in the door first. I was promoted to SWAT, then to team leader. For nearly three years, Team Four cleared more tricky situations without casualties than any other team…and then the odds caught up with us."

He let go of her hand and scrubbed at his face, then dropped his arm and just sat there, wrists dangling between his knees. "It was a hostage call, which always adds to the pucker factor because you've got civilians in there, and it was at a bank, which sucks for the obvious reasons. The robbers weren't pros, which meant they were twitchy on the triggers, and…" He shook his head. "My team wasn't in great shape—one guy's wife had just walked out on him, another guy had just found out he had a second kid on the way. They said they were good to go, that they could put that stuff aside… Hell, I don't know. I know prescience isn't part of the job description, but afterward, looking back, I could see the signs."

"I'm sorry," she said again, because it was the truth. What else was there to say?

She had guessed it had been a crisis response gone wrong, but she ached doubly for him now.

"We were in position, waiting on the hostage negotiator and a few feds who were en route, when the shooting started. Later, we found out that a construction worker had gotten it in his head to play hero and went after one of the thieves. All I knew was that we couldn't wait. We breached and went in on the intel we had at hand, which was good but not great. We thought there were four gunmen. Turns out there were five, and the fifth guy knew where to aim, how to go in over and under the body armor, and through the joints."

Thus the scars high and low on his torso. Gigi's stomach did a slow roll. "How many casualties?"

His eyes had gone dead and his voice was flat with pain. "They took out twelve hostages before we breached. Three more were wounded in the crossfire, their bullets, not ours. We got all five of them within, what? Two minutes? Three? But I lost four good officers, including the two guys who had other things on their minds."

"Other things," she echoed. "Like people they cared about."

He didn't seem to hear her. Or maybe he did and didn't know what to say. He continued: "I took a couple of bullets, lost a chunk of my liver and gained an ulcer. And after I finished rehab, I…I don't know. Tuned out, I guess, or maybe burned out. I passed the psych evaluation, but I just couldn't do it anymore. I couldn't go into a call knowing I was putting my teammates' lives on the line, and that us going in there—wherever 'there' was—could upset the balance and start the shooting again. I lasted three months with SWAT, another three in plainclothes before I quit, moved out here, found some peace and quiet, and thought I had healed just fine." He glanced at her, expression as fierce and unreadable as it had been the first time they met. "And then you showed up, and the pins and needles started."

She took his arm in both of hers, leaned against him and pressed her cheek to his T-shirt-clad shoulder, over the bullet scar. "No matter what happens next, I'm glad we got to know each other."

In such a short amount of time, he had become more important to her than she wanted to admit. He annoyed her, intrigued her, turned her on, made her look at things differently. He hadn't quit because he wasn't good enough; he had flamed out because he'd cared too much, put too much of himself into the job. She was happy that he was starting to reconnect with the people and things that had once been important to him.

And when she left… No. She didn't want to think about that right now. Tonight was tonight.

"That's the question, isn't it?" he said quietly. "What, exactly, *does* happen next?" He paused. "Just now, Jim was talking about sitting with Tanya and regretting the things he hadn't done because the timing didn't feel right. And I can't help thinking that either of us could've wound up in the same position today."

She shifted to face him as her heart thudded quickly. Although that small, cautious kernel of self-preservation inside her said to keep her distance, the larger part of her wanted to lean in.

Maybe it was the soft light and the bubbling back-drop, or maybe it was having spent some serious time thinking about death and dying, but the whole idea of avoiding the big foam finger of emotion didn't seem nearly as critical as it had a few days earlier.

Still she didn't want to let him know how huge those emotions were, how all-consuming. He was having enough trouble managing his own head, he shouldn't have to deal with hers, as well.

So she let him see she was serious, didn't let him see her yearn. "I've always said I'd rather have regrets about the things I did do, rather than the things I didn't."

"Why am I not surprised?" For a second, the super-cop was back in his expression, as if he wanted to warn her to be careful, stay back, duck and cover.

His sudden fierceness didn't irritate her as it would have before, because now she knew where he was coming from. More, seeing him in full-on cop mode set off a chain reaction of heat inside her, because for all that she wanted to be the best at what she did, it got her seriously hot when she met someone who was better.

Mixed in with the heat was tenderness, though, because beneath that capability was the weight of responsibility.

"Hey," she said softly, cupping his face in her hands and feeling the bristle of afternoon growth. "We're safe, remember? You can let yourself be off duty for a few hours."

He lifted his hands and caught her wrists, handcuffing her in place. "That's the problem. I can't compartmentalize anymore—hell, I wasn't ever very good at it. I just sucked up the stuff that bothered me. Now, though, I can't separate this case from the thing that's bothering me the most."

"And what is that?" she asked, even though she already knew. It was in the intensity of his eyes and the hard, unyielding grip that said he wasn't going to let her go this time, wasn't going to push her away.

"You," he rasped. The word both thrilled and intimidated her, making the moment feel far more important than it should, far more than she was comfortable with.

She had thought she was out of her comfort zone before, but she hadn't known the half of it.

She was outside the box, outside her usual paradigm, and she didn't care.

The firelight and candles painted him bronze and the humidity had made his hair curl at the tips, contrasting with the hard angles and intensity of his face. His damp T-shirt clung to the bulges of his shoulders and biceps, the ripples of his abs, and his pants were worn enough to drape suggestively, drawing her eyes to the flat planes of his hips and the strong columns of his thighs.

But it was that small nick of a scar below his knee that caught her attention. It was nothing compared to his bullet scars, but it was part of the history he had drifted away from. It gave him a past, marked a time in his life when he still had his parents and sister, still had dreams of going into politics. Those things were gone, but the guy who'd given him the injury wasn't. Anyone who had kept an Ian in his life all this time wasn't nearly the loner he wanted to think.

And, loner or not, cop or ranger, she wanted him. Now. Tonight.

As if her body had been waiting for that permission, heat flooded her, pooling in her breasts and core, and making her very aware that she was naked beneath the robe, that only a thin tie separated them.

His voice rasped low as he said, "I watch you, worry about you, think about you when I should be concentrating on other things." He paused, expression shifting. "Look, I know you've got other plans, and that you don't want to start something with someone as screwed up as me…so here's your chance. Say the word and I'll hole up in the bedroom until morning."

"And my other option?" Her heart tapped a quick rhythm in her chest. *Tonight is tonight,* she thought. She could do this. She could enjoy him yet protect a piece of herself.

"You're the overachiever. You figure it out."

Lips curving, she shifted her hands in his grip and moved in, conscious of the way her robe gaped at the chest as she rose up onto her knees to lean over him. Catching one of his hands, she brought it to the bend of her knee and up along her bare thigh, then pressed her hand atop his, holding him there.

His eyes fired and his fingers flexed restlessly beneath hers as he waited for her kiss. "Just do it," he rasped.

"That's a family motto," she whispered bare inches from his lips.

Then she looped her free hand around his neck and flung herself backward, yanking him fully clothed into the bubbling froth, laughing. Feeling free.

MATT SURFACED WITH A shout and found himself standing nearly chest-deep. He hauled her into his arms as warm, foamy water ran down them both. "You're insane. You know that, right?"

She latched her legs around his waist, flung her arms wide and leaned back into the bubbles. "Sanity is overrated, especially at a time like this."

She had a point—they were in an oasis of calm in the middle of a crisis, and she was in his arms. If this was crazy, maybe he *was* overrating sanity. But there was no way to overrate her wet, gleaming skin.

The robe clung to her breasts but parted between and below, flaring away beneath the bubbles, so when his hands came up naturally to catch her legs where they wrapped around him, his fingers slid without interruption along sleek skin covering gloriously toned muscle.

Murmuring approval, she slicked her hair away from her face and rose back up against him, wrapping her arms around his neck to meet him in an openmouthed, rapacious kiss.

Heat hammered through him, around him. His shaft hardened to iron as it had been that morning when he woke thinking of her.

They kissed, straining together in a clash of lips and tongues that nearly sent him over the edge then and there.

His fingers tightened on her thighs, digging in as he searched for control. He wanted to drag off his pants and bury himself in her, wanted to rise over her, pin her to the tub's edge and pound into her, claiming her as his own.

Slow down. Hold it together. He said it over and over again in his head, clawing himself back from the brink as he held her, kissed her, touched that glorious skin where it slipped and slid against him.

Her robe came loose. His free hand found a breast, and she arched into him. He cupped her for a moment, relearning the feel of a woman's body, learning the feel that was hers alone. Then he slid his thumb up and across, and caught her moan in his mouth as he brushed across a peaked nipple. He kissed her cheek, her jaw, took her earlobe in his mouth and got a raw kick of pleasure from her throaty gasp and the texture of the three diamond studs that were so elementally *Gigi*.

She reared back and peeled his shirt away. His balance teetered in slow motion, the two of them buoyed by the pulsing water that now touched his bare torso.

He let momentum carry them into the shallows, then sat where a curve in the hot tub wall formed a soft niche. It was just right for a man to sit, for a woman to ride. She straddled him, bore him back against the edge, and rose over him as they kissed.

She was naked now, her robe lost somewhere to the water, freeing him to shape the flow of her spine, the flare of her waist and the tight curves of her rear.

His head spun. His body pulsed. For the first time in an eternity, he was entirely inside his own skin and in the moment. He wasn't thinking or worrying, wasn't numb. He was *feeling*. He felt the scrape of her teeth along his throat, the press of her lips on the puckered scar atop his shoulder, bringing mingled arousal and absolution.

Then she straightened and, with an impish smile, disappeared beneath the bubbles. "Don't—" he began, then groaned at the brush of her hair against his stomach, the touch of her lips along the second, larger scar, and the sensation of her fingers at the button of his fly, and then inside.

He hissed and arched into her touch, his vision graying as her hand closed around him fleetingly, then released so she could work his pants off.

As the clinging cloth finally came free, leaving him

naked in the bubbles, she surfaced with a gasp, her eyes bright, her cheeks flushed. He reached for her and she slid up against him, so they half reclined, touching along the lengths of their bodies with her legs alongside his, her arms around his waist, the two of them locked in a kiss.

Then she rose up over him, poised above him. They traded whispered words about safety and protection, and dealt with the necessities. But his entire attention was on need and sensation, the touch of skin on skin, and the way his flesh surged up toward her opening, seeking her. He surged against her, started to shift them and reverse their positions, but she pressed his shoulders back, her lips curving in an expression that was so wholly feminine it made his chest ache.

She leaned in and whispered close to his ear, "How about you let someone take care of you for a change?"

Then she shifted down and back, and he hissed out a breath as his hard tip nudged against yielding flesh and eased inside.

"Ah," he breathed, the noise rattling in his chest. "Tight."

She murmured something against his throat, then found his lips with hers, letting him control the kiss as she controlled their union. She slid down on him inch by torturous inch, until she was finally seated against him, wringing a deep groan from him that felt like it came from his toes.

His whole body stung with pins and needles now, reawakening to pleasure at a level he had never known. His hands flexed on her hips, drawing her closer, settling her astride him until she gasped against his mouth, shuddering as he hit a spot that was sweet, tight and right.

Her inner muscles pulsed around him, waking every neuron and tickling pleasure centers he had long forgotten. Then she began to move, in just a small, wavelike motion at first, following the rhythm of the water surrounding them. Even those small shifts had him throwing back his head and bracing, trying to slow himself down.

Some part of him said that he should be doing the work and making sure she came before he did, but then she picked up the pace, and chivalry lost out to "oh, hell, yeah" as everything started coming together inside him.

Water splashed between them, around them. He let go of her hips and slapped for purchase, found handholds and dug in with his heels, which gave them an anchor but left him effectively bound spread-eagled in the water.

Heat flared where she twined around him, moved against him. He sought her mouth, felt her shudder and clutch as they hit that sweet spot together, and then, too quickly, the pins and needles were racing through him, coalescing, speeding up, threatening to detonate.

He reared up and caught her by the waist, bracing her against the side of the tub as he plunged into her once, twice, a third time, and heard her cry out as he cut loose. Bowing into her, he rode out the orgasm, emptying himself into her in a rush that blew his mind and shifted something deep inside him.

He shuddered against her, pulsed into her, and then held her close as things leveled off and the intensity of their union eased. He kissed her cheek, her temple, wanting to say something, but unable to come up with the right words. Restless, edgy energy shifted inside him; he wasn't even close to sated.

The room suddenly seemed very quiet, with only the hum of machinery, the pop of bubbles and the soft throb of jazz in the background.

It had been a long time since someone had wanted to be there for him, even temporarily, rather than the reverse. She cared for him, made him feel alive again, and he should be satisfied with that. But he found that he couldn't uncoil, couldn't relax, because deep down inside, he knew he hadn't gotten all of her just then. In controlling their lovemaking, she had held part of herself in check.

Don't complicate things, he told himself. *She doesn't want more than this.* He wasn't sure he did, either. But the edge remained.

She curled against him, her head in the crook of his neck, her arms linked loosely around him, their legs tangling as they drifted into deeper water.

"Nice," she said, turning her face into his throat. "Never would've guessed you were rusty."

That elicited a surprised snort out of him. And it gave him an opening to take what he wanted in a way she could understand.

"That's it," he growled. "Those are fighting words." In a rush, he shifted her, got her over his shoulder and charged out of the hot tub, headed for the bedroom.

She squeaked and squirmed wetly. "What are you doing?"

"Getting us someplace drier where I can do this my way."

"You're *complaining?*"

"Hell, no. But you got to go first. Now it's my turn." And this time he would take more. He wanted her to be right there with him in the crazy, illogical space they made together, the sizzle and spark that had forced him out of his comfortable routine and opened old wounds. After tonight, he didn't want to look back and know they had taken it only partway.

Tonight he wanted all of her. No regrets.

Chapter Twelve

Somewhere in the back of Gigi's mind a warning pinged, saying that this was a bad idea, that they should keep it in the hot tub, on the couch, the bolsters, hell, up against the wall. Those were places where sex stayed fun, where they were just two people burning off steam and enjoying each other. Bedrooms were more serious places.

Or did the shimmer of nerves come from the change in him? His grip had gone firm and commanding, his voice no-nonsense, and he was suddenly doing rather than checking first. He was the über-cop, the super-ranger, the guy who, when he had burned out on saving one chunk of the world had retreated to protect another.

She was a liberated female, a warrior, the best she could be. And as he carried her into a simply furnished bedroom lit by a dimmer light turned low, tossed her on the bed and followed her down to cover her moisture-slicked body with his own, she was hotter for him than she had ever been for any other man, under any other situation.

His muscular bulk made her feel small and delicate, and when he levered himself up on one elbow to look down at her with fierce heat in his eyes, her blood leaped right back to boiling, though they had had each other only minutes earlier. His look was a challenge, a dare, and it had her reaching for him.

He caught her wrists and guided her hands to the spindles of the headboard. "Not this time."

She would have argued, but he kissed the words away, traced a finger down the center of her body and made her arch into him, helpless beneath the sudden heat, the maelstrom of sensation brought by his tongue and his touch, and the leashed strength she sensed him containing as his legs twined with hers.

Her better sense told her to let go of the spindles and give as good as she got, keeping them on the same level with each other. But the inciting stroke of his fingertips teased her senses and the promise that lit his eyes when he broke the kiss and moved down her body held her in place.

He cupped one breast and had her arching against him, then took her nipple into his mouth, wringing a moan from deep in her throat. Her body heated and throbbed. Pleasure coiled inside her as she tightened her fingers around the headboard spindles and hung on for the ride.

The soft bedspread had bunched up beneath them; he pulled it free and stroked her with it, blotting her face and pushing back her wet hair, then moving down her body, alternately drying and kissing her. All the while, he whispered hot praise and dark suggestions that stirred her to the point of madness.

The sun had set, turning the world dark and making it feel as if they were the only two people on Earth. Danger still lurked outside, but the need for him—and the temptation to let him take charge—was far more immediate. He reared over her, settling back on his haunches to scrub a corner of the bedspread through his thick, dark hair, down across his shoulders and broad chest, and down farther, to where his shaft emerged from its nest of dark curls, ruddy and engorged.

She feasted on the sight of him, shifting almost without volition to rub her thighs together as he tossed the bedspread aside and bent over her.

Her senses spun and her insides clenched when he kissed her stomach, her navel, the point of her hip. Someone moaned—she thought it might have been her, but couldn't be sure. She wasn't sure of anything anymore; her whole world hinged on the touch of his lips and tongue as he moved down and settled himself between her legs.

The sight of his dark head down there made her breath go thin and the contrast of his skin against hers shot flames searing through her. Then he slicked his tongue through her folds, and every part of her clenched in a sudden surge of pleasure that had her bowing back on the mattress with an inarticulate cry.

He rasped something low in his throat—a curse, maybe, or a plea—and did it again. And again. When she strained against him, trying to move, to speed things up, he held her in place with his weight and strength, and kept going—licking, lapping, nuzzling, *taking*.

The breath backed up in her throat as he stripped her defenses and broke through to a place of pure sensation. She responded to him without inhibition or boundaries, no thought of yesterday or tomorrow. He brought her

to the edge of release again and again with his mouth
and hands, until the pleasure burned her, consumed
her, knotted her body tight and left her sobbing with
pleasure.

Her hands cramped on the spindles; her body burned
for his. She was gasping, babbling pleas and demands
that went unheeded until, finally, he looked up at her,
his eyes sharp, bright and a little wild. Voice rattling in
his chest, he grated, "Now."

"God, yes, now."

He moved up her body. His skin was hot on hers; his
scent had become theirs, and was laced with sex.

She was tight all over, needy and greedy. And when
he came down atop her, pressing her into the mattress
with his hard, solid weight, she couldn't take it anymore.
She tore her hands from the headboard and dug her fingers into his hips as he positioned himself at her center,
the thick head of his erection just nudging her opening,
which was slick and wet, and pulsed for him.

He kissed her long and deep, then broke the kiss,
pressed his furnace-hot cheek to hers, and whispered her
name as he thrust home, filling her in a single strong,
possessive surge.

In an instant, his hard flesh was seated far more
deeply, more intimately than before. He surrounded
her inside and out, pinned her, possessed her.

Then he fixed his eyes on her and she found herself
trapped in their green depths, laid bare by their intensity as he withdrew slowly, then thrust home. The first
plunge wrung a gasp from her, the second had a groan
rattling deep in his chest. He dropped his head, pressed
his cheek to hers, slid into her with delicious friction.

She was laid flat and open beneath him, but moved when and where she could, digging in and meeting his thrusts. His breath was a roar, hers a sob. If she had been on the edge of an orgasm before, now she leaped to a new plateau entirely, one that was huge, breathtaking and scary. Nothing existed except the two of them and a bed behind bulletproof glass as he drove her up toward an impossible pinnacle, one she had never before glimpsed.

She clung to him, anchoring herself to his shoulders, pressing her lips to the scarred indentation where the bullet had gone in. Misplaced terror flashed at the thought that he could have died, that she wouldn't ever have known this, known him. That brought a warning buzz, quickly lost beneath the enormity of the breathless pause that presaged orgasm.

Her body tightened, sensation rushing inward to gather at the place where he stroked her inside and out. He touched all the right spots at once, their joined flesh slick with excitement, and…and…

The world paused. Held its breath.

And she went over the edge.

A shuddering cry escaped from her, mirroring the all-consuming, wrenching fist of her orgasm. It defied logic and boundaries. She bowed into him, gasped against his sweat-slicked flesh as the radiating throbs of pleasure went on and on, sent higher by his harsh groan and three quick thrusts, then higher still when he stiffened against her and came whispering her name in a voice that was filled with awe, approval and satisfaction.

He shuddered, and bucked as her flesh milked him, the echoes of her pleasure prolonging his.

Then, even after things leveled off and their bodies began to cool, they stayed wrapped together, her arms around his shoulders, her ankles locked behind him, their faces pressed together.

Then he backed off and looked down at her, and where before there had been a challenge in his eyes, now there was only a profound tenderness that shifted something inside her.

He opened his mouth to speak, but then just stopped and shook his head. "Later," he whispered, and dropped a kiss to her brow. He rearranged them, nudging her onto her side and fitting her into the curve of his body, then pulling the bedclothes up and over them.

She let him fuss, ignoring the nerves that churned over how far she had let him in, how much she had let go. Instead, she told herself to enjoy the moment, and the man. She would deal with the rest of it later. Tonight was tonight…and for tonight, she wanted to belong entirely to him.

THE NEXT MORNING, GIGI awoke from a fractured jumble of dreams and plunged directly into sensations that were entirely different yet equally terrifying: body heat behind her, an arm across her waist, the pleasurable ache that came from a sex-filled night, her feet pressing atop those of her lover…

Her lover. Matthew H. Blackthorn. Oh, God.

The dreams—an amalgam of the crashed Jeep, the fleeing truck and the imagined scene of a furniture truck slamming into his mother's minivan—cluttered her mind as she rolled to face him.

He woke when she moved, going tense and alert for

a second and then easing, cracking one green eye with an expression that said, *Ah, it's you. No threat.*

But although she might not be on his threat radar, she couldn't say the reverse. Because as she lay there with her head pillowed on his arm and her feet still pressed atop his, she badly wanted to snuggle into him, tuck her head beneath his chin and pretend the world outside didn't exist. More, she could already feel herself storing away the small moments, the details that didn't matter when the sex was just for fun.

She knew how his eyes went dark when he was aroused, how his voice rasped on her name when he climaxed. She knew how he smelled and tasted; how he moved with animal grace one moment and a cop's blunt get-it-done attitude in the next; how he drove like a maniac but would always keep his passenger safe, or die trying.

"No regrets," he said quietly, his eyes steady on hers. It wasn't a question; it was an order. And part of her wanted to go along with him. Because if she could convince herself there was nothing to regret, that she hadn't truly given herself over to him last night, then everything would be okay.

She closed her eyes and whispered inwardly: *You're fine. You're whole. You can handle this.* But instead of confidence came the images of the Jeep, the truck speeding away, brake lights flashing.

It repeated in slow motion: the…truck…speeding… away.

Shock seared through her as she realized what she had seen, what her brain was trying to tell her. Her eyes flew open. "Holy crap. I didn't see it before, but now that I'm more relaxed," she rushed on, not waiting to look hard at the source of that relaxation, "I'm seeing the truck driving away… And I caught a partial plate number."

He stared at her for a three-count, expression unreadable. Then he nodded. "Call it in and let's get moving."

And just like that, their night was over. It was tomorrow, and they had a case to solve.

Chapter Thirteen

Matt drained the hot tub, stuck his clothes in the dryer and generally pulled the place back together while Alyssa ran the plates.

Any thoughts he might've had of a breakfast of eggs and toast with a side of "hey, that got pretty intense last night" had been shot to hell by the break in the case, but maybe that was for the best.

In the clearer-headed light of day, the mind-blowing sex they'd shared didn't change the fact that she had her sights set elsewhere and he didn't have his set on much of anything. In fact, he flat-out hated the idea of her joining a hazardous response team.

Not because she wouldn't be good at it, but because she would be great at it, and there was no way in hell he could wave her off to work and then wonder if she was coming back. The fact that he could picture himself doing just that—and imagine it driving him nuts—just proved he had gotten himself in way too deep last night and needed to back off, fast.

Meanwhile, Gigi was acting as if it was no big deal. He might have been annoyed if he hadn't seen the hint of a plea at the back of her eyes, the well-hidden desperation that said she wasn't any more comfortable with how things had gone than he was, and they should just leave it alone.

Her phone rang in the bedroom, where she was getting dressed in Chelsea's spare clothes.

"It's Alyssa," she called. "I'm putting her on speaker."

"Thanks." He moved into the bedroom doorway and leaned in, looking at the phone rather than Gigi, yet very aware of the sidelong look she shot him.

After the hellos were out of the way, Alyssa said, "Assuming these guys were dumb enough—or ballsy enough—not to switch out the plates, there's only one truck that matches the description and your partial."

"The guys in the truck were amateurs," Matt said with total certainty. "I'm not sure if they're the same ones who went after Tanya or torched the station, but these guys didn't shoot or drive like pros."

"Who's the registered owner of the truck?" Gigi asked. She had one hip propped on the edge of the mattress, as if trying to prove to herself that it was no biggie that they had shared the bed.

"Alex MacDonald. He's a sometimes handyman, always troublemaker who lives near the arena and has a fondness for off-track betting and the occasional hunting trip."

Gigi glanced at him. "Did he come through Station Fourteen?"

"If he did, he didn't make enough of a fuss for me to remember his name. I'd check the records, but..."

"They're torched."

"Right." Even with the fire threat, there hadn't seemed

to be any reason to store copies of the hiking permits online. Most of the people who came through Station Fourteen only lasted a few days, a couple of weeks at the outside.

"I'll send you a picture," Alyssa said.

"Do you have him in custody?"

"Jack is on his way over to his place right now. I—hang on. Tucker's calling in on the other line. I'm going to put you on hold. Be right back." Alyssa clicked off.

That left Matt in the bedroom doorway, Gigi on the bed and a huge elephant in the room, sitting between them.

He told himself to leave it alone, then surprised the hell out of himself by saying, "If I asked you out to dinner once this was over, what would you say?"

From the look on her face, he had surprised the hell out of her, too. Her eyes widened and new color touched her cheeks, but he wasn't sure if that was from pleasure or something else. Then her lips curved, though the expression didn't quite reach her eyes. "When this is over, why don't you ask me and we'll find out?"

With timing so perfect he suspected she had been listening in, Alyssa said, "I'm back. Jack says Alex MacDonald is in the wind, his apartment pretty close to stripped. Cassie is off on a call, so Tucker is going to pick me up and run me over to the apartment to process what's left."

"Are you sure—" Gigi began.

"I'm sure I'm going to lose it if I don't do *something* other than sit on my rapidly spreading butt and coordinate calls and manpower," Alyssa snapped. Then, a little calmer, she said, "The apartment is locked down and there's no off-road bouncing around involved in getting there. You'd need some serious firepower to keep me away, because I hate that these bastards came after you two, and it scares me to think they might try again."

"How about Gigi and I meet you there?" Matt asked. "I can discuss a few things with Tucker while you two work the scene." And it would double up on the firepower if it turned out that the apartment was a trap.

"He said you would say that. I'll send you the address. See you when you get here." The line went dead as she clicked off.

Gigi stood and pocketed the phone, then smoothed her palms down the borrowed pants, which were a little too big. "I'm ready to leave when you are."

"One minute." Going on instinct, making the sort of split-second decision that used to be second nature, he crossed to her, cupped a hand around the back of her neck and laid his lips on hers.

She stiffened and brought her hands up, he thought to push him away. But instead she curled her fingers into his T-shirt and pulled him closer, opening her mouth beneath his.

Heat seared straight through his gut at the touch of her tongue and the taste of her, which was instantly familiar yet still stunningly new. He crowded closer, so their bodies aligned, and his flesh hardened in moments, though he should have been sated.

He couldn't get enough of her. He buried his hands in her hair, ran his tongue along the rim of her ear, tugged at the studs with his teeth and made her moan. Then he eased away, brushing her hair behind her ears and watching how the shorter half of it fell forward once more. "Okay. Now I'm ready to go."

No regrets.

As Gigi followed Alyssa into MacDonald's apartment, which was a small second floor one-bedroom in a dingy three-floor apartment building in a not very nice section of town, she was still debating how much—if anything—to tell her friend about what had happened with Matt.

But the moment the door closed behind them, shutting out the two uniforms stationed in the hallway, Alyssa faced her, crossed her arms atop Baby McDermott and said implacably, "Okay, sister. Spill it."

"I… Darn it, you were listening in on the phone the whole time."

"I caught the end of it, anyway. Sue me." Her eyes gleamed. "What happened with you two last night?"

"Aren't we supposed to be processing a scene?" Gigi took a pointed look around, though admittedly there didn't seem to be much of a scene to process. The apartment had been stripped back to bare walls and plain furniture, with nothing personal that she could see.

"Yep. And it'll go much faster if you confess, so we can get started." Alyssa paused. "Or you can tell me to mind my own business."

Gigi winced. "Ouch. Low blow."

"I'll start. You slept together. That's obvious, given the way he was looking at you just now."

"I…" To Gigi's horror, her eyes filled with tears. "Oh, crap." She spun away, mortified, feeling her control start to slip. Aware that Alyssa was coming over, knowing that a kind word might break her, she held up a hand. "Don't. Please."

"Sorry. I'm pregnant, which means I can do pretty much what I want and I'll be forgiven." The blonde wrapped her arms around Gigi, sandwiching Baby Mc-Dermott between them, and said, "You don't have to be a hero with me. Not ever."

A big sob welled up, jamming Gigi's throat. She held on for another few seconds, then let go, sagging against Alyssa and giving herself permission to lose it and give in to the shakes that had eluded her the night before.

Her friend hung on. "It's okay, kiddo. Whatever's going on, it's going to be okay."

She sucked in a shuddering breath as tears scalded her eyes, but to her surprise, that was all that happened. After a moment, she lost the overwhelming urge to wail, and the tightness in her throat eased. A minute after that, she could breathe again.

Letting out a shaky laugh, she straightened away from Alyssa. "Well. That was anticlimactic. I guess...I think... Wow. It's been a pretty intense few days."

Alyssa pressed her hands into her lower back and leaned against a corner of a ratty couch that looked like a few more fibers wouldn't make any difference one way or the other. "Would that be the part where you dove back into a burning building, made it through a car chase or spent the night with Matt in the 'safe' house?" The finger quotes said she knew exactly what kind of a house it was.

"All of it." Gigi's cheeks heated. "And you could've warned me about the cabin."

"Would it have changed anything?"

"Maybe." But honesty compelled her to admit, "Probably not." She and Matt had been on a collision course. It would've happened with or without the ambience.

"So. You going to give a pregnant lady some details?"

"Only if said pregnant lady is working while we talk." Given that MacDonald had taken the time to strip the place bare, logic said that it probably wouldn't yield anything useful. But instinct itched along her spine, telling her that there was something…

Or maybe not. Maybe her emotions had screwed with her instincts. Wasn't that what Matt had been implying when he mentioned the two guys on his team who'd had things on their mind the day of the bank robbery?

It didn't escape her that his point jibed with the Lynd protocol: one thing at a time. Work, then family. Mixing the two was risky, especially if you wanted to be the best at both.

Alyssa nodded. "How about you get started and I'll catch up. Better yet, I'll observe your highly trained technique."

"Wow. You're really working it, aren't you?" Gigi sent her a look. "Or are you feeling crappy again?"

"Little bit of both." She nudged her field kit with a toe. "I'm waiting."

Gigi put on her protective gear and got to work, first taking a tour of the apartment, looking for obvious stuff and snapping some overview photos, and then coming back to the main room.

Alyssa sent her a look, then pointedly drummed her fingers atop Baby McDermott. "Still waiting."

Starting with a banged up wooden desk that had a

layer of dust on it with a laptop-shaped void off to one side, Gigi took more pictures with a ruler for scale, and then used a shoeprint-size piece of transfer paper to take a print of the laptop. She wasn't hopeful that it would lead to anything, though. Thanks to the TV shows, the bad guys had gotten way better at cleaning up after themselves. *Hello, CSI effect.*

Finally, she said, "I called my mom last night to tell her what was going on."

Alyssa raised an eyebrow. "And?"

"I couldn't tell her about it. Any of it." Gigi went through the drawers, which held nothing but lint and crumbs. "She just finally started getting behind the idea of me trying to get into the accelerated training program. Mostly because it's a tangible goal that involves testing and competition, which she gets, even if she doesn't understand why this is what I want to do."

"Dangerous professions can be harder on the family than the individual. The individual chooses the job, chooses the risk. The family members don't always get a vote."

Hearing a tone, Gigi glanced over. "You and Tucker make it work, and so do Cassie and Seth."

"Three of the four of us are analysts. And while we see more action than the norm, being in Bear Claw—or in Seth's case, a field office—the action is still the exception. As for Fax and Chelsea...well, they're different. He sponsored her into the agency, made her his partner. But..." She shook her head. "He worked under a female superior for a long time, which I think makes him more ready to accept Chelsea being in the field with him."

Gigi let out a soft sigh. "Whereas Matt has spent most of his life trying to protect the world from itself."

"He could change."

Now it was Gigi's turn to raise an eyebrow.

"Okay, maybe not." Alyssa paused. "Where did you guys leave things?"

With a kiss that had shot right to the top of her top ten, one that had made her feel strong yet feminine, like she was the supercop's girl, the center of his world. "With a 'maybe' on going out to dinner after this case is wrapped up and things go back to normal."

Alyssa made a face. "Which one of you was doing the most backpedaling?"

"I'd say we were about even." Gigi abandoned the desk and moved to the couch, which was the only other large piece of furniture in the cramped sitting area.

Alyssa shifted over to lean on the desk, moving slowly, while Gigi gave the carpet a quick scan—wincing at the profusion of fibers, most if not all of which would be totally useless.

Part of an analyst's job was making judgment calls about what to collect and what to leave behind. Each piece of evidence she selected represented dollars, man hours, storage space and analytics.

One of the things that made her very good at what she did was her instincts. Normally, she could look at a scene and know, at a gut-check level, what to take. Now, though, her instincts were humming, but they weren't telling her anything. It wasn't just Alyssa being there, either. Her head wasn't in the game.

She used a small flashlight to look under the couch, trying to make out anything useful amid the dust rats.

"When I woke up this morning, I thought to myself that if he asked me to turn down the academy and stay here with him, I would seriously consider it." She was ashamed even saying it aloud. "I've known the guy—really known him, I mean, not just to the point of avoiding each other in the hallway—for what, seventy-two hours? And we've been in each other's faces—and not in the good way—for more than half that time. So it's ridiculous for me to even think…" She shook her head. "It's ridiculous."

"Maybe, but there's such a thing as love at first sight."

Gigi snorted. "Lust at first sight, maybe, but not love. We're not… It's not like that." But she glanced over. "Was it that way for you and Tucker?"

"No way. We met. We danced. We hooked up. We realized, belatedly, that we were going to be working together. And big, bad Tucker McDermott, the original 'I'm a rolling stone, just passing through' didn't want anything to do with a girl who wanted to put down roots, so we spent the next few months snarling at each other." She shook her head. "No, I'm thinking of Fax and Chelsea, actually. When she met him, he was posing as a convict and had just helped al-Jihad himself break out of the ARX prison. He was on the job, deep undercover…and they got one good look at each other, and fell hard."

"Oh." Gigi had to swallow past the wistful lump in her throat. "Well. We already know Fax is a special case. And I'm the 'doesn't want to put down roots' factor in this equation. I still have things I want to do before I settle down."

"Why does it have to be settling? Why can't it be making a choice of one thing you want over something else you want? Or, better yet, finding a way to have them both."

Pulling the cushions off the sofa with more force than was probably necessary, Gigi probed the cracks and found the usual gnarly assortment of crumbs, old food, wrappers, coins and other garbage. "That's not the way it works in my family."

"So be the black sheep and do your own thing."

"Been there, done that." Gigi flicked at her earrings and hair.

"Those are little things."

"The job isn't."

"Maybe, but you're still doing the 'got to be the best' thing they're so into." Alyssa shifted, wincing.

Gigi's instincts flared. "You're not in labor, are you?"

"God, no. I'd be screaming my head off. And don't change the subject."

"Do you swear you're not in labor?"

"I swear. Seriously. Now let's move on."

Gigi felt her way along the back of the sofa, where things sometimes got wedged and forgotten. "Look, I know my family is whacked-out, okay? In a good way, maybe, but whacked-out nonetheless. I know there's no law that says I have to be in the top whatever percentile of the universe…but what if I want to be? My parents gave me all these great opportunities, so why not use them to shoot for the moon? I want to be on a hazardous response team. I want the adrenaline rush. I want to save lives and be an über-cop, not just date one." Love one.

Marry one and spend the rest of her life waking up as she had that morning, wrapped up in him and pleasantly satiated from their lovemaking. Maybe even riding herd on a couple of green-eyed—

Whoa, back up. Getting in way too deep there. She could feel the urgency building, the need to see him again, even though he and Tucker were just outside.

"An über-cop?" Alyssa's voice was amused.

"Oh, shut up. You know what I mean. I've got goals that are mine, not my family's, and I don't want to give them up."

"Has he asked you to?"

"Not yet." But he would. If things went any further between them, she would eventually have to decide between him and the job. She knew that deep down in her soul. "Right now, *I'm* more the problem than he is. I've got this thing going on inside me that I don't like. At all. When I'm not with him, I'm thinking about him, obsessing over him, both the good stuff and the bad." Even saying it aloud made her feel shaky and weak. "Then when I *am* with him, I go back and forth between wanting to tear his clothes off with my teeth, and wanting to slap at him because I hate feeling this way and it's his fault. Only it isn't. It's *mine*."

"Oh, Gigi. Honey."

She wound down, breathing hard, and realized she was crouched over the sofa, glaring into its sprung interior like a madwoman. Looking up, she found Alyssa watching her, wide-eyed. "See? He's making me crazy. Strike that. I'm making myself crazy over him." She pushed to her feet, wanting to pace, but not letting herself because she had a *job* to do, damn it.

"Gigi—"

"I hate this. I must look completely—" *Insane,* she started to say, but then broke off as she flashed on the prior morning, when Matt had yelled at Ian over the mayor's shenanigans…and looked completely insane doing it. "Oh, for crap's sake." She started laughing helplessly, almost hysterically as she realized she was doing the same damn thing—yelling at a friend because she couldn't deal with the amount of emotion he could pull from her. "You've got to be kidding me. We're like fertilizer and fuel, functional on our own, but put us together and *pow,* stuff gets blown up."

"I have no idea what you're talking about."

"I know. It's okay, really. I'm not losing it." She took a deep breath. "I'm just figuring a few things out." She put the sofa cushions back, then stood in the center of the room and did a careful three-sixty turn, looking for anything else that pinged on her radar screen, even if this particular scene might just be about going through the motions.

"A few things," Alyssa repeated. "Like the fact that you two are good for each other."

"Ha-ha. Try that one again. More like we set each other off, and… Well, what have we got here?" Her instincts suddenly kicked hard and she went on point. "Does that look like blood to you over there on the doorframe? Looks like blood to me."

The rusty smear hadn't been immediately obvious because the rest of the place was pretty filthy, but when she looked at it from exactly the right angle, there was a handprint pattern to the grime on the doorframe leading to the bathroom.

Senses humming, she approached the spot, ignoring the funky smell coming from the room beyond.

Alyssa came up behind her. "Looks pretty new."

The blood was dry and rusty, but the imprint was crisp, unsmudged by later traffic.

"Could've been from yesterday," Gigi agreed. "Maybe from the guy Matt shot, or someone who tried to stop the bleeding." Which not only suggested the men had been in the apartment very recently, it made the bathroom the next obvious place to search.

She took pictures of the handprint and then lifted it and took a couple of DNA swabs. She handed off the evidence for Alyssa to bag and tag while she kept going, her pulse drumming a little with the high that came from being on the verge of finding a piece to add to the puzzle.

The bathroom itself was small and scuzzy, an abstract study in cracked porcelain and rodent droppings. It, too, had been stripped of its personal items, but the trash basket held a few scraps of wax-coated paper at the bottom. "Looks like someone did some first aid in here."

"More blood?"

"Pieces of bandage wrappers. There's no obvious blood—given how good they were about picking up after themselves elsewhere, they probably bleached it to nuke the DNA." But that was okay, she had the handprint. She should be able to lift enough DNA from it to give Cassie something to work with.

After taking more photos, she picked up the trash basket and shook it to move the bandage wrappers around and see if there was anything more interesting beneath.

A piece of paper unstuck itself from the bottom of the can and fluttered to the floor.

"Hello." There went her instincts again.

Alyssa poked her head in. "Got something?"

"Maybe." Gigi took some photos and made a couple of notes, tightening up her chain of evidence in case the scrap of paper turned out to be something useful. Then she reached down and picked it up, handling it as carefully as she could.

For a second, disappointment threatened when she saw that it was just another bandage wrapper, this one mostly intact. But then she saw the bloody thumbprint on one edge and writing on the other side, and adrenaline sizzled through her. "It's a note. Numbers. Letters. And a date and time." She looked up, blood draining from her face. "Whatever it is, it's happening in less than two hours."

Chapter Fourteen

Matt took one look at the note Gigi had spread out on a rickety desk and said, "The middle numbers are GPS coordinates." At Gigi's frown, he added, "It's a military notation scheme, not civilian."

"Alex MacDonald was in the National Guard," Alyssa put in.

He caught Gigi's quick glance, but got busy pulling out his phone and keying the sequence into the GPS feature. "Who do you have that's good at codes?" The number-letter sequences almost made sense, but not really.

She photographed the scrap of paper. "I'll send it to a friend, see if she has any suggestions."

"If you're cool with it, you could hit up Ian, too. He's good at puzzles." At her nod, he rattled off the number. His GPS was taking forever. "Come on, you bugger. Load already."

"Yeah," Tucker put in drily, "Talking to it always helps." He stood a few paces away with Alyssa, who was propped up against the sofa and looked more than a little pasty. Tucker, too, was pretty drawn all of a sudden.

"Everything okay?"

"I'd be lots better if people stopped asking me if I'm okay," Alyssa snapped, then closed her eyes and shook her head. "Sorry. Crabby."

"You've earned it, I'd say." But he caught Gigi's worried look, and his gut churned slowly at the realization that as a team, they were batting a thousand on the distraction factors. "Look, if you two want to head out—" His phone rang, interrupting. He glared at the stalled GPS transfer and stabbed the button to answer. "Blackthorn here."

"We got MacDonald," Jack said, satisfaction plain in his voice. "Idiot ran his truck off the road heading up into the backcountry."

"Hang on," Matt said. "I'm putting you on speaker. Go ahead."

"One of the search parties found him and sat on him until I got here. He's light-headed from blood loss and a fever, and he's singing like a freaking canary. That's the good news. The bad news is what he's telling us: apparently he and a half dozen other local thugs, along with some out-of-town muscle, have been keeping those fires down at Sectors Five and Six going in order to tie up air support and keep the rangers focused downhill. The break-ins were theirs, too—partly for entertainment and profit, partly to mix things up and, again, to keep attention off other parts of the park."

Matt's blood iced with fury at MacDonald and the others—and whoever was controlling them. They'd destroyed thousands of acres and caused numerous casualties for nothing more than distraction.

But part of his fury was self-directed. He hadn't

caught on. The bastards had torched his station, yet he hadn't made the leap to the wildfires.

A hand touched his, making him aware that he had grabbed onto a nearby doorframe, was clutching it so tightly his knuckles were white, his fingers cramping. Gigi. He knew it was her without looking, felt the sizzle in her touch, the compassion.

But when he looked down into her eyes, he only saw annoyance.

"You don't have a crystal ball, remember?" She tapped his bloodless knuckles. "I don't care how good your hindsight is, you couldn't have seen this one coming. So just take a breath, cut yourself some slack, and focus on what we can do something about, which is what's happening right now, and what we can plan in the next couple of hours."

And the damn thing was, she was right. In three days, she had gotten to know him better than…hell, anyone in his life except, perhaps, for Ian.

He took a deep breath and nodded. "Thanks," he said quietly, privately. Then, raising his voice, he said, "Sorry, Jack. You were saying?"

"Here's the thing. MacDonald doesn't know who he's working for or why this guy—it's a guy's voice on the phone, that's all I'm getting—wants our attention on the foothills. Or if he does know, he's not saying." He paused. "Apparently Tanya saw and took something she shouldn't have, and the voice on the phone told Mac-Donald and a couple of his buddies to shut her up and destroy the evidence. The next thing they know, Matt and Gigi are on the list, too, because they're getting too close. And then…wait, hang on."

Voices murmured in the background, and then Jack cursed viciously.

Returning to the call, he said, "Okay, forget that stuff. You guys need to get on this, *fast*. Apparently MacDonald was headed up to meet up with the others and get new marching orders. They're going to hit Sector Nine this afternoon."

Matt's blood went from ice to a vicious boil. "Sons. Of. Bitches. If Nine goes, the whole damn park goes." Then it wouldn't matter what Proudfoot sold or didn't sell—it would all be worthless char.

"The meeting," Gigi said urgently. She tapped the note. "That's got to be it."

A ping sounded from his phone, indicating that the download had been completed. "About freaking time." He grabbed the phone and said to Jack, "Call us if you get anything more out of MacDonald." Toggling over to the other screen, he took a look at the map the GPS coordinates had pulled up, and nearly groaned. "Perfect. That's just freaking perfect."

"Where are they meeting?" Tucker asked.

"The Forgotten." Matt looked around the room, trying to stow his emotions and deal with the problem right in front of him, namely how they could get out there in time. "We need a damn chopper." But the functional birds were all out at Sectors Five and Six, and most of them were limping—there wasn't enough time to get one out to the Forgotten.

"What about Fax's helicopter?" Gigi said. "The one with all the bells and whistles?"

"That might actually work," Tucker said, surprised.

"Last I checked, it was at the old airfield near Station Eight, on the west side."

Alyssa was already on her phone. "Chelsea? We need your help. Well, actually, we need your chopper and your pilot."

"Come on." Matt said, heading for the door. "We'll meet them there." Entering a sort of highly functional haze that wasn't quite his old crisis response mode, he hit redial, and when Williams answered, said, "If you can pawn off MacDonald, meet us at the old airstrip just past Ranger Station Eight. Wait. What's your closest station right now?"

"Um. Ten, I think. I'm pretty far up."

"Good. Go there first. Someone will meet you with guns. Grab them and meet me at the airstrip."

He powered past the uniforms and hit the street, then turned back to Tucker. "We'll see you there?" He was asking about more than just a rendezvous.

"Absolutely," Alyssa said. When Tucker turned on her, she glared right back. "I'm. Fine."

Leaving them to their fight, he ducked into the rental as Gigi launched herself into the other side and went for her seat belt. Her eyes gleamed. "Finally, a big foam finger."

She terrified him.

Tabling that for the moment, he put in a call to his quarters, hoping someone was there. Bert answered, "Station Fourteen."

For a second Matt couldn't say anything, as the sound of the older ranger's familiar voice slammed home how far he was from the man he'd been just a few days ago. He didn't wish himself back up there, wasn't pining for his solitude. He wanted to get to the airstrip and be right in the thick of things.

He glanced at Gigi, who was on her phone, trying to get some birds diverted to fly over Sector Nine. From the looks of it, she wasn't having much luck.

"Boss? That you?"

"Yeah. Sorry, Bert. Look, I'll catch you up later. Right now, I need you to patch me through to Ten, ASAP. Get me Harvey if he's there. Once you've done that, get all of your volunteers headed for Sector Nine. There's a chance someone's going to try to torch it."

"They do that, and the whole place is toast."

"Which is why we need to make sure it doesn't happen. So get me Harvey, and get the others moving."

"On it."

As Matt steered the rental onto the highway leading out to the city and passed a big sign for the state park, the head of Station Ten came on the line. "Blackthorn? Harvey here."

"There's a cop headed your way, name is Williams. He needs whatever serious firepower you've got, with full ammo. Hook him up and then spread the word that you may have firebugs incoming to Sector Nine within the next few hours. I'll get you descriptions and more details when I can, but until then, do your best. Watch the roads, the skies, whatever it takes."

"Blackthorn, what the devil is going on?"

"Someone is trying to keep our attention off the Forgotten. That's all I know." How the mayor—or his buyer—figured into it was something they would need to look long and hard at. Later.

Harvey cursed and cut the connection. But he was a good man, a good ranger; he would get the job done.

Gigi ended her call, shaking her head. "Maybe. That's all I could get out of them. A maybe. They didn't seem to want to hear that if Sector Nine goes, it won't matter that Five and Six are burning—the whole damn place is going to go up." She was tight-lipped and grim, but her anger shifted to something more personal as she looked at him. "It's not a very big helicopter."

He nodded. "Pilot plus three if you skip the copilot. Maybe one more if you get real friendly. She's built for speed and fuel efficiency, but the trade-off is a low payload, and not much space."

Her brows drew together. "You'd better not be thinking about leaving me behind. This is my case and I'm your partner. *Right?*"

He hesitated. "Tucker's got the final say. He's got the rank, not me."

But Matt was going to do his damnedest to make sure that she didn't get anywhere near the Forgotten.

Chapter Fifteen

Gigi fumed in silence for the rest of the drive. But when they pulled onto the deserted airstrip and came into view of the sleek black agency chopper, she said quietly, "I've earned this one and you know it."

Matt cut a hard-eyed look at her. "Life isn't fair."

"You said the pilot plus four. That's you, Jack, Fax and me." When he glared, she just lifted her chin. "I'm a better shot than Jack."

"Not by much. And you forgot Tucker."

"No, I didn't." They both knew he wasn't getting on that helicopter. Even if the detective was willing to leave Alyssa, he was too far off his game thinking about the baby to be any good to anyone right now.

Matt parked out of range of the rotor sweep and they got out of the rental just as Tucker's SUV rolled into view.

Gigi came around the hood of the car and squared off opposite Matt. Her blood was running high with righteous indignation, but that didn't stop her from feeling the inevitable skitter of heat that hit her whenever she looked at him. It was stronger than ever now, and she was still storing up those damn details: she was conscious of the tight worry in his expression, the stark determination that wasn't the cop or the ranger, it was, quite simply, *him*.

"Gigi, please don't do this," he said quietly. "Not now. Later, after you're all the way trained, I'll..." He trailed off with a small shake of his head.

"You can't even say it, can you?" Her heart sank. She had known that it would probably come down to this between them. She just hadn't expected it to be so soon. She wasn't ready for the flameout yet.

Tucker parked nearby and climbed out of the SUV. Alyssa's door opened, but it was a moment before her feet appeared. Gigi was deeply worried for her friend, but she couldn't afford to let Matt win on this one. Not if she intended to hold her own in whatever happened between them next.

"This isn't about us," Matt said urgently. His eyes were stark. "It's a tactical decision. Yes, you're a sharpshooter, but you don't have any actual live firefighting experience, and we're not going to be dealing with just MacDonald this time. We don't have any intel, and there's no way to get a satellite feed in time. We're going in blind, with no clue what we're going to find when we get there. Admit it, that's not the sort of scenario you've trained on."

He was right, of course. Hazardous response, especially in the city, was all about collecting information before and during the op, and using it to make the best plans and decisions. This, on the other hand, was going to be a "hit the ground and go" scenario, with the added risks that brought.

She took a step toward him, until they were close

enough to touch each other, close enough to kiss. "Nobody is going to watch your back the way I will," she said with quiet determination. "If the roles were reversed, and I was the one who had to go because it was my territory, you'd be fighting for a spot on that chopper."

"I would kill for it," he said simply.

His stark words and the punch of emotion in his voice put a lump in her throat. "Then you know how I feel."

"Fine. Great. How about picturing this: we're on the ground, there are men shooting at us—real, live men, not cardboard cutouts—and I'm so damned terrified for you that I'm not watching my own six. Which is fine, because you've got my back. But I'm also not on top of what's going on with the others. We get scattered, pinned down, freaking *gunned* down because I can't think straight while you're out there."

She didn't know how so much aching tenderness could coexist with so much pain. But somehow it did, sliding through her and leaving her bleeding even as she wished she could back down and give him what he wanted.

She couldn't, though. In the end, it turned out she was a Lynd all the way, after all.

Reaching up, she smoothed the neckline of his T-shirt. "This is who I am, Matt. This is what I want. If you can't accept me being out in the field, right now, today, then…" she faltered, but made herself keep going, "then don't bother calling when this is over."

"This isn't about a date," he grated. "There's already way more than that between us, and you damn well know it. Why do we need to do this right now? We can take time to figure this out and find some sort of compromise we can both live with. Preferably *not* in the middle of an op."

His face was stark, his eyes as close to begging as they got. Her heart twisted—she wanted to give in to him so badly, but it was that very urge that had her standing her ground. If she gave in now, she would lose a piece of herself. "We can absolutely discuss this later, after *we* finish this op."

Matt raised his voice. "Tucker, as ranking—"

Alyssa gave a low cry, clutched her stomach, and doubled over. She might have gone down, but Tucker was there to catch her shoulders and prop her back up, his touch incredibly gentle, his face simultaneously tender and frustrated beyond words as he said, "Seriously. Are you ready to 'fess up yet, or would a nice helicopter ride feel good right about now?"

"Fine," Alyssa said between gritted teeth.

"Fine, what?"

"I'm. In. Labor." She spaced the words, looking furious, but the moment they were out there, her eyes filled with tears. She looked at him with mingled terror and exhilaration and whispered shakily, "Hey, McDermott. We're going to have a baby."

"Yeah. We are." Tucker turned to Matt, jaw set. "I'm putting you in charge, effective immediately."

Gigi's stomach sank.

"Then here are your orders," Matt said. "Take Alyssa and Gigi back to the city, and don't let either of them out of your sight."

"Matt, please." Gigi grabbed his arm, fingers digging into his solid strength as her instincts warned that she needed to go with him, be with him. "I can handle myself. You know I can."

She saw the things he had learned over the past few days battle it out against history and loss. He shook his head. "I can't. I'm sorry, Gigi. I'm..." He stretched out a hand to her, but when she backed away, he let it drop. To Tucker, he said harshly, "Take her. Watch her. I'm counting on you to...I'm just counting on you. Don't let me down."

Face haggard, Tucker nodded. "We need to go now. We can't wait for the others."

Matt nodded. "Go. They'll be here any minute."

"Matt," Gigi whispered. Her throat ached with the tears she would shed later; her chest burned where her heart had broken. "Please. Let me be *me*."

But he turned away and said harshly, "Get her out of here."

Someone grabbed her arm; she jerked back and raised her fists, then froze when she saw Alyssa. She let down her guard. "Sorry. I'm sorry."

"I know. And I am, too, but we really need to go." She pressed her hands to the sides of her belly. "And I mean now."

Gigi looked back at Matt, met his eyes, and felt his pain as well as her own. "Be careful, damn you." Then she headed for the SUV with Tucker and Alyssa, and she didn't let herself look back.

The next few minutes were a whirl: another contraction hit while she and Tucker were getting Alyssa into the car, and then they were in and moving, with Gigi propping up Alyssa in the backseat and Tucker driving like a man possessed.

Gigi waited until they were past the first hangar and out of Matt's line of sight. Then she said, "Forgive me."

Alyssa craned to look at her. "For what?"

"This." Gigi pulled her Beretta, thumbed the safety and pointed it at Tucker's head. "Pull over."

He didn't even flinch. "I can't, Gigi. He's right. Fax, Jack and the pilot all have loads more training than you do."

"Check your text messages. Jack got hung up at Station Ten and Fax and the pilot are still forty minutes out. They're not going to make it in time." She racked the action. "Pull over. I can't let him do it. *And please don't make me make this any worse.* She had the perfect hostage right there in her arms.

"Do what?"

"Go after the bastards on his own, flying solo. Literally."

Tucker hit the brake and brought the SUV to a shuddering, screeching stop. He spun toward her, and for a second she thought he was going to come over the seat at her and fight for the gun. But he snapped, "Put the damn gun away and start talking. How many chopper hours does he have?"

"I don't know. But he knew her specs right off the top of his head, and his father died in a helicopter crash. National Guard. My guess is that he got good enough not to be afraid." It was what she would have done.

"I know for damn sure he hasn't flown since he's been here."

"Then let's hope it's like riding a bicycle." She reached for the door.

Alyssa grabbed her arm, fingers digging in. "This is crazy. You can't go. You don't know for sure that he can even fly the thing. And what are you going to do when you get there? He's right—you don't have a plan, intel, enough manpower. It could be suicide!"

Gigi covered Alyssa's hand with her own and squeezed. "I'm not being stupid this time. I'm doing what I need to do. He needs me." Another, more profound sentiment echoed through her, but she kept it to herself.

Alyssa turned weepy eyes on her husband. "Tell her she can't do this. Make it an order. Do *something*."

For a second, he hesitated. Then he hit the locks and opened her door. "Go. You don't have much time."

"Tucker!" Alyssa flared.

"Enough!" he snapped back. "You think I like this? If you hadn't insisted on coming out with me—"

"Stop it, both of you," Gigi said, sharply enough to have them subsiding. She hugged Alyssa tightly, reached up to grip Tucker's shoulder and slipped out of the SUV, then leaned back in to say, "Go have your baby. Let us worry about the other stuff."

"Be careful," Tucker grated. "That's an order."

"I'll do better than that. I'll be good." To Alyssa, she said, "Ten bucks says I get to the hospital before Baby M puts in an in-person appearance." She shut the door and stepped back as Tucker cranked the transmission and peeled away.

Alyssa pressed her face to the window, spreading a hand in farewell, or maybe to wish her luck.

But as she set off through the echoing hangar, hoping to get around behind the sleek black helicopter and use the code Fax had texted her to sneak in through the rear hatch, she heard the sound of rotors and her heart stopped.

Her luck had already run out. She was too late.

MATT HADN'T FLOWN IN nearly eight years and this baby was way more than he'd ever handled before, but she was fairly idiotproof—to the point that a chopper could be, anyway. Between his having chatted up the pilot the other day, and Fax—another lone ranger type— texting him the codes when it became clear that he and the pilot weren't going to make it in time, Matt maneuvered it off the ground without too much trouble.

The chopper wobbled a little, then leveled off and got underway.

He didn't let himself look at the main road to check on the SUV, didn't let himself think about the broken grief on Gigi's face as Tucker and Alyssa had taken her away to safety. Instead, he sent the chopper hurtling toward the Forgotten and did his best to clear his mind.

Half an hour into the forty-five minute flight, when he dropped low and skimmed the treetops, he admitted it was no damned good. His mind wasn't even close to being clear.

All he could think about was her.

He hated that he'd hurt her, hated that he couldn't get past his own hang-ups when it came to her going into the field as a cop, never mind crisis response. Most of all, he hated the way her eyes had gone dead as Alyssa pulled her away, and how his insides had hollowed out at the realization that she had lost faith in him, in them.

"Damn it," he muttered under his breath, and checked the readouts. He was ten minutes out with twenty-five to spare. And with no scanners online, he was going in blind with the simplest of plans: take out any and all vehicles, identify the boss, and grab him.

It sounded simple, but wouldn't be. And he should be thinking about that, not about the woman he'd left behind.

How had things gone so wrong so fast? How had she become so important to him in so little time? It had been less than seventy-two hours since she skidded her ride into the parking lot at Station Fourteen and promptly made him eat his attitude, but in those three days she had gotten under his skin, into his heart. She had changed him, awakened him, made him *feel*.

He didn't want to lose her. But he didn't know how to keep her without losing part of himself.

"Damn it, Gigi," he said aloud. "Why couldn't you have given me this one?"

"Because it would've been the first of many," she said over the thudding engine noise.

He jolted and whipped around, swearing when he found her standing right behind him. His blood fired at the sight of her, a potent combination of fear, anger, desire, tenderness…and reluctant admiration. Because damned if she hadn't somehow doubled back and stowed away on the chopper.

"How did you—" Remembering the rear hatch—and the fact that Fax played by his own rules—he did the math. "I'm going to kill Tucker."

"Don't blame him—I made him do it. At gunpoint, no less."

Putting his attention back on the controls, he snapped, "Sit down and strap in, we're almost there." But as she came forward and fumbled with the copilot's harness, he had to ask, "Why did you come after me?" He thought she had given up on him back at the airstrip.

"Because there was no way in hell I was going to let you fly solo on this one." She glanced over. "Why did you send me away?"

"Because I'd rather watch you walk out than bleed out."

She blanched, but lifted her chin defiantly. "Those aren't the only two options."

"They are the way I see things."

"Then I feel bad for you." She turned deliberately to the panel in front of her, pulled her phone and checked a saved message.

He nearly groaned. "Fax sent you instructions for the guns, too?"

"Just shut up and fly," she said.

He growled low in his throat and thought about stuffing her in a parachute and throwing her out the door. He didn't have the time or altitude, though, so he was going to have to make sure he kept her in one piece, no matter what.

The responsibility was a heavy weight on his shoulders, the pressure a yoke around his neck. His blood burned with anger, his chest was tight with frustration... and he felt acutely, painfully alive.

He wanted to grab her, shake her, kiss her, make love to her. Watching Tucker and Alyssa drag her away from him had been one of the hardest things he had done; thinking it was over had been one of the lowest points of his life. And now, God, he didn't know what to say, how to tell her that this was it for him, she was it. That somehow they were going to have to find a compromise, because he didn't ever want to watch her walk away again. And he damn sure wasn't going to watch her bleed.

Determination firming, he checked his readouts and turned to her just as the chopper crested a low line of trees. "Gigi, I need to—" A shrill bleat cut him off, coming from the console, where a display blinked a warning.

Blood icing, he whipped back to scan the ground below them. Too late, he saw that the "treeline" was camouflage netting strung over a half-dozen tents and twice as many vehicles, ranging from dirt bikes to a huge box trailer hooked to a heavy duty truck.

"There!" she cried, pointing to the smoky trail of a rocket-propelled grenade. It was headed right for them.

For a second, he froze, paralyzed by the thought that he, too, was going to die in a chopper crash, and that he was going to take Gigi with him. Then a second buzzer went off, snapping him straight into a crisis mode that was more intense than any he'd experienced before.

Shouting, he laid the chopper over onto its side and banked, veering sharply up into the sky. "Can you see it?"

She twisted, trying to get a look behind them. "No, I—" A booming thud reverberated through the tiny cabin and she screamed as more warnings shrilled.

Matt's stomach headed for his toes and he swore as the chopper listed heavily, wallowed for a second and

then nosed down. As it did, he caught sight of a forest
service Jeep sitting beside a river a few miles away from
the camouflaged camp, nearly hidden beneath a stone
outcropping.

"Matt!"

"I'm trying!" He aimed for the Jeep, but the tail rotor
was toast, his control sluggish to nonexistent, and they
were too damn low for chutes to be any use. "Hang
on!"

Chapter Sixteen

The helicopter crashed into the dry riverbed with a terrible, rending roar of tortured metal, the scream of an overloading engine, and the *whip-whip-whip* of the main rotor blades slamming into the ground and coming apart.

Gigi cried out as the cockpit took a huge, spinning bounce and she was shaken like a ragdoll. Her harness cut into her hips and shoulders, and her stomach couldn't catch up, but all she could do was hang on and pray. As the windshield cracked and the rear door tore free, churning dust and rocks poured in, adding to the chaos.

Then the bulk of the cockpit thudded into something and jolted to a wrenching, shuddering stop. The console surged, spat and died.

"Gigi!" Matt wrenched free of his harness and lurched across to yank at hers.

Her head and stomach were spinning in opposite directions, but she slapped his hands away. "I'm fine."

Then she popped the buckles, pitched into his arms, and let out two wrenching sobs as she clung to him with all her strength. She absolutely, positively was *not* fine.

She was scared and shaken, and her emotions were all over the place. She wanted to push him away, pull him close, scratch at him, shake him, kiss him, hold on to him and never, ever let go.

She was a wreck. And so was their chopper.

He crushed her to him. *"Gigi."* They held each other for a few seconds. Then they pulled apart and he shoved her toward the ripped-open doorway. "Go!"

As if they had practiced it a hundred times, she paused at the opening, crouched and looked low while he went high. She had her Beretta out; he was ready with his Sig Sauer. They shared a look and she went through the doorway, with him right behind her.

Her boots crunched wetly on the riverbed, which had a skim of water running through the rounded stones, a slightly deeper channel in the middle. She stuck to the edge of the narrow canyon, where a slight overhang offered the illusion of safety.

"Head downstream," Matt directed, staying close and keeping his voice low. "We're not that far from the bigger river. Fingers crossed that the Jeep is drivable and the keys are in it."

Miles out of radio range, with the chopper's main systems fried and limited knowledge of its tricks, their best option was going to be to drive to somewhere they could make contact with their team.

Turning downstream and picking up a mile-eating jog, Gigi tossed over her shoulder, "Keys are optional. I can hotwire it if it's still working."

She had the satisfaction of seeing his double take, then a reluctant glint of approval as she turned back and picked up the pace. Holding her gun at the ready as she ran, she scanned their surroundings for two-legged predators as well as others of the clawed or slithering variety. The coast seemed clear, the only sound that of the air moving through the trees.

It wasn't that she'd stopped being scared—the fear was there, and not even buried all that deeply. But at the same time, going fetal wasn't an option, so she was just doing what needed to be done. *Just do it,* she thought, the words taking on the feeling of a Lynd family battle cry.

"Hear that?" he said quietly. "I think we found Tanya's waterfall."

He was right. That wasn't the wind in the trees; they were getting close to the river, and there was a cascade somewhere nearby. Excitement kicked at the sense that the case was finally coming together, though the adrenaline was tempered by the fact that they were cut off from backup.

The rushing roar grew louder, and the canyon took a sharp left, blocking their view. She paused at the turn, waited for Matt to move in close, and then looked low while he went high.

She caught her breath at the sight of a wide, rushing river with elevated banks that suggested it was far from its peak level. Both sides of the river were lined by scrubby trees that looked like an old man's hands— gnarled and bent, with tufts of wiry white fibers growing in strange patches and trailing down. The water churned through a small set of rapids just downstream from them, and maybe five hundred yards or so farther down, the world dropped away. A cloud of mist beyond sparkled subtle rainbows.

It was stark, strange and beautiful. Even better, the Jeep was maybe a hundred yards away, parked up on the bank. It looked intact and untouched. And it was on their side of the river.

"We caught a lucky break there," Matt said. "Let's hope it holds."

She looked up at him, and when their eyes met, her capable facade threatened to crack and crumble. It hadn't been that hard to hold it together while they were moving, but now, with their one real hope within reach, fear crowded close, tightening her chest and stealing her breath.

If they couldn't drive out in the Jeep, they couldn't warn the others that it wasn't just four or five hired thugs. Instead, they were dealing with a highly organized and well-armed camp. *Terrorists,* she thought. But she didn't say the word aloud, because regardless of who the militants worked for, they would be en route to the crash site, looking to confirm the kills. Which meant that the Jeep better damn well work.

"Hey." Matt dropped to a crouch, so they were at eye level. "You're doing great."

She nodded, gritting her teeth when they wanted to chatter, and forcing a smile that felt ghastly. "Don't worry. I've got your back."

"I know." Still holding his Sig Sauer in one hand, he used the other to catch the back of her neck and draw her in for a kiss.

Logic said the timing was totally wrong. But the kiss was exactly right.

The press of his lips steadied her. The touch of his tongue said *we're in this together.* The slant of his mouth across hers reminded her that when it came to dangerous situations, they were batting a thousand. And the warmth that rose in her, suffusing her body and lightening the heavy weight on her heart reminded her that she was with a man who had always believed in protecting others, even when he'd stopped believing in himself. And she, who never ever leaned, let herself lean into him for a precious second, drawing strength.

When they drew apart, he cupped her cheek in an uncharacteristically tender gesture. "No regrets, Gigi."

Remembering their lovemaking, she smiled slightly. "No regrets."

"I love you."

Gigi froze. Heat slashed through her—maybe panic, maybe exhilaration, maybe some of each—and her fingers went suddenly numb where they clutched her lifelines, him on one side, her gun on the other. "I... Oh, wow."

His grin was decidedly crooked, not an expression she had seen on him before. It lightened him up despite everything, making him look younger, more approachable, even a little roguish. Very much like a man a friend would call "Blackie."

He took her gun hand and raised the Beretta between them. "Cover me...partner."

Then he gave her hand a last squeeze and slipped past her, staying low against the riverbank as she headed for the Jeep.

She watched him go, staggered, her mind spinning. It was just the moment, she told herself. He couldn't possibly love her. It was too soon; they were too different; everything was fresh, shiny and new now, but when that wore off the cracks would show. Opposites might attract, but they didn't stick for the long haul.

I love you, too. The words were trapped deep inside her, unsaid. She was entirely out of her depth. Love was too important to get wrong. How could she know for certain if it was going to last? She had thought she was in love before, and it had nearly destroyed her when it ended. Yet her feelings now were ten times stronger, a hundred. And as she watched Matt jump lightly from the concealment of the riverbank to the open ground above, her heart pounded with fear. Not for herself, this time, but for him. If anything happened to him… No, she wouldn't think it. Couldn't face it.

But it was that fear that broke her from her shocked paralysis and got her moving. Heart drumming lightly against her ribs, she edged farther along the riverbank, the rushing roar of the water and the deeper thunder of the falls covering the sound of her movement. She stayed concealed, but moved so she could see most of the clearing where the Jeep was parked. She covered her partner—her lover—as he headed for their best hope of surviving and warning the others what was happening inside the Forgotten.

And for the first time in her career, she wasn't fighting against something—crime, bloodshed, injustice— she was fighting *for* something.

Him. And, maybe, their future together.

MATT'S HEAD WAS CLEAR, his heart full, his senses attuned to his surroundings as he slipped between the Jeep and its rocky overhang. His cop self checked the frame and peeked through the windows, looking for evidence of a trap, while his ranger half listened for changes in the rhythms around him, the sudden silence that said predators were near.

No trap, no unwanted company, you're good to go. More, he was whole, connected, and entirely in the moment.

Becoming his better cop and ranger self hadn't been about blocking out his emotions after all, it seemed. He had needed to accept them instead, embrace them.

When he had headed off to France with Ian, he had been so full of a college hotshot's self-importance, so wrapped up in himself that he'd skipped his last visit home to go to a party being thrown by a guy he barely knew, to hit on a girl whose name he didn't remember. He hadn't told his parents he loved them, hadn't teased his sister one last time—he had thought there would be time for all that later, after Europe. After college. Whenever. But then they died and there hadn't been a later. There had only been grief, heartbreak, and raw, tearing regrets.

Not this time, he thought as he eased open the driver's-side door, took a quick look around, and then felt up underneath the overhanging section of dashboard where he and his rangers left their keys. Relief kicked when he found them right where they belonged. It looked like the Jeep had gone undetected, that they might be in the clear, after all. If he and Gigi could get back into radio range, he could mobilize a full-scale response. Not even Proudfoot could ignore the presence of an armed camp in his territory. And if the mayor tried to—if he was part of whatever was going on—Tucker, Fax and the others would go right over the top of him.

And damned if it didn't feel good knowing that he was part of a team like that.

Easing partway out from behind the Jeep, he flashed a sign toward where Gigi was hiding, then held up the keys. *Stay there, I'll come get you.* He was just easing back into concealment when there was a thump and a hiss from the nearby trees, and something came hurtling straight for him.

Incoming!

He flung himself away. Behind him, the missile slammed into the Jeep and detonated. In front of him was Gigi. He bolted toward her, and—

Shockwave. Searing heat.

Blackness.

THE IMAGES BURNED themselves onto Gigi's retinas: Matt's body silhouetted against the blast, his arms outstretched, his mouth shaping her name. Then, moments later, him lying crumpled on the ground, unmoving, the Jeep in flames behind him.

No! The scream reverberated in her head and pain ripped through her chest. Inwardly, she went fetal. Outwardly, though, she bolted along the riverbank, clutching the Beretta so hard her fingers numbed.

She sobbed silently as she ran, choking on grief and guilt. He'd trusted her to watch his back, but she hadn't seen or heard the grenade launcher, still didn't know exactly where the RPG had come from. One second, she was clandestinely giving him the thumbs-up for finding the keys, and the next... *Oh, God.*

"Please let him be okay," she whispered. Then, not caring if it was reckless or not, only knowing that she had to get to him, she vaulted onto the plateau and sped toward him, staying low, her mouth souring with fear.

He'd said he loved her. And she had frozen—not because she felt nothing, but because she didn't trust the huge, overwhelming feelings she had for him.

As he'd walked away, she told herself she needed time to think it through, time for the two of them to figure out if they could make it work. But even waiting five minutes had been too long.

She reached him, and had to choke back a sob. He lay facedown. His shirt was torn, his back streaked with blood, but she couldn't tell if it was still flowing, or even if he was breathing. Beyond him, the flames had died down to inky, foul-smelling smoke.

She crouched and moved to touch him with a shaking hand. "Matt? Can you hear—"

Movement blurred *above* her. Ambush!

She jerked back, gasping and bringing up the Beretta as a man leaped down from the rocky overhang. He landed on her with both feet, knocking her down and away. They rolled, grappling, and he nailed her with a vicious wrist chop that numbed her hand and sent her gun skidding. Then he was on her, straddling her, pinning her. She tried to knee him, but couldn't shift his heavy bulk, tried to twist away, but didn't have any leverage.

She was trapped. Oh, God. Terror rose, choking her.

Her dark-haired captor was wearing hunter's camouflage, a full suit of it that looked fresh out of the catalog, along with a utility belt that held a GPS, spare ammo for a shotgun she didn't see and a couple of fist-size canisters that were either grenades or gas.

His breath was hot on her face as he leaned over her, his blue eyes dark and feral. "You're in luck, bitch. The boss said to bring him a survivor, if there were any. He wants to know how much the cops have figured out."

A trickle of strength seeped into her and she sneered, "They know about everything. The camp, the stuff, all of it. If you want to get out of here, I'd do it now, because they'll be here any minute."

"Shut up." He backhanded her, the blow made heavy and hard by the pistol he had clenched in his fist.

Agony exploded in her jaw and her head whipped to the side. She cried out, not just in pain, but with the gut-deep wrongness of what was happening, and the horrible realization that Matt had been right—it was nothing like cardboard cutouts and training spars. Real blood ran from a cut on her cheek, real tears leaked from her eyes.

Her captor leaned in and rasped, "You'd better re-think that answer. You try lying to the boss and you'll wind up dead, too."

The word hit her harder than her attacker had. Dead? No, that was impossible. Matt couldn't be dead. He had just said he loved her. And she was supposed to have been watching his back.

She let out a single broken sob and turned her head away as her captor whipped off his belt and used it to lash her hands together behind her back, then sobbed again as he got to his feet and dragged her up by her bonds.

"Move." He shoved her ahead of him, then prodded

her with the Beretta. When they got closer to the line of strange, gnarled trees, she saw a battered military-style Jeep with no top or doors, and bare foam showing through tears in the upholstery.

She hadn't heard it. Even with the roaring noise of the water, she should have heard something, seen something.

"Get in." He shoved her in, pushing her back so her hands were trapped beneath her.

Her shoulders screamed, but that was nothing compared to the terrible, awful feeling that swept through her as she craned back and caught sight of Matt's body. Her heart cracked and bled; tears ran down her cheeks at the realization that she had waited too long, that in just a few short days he had gone from being adversary to lover, and now to loss.

And regret. Terrible, awful regret.

Chapter Seventeen

Groaning, Matt levered himself up and crouched for a second. His head spun and his ears rang, but that was nothing compared to the raw rage and hatred flowing through his veins, and the burning churn of the man he was becoming combined with the chill command of the one he used to be.

Gigi. Her name was a talisman, a focal point that got him on his feet.

He had regained consciousness too late to protect her, but he had heard where the bastard was taking her: back to the hidden campsite where, even if he could get through the perimeter, he would be one man against an army. It would be certain death for both of them.

Which meant he couldn't let them get to the campsite. He had to intercept them somehow. But the Jeep was toast and his Sig was gone, lost in the explosion. He was totally on his own.

Flashing back on the brief glimpse of things he had caught from the air, he headed for the waterfall. He forced his legs to carry him because there wasn't any alternative—no backup, no intel, no nothing—and failure wasn't an option.

His heart thudded in his chest. *Hang on, sweetheart. I'm coming.* Somehow.

The falls tumbled down from a wide, rocky promontory, fell four stories, and slammed into a pool that under normal circumstances was probably good and deep, but because of the drought looked churned-up and angry. No more than a half mile beyond it, though, the waterway spread out and became even shallower. And a single set of wet tire tracks emerged on one side, showing where the bastard had come through. There was no sign of him having gone the other way.

Matt's cop self said human beings were creatures of habit, which meant the guy would leave the way he had come in. The ranger in him said only an idiot would jump. Or a man in love.

Holding the image of gorgeous gray eyes snapping with mingled temper and arousal, and remembering what it felt like to lose himself inside her, wake up next to her, he backed away from the edge, took four running steps…and jumped.

GIGI'S SHOULDERS BURNED with every bump and rattle of the Jeep, her legs ached from bracing in the foot well as she struggled to free herself from her bonds. Her captor had threaded the seat belt through the leather strap so she couldn't launch herself out of the open-doored vehicle. The narrow edges of the leather belt cut into her hands and wrists, unyielding.

He held the Beretta trained on her as he drove.

Her mind swung violently from pure terror to calculating rage and back again. One moment she wanted to curl in a ball, the next she imagined herself breaking free, grabbing her Beretta away from her captor, and unloading it into his sneering face. He was no cardboard cutout, but she could do it. Not just to escape, but for Matt.

She pictured his face, his body, the way he moved, the fierce light of determination in his eyes when he saw something that needed to be done, and the way he was always there for the people around him, even when he seemed to be utterly disconnected from the world.

Oh, Matt. She wanted to close her eyes and pretend it was all a nightmare. But she couldn't, because it wasn't. This was really happening.

How arrogant she had been, how unrealistic to think she could save other people from situations like this one. She couldn't even save herself. What was more, she had failed the man she loved.

Love. Yes, that was it.

Too late, she admitted to herself that she was in love with him—she had started falling that very first moment in the hallway, and had toppled cleanly over that night in the safe house, when he'd imprinted himself indelibly on her soul. And, too late, she understood where he had been coming from, truly understood what he'd been through as she felt the fear, anger, rage, impotence and rending, tearing grief of losing him. She gave a shuddering sob and went limp.

The leather strap gave slightly.

Adrenaline flared through her, swerving her mind back to revenge and the thin-seeming hope of escape. Pulse pounding in her ears, she tugged experimentally. Felt it give another fraction of an inch.

She had to relax and let it come, she realized; she

couldn't force it. And if that was supposed to be a life lesson from some higher power, she would deal with that particular epiphany later.

How much time did she have? Her heart raced as she made herself stay limp and worked one hand partway out of her bonds, little by precious little.

The Jeep broke through the old-man trees into a clearing near the same river they had been at before. Only it was shallower and wider here, downstream of the pounding waterfall. She held her breath when she caught sight of a rocky promontory halfway up: it was the one from Tanya's sketch, she was sure of it. But what did it mean? Was it a coincidence? A connection?

Gigi's grief didn't fade, but she could make herself think through it, using rage and regret to sharpen her senses as the driver muttered something under his breath, downshifted and gunned the vehicle into the river. Water sprayed up and in as the vehicle jolted and lurched. One of Gigi's feet slipped and she swung violently to the side with an involuntary gasp.

"Son of a—" Her captor took a hand off the wheel, grabbed her shirt and jerked her back upright. The wrench nearly yanked one shoulder out of its socket, but one wrist slipped from the wet leather. And she was free!

Still cursing, unaware that she had escaped her bonds, he fought the wheel, sliding on sprung upholstery made slick with the water that gushed over them as the four-wheeler went in deeper, bucking over the rocks.

Acting on rage and instinct, she screamed and launched herself onto her captor. She slammed a knee onto his gun hand and went for his throat, wrapping the leather around it and pulling as tightly as she could. She screamed again—a noise of hatred and heartbreak.

For a second, surprise gave her the upper hand. Then his foot came off the gas and he surged up against her, breaking her hold. He slammed an elbow into her jaw, knocking her back against the passenger's seat. Her head banged into the edge of the empty doorframe, and the world blurred.

He rose over her and aimed the Beretta point blank.

Everything came back into focus in that moment of blinding terror. She saw his cruel blue eyes, saw no remorse or pity, only a killer's calculation.

Panic slashed, emptying her mind.

"I'll talk," she blurted. "I'll tell your boss everything."

His eyes flashed. "Too late. I'll just tell him you were both dead when I got there." His finger tightened, the mechanism clicked—

A monstrous roar erupted from behind him as a figure lunged up, out of the water, grabbed him from behind and dragged him down. The gunman howled and his shot went wild, and then the gun flew free, landing in the driver's seat.

Gigi gaped as fire poured into her veins and her heart expanded in her chest. *"Matt!"*

His shirt was gone, his pants torn to the knee on one side, and blood streamed in the water that ran off his body, but he was there. He was alive!

Relief poured through her, pure and profound, but then her captor surged up, nearly tore away, and then spun back and kicked Matt in the stomach. He folded, the breath exploding from his lungs, and nearly went down.

She screamed and went for the gun.

The other man grabbed it a split second after she did, and they grappled for the weapon. She kicked at his face, caught him in the shoulder and made him howl. But then he twisted the gun free and fired.

Gigi threw herself backward out the far door.

"NO!" Matt exploded back out of the water and slammed into the gunman, driving them both against the side of the vehicle. He slammed the man's wrist against the doorframe, and there was a sickening crack. The man howled, and the Beretta went flying into the river.

"You. Don't. Touch. Her." Matt punctuated each of his words with a slamming blow that hammered his enemy into the river, until finally the man went limp, sprawled half into the driver's-side foot well, no longer a threat.

Once the guy was down, Matt yanked off his belt, cranked it around the guy's wrists and through the steering wheel, and pulled so tight that the guy's hands went white.

"Matt!" Gigi flew to him as he drew back his arm for another blow. At the sound of her voice, his head snapped up, his eyes locked onto her and his face flooded with all the same emotions that were suddenly filling her.

Relief made her sob, triumph made her smile and joy made her fling herself into his arms.

"Gigi." He caught her close, clamping on so tightly that she couldn't breathe. She didn't care, though. All

she cared about was the man holding her, murmuring her name. He shifted to kiss her lips, her face, her temple, then back to her lips again.

The kiss wasn't about seduction; it was about connection. She fused her mouth to his, poured herself into him and took his heat in return. Then she tore her lips away and said against his mouth, "I love you, too. I almost didn't get to say it. I love you. I love you. I think I started loving you that very first moment. Alyssa's right. There really is such a thing as love at first sight—and I'm in it."

His eyes burned green fire. "It's about time you admitted it. And people say *I'm* stubborn."

"What do you mean 'about time'?" Crazy exhilaration rose in her as she squared off opposite him. "It was like fifteen minutes. What if—" She broke off, new terror slashing through her at the sound of an incoming helicopter.

"Run!" He caught her hand and they bolted for the far bank. But the rocks beneath them shifted unsteadily and the water dragged at their legs.

They weren't going to make it.

A ROAR OF DENIAL BURNED Matt's throat, but he didn't have time to be pissed at the unfairness of the situation. His mind churned through hostage scenarios, negotiation tactics, something—anything—that would keep them alive. Because as long as they were alive and together, they had a fighting chance.

"Stay behind me." He stopped and turned as the rotor noise ratcheted up and his stomach sank at the realization that there was more than one chopper. Who were these people?

He braced himself squarely in front of Gigi, keeping a hand back, linked with hers to give her a reassuring squeeze. "I love you," he said over his shoulder.

Her eyes were wet and scared, but she smiled through trembling lips. "I love you, too. No regrets."

"No regrets." Because life wasn't about avoiding risk. It was about living in the present, and making each moment count.

The engine noise screamed and three choppers appeared downstream, flying low, in battle formation, weapons hot.

Gigi screamed in joy. "Look!"

The choppers were sleek, black and familiar, and wore tail numbers that didn't look quite right.

It wasn't the bad guys. It was backup.

"Hey!" He let go of her hand to wave his arms over his head. "Fax. *Hey!*"

The lead chopper roared directly over them while the other two peeled off and headed away, in the direction of the camouflaged camp. As the remaining chopper circled and headed for a landing on a small, rocky strip near the waterfall, Matt caught Gigi by the waist and swung her around. "We made it!"

She laughed and wrapped her arms around his neck, holding on as if she never intended to let go. Which was just fine with him.

The chopper settled down and the engine cut out. Moments later, the door opened and Fax and Chelsea emerged and headed straight for them. Another agent, this one wearing a pilot's headset, dropped down and headed for the Jeep, where the man they had captured had regained consciousness, and was furiously trying to escape from his bonds.

Matt and Gigi met Fax and Chelsea halfway, at the river's edge. "Thanks for the backup," Matt said. "Sorry about the chopper."

Fax winced. "That doesn't sound good."

Chelsea poked him in the ribs. "Don't listen to him. We were patched into your chopper's cameras and saw the whole thing. It gave us the leverage to mobilize agents up here as well as out to Sector Nine." She glanced from Matt to Gigi and back. "You guys both okay?"

"We'll live," Gigi said, glancing up at him. She threaded her fingers through his and squeezed, and it felt like she had just touched his heart.

They had things to work through, it was true, but after seeing her in the line of fire, he knew he couldn't keep her in the background. She was made for action, thrived on it. But at the same time, he saw a new awareness in her, and knew that the connection they had forged had brought home the realities of what it meant to knowingly walk into a critical situation. She would be more careful in the future…and she would have him to watch her back.

It was time for him to get back on the job. He didn't know what the next few months would hold for them—or for the investigation—but he knew that whatever they did, they would be doing it together.

He lifted their joined hands and pressed a kiss to her knuckles. "Yeah. We're going to be just fine."

* * * * *